CATHERINE WIMPEN
Manchester. After leaving Marple High School Catherine worked as a mental health nurse. In 1991 she completed a degree in Psychology and subsequently qualified as a Psychotherapist.

She has now retired from therapy and currently works in the family business of Lightning Protection. Her writing keeps her connected to the field of mental health and Catherine is drawn to reading and writing in the moody psychological suspense genre.

Follow Catherine on X/Twitter @CWimpeney

A CAT LOVER'S GUIDE TO MURDER

Catherine Wimpeney

Northodox Press Ltd
Maiden Greve, Malton,
North Yorkshire, YO17 7BE

This edition 2024

1
First published in Great Britain by
Northodox Press Ltd 2024

ISBN: 9781915179807

This book is set in Caslon Pro Std

This Novel is entirely a work of fiction. The names, characters and incidents portrayed in it are the work of the author's imagination. Any resemblance to actual persons, living or dead, events or localities is entirely coincidental.

To my brother, Pete,

12th Dec, 1955 to 31st Dec, 2022.

How It Ends

It's late afternoon and a hush of anticipation has settled over Courtroom Two Manchester Crown Court. Only the squeak of a chair and the rustle of paper can be heard; underscored by the rhythmic brush strokes of the court artist's pencil, as she tries to capture the strained expression on the defendant's face.

Circuit Judge, Her Honour Judge Abilene Blanchflower, removes her glasses, turns to the jury, and says, 'You have heard the defence and the prosecution case. Now it is your task to decide. Has the prosecution proved to your satisfaction that the defendant is guilty of the charge of manslaughter?

Jury members, you must find you are satisfied and sure of the defendant's guilt. You must be one hundred per cent satisfied and sure. If you think the defendant *might* be guilty, you must find *not guilty*. If you think they are *probably* guilty, you must find not guilty. If you are *almost sure* they are guilty, they are still not guilty. Members of the jury, only one hundred per cent certainty of guilt will suffice.'

Chapter One

Bella

I shouldn't be here. I'm only supposed to clean his house and do a little ironing, but the temptation to see what it was like to sleep in Graham's bed was too much. Once the idea entered my head, it remained like a squatter. I rise and jam my feet into a pair of slippers, grimacing as the pain delivers a morning herald; I'm never prepared for it. Trevor, my cat, kneads the bed covers, purring like an idling engine. He stretches lazily as I grab my cardigan and pull it on over my pyjamas. I chivvy him off the covers and he follows, making his little noises as I check around the bathroom for signs that might give me away. I make the bed meticulously, then run a small lint brush over it to remove cat hairs.

A sound from outside.

Leaning forward, I see Graham's silver Mercedes pulling onto the narrow driveway. The 'landing strip' as he likes to call it. Grey paving swallows the car up in a perfect camouflage.

The engine stops.

Trevor runs ahead of me as I rush down the stairs and out through the back door. Once in the backyard, I open the small adjoining gate to my garden, fumble for my keys, drop them, and scratch my knuckles along the paving as I retrieve them. In the safety of my kitchen, I repress the urge to giggle as I place my ear and palms to the wall, and feel the vibrations as Graham's front door shuts. Creaking tread as he climbs the stairs, brushing our adjoining wall with his case.

'Talk about extreme sports,' I say.

Chapter Two

Angela

'Phone Mum,' Angela says to Siri, her in-car virtual assistant.

'I can't find Norman in your contacts,' Siri replies in clipped pronunciation.

Sighing, Angela tries again, enunciating loudly as though talking to an idiot. 'Not Norman – Mum.'

Indicating left onto Elmwood Terrace, she exits the uninspiring granite grey of the main road and enters the lane. The sight of lush green trees and well-tended front gardens beckons, smoothing out the stress-lines etched into her face. She slows to admire the pretty pastel front doors of the terraced homes and recalls the first time she'd seen number sixty-one.

The divorce and sale of the marital home had gone through, and she'd spent months searching for the right property, 'props' to those in the know. The estate agent, enthused, overboard in her pitch. *Such a lot of interest, the need to act quickly*. Her sales talk had been white noise. Angela had heard people say that they'd known instantly when they'd met "*the one*". She'd never felt that about a man, but with the house she'd known immediately. Looking out of the bedroom window at a budding wisteria, she'd put her offer in, well over the asking price.

Chapter Three

Bella

The silvery chiffon of dawn lifts to reveal an eggshell blue sky. A morning for taking a cup of tea outside and pottering.

As I dig a hole in the peaty soil, I hear Graham's front door open. A blush starts.

'Morning Bella,' he says.

'Oh, morning.' An image of waking in his bed and I blush even deeper. 'Do you know that there's no flower grows quite as black as a pansy?' I say, diverting attention away from the red creeper on my neck.

'You have a way with those things.'

'I just enjoy it.'

'Cheers, again, for the cleaning. I didn't expect the lasagne.'

'It's fine, kept me busy.'

He holds a small carrier bag out, 'I got you a–'

My jaw falls open on loose hinges. He's looking beyond me, though, and hasn't noticed.

'Is that Trevor?' he asks.

I turn. Trevor's on the opposite side of the road. A white four by four approaches. Too big for this narrow road. Trevor's focused on a bird on this side of the road, oblivious of the approaching car. The contents of the carrier bag forgotten. I drop the pansies and run to the gate.

'Trevor, stay!'

Trevor lifts his grey shawled head, amber eyes locked on his prey. He steps into the road.

Chapter Four

Angela

'Hey Siri, phone Mum,' Angela instructs again, calmer now.

'I'm sorry, I can't find Norman in your–'

'Oh, bugger it.'

Absently reaching over to manually search, catching movement, a woman in the road, panic on her face. Following the woman's fixed stare, she sees a cat and slams her brakes on.

'For fuck's sake!' she shouts.

'There is no need for that.' Siri responds.

Chapter Five

Bella

'Oh God, Graham, is he okay?' I grab his arm, and for once I'm not self-conscious. I can barely focus. He puts his hand firmly over mine, and it hardly registers.

'I'm sure he's fine,' he says, and awkwardly ducks under the car. I can hear him, pitch altered, an appeal to a child. 'Trevor, come on, lad.'

I cross myself and pray silently. *Please God, please don't take my little boy.* My hip hurts like hell and the grit of the road digs into my knees. I bear down harder, using the pain as a distraction, peering under the car at a pelt of fur by the front wheel. Two small grey legs protrude, cushioned paws, claws retracted, still. My special boy. Fear turns into something tangible as tears slide down my face.

Graham leans further in.

'I'm so sorry, I didn't see him,' the woman says.

I'm vaguely aware of her at my side. My brain took a sort of instant picture of her when I stood in front of the car. If I closed my eyes, it would still be there, a negative image. She looks and smells like one of the cosmetic assistants in John Lewis. She stands, black shoes and tanned legs.

'I've got him,' Graham announces.

Air circulates again. I touch his back as he reverses from under the car. The woman has gone over to Graham's side and knelt.

'I'm really sorry.'

Graham ignores her. I'm glad. We're united in our approach to cat killers. He emerges holding Trevor. Standing, he passes him to me. Tears distort my vision. I sniff them back.

Trevor meows.

'Looks unharmed,' Graham says, as he inspects Trevor's legs. 'One of his nine gone, though.'

'Yes, but *I* only have the one,' I say, giving the woman a killer stare.

'Look, I'm really sorry,' the woman repeats. 'I'm Angela.'

She offers her hand. Graham shakes it. Traitor. 'Graham.'

'I've just moved into sixty-one, the house not the age bracket, obviously,' she laughs. Turns to me. 'Well, thank goodness you're both okay. Again, I'm so, so sorry. I was. I'm just not familiar with the road here.'

'What? You're in Stockport for God's sake, not Buenos Aires.'

Graham steps in. For me, or her? 'Reckon he's fine,' he says. 'But you might want to get the little fella checked over. Let me know if you need a lift. I'm in all day today.'

'Oh, you two aren't..?' Angela says.

Standing side by side, me and Graham are an unlikely couple. This woman didn't for a minute believe we were together. At least, if she did, she'd thought it an odd pairing.

'Oh.' Graham points a finger from me to him. 'No, just neighbours.'

A punch-to-the-gut comment. Graham compensates by glancing at me and adding, 'And friends.'

But the word is out, etched permanently onto the storyboard of my life. I turn away, concentrate on Trevor, his heartbeat calming though my heart deflates.

'Well, I know where to come to borrow a bottle of Pinot.'

'Wine preference noted,' Graham answers, then looks at me. I feel like his mother.

'You're a beauty,' she says, reaching out to stroke Trevor.

I pull away. 'If you'll excuse me, I need to get us both off "Deadman's Curve."' Pushing between them, I notice an old man in a black Jag trying to manoeuvre past Angela's car. He bips his horn lightly. 'I think you're causing a gridlock,' I add. I walk back through my gate, noticing the crushed black velvet petals strewn across the path.

I hear Graham leave his house at his usual time the following morning. As I glance towards the front door, the woollen scarf on the coat stand warms me from a distance. Graham said he'd bought it at the airport and would take it back if it didn't suit. I told him it would be perfect for winter. It's a shame I can't wear it yet, but I've hung it where I can see it, like a longed-for Christmas present, or new shoes when I was a child.

Instead of the noise of his engine pulling out of the driveway, I hear indistinct voices.

Moving from the kitchen into the living room, I can hear it's a woman's voice. Angela's voice, and Graham's.

I can't catch what they're saying. If I move forward, Graham might see me through the window. The cellar door is to my right. I open it and quietly descend into the small bare brick chamber. I approach the narrow window at the front, which I always leave slightly ajar. It has a wire mesh covering, so it's safe and keeps the room aired. Standing just below it, out of sight, my vantage point gives me a view of Angela's heeled feet and tanned legs. The hem of a black patterned dress sways coquettishly.

'Got her a peace offering,' I hear Angela say.

'Forty quid for the vet's bill might be more useful,' Graham answers.

Yes, go Graham.

'Oh, sure.'

I hear the doubt in her reply. Feet shuffle.

'She must be at work.'

'Not since I've known her.'

'Oh?'

'Not my business,' he answers. 'Have you knocked? The bell doesn't work.'

I'm annoyed. Their "water-cooler" conversation, happening on my doorstep.

'How long have you been neighbours?'

Trevor's followed me down and discovered an old toy. He pounces and it emits a loud squeak. He throws it in the air, it lands, he pounces again. I miss Graham's reply.

'So, no Mrs Graham?'

Brazen.

'What? No,' He adds something, but the squeaking toy drowns him out.

'Shush,' I hiss.

'You settled in?' Graham asks.

A change of subject. I wonder if he's aware I'm listening.

'Well, I've got a way to go, but getting there. I'll be working from...'

Squeak, squeak, squeak. The toy is tossed here and there.

'Doing what?'

'Therapy. I'm a…'

Squeak, squeak, squeak

'Ah, right. I could have done with you a year ago.'

'Oh?'

'Long story.'

'That's why we charge by the hour.'

Graham's amused by that. 'Yes, I'm sure.' He doesn't laugh out loud, but I can hear it in his voice.

I think the long story he's referring to is the split from his business partner. It had all become very fraught with solicitors and such.

Trevor is scratching at the square of plasterboard that covers the fireplace. When we first moved here, he climbed inside and up onto the damper and got stuck. I managed to pull him out, both of us covered in old black soot and dust, but he was unharmed. I had the top capped so that birds couldn't fall in, and Graham had helped me to carry the fifty or so bricks down so I could cover it properly from inside. I wasn't really bothered about bricking it up. The piece of plasterboard has been effective enough. It had just been another reason to have Graham's help, to invite him in, to involve him in my life. He never took the hint, though.

'Well, I'll see you.' Graham's voice fades as he walks away.

'I'll send you an invite to the housewarming.' Angela says.

A car door opens and shuts, preceded by a knocking at the door. No way am I going to be summoned. I wait until she leaves, then I climb the cellar steps, closely followed by Trevor.

There's an envelope on the doormat. I tear it open and remove a single piece of card. On the front is a picture of a British Blue, almost identical to Trevor. The caption reads: 'Time Spent with Cats is Never Wasted, Sigmund Freud.' A note is scrawled inside:

Please accept my apologies for frightening Trevor. I have bought him a small toy.
I hope he's alright.

Angela Maynard, your new neighbour at number 61.

'Frightening us? She bloody nearly killed us.'

Surreptitiously opening the front door, I see a small parcel on the step and deftly pick it up and close the door again. It's wrapped in trendy brown paper. Tearing through, inside I find a small furry toy with green feathery bits stuck to it. The label reads: *for small dogs and puppies aged two to three months old.* I pop the pedal bin open and drop the card and gift in.

'No wonder the stupid woman nearly ran us over, Trevor. She's half blind.'

Trevor effortlessly raises one leg over his head and starts licking his bottom. Removing some tender cooked chicken from the fridge gets his attention. He drops his leg and saunters over.

'There you go. Take that nasty taste out of your mouth.'

As he hunkers down and tucks in, I walk over to the window. A white rental truck is parked outside sixty-one. A relay of people carries items of furniture into the house.

'Who does she think she is?' I say to Trevor. 'All false tan and eyelashes, smelling like Saturday night in a Turkish harem. Graham will see right through all that. She's brazenly trying to edge herself in, but it's me who he's entrusted to water his plants. When a man asks you to care for his ericaceous specimens, Trevor, he's interested in more than just moist compost. And what would she know about Pieris Japonica, eh? Or Baby's Tears?'

On Wednesday, my washing machine stops working mid-cycle. Any more excitement in my life and I couldn't stand it. I empty my bed sheets into the sink and use the drain cycle to see if I can clear it, but it makes a noise like grinding metal. It's out of warranty, so I knock on at Graham's and ask him if he can help.

He nods, checks his watch. He pulls his door to, and steps over the narrow grass boundary that divides us.

'I can have a quick look, but it'll probably need a pro.'

He follows behind me. 'Hey, gorgeous.'

I smile and look back, then quickly turn away. The "gorgeous" comment is not intended for me. Its actual recipient is on the other end of Graham's phone and says something that makes him laugh and look at his feet. 'Well, tell him I called. Need him to look at a neighbour's machine.'

There must be something hilariously funny about that, because he laughs again before saying, 'Bye.'

He remembers where he is. He tidies his face up. 'No worries, Bell, sit tight. Nick's wife said she'll pass the message on.'

Nick the plumber arrives within the hour with an array of replacement parts, and my machine is as good as new while there's still enough sun in the sky to dry my sheets.

As a small thank you, I buy Graham a vanilla slice – his favourite – from the village bakery and leave it on his kitchen table after I've finished his ironing. It's these little acts that make our relationship what it is today. I'm thinking this as I close my bedroom curtains. It's eleven o'clock at night, but still all the lights are on at number sixty-one. I can see Angela sorting through things in her curtain-less front room. My mood suddenly changes as my brain switches track. The thought comes to me, filling me with dread. Everything changes, *nothing stays the same.*

Chapter Six

Bella

Four Weeks Later

It's a beautiful morning, the sky is washed with pale pink brush strokes. Trevor is up and about and comes in calling for his breakfast. We always begin the day with one of his tubes of yoghurt. I swear he's an addict and I'm his enabler. I sit and he jumps into my lap. Impatiently, he places his paw on my hand as I rip the top off. He laps up the contents, golden eyes half closed, relishing.

'It's a beautiful day for cats,' I say to him. 'Look at that sky. What wonderful adventures have you got planned?'

He finishes the yoghurt and I kiss him on his grey head like I'm seeing my child off to school. He jumps down and slips lithely through his cat flap. I watch him saunter around the garden, then turn my attention to my own breakfast.

'Gloria,' arrives in the post. I unfold the white tissue paper and lift out the plastic zipper bag. My heart does a little flip. The wig is flattened by the packaging, but the waves spring to life when I give it a good shake. It's not a real hair wig, but it's heat- resistant, cappuccino with blonde highlights, and a side swept fringe. The soft strands slip through my fingers like cool water.

As the result of a car accident, my late teen and early twenties were a time of treatments, ops and physio. The injuries I sustained still impact my life and I can't stand for any longer than half an hour. Despite the slight limp, sore limbs respond to the beat of Dolly Parton '*Working nine to five, what a way to make a living*'. I dance over to the mirror. The wig has stayed secure and I'm confident it won't slip during my normal day-to-day activities. I normally avoid mirrors because, despite three skin grafts, facial scarring altered my left side profile. My cheek area has a deep indent and my jawline ripples on that side when I smile. I use a little foundation to cover it and pull the hair forward as a screen.

Later, with my spirits lifted, I take some pain killers and have a shower. I change into a floral dress. Gloria tops off my look. Trevor lies on my dressing table and plays with a hair grip, batting gently with his paw as he pushes it to the edge. He leans his head over and watches it fall to the floor, his tail slowly waving as he decides whether to pounce.

Glasses on and a final check in the mirror, I sigh 'Well Trevor, I've made the best of it.'

Tea towel covering my home-made lasagne, I make my way over the road to number sixty-one and Angela's housewarming barbeque. Voices and music greet me as I walk down the side of the house. Doubts about coming here flood back in. I don't do well in social situations. I seem to run out of myself very quickly. When I emerge into the back garden, I see Graham has already arrived. He tilts his head back as he swigs beer from a bottle and chats to a guy expertly turning sausages on the barbeque. Angela's boyfriend? He looks the type. Speak of the devil. Angela comes from the back of the house with a bowl of food in each hand. Graham turns, hurriedly puts his bottle down and takes a dish from her. Angela's dark hair is piled into a chignon and she's wearing a white cotton dress and gold sandals. My head is sweating and itchy, my flowery dress is all wrong. Feeling self-conscious, and out of place, I turn around to leave, but my exit's blocked by Sue, a woman who lives a few doors down from me.

'Ah, hello.'

The corner of the tea towel has blown off the dish. Sue looks down and inhales. 'That smells delicious. Have you just stolen it from the food table? Good choice.'

We face each other awkwardly for a moment as I try to sidestep her. She smiles kindly and takes my arm.

'Come on, we can get drunk very quickly, then make our excuses.'

'Ah, hi there,' Angela says as she walks over. She surveys me from top to bottom in a deliberate way. 'Thank you both for coming.' Taking the lasagne from me, 'This looks great Bella, very kind of you. Come and meet some of your neighbours.'

'I must see your new kitchen,' Sue says.

'Go through, both, help yourselves to wine,' Angela answers. 'Be with you in a mo.'

'Come on,' Sue says, as she guides me through.

A couple of women holding glasses of wine are already inside. I look back and see Graham, smiling and chatting easily with Angela as she lays my lasagne on the food table. I'd wanted to show it to him, but Angela seems to be taking the credit. Graham says something and Angela leans into him and laughs. Her laugh starts off low and goes up in octaves, like an opera singer practising a scale.

'Don't put your fingers under that,' a woman with short auburn hair says to Sue, pointing at a high-tech-looking tap. 'Instant boiling water. I looked all over for the kettle, gave up and went on the wine.'

I take the opportunity to escape and wander around the house. The front room door's ajar and I push it open. Soft pastel walls and a cream rug. An angular lamp with an elongated neck and pink shade hangs elegantly over a grey settee, like a wading flamingo. On the other wall are framed certificates. Fancy scrawl naming Angela Maynard as their recipient. There's a grey filing cabinet. A recessed bookcase holds neatly stacked publications with titles like, "Dealing with Loss;" "Overcoming Low Self-Esteem;" "Mind Over Mood." A hefty tome called

"The Diagnostics and Statistics Manual" serves as an effective bookend. A sense of loss surfaces, reminds me of what was taken, everything I don't have. I recognise the acid of envy on an empty stomach.

'Ah, there you are,' Angela says from the doorway.

'Oh, sorry. I wasn't–'

'Do you like it? It's for my sessions.'

'Yes, it's nice.'

She walks further in and runs her hand over her desk. 'I've never worked from home before, always at the hospital, or with a team.'

'It'll be different then,' I say. It's all I've got.

'Certainly will. I won't have anyone with severe risk or anything like that. Just the walking well.'

'What's the therapy?' I ask, hoping I'm not showing my ignorance.

'CBT mostly. Keeps it simple, short.' She does a little wave with her manicured hand, adding, 'Six sessions and thank you very much.'

Considering she's a therapist, she doesn't seem to have a lot of empathy.

'You lived here long?' she asks, looking out of the window towards my house.

'A few years.' I don't know what it is about her that makes me unsure of what's going to come out of my mouth, but I add unnecessarily, 'I won't move again.'

'Hm,' she says, reaching out with her forefinger she dabs at something on the table then examines her fingertip. 'Graham said you clean for him.'

I have never thought of myself as simply Graham's cleaner. I see myself more like his personal assistant. I want to say as much, but she jumps in. 'Only I could do with a cleaner and I'm sure you could use the money.'

'I help him out because he's a friend. It's not my job.'

'Oh?' She looks as though she hadn't contemplated that I

might have a say. 'Okay, whatever, but...' She moves to the filing cabinet and straightens some books that have slumped sideways. 'I'm just saying, circumstances change. If they do, you could always pick up a few hours here.'

A series of short buzzes fills the room. I follow her gaze to a wall-mounted screen. A couple holding up a bottle of wine smile into the camera. Angela presses a button and says, 'Hey guys, the party is at the back. Come around.' She turns back to me. 'Well, better go.' She walks to the door and waits for me. 'I like your hair, by the way.'

The compliment is delivered with a mocking twist to her lip that rather disturbs the perfect symmetry of her face, and I realise there isn't a modicum of friendliness about her. My scalp tingles uncomfortably as I pass her, and I make a concerted effort not to reach up and adjust Gloria.

The young couple with the bottle of wine are Guy and Raita. Guy, it turns out, is Angela's nephew. Guy and Raita are in love. They glisten with it. Moving and thinking as one. We onlookers treat them as though they are rare and special beings. Which they are, because there is a shared understanding that Guy and Raita's bubble will eventually pop and they too will be reduced to onlookers, the same as the rest of us.

As I pick at the food on my plate, I try to initiate conversation with Graham. His replies are brief, economical. He's clearly enraptured by Angela, as most of the men are. Her background in psychology is the favoured topic.

Angela's loving it. She twirls her Nigella Lawson hair around her fingers. I imagine her like a southern belle, being unhooked from her corsets by her maid and complaining of how tiresome it is to be so doted upon.

'Who's the worse person you've ever treated?' Barbeque guy asks, 'You treated any murderers or psychopaths?'

Angela keeps her responses vague, says she could tell us, but she'd have to kill us. Everyone laughs at that.

'How hard can it be?' I ask, surprising myself. Everyone turns to look at me. There's just the sound of sausages, sides splitting on the barbeque. 'I mean, you're just listening to people's problems. It's no big mystery, is it?'

Angela sits up a little straighter with a bemused expression on her face. 'Well, I suppose you're right, Bella. Any fool could do it. You should give it a go.'

They all laugh again, even Graham.

'You asked for that,' he says.

And I realise with gut-dropping certainty that I'm on my own. He's shown his colours, planted his flag.

Angela is looking at me with that half-smile. She blinks slowly and turns away.

Sue is true to her word and gets tipsy very quickly. 'I think I'd better be going,' she says. 'I'm up early in the morning, and I think I've overdone it on the prosecco.'

I seize the opportunity. I've been uncomfortable on the plastic garden chair but didn't want to ask for a cushion. My dress sticks to my bottom and legs as I stand up and I quickly pull at it, hoping no one has noticed. 'Yes, I need to go too.'

'Oh no, so soon?' Angela says.

'I need to get back to Trevor, and I think I've overdone it on the caffeine.'

The group seem amused by that, even though I didn't intend it as a joke. While everyone else has been drinking wine and beer from glinting flutes and bowl-shaped glasses, I've been drinking tea.

'Walk with me?' Sue suggests as she rises. 'I have some cat food that Molly won't eat. Maybe Trevor will like it? It's Pharaoh's, expensive, all natural, but you know what they're like.'

Angela rises and thanks me for the lasagne and tells me she'll drop the dish off tomorrow. I look back and call goodbye. Graham is engaged in a conversation with someone, oblivious.

Sue links my arm like we're old friends. 'She's a good act, but she's on too long,' she says conspiratorially when we're away from the house.

At her house, Sue hands me a carrier bag full of cat food.

'You should find another interest, you know.'

For a moment, I think she's referring to Trevor.

'You're too obvious,' she adds. 'Too up close. He can't see you.'

Her comments make me wonder whether anyone else at the barbecue noticed my obsession with Graham. But I suppose obsessive behaviours are hard to hide.

The second I step into my own house and close the front door, I drop the bag of cat food, pull Gloria from my head and have a good satisfying scratch. God, what a relief. Upstairs, Trevor is curled up on my bed. He looks up at me through half-closed eyes and makes a little noise, which I take to mean, 'Don't worry, I still love you.' Then he smacks his tiny lips together in contentment, stretches out, and closes his eyes again. From under the waistband of my skirt, I remove the booklet called "Overcoming Low Self-Esteem" which I took from Angela's pretentious consulting room. I lie down on top of the bed, stroking Trevor's head as he snores.

Chapter Seven

Bella

Monday morning gallops in astride blustery winds and heavy rain. I had planned to go shopping, but the weather aggravates my pain and I decide that shopping can wait. Instead, I switch the table lamps on and light the log burner.

The living room isn't large, but it's cosy. The settee's a violet plaid fabric. It came with two accent armchairs which flank the fireplace. The suite is at least ten years old, but it's proven to be a good buy. Mind you, it's hardly like I've raised a brood of teenagers on it. I've probably sat on the armchairs a handful of times over ten years.

With a cup of tea and a plate of toast, I sit on the settee with my feet resting on the coffee table and flick through the purloined self-esteem book. I vaguely register the click of the cat flap as Trevor leaves for his morning exploration.

The opening chapters discuss the impact of early experiences. It says that you don't have to have been the victim of abuse to have depression and low self-esteem: a lack of interest from parents and significant figures can cause it. I've been enjoying my toast, but it starts to feel like a piece of foam, spongy and tasteless on my tongue. I've read before that girls get their self-esteem from their relationship with their fathers. It makes sense to me because my father hardly ever spoke to me. For years, I endured his misogynistic attitude, not understanding what I'd done wrong. 'He would have preferred a son,' my mother said, when I asked her why Dad didn't like me. I wonder about Angela's background, her relationship with her father. She has that indefinable quality, the assumption that she will be liked. That people will listen when she speaks.

I catch a movement at the window, something blocking the light. Then knocking at the door. Rising, I carry the tea tray into the kitchen, before checking myself in the mirror. This morning I'm wearing my usual, Audrey. She doesn't itch as much as Gloria and has slightly darker streaks.

A large lady stands at my door holding a red umbrella, which lends a healthy pink glow to her face. She looks to be in her late thirties, maybe early forties, like me. She has blonde shoulder-length hair and little, red-stained cupid-bow lips.

'Hi, I'm Jenny Moorfield,' she says, as though I should know her.' Angela Maynard?' she asks.

Ah, I realise her mistake. I'm number sixteen, she's looking for number sixty-one, Angela's. It's not the first time this has happened. I've received mail for the previous occupants of sixty-one in the past. My intention is to re-direct her, but I'm also intrigued, read nosey if you like.

'For a therapy session?' I ask.

She assumes my question is rhetorical because she closes her umbrella, an expression of relief on her face as she waits to be invited in. She seems vaguely familiar, but she doesn't appear to register any recognition for me. I look across at Angela's, resenting her because she's taken so much from me. I hear Sue's words on a repetitive spool: *"Be less obvious. Find another interest."* How hard can therapy be? It's so tempting.

I invite Jenny in.

Chapter Eight

Angela

Angela stands at her front room window, straightens her skirt with the palms of her hands and checks her phone again. Scrolling through her contacts list, she locates Jenny Moorfield. It's Jenny's responsibility to inform *her* if she's going to be late. She decides to give her another ten minutes.

She surveys the room as she sips coffee. Books are slumped sideways on the shelf. She puts her cup down and walks over and straightens them. Returning to her desk, she checks her phone, sighing and shaking her head. 'Really annoying,' she says.

At that moment, her phone rings. It's Steve, her ex. Out of habit, she answers. 'Hi,' she says flatly.

'Hey.'

His bright tone is very annoying but, she supposes, that's what waking up next to a different girl every few weeks does for you.

'You settled in?' he asks.

'Sure, getting there.'

'Haven't got my invite to the housewarming yet.'

'No? It's in the post. Is it something urgent, only I'm waiting for a call?'

'Good for you. Straight back in the saddle.'

Angela shudders, stays quiet, and waits.

'Right,' Steve begins. 'Just wondering if you'd got those curtains?'

'What?'

'Green, with the pattern thing. I've just moved into my new flat, Wilmslow. You should come and have a look. Anyway, I've no bedroom curtains. This morning, everyone on the number three-five-seven bus got a good look in while I was in my boxers. The bus stops right outside the flats. It was there for about five minutes. I had to duck down and wait for it to go.'

Unbelievable, Angela thinks, aware that the safest way to deal with Steve is to send him the bloody curtains, even if she has to buy some and post them.

'How big?' she asks.

'A double-decker.'

'The curtains, idiot.'

'It was a joke.'

'Look Steve, I've got another call. I'll have a look and text you back. But can you keep the calls down please now? There's no need for us to be in contact.'

'Great, yeah, sure, I–'

She cuts him off, 'Knobhead.'

Chapter Nine

Bella

What am I doing?

I haven't thought this through. Jenny hands me her coat. I turn away to hang it as a hot flush grips me.

'Where do you want me?' she asks.

I direct her to the settee and offer her a cup of tea. My heart thumps in my chest like it's trying to kick its way out.

It's still not too late. I can just say I made a mistake. I'll appear strange, but no real harm done. But then she'll tell Angela, and Angela will tell Graham. They'll have a good old laugh.

I hurry into the kitchen and flick the kettle on. With a shaking hand, I prepare a tea tray. A mundane act, suddenly complex. How do I extricate myself? Pretending to *be* a therapist is one thing, but she thinks I'm Angela. I will have to be Angela. It's wrong on so many levels. With no idea how I'm going to explain it, I return to the living room.

'I'm so sorry Jenny, I'm not–'

'Oh, my goodness.' Jenny exclaims, as Trevor jumps onto the settee. I hadn't heard him return. I'm about to rush over and remove him: she may be allergic.

'He's just beautiful, a British Blue?' she asks, as Trevor leans his head into her hand for an ear-rub. Unusual; he's not normally affectionate with strangers. 'I just love them. I have two rescue cats, mother and son,' she adds. 'To be honest, I was very nervous about today. I nearly didn't come. I mean, it's a hard thing to do, isn't it? Bare your soul to a stranger. But now I know you're a cat person. Cats go where they want. They stay with who they want to stay with. No one person really owns them. If he's with you, he's with you for a reason. That's good enough for me.'

I had known what I was going to say, but Jenny seems so friendly, and she's a cat lover. Maybe I could get away with it?

The decision's made for me. I return to the kitchen and Trevor joins me, waiting for his breakfast, pleased with himself as if he's just closed on a big deal. I place some food in his bowl and then root around for a box of French fancies.

Jenny calls through. 'So, I've brought my food diary, as you said. It's so embarrassing to write it all down.'

I pop my head around the door and see her rummaging through her bag, emptying its contents onto the coffee table.

'It's in here somewhere.'

Returning to the tray, I quietly remove the plate of French fancies and replace it with my writing pad and pen. I inhale, exhale, and try to focus.

'Okay, Jenny. I like to start my sessions with a nice pot of tea, perfect therapy for mornings like this.'

So far, so good. Jennies hardly stopped for breath, while I've made a few notes on my writing pad. I nod occasionally, feel real sympathy, very aware that Jenny thinks I'm Angela. That I'm a fake, while she continues to pour her heart out.

'I've got a hairdressing business.'

'Oh?' I become aware of Audrey. An experienced hairdresser could probably spot a wig from outer space. But Audrey wasn't cheap. Apart from my house, and Trevor, she's probably the most expensive thing I own. I almost reach up and give her a reassuring pat; too much time with cats.

Jenny continues, 'I'm on my feet all day, but it doesn't seem to make any difference. The trainees are so skinny, and they can eat anything. There's always biscuits and snacks around. If anyone offers me anything, I go through this whole routine. Should I have one? Will I be judged if I take one? They'll think I'm greedy.' Stopping to draw breath, she glances down at her hands in her lap. 'I mean, it's just a flipping hob nob.'

'It sounds like you simply enjoy food like you're supposed to. Are you over-thinking everything?'

'Well, that's how it gets you. I've tried every diet,' Jenny says, 'Atkins, paleo, the zone, south beach, you name it. Hilarious., If they worked, I'd be in a bikini on the south beach like right now, not here.' She hands me a piece of creased paper. 'I've written it down from yesterday, but I've kept food diaries in the past. They don't work for me, just make me feel guilty, then I eat more.'

I take it from her and smooth it out.

She says, 'Look, Angela... Can I call you Angela?'

Guilt ripples through me. Instinctively, I want to correct her. I'm about to, but she continues, oblivious, 'I don't think I can sit here while you read it. Can I use your loo?'

Directing her upstairs, I try to picture how I left the bathroom. I'm a tidy person, so I'm confident it's presentable.

The list of food is hard to decipher. Removing my glasses, I give them a good wipe, before returning to the list.

'Oh look,' I say to Trevor, who's curled up on the sofa, '*Wagon Wheels*. I love those.' He lifts his head as a low buzzing noise begins. I look around. Jenny has left her belongings spilled out on the coffee table. It's her phone. Leaning forward, I see that the caller's name is Angela Maynard. I panic: what do I do? I pick the phone up and stand and look around. Should I hide it? Where? It stops ringing. A second later, a notification appears: *message left at 11.20*. With shaking hands, I listen. Angela's voice, she sounds stressed, annoyed, not in a good place: '*Hello Jennifer, we had an appointment at eleven. Please could you let me know if you're not attending? Thanks*.' Then a calmer voice: '*To return the call, press one, to listen to the message again, press two, to delete the message*–' I press three. '*Message deleted. End of messages*.'

The toilet flushes.

I scroll through the contacts until I find Angela Maynard.

Trevor watches.

The bathroom door opens.

I edit the number, amending it to my own.

Jenny's footsteps on the stairs.

I press save and almost throw the mobile down on the table. As I sit down, Jenny re-enters.

'You look shocked,' she says. 'I told you it wasn't good reading.'

Remembering the list, I'd only got as far as Wagon Wheels.

'Look, Jenny.' It's on the tip of my tongue. It's here. I'm about to tell her the truth, that I'm not qualified for this. I'm so out of my depth.

Knocking at the door.

Oh God, what now? Rising, I go to the window and see Graham. Normally, I would be rushing to open it. He looks up and I think he may have seen me.

'It's just a neighbour,' I explain. 'I don't answer the door when I'm in a session.' It feels the right thing to say. Angela wouldn't answer the door during a session, would she? Let him knock. The moment for truth has passed. I pick the list of food up and rip it up.

'No more food diaries,' I say.

'Okay, great,' Jenny answers. 'So how?'

Recalling Angela's words, I say, 'We keep it simple, focus on eating properly, regularly. No food diaries and no diets.'

Jenny tells me about her difficulties with eating, that she goes for long periods without food, then rewards herself with treats. I find myself totally engaged in what she's saying, as though we're friends chatting, problem-solving, then I suddenly feel detached, as though I'm watching us from another part of the room.

Unsurprisingly, her weight loss efforts aren't working, but I haven't a clue what to suggest. I've vetoed the use of a diary, which I thought was a great idea. If it doesn't work, what's the point? The only insight I have is my personal experience with weight and food, so I use that. 'I have to ask you, Jenny, how prepared are you to change?'

'Very. I wouldn't be here otherwise, would I? There's no other help on the NHS. I wouldn't be paying seventy quid a shot to you. No offence, like.'

I'd overlooked that: she'll need to pay me. I hold eye contact while she talks, but I'm elsewhere, imagining the end of the session. How can I possibly take money from her? Manage weekly appointments? I zone back in and realise that she's expecting a plan of some sort.

'Okay, here's the plan,' I say. Even *I'm* interested in hearing what it's going to be. Seeing her phone on the table sparks an idea. 'No food diary, but I want you to record on your phone when you're going to eat something and what it is.' I sit back and wait.

'Record my food on my phone?'

'Yes.'

'That's all?'

'For the first week,' I explain. *Until I can come up with something else.*

She picks her phone up. 'Okay, I think I can do that It's still a food diary, though, isn't it?'

'Well, yes.' I cast about for plausible reasons why it might be different. 'But you're talking to me, telling me what's going on, what's worrying you. How you feel.'

'Ah, okay, like you're just on the other end.'

'Exactly.'

'I'm not having to see it written down. See how greedy I've been.'

'Well, I would never call it greedy. You need to stop that.'

She looks shocked at my tone. I've gone too far.

'No,' she says.

I think she may walk out now. Why didn't I think of that in the first place? I could have just spent an hour insulting her and she would never have returned.

'You're right,' she adds. 'It's a horrible word. I wouldn't let my daughter call herself that.'

At twelve o'clock she looks at her watch and I realise she's waiting for me to end the session. I'm reluctant because of the awkwardness around money, but my back has begun to spasm, and I know I need to move around. I stand slowly, trying not to grimace, and say, 'Thank you, Jenny. If you want another appointment next week, just ring me.'

She rises and says, 'Thank you so much, Angela.'

I stop myself from reacting.

'It's been good to talk,' she adds, as she rummages in her handbag and brings out her purse.

Placing my hand over hers, 'No, thank you, Jenny, no money, this one is on the house.'

'Oh, are you sure?'

'Absolutely. One cat lover to another.'

'That's so kind of you.'

As I help her with her coat, I realise I've really enjoyed her company. I open the door and Jenny extends her umbrella.

'See you next week,' she says, just as Graham approaches, head down against the battering wind and rain. He lifts his head and nods at Jenny as she passes.

I step back, allowing him enough space so that he can shelter in my doorway.

He smiles, 'Bloody awful weather. I'm glad it's summer, the rain's warmer,' he says.

'I'm busy, Graham. I need to get on.' My guilt and pain make me sound curt and offhand. I register the fleeting crease on his brow.

'Sure. Just letting you know I'm away for the night tonight. Just over at Ant's.' Anthony is Graham's younger brother, who lives with his wife and children in Matlock. I have met him. 'But' he continues, 'I'm off to Brussels on Friday for a long weekend. Be good if you could' – stupidly, I imagine he's inviting me to go with him – 'watch the house, the usual.' He smiles again. He's so sure of himself, of me.

I smile back. 'Course. I'll clear my diary.'

Chapter Ten

Angela

A weekend of late nights and too much alcohol had left Angela imagining a fug hanging over her head, following her like a cartoon cloud. While working on a medical report, she absently dragged her fingernails over her scalp, feeling the build-up of dry shampoo masking the week of unwashed hair. Leaving the report, she walked to the mirror and examined her parting. Pulling the hair flat, she could see the landing strip of grey showing through and wondered if she could get a hair appointment at short notice.

Thankfully, the days of Steve's criticisms about her appearance were over. His high expectations had been taxing. Steve wasn't a romantic in a Billy Joel *'Don't go Changing'* or Bruno Mars *'Just the way you are'* way. He was more of a Shaggy *'It wasn't me'* man.

She had often thought that their marriage had been borderline abusive but had never said it out loud. If one of her clients described abuse, Angela would set them straight. No grey border, no room for denial. Abuse always appeared much more clear-cut when it was described by other people. Steve had never laid a hand on her, but each infidelity had been like a physical assault. After ten years, they were at an impasse. Steve wanted children, but Angela didn't because of his betrayals. Steve promised that if they had a baby, he would change. It had been a physically and emotionally exhausting few years.

The doorbell rang and, looking out of the window, she sighed, grateful that she'd installed an intercom system. She pressed the 'speak' button.

'Hello.'

'Angie, it's me.'

'Steve. It's late.'

'I've come for the curtains. I'll be straight off.'

'I said I'd post them.'

'I'm guessing you haven't?'

Angela considered the bag of curtains in the hallway. She supposed it would be easier and cheaper to hand them over.

'It'll save you the cost of the post,' he added, then laughed.

You could tell when people feigned laughter because it didn't reach their eyes. Strangely, Angela thought, when Steve laughed, it never reached his voice. She could see him through the monitor. He remained on the path the whole time, checking his watch. Angela guessed he is in a hurry himself.

'You're probably right though. It's a bit late. I'll leave you to it. I was just passing,' he said, and turned to leave.

'Steve, here. Take them,' she said resignedly, and opened the front door.

'You sure?'

She hefted the bag up from the bottom of the stairs. He rushed to help. 'Thanks,' he said. 'Sorry, forgot you went to bed after *Corrie*.'

'It's okay. Just no more soft furnishing, alright?'

'No problem.' He rolled the bag up and holstered it under his arm as he looked around. 'Looks nice. You going to invite me in?'

Chapter Eleven

Bella

Trevor comes in at nine mewing for something to eat. Grateful for the distraction, I get up and put some food in his bowl. He gulps it down gratefully and before joining me on the settee as I flick mindlessly through channels.

It's after two in the morning before I wake up with my neck at an awkward angle. It takes a moment of rubbing before the cramp eases off. I switch the tv off and, for some vague reason, I'm drawn to the window. I part the curtain and look up and down the road just as Angela's front door opens and a strip of light from her hallway illuminates her front lawn, injecting a brush stroke of green into the colourless night. With one arm against the door frame, she leans out. I notice the man walking from her house to a black car parked on the narrow kerb. Still a bit groggy, I think it might be Graham, but he's out for the night and the man's gait and shape don't fit. He's carrying a large parcel and opens his boot and disappears for a moment. When he emerges, he says something that I can't discern. Angela shushes him and looks over towards my house. I let the curtain fall back in place. The car engine starts up. Slowly, I peel the curtain back and watch it disappear down the lane. Angela stands for a minute. I think she's looking at me, then I realise she's looking up at Graham's bedroom window. A second later, she closes her door, and the thin strip of green disappears. Once again, the road is in darkness.

Chapter Twelve

Bella

The bookshop has two walls full, top to bottom with books on dieting. I pull a few out. Colourful photographs of vibrant foods adorn each page. On page thirty, the '*Dairy Free, Gluten Free, Cake Recipe Book*' has a photograph of a glistening sticky toffee pudding which makes my mouth water. I almost dribble onto the page.

The picture of an attractive woman surrounded by young children, who are all helping her to bake in her middle-class designer kitchen, stares at me from a book called '*Yummy Mummy, Scrummy Tummy: Recipes for Rainy Days.*' It's all a far cry from the recipe book called '*A Hundred and One Things to Do with Condensed Milk*' that my mum used to have.

I move over to the "self-help" section and find a few books on depression and anxiety, including '*Free Your Mind and Your Body Will Follow: A guide for losing weight using relaxation*'. I read one title, thinking I must have misread. I move on, I take a step back to check. Yes, it's called '*Angel Therapy.*' The back of the book explains that it combines traditional psychological counselling with teaching people how to contact their own guardian angels and listen to their guidance. The price for this enlightenment is twenty-four pounds and ninety-nine-pence. I have a sense that all the saints and angels are screaming at me to look for something cheaper. Eventually, I settle for a few books in the '*Overcoming*' range.

At the till, the cashier places *Overcoming Binge Eating*, *Overcoming Bulimia* and *Overcoming Anxiety* very carefully into a bag for me and gives me a pitying smile as she takes my money.

When I arrive home, I see that Graham's car is back on the drive and remind myself to ask him how Ant is. Inside, Trevor's asleep on the settee. I say hello and he lifts his head and blinks slowly, yawns and tucks himself back into the curl of his body. I busy myself with unpacking my books and have a read through the binge eating book. I notice that Trevor hasn't shown interest in his food, so I go to him and pick him up. As I do, he lets out a little cry and struggles to get free. I lower him slowly to the floor.

The vet diagnoses a tail pull injury and tells me that these injuries are usually caused by being caught under a car wheel or just by being pulled.

'Keep an eye on his bladder: you might notice some dribbling. But from the x-ray, I'd say it's a mild pull and will heal in a week or so.'

I order a return taxi and leave the vets in a perplexed state. He has never had such an injury. I know he doesn't wander far from home as he's always in calling distance. The cars on our road are usually travelling at a slow speed because of the cul-de-sac. I think back to the day Angela arrived and the near miss. She hardly showed any remorse. A thought enters my head. Could she have..? But she's been nowhere near our house.

During the journey home, Trevor calls to me from his carry basket and I put my fingers through the gaps and try to placate him by making soothing sounds. 'It's okay, boy, you'll be fine, nearly there.'

At home I feed him a *lick-e-lix* and make him comfortable. I go to fill the kettle, but think I can hear voices. I turn the tap off and incline my head, like a satellite locating the direction of noise. I move towards the adjoining wall and press my ear to the plaster. The voices are coming from Graham's. The tone of conversation is lively, the speech continuous, no pauses. Then there's a woman's laugh. It starts off low and goes up in octaves, like an opera singer practising a scale.

Chapter Thirteen
Bella

Jenny arrives for her next appointment and this time, I'm ready. I've taken some analgesics and I have a notepad and pen handy. I've also copied a short questionnaire about eating habits from the book about binge eating. I was always a good student.

I get a better look at her today. Her hair is tied back in a ponytail and she's wearing eye liner that accentuates the pale grey of her eyes. Her thighs and bust are generous, but she has a waist. I think her outfit – jeans and white jumper – suits her shape. I don't see anything wrong with her size.

'What kind of a week have you had?' I begin.

'Not bad,' Jenny says as she scrolls through her phone. 'I recorded my food on my phone, like you said.'

'How did you find that?' I ask, keeping it casual but hoping to God that it was worthwhile.

'It was okay. Felt like I was talking to myself. Not unusual for someone with three kids. It stopped me in my tracks a couple of times. Like, Jenn, is that what you're really thinking?'

She looks at me, eyes wide. I think there may be tears in them. She continues, 'As if I've never been aware of what has been going on in my own head.'

I nod at her. I can see the importance of this revelation in her face, but a response deserts me. Maybe it's the sudden eye contact or behaving as though this is perfectly normal. It all crowds in on me at once. I look at Jenny as she looks back at me expectantly. In my hand is the questionnaire and I'm so grateful to be able to refer to it.

As we explore the questions, I know that I should have asked what thought had stopped her in her tracks, but the moment has passed. It was probably incredibly significant.

All isn't lost, though. The questionnaire kicks up some interesting stuff around Jenny's childhood. Trevor is settled on the settee next to her. He's moving a lot easier now, but I've kept him in for the last few days. She strokes his head. He makes his little mewling noise, before yawning widely, exposing his coral sharp canines, before stretching out and closing his eyes. Cats need at least sixteen hours of sleep a day. I don't judge him.

Still gently stroking Trevor's head, Jenny tells me that when she was twelve her mum put her on the same *Slim Fast* diet as she was on.

'She thought it would be something we could do together.'

The harm mothers do, I think. I say nothing.

She continues, 'Whose mum does that? I thought I was fat. But I look at photos of myself from then and I was normal, yet she treated me like I was terminally fat.'

'When we're young, we're never as fat or ugly or stupid as we, or our mothers, think we are. Could you bring those photos to the next session?' I suggest, thinking it will be nice to see a few photos. It'll give me a focus.

'Sure.'

'What about your dad?' I ask.

'Oh, Dad had hollow legs. He'd sneak food to me, toffees, and that. They had arguments about it.'

'What about brothers? Sisters?'

'I have an older brother, Hugh. He was fine. She didn't put him on a diet.'

'Did you lose weight?'

'Oh, you know, like two pounds here and there. I don't think Mum did, either. It was all about the diet. Cut out this and that. No sugar, no cake, no sweets, weighing ourselves every day.'

I glance down at the notes I made from the binge eating book. 'How do you think that affects you today?' I'm really pleased with this question. As the books say, focusing on here and now is one of the *core methods* of the therapy. I'm actually doing therapy! I feel something stirring in my blood stream, akin to the surge of caffeine from my first cup of morning tea. I refocus.

Jenny puffs her cheeks out and blows. 'I think about food all the time but try not to. I go for long periods without, sometimes to test my self-discipline. I'm kind of all or nothing. Anyway, I need to cut down to prepare for the surgery.'

'Surgery?' This is news to me. She sees my confusion.

'I'm on the list for the gastric bypass. Sorry, I thought I'd said.'

I stare at my notes to give myself a moment. 'Yes, course you did.'

'I need some therapy first. It's part of the criteria. Mike, my other half, doesn't want me to have it.'

'You sound determined.'

'I am, so please don't try to therapy it out of me.'

The hour passes very quickly. At the end, I make sure she has a clear, regular eating plan. No more long periods of not eating, as outlined in the book. I ask her to send the recordings of her thoughts around eating to my phone, and any subsequent recordings, the day before each session, so I can prepare. I'm learning fast.

As she reaches for her purse again, I flush. I shake my head and explain that I've decided not to charge her for the sessions. Instead, I've come up with an idea that I think she'll be happy with.

'Are you sure? It's very kind of you.'

'Yes, I'm sure. I suggest it to a few of my clients.'

Chapter Fourteen

Bella

I let myself into Graham's and Trevor follows close behind with his tail high in the air. A sign that he's happy. I close the back door and place the keys onto the kitchen counter, where Graham has left a brown envelope with my name on it. I love to see my name in his handwriting. It's only the payment for ironing, but it's something between us. I put my hot pot in the fridge for later, take my holdall upstairs and lay out my nightdress carefully. I'm looking forward to another night in Graham's bed. I'll have to be careful with Angela being just over the road. I usually draw Graham's curtains at night when he's away, and open them in the morning, so it won't seem odd if she sees me here.

The kitchen's tidy. Surfaces have been wiped down, and there's a sharp smell of lemon in the air. I place my keys in the cat-shaped keyholder similar to mine. I bought it for Graham and it's a fixture now. There's a couple of keys on a red leather fob that I don't recognise. One from Graham's office, no doubt.

I walk through the open-plan kitchen-diner into the living room and see the track marks where Graham's hoovered. It sounds stupid, but it feels intimate. Only I would know that Graham hoovers across the rug, side to side, not top to bottom, as I would. He hasn't asked me to clean for him this time, just to do his ironing.

Sir Trevor jumps up onto the window ledge and looks out. I pour some water into a saucer for him and place it in his usual spot at the back door. Before I start the ironing, I choose a film from the array on Netflix. As I turn back, I spot a greetings card on the mantelpiece. Puzzled, I wonder if I've missed his birthday, but his birthday is in November and it's only June. I pick up the card for a little sneaky peek. The handwriting's familiar. Then I see the signature. The room mocks me as I read. With a head full of wasps, I falter. Dead-legged, I drop backwards into the chair and stay there a moment until the buzzing stops.

As I stare at the card, Trevor jumps up into my lap. The sudden movement breaks me out of heart-lock, and I let the card drop to the floor. He pushes his head under my hand, and I stroke him on autopilot while my insides churn.

'What an idiot I am.'

Gently lowering Trevor to the ground, I slowly stand, retrieve the card from the floor, and place it back on the mantlepiece. I grab my keys and open the back door. Trevor runs past me and knocks the saucer of water over. It puddles on the laminate floor. I leave it there.

'Hi, Angela. It's me. So, I think talking to you is helpful. Like, it's mad to realise all this dieting crap started a long time ago with my mum. It makes me really pissed off. It's other people's stuff, isn't it? Always other bloody people.'

It's so very gratifying to hear Jenny thinks that talking to me, an untrained novice, is helping. I press *stop* on the recording she's sent me and jot down a few notes. The words that resonate, though, are those about other people. Jenny's right: a lot of problems are caused by others. A mental picture of Angela surfaces. I try to refocus, reminding myself that I'm supposed to be listening as a therapist and not as a voyeur. It's not all about me. Is it?

Later that day, I relent. I return to Graham's, clean up the spill and collect my holdall and nightdress. Then I do his ironing, water his plants, and have a general dust around. He's paid me, after all, and I realised that not helping him anymore would be playing into Angela's hands. I need to fight back, but I'm not sure how. The gloves might be off, but I don't know if

I'm even in the ring.

I study the card again. A plain white card. *'Thank You'* on the front in gold lettering. Classy, understated. Only three sentences written inside.

Graham, just a little note to say thank you for the lovely meal. It's a long time since anyone cooked for me. Really looking forward to Brussels. Angela xx

So much I'd seen and heard and denied.

So much for playing the long game.

I place the card back on the mantelpiece, resisting the urge to avenge the rip in my heart by tearing it in two.

I come home and switch my computer on, seized by the need to look at Angela's website. I hold my breath as I search, and wonder irrationally whether, through some primitive spider sense, she will know what I'm doing.

Its presentation is simple, though sophisticated. A couple of Corinthian columns sit either side of a quote: *'I think, therefore I am.' René Descartes*. The following pages explain her specialities. Depression, anxiety, PTSD, eating disorders. There is a watermark of the head of a Greek Goddess running across each page. I'm not sure what the significance is, other than the annoying similarity to Angela. I feel like a lovestruck fan as I search the pages for her photograph. Thankfully, there is none. I close my laptop and sit back.

I knew that looking on her website would make me feel bad, but I wasn't sure how. Her house, her looks, her qualifications. Now she has Graham, too. The jealousy courses through me like a shot of whisky.

In the afternoon, I gather my gardening gloves and kneeling pad and go into the front garden. After half an hour, my knees are screaming for mercy, so I stand up slowly, grimacing as my limbs adjust to being upright. There is a man at the front of Angela's house, cupping his hand around his eyes and staring into the front window.

Ever the watchful neighbour, I leave my garden and cross over the road.

'Hello,' I say.

He turns. 'Hi,' he answers, as he crosses the path towards me. Tanned sockless feet in moccasin shoes. He's handsome, expensive teeth and good bone structure. He's holding a bunch of pink roses.

I smile back, though my smile is the cheaper, NHS version. 'I'm Bella, I live over the road. Are you looking for Angela?'

'Yeah.'

'For therapy?'

'I probably should be,' he laughs. 'I'm Steve.' He holds out his free hand. I shake it as though it's the most natural thing in the world. 'Ex-husband,' he adds.

'Ah, yes.'

'Angie mentioned me, then?'

'Of course.'

Steve looks back at Angela's, shrugging. 'No answer. I'll come back later.'

'Probably best,' I say, 'but I'd leave it until Monday, Steve. They won't be back before then.'

'They?'

The brightness of his smile disappears like a missing ornament.

'Angela and Graham.' I wave an arm in the direction of Graham's house. 'Graham lives next door to me. He's eighteen. House number, not age, obviously.'

His smile returns. 'Oh, ha ha, sure.'

'I hope I've not spoken out of turn?' I say. 'Caused any trouble?' Feeling the poison in my heart bubble and pop with the possibility that I have.

'Not at all. Angie told me all about him.'

Like hell she did.

'I'm just glad she's happy. You know how it is,' he adds.

'Oh yes, so much easier if you can stay friends.'

'She's been with him how long now?' he asks.

'Since she moved in. They've been inseparable.'

Steve puts the flowers on the bonnet of his car, leans back against it and pulls a vape cigarette out of his pocket. As he exhales, I get a whiff of coconut. It reminds me of suntan lotion and burning-hot sands.

'She tells me he's a nice guy, this… er...'

'Graham.'

'Yeah.'

'It's good that you're looking out for her, Steve. Very admirable. But you've nothing to worry about, they're very happy. It's as though they've known each other for years.'

I watch his reaction carefully as the implication sinks in.

'Listen, Bell.' He reaches into his inside jacket pocket and pulls out a business card. 'This is my number. If you need to call me about anything. I'm only keeping an eye out for her. Angie doesn't need to know.'

I take the card, flattered that he would consider me a confidante.

He grabs the roses from the bonnet and hands them to me. 'Here, find a nice grave for them.'

Then he winks at me and gets back into his car.

Jenny arrives for her session at eleven. She removes a light jacket under which she's wearing a wrap-over dress.

I'm happy to have her company again, but I wish it were as a friend not as a fraud. I try to get into the right mindset, but I'm thinking of Graham with Angela, and my chat with Steve, which I'm still trying to figure out. Like Jenny said, *it's always other people.*

I remember to start the session off with a mood rating out of ten. I remembered it last week but forgot to get one at the end of the session for comparison.

'Four,' Jenny answers. 'Me and Mike argued.'

'About the surgery? I listened to your recording.'

'So, when I got back from work on Thursday, he'd gone and brought himself a motorbike. I hate the things.'

'Why is having a motorbike such a bad thing?'

'Scuse me?' Her voice rises as she speaks. 'Like, because they're dangerous.'

'Isn't that how Mike feels about your operation?' I gently suggest.

She sighs. 'Sounds like you disagree with the surgery, too?'

'Not enough to buy a motorbike.'

She looks at me and laughs. I'm relieved. I don't deal well with angry people.

Jenny reports eating more regularly and not weighing herself every day. She remains dubious about whether she's lost any weight, even though she's told me that my treatment plan echoes the advice the dietitians gave. They must be reading the same book as me. I re-iterate that the goal isn't weight loss. It's to understand her eating patterns and to establish more helpful ones.

As the session proceeds, I feel the strain of her unhappiness. I find the pressure of thinking on my feet in the session very draining. I wonder how real therapists manage to see five or six clients a day and not end up peeling themselves from the wall at the end of the week.

I've exhausted the notes I made and reverted to discussing Jenny's childhood. With twenty minutes to go, the pain in my side is building and I need to move. I decide to take some radical action.

'Come on, Jenny,' I say, as I head over to the record player. We need to shake this mood off with a bit of movement.'

She looks doubtful, but I've discovered that therapists can get away with a lot because people don't know what to expect. I've also learned a new term: '*Evidence based*.' I use it now.

Shaking the tension out of my arms, I tell her, 'There's a strong evidence base which shows dancing releases feel-good endorphins.'

It's initially awkward, but eventually we're chatting while we move. Nothing too strenuous, just side to side. Occasionally Jenny joins in the lyrics to *'Man, I feel like a woman'*. When the songs ends, she flops down in the chair.

'Okay,' I say, 'that's it for today.' I ask her to re-rate her mood.

She thinks for a moment and, still a bit breathless, answers, 'I find it hard to put a number on this stuff. Maybe six?'

'Could you do it at home? Ask hubby?'

She looks at me doubtfully as she stands and picks her jacket up. 'The dancin'? Are you kiddin'? He'd have me committed.'

'He's not supportive?'

'Oh, he's not bad. It's just he's not psychologically minded. He thought the Oedipus Complex was a shopping centre just off the Runcorn bypass.'

I laugh with her, but in truth I'm impressed. I'd heard of Oedipus but have only recently read about Freud's theory. I found it ridiculous. Still, it's a timely reminder for me not to underestimate people.

Chapter Fifteen

Bella

On Monday evening, the diesel clatter of a taxi engine proclaims that Graham and Angela have returned. The taxi leaves and I lean forward and see them together on the pavement. Their low voices sound like humming on the warm evening current. Then I hear Graham's front door open and close. I lean forward to see if Angela is walking towards her own house, but the road is empty. Moving into the kitchen, I wait for the sound of the case being hefted upstairs, but there's only silence.

Minutes pass. Imagining that they know I'm listening, I pull away from the wall and turn the tap on full. I busy myself with washing the few pots in the sink and switch the kettle on. I toy with the idea of knocking on Graham's door to tell him something urgent, like my heart has broken. Instead, I turn the volume up on the tv.

From the day I moved in here, I've fancied that me and Graham shared the same house. With only the wall dividing us, it was easy to imagine. Now Angela has entered the picture, that fantasy is sullied, inaccessible. Trevor jumps up onto my lap and I take great comfort from having him there. I hardly notice that I'm crying.

On Tuesday morning I awake feeling like I've slept in a tomb. One of the books I'm reading advises the use of positive visualisation and mindfulness. Before I get up, I imagine that I'm breathing in clean, positive energy and expelling the ashy dust that's settled overnight, weighing me down.

After breakfast, I play with Trevor for a while. I watch him leap up, swatting at the neon feathered bird on the string as I swing it around. He's completely recovered and is agile, focused, and deadly. When he catches the bird, he wrestles it to the ground, clasping with his front paws and kicking with his hind legs, like he's trying to eviscerate it. After twenty minutes of this workout, I put the feathered toy away and take my gardening tools outside. The early morning chill is refreshing, and the pale expanse of sky helps to put things in perspective.

I bought the toy fire engine when Trevor was just a kitten. Attempting to sit him in it and pull him along was impossible. He writhed, slipped, and slithered out of my hands like cooked spaghetti, thus skilfully evading the promise of fun and bonding between cat and owner, as suggested on the box. I gave up and instead planted some aubrieta kitte in it and placed it in a covered area of my back yard. The purple-blue flowers have lasted well this year. I decide to move it to the front doorstep, where it can have a little more sunlight. Trevor looks on as I remove some of the dead petals.

I lean to the peonies and inhale the soft rose scent. Reaching to cut some for my kitchen vase allows me to angle my head towards Graham's bedroom window. The curtains are still closed.

For the next hour, I carry on with weeding, turning the soil and pulling out threads of vegetation. As I lean back on my haunches and reach for my mug of cold tea, his front door opens. I look up as Angela appears and I catch the tail end of their discussion.

'If you need me there,' Graham says as he emerges, his thumbs hooked into his jean pockets like a cowboy.

They haven't seen me. As much as I'm tempted to eavesdrop, I don't want to look like a Peeping Tom, so I stand up with as much dignity as my knees will grant me.

'Morning.'

Angela turns, surprised.

Graham looks up. 'Morning, Bella.'

'Nice break?' I ask, smiling at Angela.

'Yes, thanks,' Graham answers.

'Hm-hm,' Angela answers with a dead-eyed expression. She turns her smile back on when she speaks to Graham. 'See you later.'

She passes me with a sidelong glance as the wheels of her case rumble brazenly across the paving. I maintain my rigor mortis smile as I watch her cross the road. Then I turn to Graham. His admiring gaze follows Angela all the way. He raises his arm in a ready wave. I twist around and see her step inside her house, pull her case in, and close the door without a backward glance. Graham lowers his hand quickly and returns it nonchalantly to his jean pocket.

'Thanks for the ironing.'

'No problem. Looks like it might be nice today.'

'Yes. Well, I'd better...' He turns away awkwardly.

'Yes, sure.' I say, smiling as the front door closes.

I carry on weeding, pulling vigorously at deeply bedded mares' tail. I jab at the ground with the trowel, feeling the heat rush through as the sun gets higher. I grunt and mutter under my breath. I'm just about to pack up when a shadow falls across me and I lean back and squint up at Angela.

'Quick word about your cat,' she says.

I look around for Trevor. 'What..?'

'I'd appreciate it if you could stop him crapping on my lawn.' She dangles a small, tied bag, weighted by its contents. 'It's not nice to come home to.'

I move onto one knee to stand, but pain shoots through my hip, and I pause. I end up looking like I'm about to propose.

'But he always comes in to use his litter tray.' I say to her eclipsed head. Sun glints intermittently as she moves, bright to dark, bright to dark.

'I saw him.'

'You can't have. He always uses his litter tray.' I repeat.

'Obviously not.'

I have a surge of indignation and use it to push myself up to a standing position. At full stretch, I'm as tall as her. 'And he hasn't been out of the house for two weeks,' I add.

Graham's door opens. It silences us. He steps out.

It feels like a stand-off. I'm Gary Cooper, trowel in my hand, a drawn gun.

'Everything okay?' he asks, looking from me to her.

Angela moves to his side. 'Bella's cat did its stuff on my grass again.' She holds the bag up for him as proof. He frowns and leans away from the offending article. I see irritation in his face. 'I don't want to fall out about it, but it's not nice,' she adds. Her tone is more reasonable now Graham is witness.

'Trevor always uses his litter tray,' he says.

I'm taken aback. I'd expected him to defend Angela straight off. 'Yes! *And*,' I emphasise, 'he's been poorly so I've had to keep him in. In all these years, Graham, have you ever seen him do that?'

'I'm not looking out of my window all the time, am I? But no, to be fair. Can't you just bin it? You can't be sure,' he says to Angela in a lowered tone.

She looks at me, realising she's lost any high ground but trying to maintain her footing. 'It's a filthy habit,' she says, as if I'm the offender.

He lays a hand on her arm. 'Fancy a drink?' She turns and reluctantly concedes, but not before throwing a tight-lipped glare my way. I wonder what I've done to warrant her dislike. She's the one being invited into Graham's, not me. I'm here with a sweaty face and knees shouting for pain killers. He takes her wrist and plucks the bag from her. 'I'll dispose of this,' he says. When she's gone inside, he steps towards me and holds the bag aloft. With an appeasing tone, he asks. 'Could you please do the honours and dispose of this?'

He asks nicely, but I'm affronted by his nerve, and this is *High Noon*. 'No way,' I answer, 'possession is nine tenths of the law.'

Chapter Sixteen

Jenny

Jenny makes her way down the blue-carpeted corridor. She knows the way to the surgeon Mrs Nadia Halder's room, having attended her initial assessment appointment over a month ago.

The consulting room has clean white walls which bear a picture of the human body cut in half and labelled like the Central Line on the London Underground. She wonders whose benefit the picture is for: it's hardly art, and hardly reassuring.

A blue-striped curtain is pulled halfway alongside an examination table. Next to it a silver trolley, with all the paraphernalia she'd expect: a box of examining gloves, face masks, tissues, a stethoscope. To her right, a rack of shelves containing boxes of needles, their various sizes marked with plain black and white labels. The sight of them makes Jenny's blood run faster through her veins. The room smells pleasant, though, and belays any further thoughts about operations and such.

Situated to the left of the room is a wide desk holding a laptop, files, and pens. Seated behind it is Dr Halder. She has brown eyes and auburn shoulder-length hair. She's dressed smartly in a rust-coloured jacket over a black dress. Jenny gets another soft waft of vanilla and spice, the perfume which prevents the room from smelling too clinical.

'How have you been?' she asks, greeting Jenny with a warm smile.

Jenny says she's been fine and is still determined to go ahead with the surgery.

After some discussion, Dr Halder weighs her and informs Jenny that her weight hasn't changed. She notices Jenny's disappointment. 'It's realistic for the moment. But, as you know, your eating habits will have to change massively, especially before the surgery, when you will be on a very low-calorie diet.'

'Why is that? I mean, if I'm having the surgery, why do I have to go on a diet first?'

'I know that sounds all wrong.' Dr Halder picks up her pen and begins to sketch a diagram of the anatomy involved. 'The diet is to shrink your liver. It makes the stomach easier to access for surgery. Cutting down now will help you to cope with fewer calories afterwards.'

'I know, I'm trying. Like, I've found a therapist like you suggested.'

'Good. Is it helping?'

'Early days but hmm, think so. The group, the dietitians an' all, it's all good. But this is more personal. I can talk about things I wouldn't in the group.'

'Course.' After clicking her keypad, Dr Halder offers Jenny August the sixteenth.

Heart thudding, Jenny writes the word *surgery* with a trembling hand in her week-a-page-diary.

When the assessment is over, Dr Halder says, 'Oh, nearly forgot, could I take the details of your therapist?'

Chapter Seventeen

Bella

I cover my head with a scarf and tidy the cellar. I run a telescopic duster around the top of the walls. Cobweb trails festoon the air and dust catches the back of my throat. I go back to the kitchen for a glass of water and to allow the disturbed dust to settle, then I carry the mop and bucket down and swab around until the water is black. I stand back to review my handiwork and try to imagine the room transformed into a small office. It has potential, but the bag of cement and bricks against the fireplace will have to be dealt with.

The dark wooden chest of drawers was here when I moved in. It stands solidly against the wall opposite the stairs. I open the drawers and find some oddments which I bag up in a bin liner. I push the drawers along the wall to make room for a small desk, excited by the prospect of transforming the room into a useful space. I glance at the pile of bricks again. I will not lower myself to ask Graham for his help in bricking the fireplace up. I'll look online.

On Friday, Trevor comes in complaining loudly about the rain. He brushes up against my leg.

I pick him up and take him over to the settee, where I brush his coat and remove a large clump of hair and some sticky buds. As I do, a black clump of hair comes away in the comb to reveal a patch of skin which has clearly been bleeding. I gasp. 'Oh no.' Trevor meows, as though he's telling me about what happened.

A quick trip in a taxi and Sharma, the vet – we're on first

name terms now – tells me, 'There is some grit in here. Looks deliberate, though he could have sustained it in a fall.'

I'm close to tears. 'What can I do?' I ask as she cleans the wound. An image of Angela comes, and cold conviction grips me. 'What if it's someone I know?'

She stops her cleaning and says a gentle, 'Good boy,' to Trevor. Then turns to me.

'This is the second time in a few weeks, isn't it? You could report it to the police, but you'd need proof.'

'I don't have it. It's just a… feeling.'

'Unfortunately, cats are more often abused than dogs. They're not as obedient or easily trained. I have a house cat. I see too many things in here, y'know.'

Trevor has a small dressing on his cut and suffers the indignity of a neck cone. Sharma said he would only have to wear it for a couple of days. He shook his head and tried to paw it off at first, but I think he's become resigned to it now. He's currently lying on the settee, staring at me with displeasure. I'm reluctant to leave him again, but I've planned to go shopping for some paint for the cellar, and I want to crack on with it.

I pull my trolley on wheels out of the kitchen cupboard and give it a wipe over. But an image of Angela throwing something at Trevor sends a wave of anger through me like a radioactive current. Hatred punishes the hater; it's made me anxious and restless. Before I go out, I search online and find a company who erects garden fencing specifically designed to prevent cats from climbing over and getting out. I request an estimate. When the rain has abated a little, I pull on my raincoat and waterproof bucket hat. I tell Trevor I'll be back soon.

Outside, the peonies hang their heads as large water droplets run over their smooth petals, their perfume intensified by the rain. I'm always surprised by how resilient they are.

Bad timing: Graham pulls his front door closed behind him.

He sees me and I almost duck back into the house. Too late.

'Afternoon,' he says.

'Hi.'

'You want a lift?' he asks, as he walks to the car. He obviously thinks I've been watching out for him.

'No,' I answer, rather harshly. 'Trevor's been hurt again.'

'Oh no,' he says. He looks properly concerned and I feel myself give a little, like I'm not in charge of my heart. Maybe I should have some fencing around it too.

'Looks like it was deliberate,' I add.

'But who could…'

'If you can think of anyone, let me know,' I answer. I wonder if he can read my loaded expression through the veil of drizzle.

'We're getting piss wet through,' he replies. 'Sure you don't want a..?'

I click the automatic button on my umbrella. It fans open with a satisfying 'puff' like it's speaking on my behalf. Rain bounces off it as I open my gate. 'Have a nice day,' I say.

Lulled by the expanse of space in my shopping cart, the bright lighting, and up-beat DIY store music, I pick things up here and there. It's years since I've done this. My house is like me, low maintenance. And I don't mind a bit of wear and tear. I find it reassuring. It's evidence of life.

'No Nails' glue is three for the price of two and therefore irresistible. As is the turquoise desk organiser, which, I decide, will determine the colour scheme for the cellar walls. I go in search of paint and rollers.

Pride is all very well, but as soon as I get out of the store, I regret not swallowing it and accepting the lift off Graham. My shopping trolley isn't wide enough to hold the paint, and the carrier bag is cumbersome.

I have an inner wrangle about whether to ask Graham to pick me up, but he was on his way out, wasn't he? And, if he did come, questions about my cargo would be inevitable. So, I decide to be extravagant and order a taxi. When it pulls up, the driver instructs me to get into the cab as he unloads my shopping into the boot. The taxi is roomy with black leather seats and smells of apple air freshener.

'Where to, love?' he asks as he climbs back in.

I give him my address.

'Doing some DIY, love? he asks, as we pull away. 'I'm tiling my bathroom at the moment. I mean, it's not hard, is it? It's just the time factor. You wanna come in and sit down, put your feet up, love, don't you?'

He seems to be a having a conversation all by himself, so I simply nod and smile. When we're on the main road, he quietens down. I'm glad. I want to enjoy the feeling of independence that booking a taxi has given me. I doubt that flying first class British Airways could give me more pleasure right now.

I've spent more money today than I have since I moved in. Rarely do my bills or food shop exceed the forty-pound mark. Today I've tripled that. The thought makes me a bit giddy. I realise I will have to rein it in, especially if I won't have the little extra that Graham pays me.

My phone rings. It's a number I don't recognise. I catch the driver's eye in the mirror and feel pressure to answer it.

'Hello?'

'Hello,' a woman's voice. 'I'm phoning about therapy. Have I got the right number?'

Who does she think I am? How did she get this number?

'Oh dear, can you hear me?' the woman says, followed by, 'I think she's gone.' I hear another female voice in the background.

'Hi, yes that's right.' I reply.

'Oh, you are there. Doctor Halder gave me your number.'

Halder? Is that someone I should know? Angela probably would. I want to ask: who? when? and where? She answers all the questions for me with her next sentence.

'Is that Angela Maynard? Dr Halder said to try your number for therapy.'

I can only assume that Jenny must have shared my number. *Why didn't I see this coming?*

'I don't think she can hear me,' The woman says again to the person with her.

Maybe it's because she sounds nervous, or maybe I want to impress the taxi driver. Whatever. I run it by myself. Could I take another person? Could I help her? Because if anyone sounds like they need help, this lady does. I can't help myself. 'Yes, that's right. This is she.' I resist using Angela's name.

'How much does it cost?'

We're at the lights and the taxi driver can't help but overhear. I lower my voice and ask the deal breaker question.

'Do you like cats?'

Silence.

He's watching me through his mirror.

I think she may have gone, but then, 'Well, I don't dislike them.'

'Just checking. There's no charge for the first session. Why don't you come and have an initial chat, and we can take it from there?'

Another beat. 'Okay.'

She's Mrs Zeta Cronshaw. I give her my address and we agree a date and time.

'Busy day,' the taxi driver says.

'No rest for the wicked,' I answer, as my stomach does a back flip.

Chapter Eighteen

Bella

Insight is a word I've been using a lot lately. It's useful, the book says, for encouraging clients to examine the motivations and emotions behind unhelpful behaviours. I know how this situation happened, but I'm unsure of the why bit, except, maybe, I need to be needed. I scrub over these trails of thought, like a convict covering her tracks with a branch. Instead, I search online for CBT courses. It's clear I don't have the depth of knowledge to get me through this convincingly. I'm the fool Angela referred to.

Scrolling through, I'm drawn to 'The Therapeutic Principles of CBT' and 'CBT for Eating Disorders.' Both courses offer videos and downloadable work sheets for the sum of thirty US Dollars. Paying in dollars makes me feel like an international criminal. The conversion rate comes out at a reasonable twenty-five British pounds.

I begin the first course, and by six o'clock, I've completed three of the lectures and watched a CBT demonstration video. I decide to call it a day when Sir Trevor comes through the cat flap and meows loudly for his supper. Afterwards, I fall exhausted into bed.

The following day, I try to follow the video on helping a client to keep a thought record. As I don't have a printer, I sketch a record out.

***Negative thought**: I'm an evil person for impersonating Angela.*
Emotion/feeling Rate 1-10: Sadness 8, Frustration 8, Enjoyment

9, Satisfaction from helping someone 9.

Evidence for the thought: *I'm impersonating someone, it could be illegal.*

Evidence against the thought: *Is it a thinking distortion? What would a close friend say? Is a thought a fact? It doesn't make me evil, just lonely.*

More balanced thought: *Nope, still evil. But apparently enjoying it.*

Re-rate emotion:

I find it impossible to challenge the negative thought that I'm an evil person for doing this. I don't think loneliness is a good enough reason. One of the techniques suggested is to imagine how a friend might describe you. I wonder if Graham would think of me as evil if he knew what I was doing? Maybe. Probably.

The book suggests that the therapist helps the client to challenge this thinking and discover 'more helpful alternatives.' Maybe it is possible to change someone else's thoughts by challenging them? Now that's what I call a superpower.

Scribbling over my attempt, I decide I'm not a good subject; the exercise will be far more useful for Jenny or Zeta.

The eggshell blue I chose for the cellar walls doesn't disappoint. It looks so fresh it almost chirps. My mood lifts as I roll it on and listen to the radio. Fine flecks land on me as I work the roller up the wall. I'm not concerned. I've covered my head with an old scarf, tied on in a 'land army' style.

Trevor doesn't like the smell of paint and watches from the top of the stairs, tracking the sweep of the roller, making of it what he will. His head cone has been removed now, and the wound has healed well.

I shove a plastic storage box with my foot and find a dead mouse. I look up at Trevor. He lowers his head, and his eyes widen as I pick the mouse up gently by the tail. I'm filled with sadness at the sight of the still body and remorse for the terror that froze its tiny heart mid-beat. I tell the mouse I'm very sorry and look up at Trevor.

'No,' I say as I pass him on the stairs.

Outside, I lean over the fence and place the mouse deep inside the other, next door's rhododendron bush. As I turn back, I'm startled to see Graham at the adjoining gate.

'Hey,' he says. 'Sorry. Didn't mean to shock you.'

'Oh,' I answer, clutching my chest. 'It's okay. Just wasn't expecting…'

'You alright? Only I've not seen much of you.'

'I'm fine. I've been staying in with Trevor. He keeps getting hurt.'

'How is he?'

'He cries at the door, but what can I do?'

'Not happy, eh?'

'The vet said it was a stone thrown at him. You didn't see anything? Anyone..?'

He shakes his head but doesn't look at me. 'Not a thing.'

I feel uncomfortable for him and think of a change of subject. I'm about to tell him I'm painting my cellar, but I stop myself. Sharing personal things is like entrusting people with your valuables. I no longer trust Graham to handle them with care.

'You're not avoiding me, then?' he asks.

I raise my eyebrows. Lesson 101 in how to feign incredulity. 'Course not,' I say.

'Ok, it's just that it's felt a bit awkward since Brussels.

He makes it sound like an intimate weekend away we'd had. *Ah, remember Brussels!*

'You're happy, aren't you?' I'm glad to see the question take him off guard.

'Yes, me and Angie shouldn't change things.'

Angie.

'I couldn't care one way or another about your private affairs.

It's the lack of honesty.'

'Honesty?'

He looks genuinely surprised, and I feel the hypocrisy of my self-righteous outrage. I pull back like a retractable blade.

'Well, I'm happy for you two, obviously, but I wish you could have said at the time you were going on a holiday. I thought it was a business trip.'

'What difference would that have made?'

I can't think of anything. Except maybe I wouldn't have deliberately burned one of his shirts with the iron.

'I think that you could have told me.'

'About me and Angie?'

God, that name.

'Yes, you could have taken me into your confidence, that's all.'

'Okay, sorry.'

He nods as though he understands. But I can see he doesn't get it. He's only smoothing things over, preparing the surface for something.

'I'm going to Holland for a few days, business trip Tuesday to Friday. Will you do the honours?'

'Is Angela going?'

'Why?'

'I'd be able to let Trevor out without worrying.'

'That's not fair,' he says, as he picks at a splinter of wood on the gate.

'Five years, never a scrape. She moves in…'

'Bella.'

'Is she going? Simple question.'

'No, she's not coming to Holland.' He turns away, then turns back. 'So, we're, okay?'

'We are.'

Chapter Nineteen

Bella

Step one. Establish an agenda.

'It's so buggeringly loud, if I can say that?'

Jenny arrives today in a fluster. She sounds like she's moving through emotional gears herself as she complains about the motorbike Mike has bought.

'Is that what you want to talk about?' I ask, pen poised.

'No, not really.'

'So, what do you want to focus on?'

'It had to be something that didn't include me, though.'

'Shall we talk about that?'

'No.'

'Okay.'

Step two. Review the last week.

'How have you been over the last week?'

'I got weighed by Doctor Halder. I've not lost anything.'

So, my guess was correct. It was Jenny who gave Doctor Halder my number. *What have I started?*

'Shall we talk about that?' Jenny looks at me quizzically. I've never asked her that before. I've always gone with the flow. 'I'm trying to find out what's concerning you the most, that's all,' I explain. 'The motorbike was bothering you as you walked in.'

She examines her hands for a moment. Her nails are a glossy red. 'Can you imagine me on it? Pillion? Pillock, more like.'

'Do you really think he bought it *just* to annoy you?'

'Not really. He's too selfish to do something just to piss me off.'

'Why then? I mean, have you both talked about it? The

surgery?'

'He knows where to find the information, if he wants it.'

'You haven't talked about it?'

'Don't need to. I know he thinks I'm an idiot.'

I've been itching to use the thought record and seize the chance.

When we've successfully challenged her belief that '*Mike thinks I'm an idiot for wanting surgery*', Jenny agrees to share the information she has about surgery with him when they are alone tonight.

'What's the worst that can happen?' I ask.

'We argue again. He rides off into the sunset. He has enough stress with his job.'

'What does Mike do?'

'Haven't I told you? He's a detective with Greater Manchester Police.'

My heart beats speeds up and I feel heat spreading through me. This new information sinks in. Life as an imposter just got a little more interesting.

'Stay calm and give him a chance,' I say, not sure if I'm talking to myself.

She sits back in her chair. 'I'm exhausted.'

'Come on, get up.' I switch the record player on and line up Neil Diamond '*Forever in Blue Jeans*. 'You'll feel better.'

She drags herself up reluctantly and begins to move to the music.

'Do we put our handbags on the floor?' she asks dryly.

I laugh. I do feel a bit foolish. 'I'll get a disco ball for us for next time.' We sing a couple of lines in unison, then I ask, 'Have you spoken to other members of your family about the surgery? Like your mum and dad?'

'Nah. Dad lives in Spain now, and it's a sore subject with Mum.'

'They split up?'

'Years ago. It was hardly headlining news. There was no trauma.' She pauses, holding her dance pose. 'Maybe there was,' she picks up again. 'I was only sixteen. It was all very civilised. Mummy and Daddy still love you; we just want to kill each other. That kind of stuff. It worked out well for us kids on birthdays and at Christmas.'

The song ends and Jenny backs towards her chair.

'Hang on,' I say. She lurches forward again. 'I've got some Abba.'

She knows all the words to '*Take A Chance on Me*' and I let her simply move to the music and enjoy it. Finally, I allow her to sit down again. It's enough exercise for my hip, anyway.

'By the way, Dr Halder wants a letter from you. Y'know, like an update, part of the criteria,' she says, when her breathing has slowed.

'Yes, course.' I answer confidently. 'I'll give it to you next time. You bring your photo and I'll give you the letter.'

'I'd forgotten about that. Oh, and I gave her your number.'

Now she tells me.

'And she said she had some other people to refer,' she adds casually. 'I should be charging commission.'

This session has not gone to plan at all.

The squeak of the metal loft ladder attracts Sir Trevor, and he paces around the lower rungs, assessing, measuring. Then sensibly decides to keep all paws firmly on the floor. I flick the light switch. The bulb doesn't exactly illuminate the loft, rather it casts a flat yellow pallor over the haphazardly placed contents. The dust pricks my nose and I sneeze forcefully three times and hope I haven't inadvertently summoned a malevolent spirit.

I shuffle into the eaves on my knees and eventually find what I'm looking for. The brown suitcase's latches are rusted and resistant, but eventually they relent and surrender their treasure. I lift the lid and am assailed by the musty smell of old things contained in an airless space for too long. Yellowing documents, empty Boots holiday photo packets, scattered negatives which reveal family silhouettes, like fossils trapped in amber. Interspersed with these are old bank statements and correspondence pertaining to disability living allowance.

I find the letters, written by an orthopaedic surgeon many years ago. Their tone authoritative, professional, and beyond challenge. I think I can lift a few of the phrases from them. I'm about to close the lid when something catches my eye. The blue of my old school uniform stands out against the disturbed contents. I move them aside and stare at my end of year school photo. I must have been around twelve years old. I feel the tendrils of temptation reaching up, drawing me in. I have a strong desire to surrender, to lose a perfectly good afternoon indulging in unhappy memories. I shut the lid and suffocate it.

Chapter Twenty

Bella

I've spent the morning searching online for more printable questionnaires and have found one pertaining to something called 'Schema Therapy'. It looks interesting but possibly too advanced for me. Still, it can't harm.

Rubbing my eyes, I go into the kitchen and catch a movement in the back yard. A flash of yellow just beyond the fir tree. Molly, Sue's Siberian cat.

The first time I met Sue was about two years ago when she knocked at my door and said Molly had escaped. She scrawled through photographs on her phone to show me a picture. It wasn't necessary. Molly is a striking cat. A cat who would stop you in your tracks if you saw her on the street. After a short search, we found her only a few feet from her back garden.

While keeping my eyes locked on her, I locate Trevor's food bowl and realise with dismay that it contains remnants of the Pharaohs cat food that Sue said Molly wouldn't eat. Still, I carry it low and approach. I place the bowl down gently onto the path, then retreat. She watches me with large green eyes. Her long fur is a mix of orange, cream, and brown, and makes her head look like an exotic flower in amongst my marigolds. Amazingly, she approaches and cautiously sniffs at the bowl. Then she begins to eat, picking at the food like a delicate debutante.

I approach slowly. 'Hello Molly,' I say, in the voice I use for Trevor. Then I grab her.

'*Thank God!* Thank you, thank you.' Sue takes Molly in her arms and kisses her head, holding her close, her shoulders raised like a child holding a precious doll. Molly appears unperturbed. 'She must have escaped when I was putting the washing out early this morning. Come in,' she says. 'I've been all over. I just need to phone the vets. Tell them I've found her.'

I follow her through the small hallway, and a buttery vanilla smell surrounds me. There's not a hint of cat lady about this house.

Despite the cat's size, Sue seems adept at putting the kettle on with Molly draped over her arm. Molly's green eyes track every movement, the water from the tap, the cups from the cupboard.

'She's fine,' I say. 'She didn't get far.'

Sue pulls out a cushioned wooden chair for me, then joins me at the pine table as we wait for the kettle to boil. With Molly in her lap, she picks her mobile up and I hear a woman's voice answer, *'Greenway Veterinary Surgery.'*

The kitchen is the same configuration as mine, but Sue has chosen bold colours. The old cast-iron fireplace is still in place and the walls are painted a deep blue. A green, leaf-patterned Roman blind hangs halfway down the window and the ledge is adorned with a variety of spider plants. Little off-shoots trail onto the draining board.

On the wall is a calendar. The picture for July is of a white sailing boat cutting through calm blue water set against a turquoise sky. There are entries on various dates, sometimes two. I read one that says, '1 pm C'. I wonder who 'C' is: a lover? Or maybe a friend she's joining for lunch in one of the chic little bistros on the high street. It could be a trip to the chiropodist to have her corns treated, but still, I feel a stab of envy at her busy life.

Sue finishes the call and places Molly carefully into her basket. I marvel at the cat's compliance. If I did that with Trevor, he'd quickly jump out and find his own spot to lie on, thank you.

'I owe you big time,' Sue says with her hand over her heart. 'Now, tea or coffee?'

My preference has always been tea, but coffee feels more

adventurous and sophisticated, so I ask for that.

'I was only at the vets yesterday with her,' Sue explains 'I always get her checked before we go away. Molly comes with, don't you, girl?'

'Does she travel okay?'

'It's not her favourite, but it's only a short flight. I have a house in Spain, had it for years. She settles once we get there.'

'She goes on the plane?'

'Sure, she goes in the footwell. She complains, but I'd rather keep her with. Do you have a cat-sitter?'

'What? Oh, no.'

'What do you do if you go away?'

'I don't. I went to the seaside with Mum and Dad. And I went to Malta for a week with the school once. Not been abroad since then, too expensive.'

'Well, I know, but I wouldn't cope without that bit of sun to look forward to.'

We sip from large white cups. I start to become aware of myself and the fact that I'm here in Sue's house and having a chat like we're good friends. It occurs to me that I should reciprocate and invite her for coffee at mine. I didn't think I would ever be able to entertain anyone in my own front room, but I'm doing that with Jenny, and I seem to be okay at it. I imagine us – me, Jenny, and Sue, and Zeta – enjoying a meal around my dining table (I would have to have both of the extension leaves out), with the record player on in the background, just loud enough for Graham and Angela to hear.

'I bumped into Angela when I was out last week,' Sue says. 'She had a trolley full of white wine. Hardly anything green in it, unless you count the bottle. Who is so busy they can't chop a lettuce up?'

Sue has a very expressive forehead and uses her eyebrows to full effect. They rise in unison, then alternate, one up, one down: surprise, questioning, irony. I become aware that I'm moving my own to mirror hers and make a concerted effort to stop.

'All this convenience food,' she continues. 'If she were alive today, my mother would turn in her grave. Which reminds me.' She stands and removes a blue cake tin from the kitchen shelf. 'I only made these yesterday.'

She lifts the lid, which releases lemony aromas into the room. I haven't eaten any breakfast yet, and the back of my jaw begins to tingle in anticipation.

'Lemon drizzle bun?' she offers.

I thank her as I remove a large golden coloured cupcake from the tin and pull away the papery casing. I eat in silent appreciation as Sue hands me a small plate to catch the crumbs.

'Did she say much?' I ask in between bites of cake and sips of coffee.

'Not really. I asked her how business was, she said it was growing. I asked her if she was in a relationship, but she got a bit guarded, like I was out to trick her. I suppose she doesn't really know me; I understand that. I'm an open book. You could ask me anything. What about you?'

'Me? I'm still on the shelf.'

'Ha ha, good answer.' She looks at me knowingly. 'I can keep a confidence,' she adds.

She takes me off guard and a crumb catches in the back of my throat. I cover my mouth with my hand and cough to dislodge it.

'I hope you don't mind me saying this?'

'Go ahead,' I answer, squeezing the words out. I take a sip of coffee and the tickle subsides.

'You don't like Angela, do you?'

'Well.'

'She doesn't like you, either. Hoity toity, my mum would have called her. She's attractive, but she knows it, and that's just not good manners in my book. There's nothing more attractive than someone who is unaware of their own beauty.'

She looks at me pointedly, both eyebrows raised, equable.

You could hold a spirit level to them, and the bubble would be dead centre.

'I was pretty when I was younger,' I say shyly. To ward off any challenge, I add, 'I have photos.'

'Ah, yes, same here. We have more than we know when we're young, don't we? Youth, it's the only real luxury that we *all* get to experience.'

'Why do you say Angela doesn't like me?' I ask. 'I mean, I don't like her because she nearly killed Trevor.'

'Really?'

'Yes, when she first moved in. She ran him over.'

'No.'

'Hm hm.' It's only a tiny lie.

'Oh, I didn't know that. Is he okay?'

'Fine now.'

'I thought it was… something else.'

She raises her cup to her mouth, holding it with two hands. Her head dips, but she keeps her eyes on me.

'Something else?'

'The chap. Graham.'

I breathe out again. Though this is hardly something I'd planned on discussing today. Sue's prodding at my secrets with a sharp stick. 'Well, partly.'

'That's why I think she doesn't like you. She likes the competition but not the competitor. Women like her thrive off it.'

I take an ungainly gulp of my drink. Replies spinning away like frisbees. 'I was here first.' I answer like a ten-year-old.

'That's what she doesn't like.'

I place my mug down on the table across which Sue regards me. We sit in silence while I wrestle with sentences. Arranging and rearranging words. How much do I tell her? Will I be judged as harshly as I judge myself? After all, I'm at my own mercy and can be lenient or harsh as the mood takes me. Finally, I speak. What should I do?'

Sue places her mug down carefully and regards me closely. 'Do you really want him? Really love him?'

The last time I had a conversation like this was with my aunty when I was in my early twenties. I nod.

'Is there anything wrong with your heart?' she asks.

I shuffle in my chair. 'What? No, I don't think so.'

'Well, what do you think it's there for? It pumps your blood around, sure. But it's also supposed to ache with love, desire, passion. I've worn mine out with it. Not with aerobics or step-up classes, with agony and ecstasy.'

'Were you married?'

'Many years ago. A good man, but it wasn't him I loved.'

'Oh?'

'A teacher at the school I worked at.'

'Was he married too?'

'She, Julia, and no, she wasn't married. I left Carl for her. Caused a lot of pain to a lot of good people.'

'Where is she now?'

'Died, cancer, five years ago.'

'I'm so sorry.'

'For the fifteen years we were together, we were that clichéd blissfully happy couple. We must have been unbearable company. Anyway, me and Jules, we *hoped* that hurting people for the sake of our own happiness had been worth it. How can you ever be sure? It was only when she was dying that we knew it had absolutely been worth it. Imagine if we hadn't taken the chance? What regrets we would have had. So, if you want something in your life, you need to act. Put your heart to use. Stretch the muscle. Share it with someone other than Trevor.'

'Graham doesn't want me and it's too humiliating to fight against someone like her,' I reply defeatedly.

'Well then.' She stands up and removes my plate from the table. 'You want the crumbs?'

Home again, I find Trevor asleep on the settee. I pick him

up and give him a cuddle. As I make some toast, I think about my chat with Sue. She's made me question everything and I realise I've been locked inside my own little world for too long. Denying myself. Afraid of being hurt again, settlings for the crumbs. I hoard my thoughts and feelings to me like shameful things, rather than treasures to be shared. Sue was challenging me to be authentic, be true to my feelings.

Chapter Twenty-One

Bella

Overcome with the desire to retch every three minutes, I set the table for two at Graham's house. He's due back from his business trip any time now.

I've put a black dress on, the only cocktail dress I own: 'Oscar de la Renta.' Fifteen pounds from the charity shop. The lady said they cost hundreds of pounds when they were new. I searched online when I got home: she was right.

I apply some "raspberry snog lipstick", ten pence, unused from the charity shop. I don't have the lips for it, so I rub it off, but it leaves an ice lolly type stain around my mouth. Flipping heck. I bet Angela never has these problems.

I found my lasagne dish in Graham's cupboard. I feel insulted that Angela couldn't have knocked on my door and returned it. She must be avoiding me. But why? I've not done anything to her. Well, nothing she knows of. I hope.

I take the lasagne out of the oven to rest, just as Graham's car pulls up. My throat constricts and I feel like I could cough a hairball up myself. I try my breathing exercises. *What's the worst that can happen?*

Hastily, I return the lasagne to the oven. Taking it out again will give me something to do. The front door shuts and the wheels of his case rumble over the threshold. He's holding his phone to his ear as he enters. He stands in the doorway, surprise on his face. I can hear the dialling tone of his phone.

'Hi,' he says and presses his phone off.

'I'm waiting for the lasagne,' I explain, haistily. 'I thought it would be nice for you to come home to.'

'Well, that's good of you,' he says hesitantly, taking in the table setting for two. 'You didn't need to do this.'

'Oh, it's my treat.'

'Angie will love it.'

He's looking at his phone, so doesn't see my mouth open then shut. Bringing the lasagne out of the oven gives me time to reorganise my face.

His phone rings. 'Hey,' he says. 'Yep, all good. How would you like to join me for dinner? Bella's made lasagne.' He gives me the thumbs up. 'See you in two.' He pulls his tie off and opens the fridge door. 'Salad too? Bella, you're spoiling me.'

'I'd better go and sort Trevor out.'

'Hey, why don't you stay?' he says as he opens a bottle of wine.

'What?'

'Sure, join us. Looks like there's plenty.'

'I don't think…'

The doorbell rings.

'You're staying,' he says.

I hear Angela arrive and the soft putt of a kiss. They talk in a whisper. I should leave now.

Angela enters ahead of Graham. She's wearing a flowery sleeveless dress, nipped in at the waist. Her hair is loose and sits softly on her shoulders, shiny as a fox fur.

'It smells delicious,' she says, looking me over.

Graham is behind her, hands on her waist, and guides her to the table. He pulls a chair out and she sits down. Then he comes around to me and pulls another chair out.

'Bella.'

I sit.

He rummages in the kitchen drawer and lays another setting for me. Then picks the lasagne up.

I stand up. 'I'll get the salad.' We almost collide and laugh awkwardly. He lifts the lasagne and I duck underneath him,

Angela watching.

When we're seated, Graham pours wine into our glasses. Angela waits with hers poised in the air.

'Cheers,' we say.

I take a sip. It's the most I'll have. A sip of politeness. I'm still thinking of ways to excuse myself, but my brain feels low on battery power.

'You're all dressed up. Are you sure this wasn't just for you two?' Angela says and does that annoying laugh.

'Don't be an idiot,' Graham says, and winks at me. 'I like the dress. You look nice, Bella.'

'I was going to meet a friend,' I fib. 'But they cancelled, last minute.' I know this lie won't bear scrutiny, so I hastily add, 'I've cooked for Graham for years now, Angela. I have a key, so…'

'How was Holland, Gray?' Angela asks.

Gray? Oh, for God's sake.

Graham puts a forkful of lasagne in his mouth and nods his head appreciatively as he chews. He takes a sip of wine to wash it down. 'That's good, Bella. Yeah, Holland was good.'

'Not as good as Brussels, though, hey?' Angela says.

This time, it's her turn to wink at me. I've never seen a woman do that before. I'm not certain of the meaning. I pick at my food and wonder how I'm going to remove myself from this excruciating situation.

'Graham says you're very good with plants. Green-fingered,' she says, making it sound like an insult.

'She is,' Graham agrees, as he helps himself to more salad. 'And cooking.'

'I'm surprised you've not been snapped up, Bella.'

It's like there's a sniper on her tongue: every time she opens her mouth, she takes a shot.

'There's more to life than marriage, isn't there?' I answer. Hardly rapid return fire.

'Like cats?' she says.

Graham appears oblivious as he pushes his chair back and grabs another bottle of wine from the top of the fridge.

'Your ex-husband seems nice,' I answer. 'Steve, isn't it?'

Angela coughs suddenly, food catching in her throat. She hacks a few times into her napkin, then picks her wine up and downs the remnants.

'You've met him?' Graham asks, turning to me, brow furrowed.

'Yes, sorry,' I answer innocently as Angela recovers. 'I should have mentioned. He was over at yours, Angela, when you were in Brussels.' They exchange a quick glance. 'He said he'd left something at yours. Brought a lovely bouquet for you.'

'Hm Hm,' she answers, as she shuffles in her chair. Seems the sniper has left the building.

'More?' Graham asks, holding the bottle of wine up.

'What?' she asks sharply.

'More wine?'

'Oh, much more.' Her eyes hold mine as he pours. 'What did he say, exactly?'

'He was asking where you were. I told him you were both in Brussels.'

Angela places her glass down and rubs her forehead as if she has a headache.

Graham looks from her to me.

I stop eating and feign innocence. It's a convincing act because I usually am. Usually. 'Oh, I'm sorry,' I say. 'I hope I didn't speak out of line?'

Graham briefly touches my arm. 'It's fine.'

'Excuse me a minute,' Angela says and rises from the table. She removes a packet of cigarettes from her bag and walks to the back door. I didn't know she smoked. Graham must really like her if he's overlooked that foible.

I feel a draft around my legs as soon as she opens the door and steps outside.

'Can you pull it to, please, Angie, so the smoke doesn't blow back in?' Graham asks.

He turns back to me and smiles awkwardly. He's always said he detests the smell of cigarette smoke.

'I'll clear up,' he says, as he transfers the plates to the draining board, signalling that the evening is over, as far as I'm concerned anyway.

'That's my lasagne dish,' I say. 'I'll take it with me, if you don't mind.'

Back home, I kick my shoes off and put the lasagne dish in the kitchen sink to soak. While Angela was in the back yard, Graham said that, as there was still lasagne left, he would wash the dish and return it. I'd been caught out by that ruse before, so I suggested he put the remaining lasagne in a plastic takeaway tray and freeze it. I emphasised that it would only be enough for *one* person.

Before mounting the stairs, I pause in front of the mirror and slowly wink at my reflection. It looks ridiculous and I vow never to try it again on man, woman nor beast.

I can hear their murmurings next door. It can't be described as shouting, but volumised in the way that too much alcohol affects your voice. If Angela had left me alone, I wouldn't have said anything. But she asked for it. It seems I've found my voice.

Chapter Twenty-Two

Bella

Zeta has a love story. She is a petite woman, around seventy years old with a cumulus of short blonde-grey hair curling away from her forehead. A grown-out perm, perhaps. Lavender-shadowed eyes dart around nervously. She's wearing a navy fitted jacket over a cream top, blue trousers and brown court shoes. Understated chic.

I point her to the settee. She places her handbag on the floor and sits down, adjusting the cushions behind her.

When I began this charade with Jenny, I had no idea that I was supposed to address risk at each session. I'm learning. But, even if Zeta tells me she's suicidal, and I sincerely hope she isn't, who would I share it with? The postman? She will have to go back to her GP. Cat lover or not.

Zeta shakes her head. 'Oh no. I'm not about to kill myself.'

Thank God.

'And I don't know anyone who is. I mean, I know that people do if they're mental and what have you. Apart from anything else, it's a moral sin.'

Does she mean mortal?

I run through a couple of questionnaires with her and learn that the reason she wants therapy is because she feels stuck after her husband Frank's death.

'I can't seem to,' she makes air quotes, '"move on". I'm very sad, but I'm not immoral. I wish I were,' she continues. 'I'd throw myself off the Thelwell Viaduct and be done with it.'

'How do you know you haven't moved on? What makes it a

problem for you?' Both classic therapy questions.

Her eyes search the room, the right corner, then they move to the left. She tells me she met Frank when they worked together in an industrial freezer production company. He was on a trajectory to top management; she worked in admin.

'I don't believe in love at first sight, Angela, do you?'

'Oh, erm, I don't know.' I push an image of Graham aside.

'No such thing,' she states. 'It's easy to believe in it when you're young and your cuddle hormones are at high tide. I loved Frank at *last sight*. That's when it matters, when you're old and your buttons are fiddly. We were happy. The children grew up and left home, and we resumed where we'd left off pre-kids. No empty nest, but a home full of memories and boxes of their favourite cereals for when they visited. Frank got one of the last good pensions and we travelled. Our last holiday was on the *Queen Mary*, transatlantic crossing. We sat at the captain's table. We were planning a Mediterranean cruise when Frank died. Last time I saw him alive was four months ago on a Tuesday morning. He was off to Morrisons. I asked him to pick up some oat milk for me and some digestives. I like one with a cup of tea in the morning. The next thing I knew, he'd had a massive heart attack. They called an ambulance, but he was dead before I got to the hospital.'

'I'm so sorry.'

'The thing was, he'd paid for the shopping, so the assistants bagged it up and gave it to the ambulance and they passed it on to me. So, I could still have my cup of tea and digestive. Just no more Frank.'

'That must have been terrible for you.'

'It was decimating,' she sniffs. Reaching into her handbag, she grabs a handkerchief as an unshackled sob escapes her. The power of it rocks her small frame. She buries her face in the hanky, muffling her words. 'I'll go into Morrison's in the hope that I'll catch him there. Maybe it's possible that I keep missing him because I'm not in the right place at the right time?'

'Grief is hard,' I add, for nothing. I know about grief. It's horrible, like climbing stairs to a room and opening the door expectantly, only to find the building next door has been demolished and there's only a stomach drop into nothing. Everything that should be there has gone.

Witnessing her pain reminds me of my own. I'm drawing in too close, feeling too much. A therapist would know how to guard against this. I stand up to get a different view of the room. I place my hand on her shoulder. 'It's okay, just let it out.' I could cry with her. 'I'll make us a nice pot of tea, shall I?' I wonder about offering her a biscuit. Would it be insensitive? 'I've got some Rich Tea, if you'd like one?'

Still holding the hanky over her nose, her eyes meet mine. The redness from crying emphasises the blue. 'Lovely, thank you,' she says.

I break away and escape to the kitchen. Zeta's vulnerability prods at my guilt, and rightly so: it would be arrogant of me not to feel self-doubt.

Over a cup of Earl Grey, I discover that gardening used to be one of Zeta's hobbies. 'I've no interest now,' she says.

I show her to my back yard. It's a still day. The sky a flat grey, no interruption of clouds, or birds, for the moment. It would make for an uninspired watercolour.

'Oh, it's an oasis,' she exclaims.

She admires the deep evergreen foliage and flower spikes of the monkey grass. The contrast of its purple leaves growing beside the Hosta. She can identify everything in my borders. When we return inside, Trevor follows us in and jumps up next to her. I wait with bated breath for her reaction.

Scratching him under his chin, she says, 'Hello chicken, and who might you be?'

'He's called Trevor.'

'Very pleased to meet you, Trevor,' she says, using her pet

voice. 'We used to have a cat called Herman.' She cups her hand around her mouth on Trevor's side so he can't hear her. I like her more for that. 'He was run over.' She drops her hand, and her voice returns to normal. 'We said we'd never have another one. Too heart rendering.'

To avoid the pity from the girl in the bookshop, I've started to order therapy books online. Overcoming Grief arrives in the afternoon, and I spend the rest of the day reading. There's some useful information about the distinctive features of complicated grief.

There's a tick-box list:

• *Intrusive memories or fantasies about the departed loved one. Strong pangs of emotion related to the lost relationship.*

Zeta certainly has those.

• *Strong yearnings that the departed person is still present.*

Another feature of Zeta's grief.

• *Intense feelings of loneliness or emptiness.*

Something stirs in me. It seems to come from the back of my brain and wind its way forward.

• *Avoidance of people, places, or activities that remind the sufferer of the deceased.*
• *Sleep disturbance. Loss of interest in work, socialising and hobbies.*

I become aware of a creeping cold and pain in my hip. I glance up and check the door is closed. As I do, an old image hits me so unexpectedly, I gasp, as though I've inhaled ice. A faded memory arrives in sharp focus. A spectre shaking me awake.

I stand, and the book falls to the floor. Startling tears spill from me. I hurry to the kitchen and gulp down some water. The image has gone, but it resonates, as it always does when the past gate-crashes the present.

In the evening the office furniture I ordered arrives. Trevor loves a cardboard box, so I put a couple of his toys in one of them and he plays for a while, but soon becomes more interested in my flat-pack skills.

I have a new lamp and a swivel chair, which was a nightmare to assemble. I can't get the lever to work, so I'm sitting a bit low at the desk. A cushion soon rectifies that.

Sound and movement from next door resonate in the cellar. The opera-singer laugh echoes from above. I've doubted my own motivation for continuing with this rash course of action, it seems like something a crazy person would do. But the sound of that laughter acts like a grater on any doubts: they become smaller, more justifiable.

Since the dinner at Graham's, my dislike of Angela proved overnight like a bread dough, and has baked and hardened my resolve to continue. She's taken Graham from me, that's clear. Even more unforgivable, I'm convinced she deliberately injured Trevor. I'm evening the score by taking something from her. She's lucky I'm only doing this.

My knees begin to stiffen, and I stand up and stretch my arms above my head, fingertips touching the ceiling. I get down on the floor and lean back against the wall, extending my legs out. It's odd seeing the room from here. Trevor's perspective, so different from mine. The legs of the table, the chair, the stumps of the drawers. The floor looks coarse and chipped. I think it may benefit from a coat of paint and a new rug. Trevor takes the opportunity to come and lie on me, and I'm grateful for the cuddle. He's not really a picky-up cat. I must wait for him to come to me. I'm always flattered when he does. I scratch his head and under his ears. Exhausted from his sudden burst of energy, he's soon snoring. I follow suit and focus on my breathing: in through the nose, out through the mouth. Trevor's fur is a deep bluey grey, thick, warm and soft between my fingers.

The muted tread of feet climbing Graham's stairs. I try to stay in the moment. In my freshly painted cellar. I'm making changes, making new friends. I have Sir Trevor and people are relying on me.

Philip Haslam phones the next morning. I sit at my desk and scribble notes and listen. They're not really notes. (I asked him to spell his name and I've written it out about twenty times). I like the feel of writing something as he explains, it helps me to think. He tells me that Jenny suggested he contact me because they attend the same weight support group. He's also considering having a gastric bypass.

I struggle with my conscience. It's one thing to have hatred spur you on, but my gripe isn't with this man. I'm frustrated that I can't get at Angela more directly and I can't prove she's the one who is hurting Trevor.

'I've tried everything to lose weight,' he says. 'But I suppose you hear that all the time.'

Hmm, A lot less than you'd think, actually. I have my doubts about having a man I don't know coming into my house. Those men usually have ID cards you can check and are here to fix something. (The exception being the nice woman who came to sort my broad band out). If I let Phil come here, it will be the first time a man has been here; but it'll be me doing the fixing.

'I'm sorry Phil, but…'

'I like cats,' he adds, out of the blue.

'Oh?'

'My mum has two.' He says it as though he's uttering the secret password for an exclusive club. Which it is. I wonder What Jenny's told him exactly.

All the literature says that the first chat is always an assessment to see if the client is suitable for therapy. Whether they could make the changes and whether you could get along. It doesn't say anything about them being a cat lover.

'How ready are you to make changes, Phil?' I ask, like a professional.

'I'm open to anything,' he says. I hope he's not being suggestive, but I remind myself that if a woman made that comment, I wouldn't bat an eyelid, so I'm being unfair to Phil.

'Okay, I do have one appointment slot for Thursday. But it will be for an assessment.'

'Fair enough. Do you want me to bring anything?'

'Yes, bring a notepad and pen. Also, bring photos of your cats.'

I'm not a complete pushover.

My life seems to be changing out of all recognition. I have three potential friends (besides Trevor, obviously). Four, if you count Phil. Three, if you don't count Graham. And I feel like I'm counting him less and less as the weeks pass by. It saddens me. There's a spare bit of my heart that was his.

With Jenny and Zeta in mind, I've started to keep notes. General notes for my own records. Notes on mood scores. The comments made that I remember afterwards but forgot to ask about in the sessions. I know I'm avoiding certain areas. Such as Jenny's relationship with Mike. Or any personal stuff, like sex. That stuff. A real therapist wouldn't avoid it. They'd dig down until they hit rock. Then continue excavating with delicate implements. But they're trained, and I'm not. I have the blunt tools of a novice.

Something I have noticed, though, is that I'm remembering more stuff about my past. I'm dreaming more. I've woken twice in the last week with that horrible screeching noise reverberating in my head. Feeling I've been shaken like a collection tin. Memories I've managed to avoid for years. Why now? I ask myself. Why now?

Chapter Twenty-Three

Bella

Phil's a large man with a mop of black hair and stubble, which spreads down his neck and under his collar. But he's not unattractive. Mind you, I've realised that there aren't many people I think are unattractive: they are just undiscovered. He's wearing dark track suit bottoms and a light grey jacket over a loose black polo shirt, which he constantly pulls away from his stomach.

When I'm seated across from him, I pull my cardigan across my chest like a strict landlady. Then check my posture. I need to be open and welcoming, but I feel nervous too. Phil's such a big man. A man's man who takes up a lot of room. Louis Walsh used to say to contestants on *The X factor* that they 'owned' the stage: well, Phil 'owns' the room.

'So, Phil, have you ever had any therapy before?' I ask, as in, could you spot a fake?

'Er, no, no. This is the first time.'

I run through some of the assessment questions and learn that Phil is thirty-two years old. He tells me he weighs nineteen stones and has been advised to shed seven of them. He says the weight crept on slowly after he lost his job in IT two years ago. His dad died when Phil was only six, and his mum has mobility problems. He's her main carer and he has three siblings. He has his own flat in Stockport. He isn't married but hopes that losing weight will help him to meet someone. He's now got a part-time job in a garage. The more I learn about Phil, the more I warm to him.

'And you're going to have the surgery?' I ask.

'I'd prefer not to, but I just can't lose it,' he says, studying the carpet.

'Jenny said the same thing,' I say, then I almost gasp as I realise,

I've crossed an ethical boundary. Discussing another client is a massive no-no. Phil doesn't seem to have noticed, but I blush a deep red. 'I mean, everyone says the same thing.'

'I would have done it privately, but it's a lot of money.' He reaches into his pocket and pulls out his phone. Two adorable ginger moggies are his screen-saver picture. 'This one is Luna, and that's Nala,' he says, pointing. 'I can't have pets in my flat, so my mum has them. They're company.

'They're beautiful,' I say.

I tell him about Sir Trevor. I have a photograph on the mantelpiece anyway so anyone who comes in here knows he's my special boy. I suggest to Phil that, instead of paying me, I would like him to make a regular donation to The Cat's Protection League.

He smiles shyly and says, 'I was hoping you'd say that. Jenny said you see people for free if they like cats.'

'Well, keep it to yourself now,' I say, thinking I need a word with Jenny. The risk of discovery increases with each client I take. Phil will have to be the last.

'It's unusual, that,' he says. 'Kind.' He looks around the room.

'It's not all about money, is it?' I say.

His gaze settles on one of my old cushions. He nods his head and says, 'No.'

We proceed with the session, and I observe that Phil shakes his legs a lot. He opens and closes them, banging his knees together in a nervous jiggle, like a five-year-old who is dying for a wee. It's very distracting.

'What do you want to get from coming here?' I ask. Classic.

'Erm,' jiggle jiggle, 'I've always wondered why I can't get food under control. I go around in circles. Always fall off the wagon.'

'So, what do you want from this?' I persist, as he hasn't answered my question. I would have missed that a few weeks ago.

'I want to know why…' He pauses. His voice drops to a whisper. I lean forward to hear. '…I keep failing.'

'How many diets have you been on? Just an average number.'

'Oh, God, now you're asking, phew!' he exclaims, blowing the forelock of black hair up off his forehead. He looks very vulnerable, belying his size. ''Bout thirty.'

'What if you're not failing?'

He stops jiggling. 'What? Look at me,' he says, casting his eyes down and tugging his shirt away from his stomach. 'Not exactly a picture of success.'

'No, I mean, what if you're not failing at dieting? What if dieting doesn't work?'

I ask him if he's heard of 'The Cycle of Dieting'. I found it in one of my books. I'm happy when he says he hasn't because it gives us a starting point and I don't think Phil will be up for *Dancing Queen* just yet.

Chapter Twenty-Four

Bella

The cellar floor is the same blue as the walls now and it's easy to imagine I'm descending into a 1950s movie star's abandoned swimming pool. I'm so glad I didn't go for the deep red.

Trevor is close at my heels. He's spent the morning chasing a crisp packet that I folded into a whirly gig. Now he's ready for a morning nap. He lies in my lap for ten minutes, then climbs down and finds a place to curl up on the rug.

I begin by skipping through some of the CBT stuff, looking for things to expand my repertoire, as they say. A list of 'Negative Thinking Errors/ Distortions', catches my attention:

Black and White Thinking [seeing things in the extreme]: Emotional Reasoning [interpreting feelings as facts]: Over Generalising [one event means you apply it to other situations]: Personalising [it's all about *me*]: Mind Reading [being sure what the other person is thinking]: Jumping to Conclusions [being sure a thing will happen].

Reading through them, I wonder how I've managed so far in life. My thinking is mostly cobbled together with these distortions. We all see a blinkered version of the truth, don't we? Only God, or some omnipresent being, could see every version of the truth. I wouldn't want the job.

Reminding myself that this isn't all about me, I think I might be able to help Phil challenge his thoughts about failing. Though I'm not sure which thinking error, this is. Personalising? Generalising? I'll let him decide, let him do some of the work. After all, he's not paying me, and he gets free tea.

Two days later, Jenny arrives for her session and sits on the chair opposite, nursing her cup of tea. She looks very stylish. Style is something I don't do. When I was younger, I was 'fashionable,' but neither a slave to, nor master of.

According to a magazine in the surgery waiting room, style and fashion are two different things. No matter. Style to me is using a special *'Grips Fur Lifter'* to remove the cat hairs off my clothes before I go out.

Jenny's been distracted during the session. Despite her telling me that talking is helping, I get the feeling she's losing confidence but doesn't know how to tell me.

'You know, I'm sure I know you from somewhere. Which school did you go to?'

The question explains her pre-occupation, but it's an unwelcome one. Off my stride and rummaging through my notes, my face heats up. 'Fine, if you want to spend the session talking about me, but,' I fiddle with my watch. 'We only have fifteen minutes left.'

'I'm on my break,' she says, holding her cup up to me as evidence. She doesn't seem to notice my discomfort.

'Well, I was going to say that it's your money and your time. But as I'm not charging you…'

Jenny sighs. 'Okay, fair enough. My head's not in it today, though. Don't you ever get like that? Don't you just want to chat sometimes? Shoot the breeze? It must be wearing, listening to other people's crap all day?'

'Changing the subject, Jenny?'

'I know, avoidant.'

'You were saying your mum suggested a diet for Chloe?'

'Can you believe it? Chloe is like *that*,' holding up a little finger. 'Straight up an' down. I told her to back off.'

'Did you tell her how it affected you?'

'It's too late for that. You know, during the start of Covid, everything went pear-shaped? Well, so did she. Now she's heavier, she even more preachy. She says, if she can't be a good example, she'll have to be a terrible warning. So, she turned her attention on Chloe, and I'm not having it.'

'So, it affected your relationship?'

'I was aware of everything I put in my mouth when she was around, so I tried not to be around her. Still do, but it's hard because I want Chloe to know her Grandma. Still, me and Chloe are talking about it now.

'Excellent.'

'Yeah, all good.'

I feel very proud of Jenny and of myself. This is what it must feel like to be a real therapist.

'Did you go to Marple High?' she persists. 'Sorry, it's just…'

I stand to avoid her gaze as the blush reheats, 'Music, I think.'

'Oh, flippin' 'eck, me an' my big mouth.'

'Come on, you enjoy it really.' She loves Bruce Springsteen, so I put *'Dancing in the Dark'* on.

'Oh sneaky,' she says, as she stands up. 'We have Scottish blood in us, you know, on my dad's side. My grandpa used to say that the best way to torture a Scotsman was to nail his feet to the floor and put a Jimmy Shand record on. I never had a clue who Jimmy Shand was, but I always laughed.'

I've steered the conversation away from me. But the pain in my hip breaks through like a child yanking on its mother's skirts. So, I suggest that we end the session early.

'You weren't feeling it anyway,' pain speaking for me, peeved and childish.

'Sorry,' she says. 'I know that sounded ungrateful, but I just thought it would be good if I knew something about you too. I wasn't being nosey or anything.'

'No, no Jenny, it's just that we only had a few minutes left. I'll talk about me for the whole hour next time. You won't be able to get away fast enough.'

Jenny agrees to continue recording her thoughts, and she

decides she's finally going to talk to her mum about the diets she put her on. Jenny thought of this herself. I wish I'd suggested it, but it seems that Jenny is becoming her own therapist.

As soon as she leaves, I rush into the kitchen and down two pain killers. Then I pick my little boy up and sit, waiting for the stinging to ebb. I put the tv on and skim-watch *Countdown*.

I thought Jenny was familiar to me, too, but I don't know her maiden name, and I don't want to ask because that conversation will surely take us back to school days and more deception.

On Thursday I answer the door to Zeta and glance towards Angela's, wondering whether she's as busy with clients as I am.

It's surprising to me that Graham hasn't once mentioned the increase in footfall to my front door in the last few weeks. But he's always been one to mind his own business, which I've always considered a virtue. Then again, it's not so much of a virtue if you're genuinely not interested, is it?

Zeta clears a space on the coffee table as I carry the tea tray in. We both reach for the cups and catch hands, then snatch them away and laugh. She slaps her offending hand with the other and says to me, 'You be mother.'

I like this part of the session. Two people sitting down for a catch-up, savouring tea in comfortable companionship. I've made a note for myself to establish Zeta's goals. Back-peddling because I should have done it at the beginning of each session.

When I put the question to her, she picks at something on her sleeve, then looks around the room. 'Frank alive again. That would be my goal.'

I write it on my notepad and nod.

'And if we can't do that?'

She looks properly disappointed in me. She squeezes her eyes shut and looks like she's smiling, but tears roll down her face, tracking through her foundation. The timely dab of a tissue in her shaky hand stops them.

'Then stop the pain of missing him,' she cries, head down, her hair a thick bundle of white curls.

My instinct is to sit with her and hold her hand, but I'm not sure whether I'm supposed to maintain a distance. Should I do it anyway? It's normal for her to be upset. I need to sit with it.

'Don't you think it's normal to miss him?'

She lifts her head. The tissue in her hand has all but disintegrated. Tiny white particles fall into her lap. I pass her the box, pulling a more substantial wad out for her. She takes it and bunches it up with the remains of the used one.

'I want to go to sleep and wake up in two years when it doesn't hurt as much.'

'Sounds like a plan.' I smile, 'but what else might you miss if you do that?'

'Erm,' she looks at me as though I'm being tricky and says, '*Cash in the Attic*?'

A smile tickles my cheeks, and I look away to stop it from spreading into a grin.

'I was thinking more in the way of…' Zeta's anxious expression stops me and I re-think how I'm going to phrase this. It's so easy to veer into chat that doesn't go anywhere and forget that something is expected from the sessions. From me. I start again. 'Someone once told me that the pain of grief is just the sting of good memories being engraved onto your heart. It's all we have, apart from now, this minute. Bypassing that pain through drugs, alcohol, sleep, whatever your poison, means that those important memories can be lost or clouded, or unprocessed.'

Zeta regards me again, and the room is still, only the sound of the ticking clock. Time passing by, unnoticed to noticed. 'You lost someone?' she asks,

I wonder how truthful to be. I've realised that I enjoy being a therapist most because I can find out about people without being under the spotlight myself. I can turn the questions back. I've always been good at that. I don't like a winding road of conversation. I'm more a cul-de-sac conversationalist.

Some honesty is required here, though. 'Yes,' I answer.

'Who dear?'

The ticking of the clock. Paced and patient.

'Well, just about everyone,' I answer, trying for a light tone.

Zeta frowns, concerned. Not what I intended.

'I'm fine, Zeta. Really.' I smile and try not to sound patronising. 'I'm saying that the pain is normal. You learn to ride it. Saddle up and hold on cos it's a bucking bronco.'

'It can throw you off.'

'Yes, but that's where friends and family come in. They're like the crutches you'd use say, if you had a broken leg, but for the mind.'

'Psychic crutches.'

'Kind of.'

She nods and pushes the tissues up her sleeve.

'No Trevor today?'

'He's around somewhere.' I say with a glance around the room.

'I should get a little rescue cat or dog to rescue me,' she says. Watching me to see if I get the joke. She makes a *hrr hrr* sound, which I have come to recognise as her laugh. I smile to show I have. She continues, 'I said never again, but that was before. Do you think it would help?'

'I think animals always help, but I'm biased. They're a big responsibility if you like to go on holidays.'

'Well, I don't suppose that's going to be happening now, is it?'

I should have seen that coming. 'Have you been into Morrisons again?' I ask.

She nods and pulls out the bundle of tissues. 'The Earl Grey tea has gone up by ten pence. I had a mind to go to Lidl, but I'm habitual and Frank wouldn't hear of it.'

'Is it still Frank's decision where you shop?'

'No, but you wouldn't catch…' She stops, frowns. 'I was going to say, you wouldn't catch him dead in Lidl. It just hit me. That's exactly what I'm trying to do in Morrisons, catch him dead.'

Silence can be useful. Which is a good thing. Zeta's sudden lightbulb moment has thrown me off my stride.

Zeta thanks me as she leaves and says the session has given her some things to digest.

I hardly did anything. I must be a natural.

I take the tray of teacups into the kitchen and look out of the window towards the new fencing. The work began early one morning last week and was done by three in the afternoon. The top of the fence curls over so Trevor can't jump up and over it. He spent a few hours distrustfully examining the perimeter, and scratching at the base, but he seems adjusted to it now. It was expensive, but worth it to know that he is safe. I can see him now, lay under the fir tree, intent on something in the branches. I breathe in and tell myself to be grateful for all I still have.

Chapter Twenty-Five

Jenny

The information evening is being held at the local hospital and Jenny and Mike arrive late due to parking problems, and slide into two vacant seats on the back row.

The room is bright and airy, surrounded by windows dressed in cream slatted blinds, angled to block out the low evening sun. The woman speaking is called Deb. She is one of the specialist dietitians with the Weight Management Team.

'One of our gentlemen, Barry Thomas, who is now ten months post-op, has kindly offered to talk to us about his experience. Thank you, Barry.'

Barry joins Deb as applause echoes around the atrium. He is about thirty and wears a blue polo shirt and a pair of denims. Jenny can tell he's lost a lot of weight by the loose skin around his neck and at the top of his arms.

She knows from talking to the dietitians the process doesn't end with the bypass. The resulting weight loss often leave drapes of loose skin, which requires further surgery to remove. She can just imagine Mike's reaction to that. He'll probably threaten to take up cage fighting, she thinks, despondently.

'Best thing I ever did,' Barry says. 'But hardest thing too. I've lost a total of sixteen stone and I'm eating normal-ish food. I still go back to ramekin-sized portions every now and then. Dumping will let you know if you've overdone it.'

A groan sounds through the room. Jenny has heard about dumping syndrome from the dietitians. It is one of the least attractive features of the bypass and happens if you eat too much refined sugar. The advice is to eat small meals through the day and stay off cakes and bread.

'Aye, the dreaded dumping,' Barry continues. 'Learn from my experience. Don't do as I did when I ventured out on my first date in six years and omitted to mention the surgery. After the meal, when the lady suggested we share a large knickerbocker glory, I said, why not? Needless to say, the glory was very short-lived.'

Although people laugh, Jenny feels her stomach turn at the thought of being caught short in a restaurant. Someone at the front asks Barry a question. It's inaudible from the back of the room.

'This lady has just asked how I deal with hunger ten months on,' he repeats helpfully. 'What I will say is that I think I get normal hunger now.'

Jenny turns to the lady seated to her right and whispers. 'What's normal hunger?'

The lady shrugs. Jenny does the usual and tries to estimate if the woman is fatter or thinner than her. She believes the woman is probably doing the same.

Barry continues to speak for a further ten minutes, emphasising the importance of family support. Jenny notices a high number of couples are present, there to support partners in one of the biggest decisions of their lives. She exchanges a glance with Mike, and he squeezes her hand. Encouraged by Angela, Jenny had finally opened up, and he'd listened. He still wasn't one hundred per cent on board but had agreed to accompany her and find out more from the group.

When Barry finishes speaking, he receives an enthusiastic round of applause.

'Thank you, Barry,' Deb says, as she glances up at the wall clock. 'Just to add that Dr Halder will speak next. Also, some of you will be familiar with Olga Thomas and Angela Maynard, therapists who have agreed to answer questions on CBT. They'll be available throughout the evening. Right, this might be a good time to break.'

The sound of scraping chairs and general chatter echoes around the room, forcing Deb to raise her voice over the escalating babble. 'Reconvene in fifteen minutes.'

Jenny is surprised to hear Angela is present. Neither mentioned the meeting at their last session. She strains to see the front row, but her view is obscured by the hovering and dawdling attendees. Mostly women, dressed in summer clothes, their exposed fleshy upper arms reminding Jenny of a butcher's display of lamb leg joints. She looks around for Phil to ask him how his session with Angela went, but then remembers he'd said he wouldn't be at the group because he was helping his mum to decorate.

Nadia Halder reaches the refreshments table and spots Angela at the far end. A couple of people are waiting to talk to her and causing a jam. She manages to catch Angela's attention and watches her make her excuses and weave her way through the queue.

'Hi Angela, I wanted to catch you. I'm Nadia Halder.'

They find a quieter spot where they discover that they worked in the same health centre for a short time, just before Angela set up privately.

'This coffee is terrible,' Angela says, screwing her face up.

Nadia considers her black coffee and sips again, as though sampling a fine wine.

'I think the boiler needs de-scaling.'

'My tongue does now, too.'

'|You get used to it. How are you doing, working from home?'

'It's okay so far. I miss the banter.'

'Yeah, I can imagine, though sometimes I can't wait to get away from it. By the way, one of my patients, Jenny Moorfield, said that she's seeing you and I got your number from her to refer someone else.'

'Moorfield? I recognise the name for some reason, but she's not one of mine.'

Deb calls out to the group. 'Excuse me everyone, can we

make our way back?'

'I'm sure she said she was seeing you,' Nadia says, as she scans the room. 'Over there, the lady with the red hair, in the blue dress.'

'Nope, definitely not one of mine.'

'How strange. I'm sure she said...'

'Okay everyone,' Deb begins, as people resume their seats and the chattering lessens. 'Dr Halder, a surgeon, is going to talk to us about the operation. This is mostly for family members, so please be patient, even if you think you know it all already.'

When they return home Jenny drops her bag on the hall table, and heads for the kitchen. The box of photos, which she'd been searching through for her session with Angela, remain on the large wooden dresser where she'd left it.

'You want a coffee?' Mike asks as he fills the kettle.

'Yeah, why not?'

'Is everything alright?'

Jenny nods distractedly. 'Fine. I'm just looking for… It was here…'

'The group was interesting tonight,' Mike says, pulling a piece of sliced ham out of the fridge and lowering it into his mouth. 'I'll come again, if that's okay?'

Jenny nods and pulls a photo from the box. 'There you are.'

Chapter Twenty-Six

Bella

I have a feeling Jenny will ask for the letter to her doctor at her next appointment, so I printed it off at the library. I read it aloud:

> *Dear Dr Halder,*
> *Re: Mrs Jenny Moorfield DOB 12/10/1980: 29, Glenview Crescent, Heather Bank, Stockport SK7 4PQ*
> *I am writing to you regarding your patient Mrs Moorfield, who is planning to have bariatric surgery and is attending CBT sessions to fulfil the surgery criteria.*
> *Jenny has now attended four sessions and is making good progress. She has established a regular eating pattern and is learning to challenge negative thoughts.*
> *She has two further sessions before she is discharged.*
> *If you require any further information, please do not hesitate to contact me.*
> *Signed*
> *A Maynard CBT Therapist*

I lifted the phrases from a letter signed by a surgeon who treated me many years ago. She has lots of qualifications after her name. They look like a *Countdown* conundrum. I have no idea what letters Angela has after her name. I can probably find out by checking her website again, but for reasons I can't explain, I'm afraid to look.

I sit at my new desk, the lamp casting a cool light over

everything. The smell of fresh paint remains, but it doesn't mask the musty spice of the brick. My fingers tremble when I pick up my new fountain pen and put it to the paper. I hold my breath. Gripped by fear and cowardice, I cannot sign Angela's name.

I push up from the chair and step back. I look around the cellar. *Really* look. I scrutinise it like a forensics expert. The cheap plywood desk and the notes copied from various textbooks. My scribbles look childish, amateur. The certificate in a 'Basics' frame. The handful of books in my 'library'.

Not so much a moment of clarity; more a punch in the face, a bloody-nosed awakening. I wonder how I've managed to go so far with this. I slump back heavily into the chair and catch my hip and grimace.

Almost signing my name (or should I say, Angela's name) to something brings the risks home to me. I'm a pale imitation of Angela. I screw the letter up, twisting it at both ends. Then I pull at it, ripping it to pieces, and watch as the shreds of it fall across the desk and onto the floor. The blue room feels cold. I have the urge to surface for air. I traipse drag-legged upstairs, Sir Trevor ahead. He waits at the top so he can surprise me with a quick swipe of his paw to my ankle before he runs off.

Later on, there's banging at my front door. Someone's fist rather than the knocker. Trevor shoots off the settee. His expression tells me 'run' as he darts out through the cat flap. I consider following him.

Another barrage ensues. I'm frozen in a state of fear. Should I call the police? But what if it's Angela, and she's discovered what I've done? What if she's told Graham? The banging repels me. I back away and watch the door, expecting it to burst open. Each thump reverberates and my heart matches its urgency and pace. Explanations and excuses orbit my head like quarrelling particles I can make no sense of. The banging comes again, and I'm shocked out of my paralysis and move towards it.

'Who is it?' I call, my voice shaking.

'Jenny. Open the door.'

I'm confused and uneasy. It sounds like Jenny, but the tone of her voice doesn't bode well. 'It's late, I'm ready for bed.' I call.

'I need to speak to you. Now.'

'You need to calm down first.'

All goes quiet. After a moment, she says, 'I'm calm. Let me in. Please.'

Unable to see a way out of this without drawing the attention of the neighbours, I open the door.

I hardly have time to register her as Jenny pushes past me, her arm brushing my shoulder. I see my chance of escape through the open door, but where would I go? I close it. Jenny stands in the middle of the room. Her jaw set, face white. She seems expanded by her anger; it emanates from her like hot thermal currents.

'My mood today is off the scale,' she says. Then adds, 'What a complete dick I must have looked. Telling you everything, trusting you.'

Oh God.

'You're a liar, a fake.' Her voice is shrill, her words a firing squad of contempt. I put my hand on the back of the settee to brace myself.

'Please, let me explain,' I say.

'I probably wouldn't have twigged it was you, but I met the real Angela Maynard tonight, but we'll come to that.' She's pacing back and forth, shaking her head.

I'm filled with self-loathing and shame. 'I was going to tell you.'

'How could you do that to someone? It's weird and cruel. I trusted you. My God, Angela. Jesus, fuck, what am I saying? You're not Angela, you're a fake. I should go to the police with this. What if I'd been suicidal?'

'Jenny, please.' I feel faint and lower myself onto the settee. 'Please give me a minute.'

My plea quietens her. I place my hand on my chest and try to breathe normally.

'That's right, you try one of your CBT techniques,' she says.

I don't look at her but can hear her tone has lost its *Psycho* screech.

'I'm so sorry, Jenny, but everything we did in here was a recommended treatment. I didn't make anything up.'

'Didn't make anything up? You made more stuff up than Disney.'

'I mean, I learned about CBT. I tried to...'

'So that makes it okay?'

'No, I didn't mean...'

'I should have twigged it.' She leans towards me and adds, voice lowered, 'Dancing. You had me friggin' dancing.'

'I need some water,' I say.

Jenny shakes her head at me and turns away. I stand on shaking limbs and go to the kitchen. I lean briefly on the counter and pour a glass of water. Through the black of the window, I see my reflection: another realm, everything in shadow, opaque and vague, perhaps the truer echo of my life.

I hear Jenny on the phone, speaking to her husband, probably. I catch a few words. '*I'm fine… unbelievable… phone when I'm leaving.*'

I brace myself for returning to the front room. When I do, Jenny is pacing, hands deep in her pockets, clenched fists pushing them out of shape.

'Jenny, please, can I…'

'I've got a photo,' she says. 'You asked for one for therapy. Well, here it is. Let's see what you make of it.'

She delves into her bag and pulls out a ten-by-ten glossy print. I feel like I've been doused with cold water. I thought I recognised her that first day but couldn't place her. You know that feeling where you see someone out of context? Seeing the blue blazer and gold insignia brings it all back. I sit down heavily as the realisation hits me. *I know Jenny; and she knows me.*

'This is a Marple High School photo for 1990. That's me there.' She points to a girl with red hair and a ponytail. She holds the photograph closer to her face and examines it, really studies it, like she's just spotted something that isn't to do with me. 'I don't look overweight, do I?' she says, more to herself.

'No,' I answer, quietly.

She continues, 'I'm standing next to my best friend, Janice Moran. Died of breast cancer when she was only thirty.' She flips the photo over. 'My mum insisted I wrote everyone's names down on the back. You see anyone you know?' she asks. She waits, eyebrows arched, lips pursed.

I feel the hard fix of her eyes on me.

'Well?' she says. 'Look. Do you recognise her?'

'Yes,' I say, suddenly very tired, wanting to get it over with. 'That's me.'

'I know that,' she says. 'Annabelle Pearson, right?'

'Yes, but I call myself Bella now.'

'Do you, indeed?'

'Could you give me a minute to explain?' Now that the atmosphere is less charged, Jenny looks as worn out as I feel. 'Please?' I add as Trevor reappears, jumps nimbly onto my lap, and curls up. His warm body is solid and comforting.

'Go,' she says as she sits. Not looking me in the face.

'Angela Maynard has just moved in over the road from me at number sixty-one.'

Jenny gets out of the chair and moves to the window, pulling the curtain aside.

'The one with the white car on the road,' I add helpfully.

'Right, so.'

'So, you came here by mistake.'

'So, it's my flippin' fault?'

'No, Jenny, never. It's all my fault, all my doing. It sounds ridiculous, I know, but when you came to my door, I saw it as a sign from the universe.' A sob cracks in my throat. 'I admit, I was lonely. Once you were in the house, I didn't know how to tell you I wasn't Angela. So, I didn't. And I really thought I could help you. I read all about CBT. It wasn't about money.'

She sighs. 'God.'

We are quiet for a moment.

'I thought it was unusual to ask for donations to The Cat's Protection League instead of a fee. I should have realised. Are there any others, apart from me and Phil?' she asks, as she sits again.

'Erm…' Hovering over the lie gives me away. 'One other. I have one other lady.'

'Jesus aitch Christ.'

'I promise I was going to stop. I was going to tell you today.' I grab a handful of tissues and blow my nose. 'I can't go to prison. What about Trevor?'

Jenny shakes her head and sighs deeply. 'Listen, I didn't speak to Angela. There wasn't enough time.'

'Thank you.' It's all I can manage through the sobs.

'You need to tell the other clients.'

'I will.'

She rubs her face and sighs again, then asks, 'Why?'

I explain how Angela nearly killed Trevor. I'm glad Jenny's a cat lover, because my account seems very flimsy in the re-telling.

'And that's it?' she asks when I'm done. 'You wanted company, and she'd run Trevor over. Did she hurt him?'

'Well, she…' I don't get the chance to finish.

'You've not really convinced me. I mean, this may be a matter for the police, and Angela, obviously.'

I shake my head. 'Please Jenny, don't.'

'Like, what if I'd been suicidal, or Phil had, or your other lady?'

'I would have…'

'It's dangerous, what you did. It's weird, odd.'

'You said.'

'Well, it is,' she says, finally looking at me.

'I'm so, so sorry, Jenny.'

'There must be more to it?' She considers me for a moment, then lifts the photograph up again. She runs her finger along the line of faces. The red tip stops at a young man with a flop of dark hair and a wide, confident grin.

'And him?' she asks.

My head starts to throb. 'What about him?'

'I recognised him from the other week, coming up your drive. That's Graham Dewsnap, isn't it? Your next-door neighbour, Dewey, as I remember him. He was mates with my brother Hugh.'

I nod. Graham's old nickname has triggered a memory. They called him Dewey and his friend Hugh was Hughie. I didn't realise he was Jenny's brother. It's all coming together, that sense of familiarity I've had about Jenny from the start. The fragments attracting each other.

'I remembered you from this photo,' Jenny says. 'You look different now.' She tries not to look at my scars, but trying too hard gives her away. 'You came to our house once. I must have been about nine and you were fourteen-ish. You had all been swimming and Hugh asked if you and Graham could stay for Sunday lunch. We were all at the table when my mum put some chicken on your plate, and you said your dad liked to chew the parson's nose. I'd never heard of it. I laughed so much that everyone else laughed too.'

It's strange to hear when someone possesses a memory of you and your life that you don't have. It reminds me that I didn't live in a bubble. I was seen by others.

'Where's Hugh now?' I ask, realising I should know this already.

'Emigrated. Australia, nearly ten years ago. Got dual citizenship.'

'He was very kind and gentle. Say hello to him for me?' I ask, then have second thoughts: 'but don't mention this…'

'I remember some talk about the accident.' Jenny says. 'It's all a bit vague, though. Hugh lost touch with Graham when he went to uni. But something bad happened, didn't it?'

I don't know if I want to open this old wound while I'm still bleeding from the current one. 'It's late,' I say.

'Yes,' she says, checking her watch. 'But I've told you my life story, and then some.'

And she's right again. She's trusted me with intimate details of her life. I feel the shame piling up like a snowdrift blocking me in. I don't have much choice; I don't want her to leave here still angry: God knows what she would do.

I make us a pot of tea and begin by telling her about my old school. It feels like a good place to start because I remember it as the positive start to my life. If it had continued, who knows what might have been? But who doesn't ponder on that at some time, turning the mysteries of life into clichés?

'I'd been at the Catholic school in Glossop,' I begin. I pause to gauge her reaction. She's looking at her hands, which are placed one over the other on her lap. Her legs are crossed, one foot wiggling back and forth. She looks up as if waiting and I take it as permission to continue. 'I was top of my class in every subject except maths. I had a good friend, Yvonne. I always associate her with that Sinead O'Connor song. "*Nothing compares to you*"?'

'I know the one,' she nods.

'We sang the life out of it, even though neither of us had ever had a boyfriend. Literally, we had *nothing* to compare anything to.' I smile at my joke, but Jenny isn't smiling. 'Anyway, my mum moved me to Stockport High, and that's where I met Graham.'

'Right, I know all this.'

'I know, but this is the straightforward part and I need a long run in.'

'Not so easy, is it?'

I shake my head. I deserve her jabs.

'Go on.'

Trevor stretches and comes to me. I scratch him under the chin and the action seems to settle me a little. 'I was only fourteen, but we were serious.'

'I'd freak out if it was Chloe. How did your mum deal with it?'

'"You can take the girl out of a school, but you can't take the girl out of the girl."' I mimic my mum's stern reproach. It's a close enough impression. As close as I'd want to get, anyway.

'The girls in my class used to talk about you. You were famous in the school canteen.'

I check for memories, but there's nothing about being the subject of gossip. I must have been consumed, blinkered.

Graham Dewsnap.

To say I loved Graham from the first moment I met him might be a little dramatic, but for a teenage girl, there is nothing to distinguish a physical attraction and surge of hormones from deep enduring love. What else is there to go on? Ever? Loving him kept me safe from the frequent emotional kicking that falling in and out of love visited on my friends.

Jenny's foot has paused its wagging as she waits for me to continue. I pick up from where I left off. Though it's difficult to condense something that I remember in such detail.

'Graham turned sixteen before me and got a part-time job in the local Spar. He said he was saving so we could rent somewhere together when we were old enough.'

'You're not telling me anything I don't know. I spilled my guts to you.'

'You don't make a very sympathetic confidante.'

'There are so many responses to that I don't know where to begin.'

Trevor looks up at me as though to say, '*She has a point.*' Then he turns full circle in my lap and settles down again.

'On the run-up to my seventeenth birthday, my mum announced she'd booked a holiday for us in Cornwall. She said it would be good for us as a family. She had very few friends and I think she missed me being around to chew out. In Cornwall she'd have a captive audience. I agreed to go because, when I returned, me and Graham were planning to rent a one-bedroomed flat over Rumbelows on Market Street.'

Jenny sighs impatiently. She's one wrong word away from another rant. I raise my voice a little and hurry on. 'I think Mum sensed it would be our last chance. She was right. On our way home, a tyre blew on the motorway, and we crashed into the safety barrier. The last thing I remember is the sound of screeching metal reverberating through my skull as I bit down on my tongue.'

Jenny puts her waggling foot down and unfolds her arms all in one motion. 'Oh God,' she says.

'I woke up in intensive care with a smashed pelvis, neck and facial injuries. As I lay in the hospital bed, the nurse held my hand and told me my mum had suffered a fractured skull, a broken arm, a herniated disc and three broken ribs.'

'Angela, sorry, Bella, I knew there had been something. I'm so sorry. You can stop if you want. I don't need to…'

But the gates have opened, and memories are pouring out like freed captives. I continue. Tears have their own way now; their slow progress tickles my face and Jenny hands me a tissue. I don't think the irony is lost on either of us. 'My dad died at the scene.' I explain.

'That must have been awful.'

'I felt sad for my mum. Mum had lost her husband, but I had nothing for my dad. Maybe the pain killers had numbed everything. Even in my doped-up state, I remember the look on the nurse's face when I told her I would be okay, because my dad had been dead at the scene for most of my life. Wasn't that a terrible thing to say?'

Jenny moves from her chair, kneels with some effort at the side of mine and says, 'Bella, I think I've punished you enough. Shall I do us a cuppa?'

I can hear Jenny searching the kitchen cupboards, opening the fridge. Trevor's ears have pricked up and I can sense he knows something has changed. I stroke him as the sounds of Jenny moving around and the boiling kettle fade away and the ticking of the clock seems to follow me to a distant open space.

I'm recovering in hospital. I have repetitive dreams about flying. Gliding on warm currents, wings outstretched in symmetry, the sun catching the blue and green shimmer of feathers. I land smoothly, elegantly folding my wings into my back. Other times I tumble painfully to the ground and curl up into a ball, screaming as the pain punches a hole through the barrier of morphine. It's following one such dream that I awake with a jolt to find my Aunt Betty sitting by my bed. She leaves the room and a moment later returns with a nurse who delivers a sharp shot of pain relief. When I am comfortable again, Betty helps me to sips of water and says softly, 'You mustn't worry about anything. I'm going to move into yours for a while and look after you both.' Comforted by her presence and the gentle pressure of her hand on my good arm, I fall back to sleep.

A *long and painful period of rehab follows. Literally, a one step forward approach. Aunty Betty sells her house and moves in with us permanently as a full-time carer. She has a cat called Cleo, old even then. She sleeps on my bed and when I awake at night, watching the rise and fall of her breathing helps me to gain control of the pain. Graham visits me as soon as he can. But I refuse to see him because of my injuries, apart from the scarring on my face, I've gained two stone, and walk with the stiff gait of C-P3O. I'm so unhappy. One afternoon I awake with a gasp, realising that I am becoming like my father, uncommunicative, sullen, withdrawn.*

'Where's the sugar?' Jenny calls and I'm seized by the firm grip of the present. The opening and shutting of a cupboard door remind me that Jenny is still holding the remnants of anger. I want to get up and take over, but I don't want to interfere.

'Top left cupboard. Green cannister.'

Jenny returns with the tea and Trevor moves off my knee as I accept a steaming mug. It's a guest mug, but I'm not about to mention it.

'You okay?' I ask, wondering if I've done my penance.

'Getting there,' she answers.

There's still a fix to her chin and a hardness around her eyes. I miss the old Jenny.

'I'm just trying to get my head around it,' she adds as she sits down. 'I mean, it sounds awful, what you went through. But how does it connect to this?'

I sip tea and place the cup down again on the table as I wait for words to gather.

'I was meant to be studying for A levels, but I couldn't concentrate on anything. I watched films from Blockbuster, ordered take-out food. My Aunty Betty had moved in by then and tried to encourage me to let Graham stay by making the spare room up so he could sleep over when he wanted. But I couldn't bear him to see me. And I wasn't good company.'

'No, but you had been through a lot.'

'Graham stopped calling all together. My friend Josie had stayed in touch and told me he had started going out with a girl called Alison, who he'd met in college. It felt unreal, unacceptable. I convinced myself he'd come back to me when I was fully recovered. Shortly afterwards, I began to pull my hair out in tiny clumps. Trichotillomania is what the doctor called it.'

'Oh no.'

'Anyway, Aunt Betty persuaded me to go for a coffee on Market Street. When we got there, Betty stopped to look in McKay's window. Through the reflection, I saw Graham. He was walking directly towards us. I was totally unprepared. The scarring on my face was much more evident then. I considered hiding or going into the shop, but instead I turned, and smiled, keeping the left side on, bracing myself. He walked past me without a sign of recognition. I watched him walk up Market Street and go into the side door at Rumbelows. He'd taken the flat on his own.'

'So that would be about1998?' Jenny looks like she's trying to line her own memories up with my own.

'Around then.'

'I remember, the car accident made the local paper,' Jenny says. 'I knew you, but didn't know you. If that makes sense?'

'Yes, same here.'

'Where's your Aunty Betty now?' Jenny asks.

'Died. Ten years ago. She left me a bit of money. That and the sale of mum's house helped me to buy this place.'

'Where is your mum?'.

'She went mad, and we shot her,' I answer glibly, surprised to hear myself using one of my dad's lines.

'Pardon?'

'Sorry, she passed away in a nursing home many years ago.'

'Sorry.'

'So, it's just us chickens,' I say, as I scratch Trevor under the chin. 'Graham married Alison when he was twenty-two. They divorced sixteen years later.'

'You kept track of him all that time? You never married?'

'Yes and no. I see Josie every now and then, out shopping. She mentioned that he'd moved here. I used to walk past as often as I could. Then I saw this come up for sale and I bought it.'

'Angela, I mean Bella, we're going back, God, how many years?'

'Thirty-two, I'm counting.'

'Thirty-two years you've held a candle for him?'

'Yes, it's one of those trick candles that you try to blow out, but it keeps re-igniting.'

'Oh Bella,' Jenny says, her voice full of sadness.

'Don't worry, the joke's on me. No one else was hurt.'

We're both quiet again as I stroke Trevor. I feel tears welling, one hovers precariously, and I wonder why we can't draw them back into our eyes, like we can sniff back a runny nose.

'Does he know? Have you spoken about it?'

'With the risk of sounding even weirder,' I say.

'Wow, can't wait for this.'

'I've not actually told him who I am.'

'What? Why would you need to? He would know. Surely?'

'Really? He didn't recognise me then. Why would he now?'

'Are you telling me he doesn't know who you are?'

'Yes, I don't think so.'

'Bella, you…' She looks down and shakes her head. 'How can

he not know?'

'You didn't.' I answer.

'…it's like a story from *Chat*.'

'I always intended to.'

'You've been living here, what, five years?'

'I look so different. I've left it too long. Like being late with a birthday card.'

'It's hardly the same flippin' thing.'

'It is though. Etiquette allows a pocket of time where it's still okay to send an apologetic belated one. After that, the excuses get harder, less believable. You instinctively know when it's *too* late. And anyway, he's only interested in Angela now.'

Jenny's eyebrows shoot up. 'Ah, there it is. The real reason for all of this,' she says, as she thrusts her hands out in front of her. 'Look, you've gotta tell him, end of. For your own dignity, for your… sanity!'

That memory of being outside McKay's comes flooding back. I told my aunt later, but at the time I just limped into the shop and hid in a cubicle, crying, pretending I was trying something on.

'There is no sanity in any of this, Jenny.'

'No, that's the thing. Can't you see…? The effects of this…?' She sits with her elbows resting on the chair arms, her hands clasped in front of her. A facsimile of how my dad used to sit. 'Okay,' she says, finally. 'Here's the deal. I don't think you've done me any long-term emotional damage, apart from maybe the dancing. You might even have helped me. It's all a bit weird. I won't tell Angela, or the police.'

'Thank you,' I say. I want to hug her, but I resist. Trevor raises his head and meows, then jumps off my knee. A second later, I hear the cat flap. As though he's been waiting for the verdict before going out. The relief is indescribable, but it's short lived.

'There's a condition, obviously,' Jenny adds.

I lean my head back and close my eyes.

'Bella?' Jenny says.

'Yes.'

'I'm doing this for you. You have to tell Phil and your other client.'

'I had already decided to, I swear it.'

'And. Your mission, missus, if you choose to accept it?'

'Go on.'

'You have three days to tell Graham.'

'That's blackmail,' I answer, seeing my stupid, disfigured, fat reflection again.

'Maybe,' she answers, standing up and straightening her skirt, 'But what did you say to me, nearly every week? What's the worst that can happen?'

Chapter Twenty-Seven

Bella

Thursday dawns, the morning sun shines through the blinds, painting narrow yellow stripes across the duvet, trailing up and over Trevor, who is curled up asleep in the middle of the bed, a grey sand dune. I have one more day: if I haven't told Graham who I am, Jenny said she'll knock on his door and make the introductions herself. And I'm afraid she'll tell him how she knows me now.

Courage hasn't materialised. I'm in the same state of fear that I was in five years ago on the first week I moved here. I had worn a nice wig and done my make up. I had become expert in addressing people right side on. I hardly had to think about it anymore. I still wasn't what you would describe as skinny, but I 'scrubbed up well,' as my aunty Betty used to say. I had knocked on Graham's door and said 'Hello, I'm your new neighbour.' I waited for the recognition. The time lapse was excruciating. Then he answered. 'Hi, I'm Graham,' and shook my hand. I had meant to say, 'Hi it's Anna,' but I became flustered by the touch of his hand and his proximity. I hadn't accounted for the flush of emotions, the rush of heat and blankness of mind. I mumbled the name 'Bella' and made a swift retreat to my house. Since then, I've waited for opportunities, for hints, for openings. But I have never been brave enough to start an honest conversation about who I am. I think I'm afraid of my feelings. Maybe it's the same for him.

I switch the kettle on and make a strong black coffee. As I sip the bitter drink, I run through my options. I wonder whether I should allow Jenny to tell him anyway, but then I dismiss that as too adolescent, and there's a risk she will tell him I've been pretending to be Angela.

Phil has an appointment next week, but Zeta has one today. I haven't decided how I'm going to handle that yet. My head is too befuddled by all of this. I'm loath to let her go after only one session. I feel I made a real connection with her. I ponder my options. Zeta seemed a kind person and I'll appear like a smooth operator. She could go to the police, but so could Jenny. All she needs to do is turn to her husband over dinner and, to use the vernacular, I'm busted. I need more time to think how I'll manage it. I have enough to think about with the Graham situation for now.

I phone Zeta and tell her I'm unwell and ask her if we can meet in a coffee shop next week. She falters for a moment.

'Hmm, yes, whatever integrates with you.'

Chapter Twenty-Eight

Bella

Grahams' home. I've heard him moving around this morning and his car is on the drive. I try to remind myself that he's a friend. I need to trust him. Trevor meows and struts past with his tail held high. He has food in his bowl, so I take this as a cue that he'd like to play. I pull the *Mouse Under the Mat* game out for him and switch it on. He crouches and watches as a small tail pokes out from under a cover and moves in a circular motion, stopping and starting. He pounces and rolls over, clutching the tail between his paws. It's not a robust toy, and the cover comes off and the batteries drop out. I gather up the pieces and try to re-assemble it, feeling his disappointment in me.

'Don't look at me like that,' I say. 'Life is hard for us humans.'

I wash the few breakfast pots and put them away. 'Wish me luck,' I say to him as I push my feet into my shoes.

I call at Sue's hoping for some encouragement. She will tell me straight if I'm doing the right thing. But there's no answer and I assume she's still in Spain.

Heart pounding, I step over the dividing boundary and knock on Graham's door. If my emotions were pigments, they would make an unattractive puce. I wait a moment but can't hear any movement from inside. I knock again, lighter this time, courage ebbing. I step back over the paving. He opens the door. I turn back. I must look very guilty.

'Hi,' he says.

'Oh,' I say.

'Sorry, I was in the back. It's just started raining.'

So it has.

He waits expectantly.

'I, er,' I falter. 'Can I talk to you for a moment?'

'Sure.'

'Inside?'

'Oh,' he steps aside. 'Sure.'

I enter the living room ahead of him and take a seat. Graham stands at the door, thumbs tucked into his jeans pockets.

'Is everything alright? Trevor alright?'

'Yes, fine.'

'Washing machine still working okay?'

It's come to something I think when the list of things that could be wrong revolves around my cat or my plumbing.

He waits, then seems to grasp the difficulty I'm having and takes the chair opposite.

Thoughts crash around in my head like waves against a flood barrier. How do you begin something like this?

'I need to tell you something.'

'Okay.' He sits forward, brow creased with concern. He's waiting for me to tell him I have a terminal illness or something. I almost wish I had, because then his reaction wouldn't be such an unknown quantity.

'I...'

He turns his head; he's slightly deaf in his right ear.

'We... you and I.'

'Yes?'

I take a breath in and exhale. 'Graham, don't you know who I am?'

'What?' The ruffles in his brow deepen like an accordion. 'Bella. You're Bella.'

'No, Graham, I'm Anna, Annabelle Pearson.' Saying my old name out loud sounds strange even to me. I wait as time and place shifts around us like scene changes on a revolving stage. In the library studying, our heads almost touching as we share a textbook. The scene turns and slowly reveals Graham's parents' house: bright colours, modern, inviting. Then we're at the traction fair, the distinctive smell of oil and steam from the old engines. The memories serve to remind me that this is Graham, my Graham, I'm safe with him.

The frown clears. 'Annabelle,' he says softly.

'Yes.'

'I know who you are. I've known since the day you moved in.'

What?

His words are like an assassin's knife to the heart, swift in and out, the pain takes a moment to register. *He knew. All this time. Why didn't he say anything?* These thoughts chase around until I'm dizzy and can't distinguish which one is chasing which.

'Why didn't you say anything?' It comes out in a whisper.

'I suppose it was because you introduced yourself as Bella. I thought it strange, but assumed you wanted to be anonymous.'

'All this time?'

Silence.

'Where do we go from here?' My question is both innocuous and loaded. I'm willing him to say more. How can I put the words in his mouth that I want to hear? Say them myself? I don't dare. He's known who I am and there have been no pent-up declarations of love bursting from him. He's been happy to let me stay incognito.

He sighs and rubs his face. 'We just go on as we were. It was fine, wasn't it? We both knew all the time anyway, so what changes?'

I feel humiliation mixed with a tinge of insanity.

'Nothing.'

'Exactly.'

He puts his hands down flat on his knees, signalling that business is over.

'It means that now we could get together and talk about the past,' I suggest, trying to delay the inevitable. I know I won't have the courage to broach this again.

'My past?' he asks, poking a finger into his chest.

'Our past,' I say.

'Ours? Blimey. We were just kids.' He waves his hand like a traffic cop signalling to traffic to pass. 'It's so long ago it's the past and keep going. I like to focus on the future. It's kinder, a place I've not made any mistakes.'

Then he tells me he's asked Angela to marry him.

Chapter Twenty-Nine

Bella

I crossed a threshold into another realm this morning and returned home this afternoon with only half of myself. I sit on the settee and look around. Nothing in the room has changed, but it's different. I've been able to fool myself that our houses were bound together like a nuptial home, divided by only a cavity wall. Sharing and caring for Trevor. Both of us moving in harmony, body clocks in sync. But I've seen what I wanted to see, fooled myself. Without a hint of encouragement, I've projected my idealistic, sentimental hopes onto Graham. I wonder, if emotion is energy, where does it go when it's redundant? Does it linger in the walls and ceilings, trapping melancholia in crumbling mortar?

Trevor jumps up onto my knee and meows. His beautiful golden eyes are wide, no trace of sympathy there, but I know he senses my unhappiness. His fur is wet from the rain, and I rummage around down the side of the settee and locate his comb. I pull it through his coat and say, 'It's my own fault. I should have been up front from the day I moved in. I clearly have problems with being myself.'

I feel out of step with the day and unsure what to do next. I go upstairs and into the bathroom, where I gaze at my reflection. I'm worn so thin that I may as well be a ghost. Unseen, transparent, weak, and brittle-boned. I return to bed and pull the covers up around me. Sir Trevor lies with me for a while, but the lure of the hunt calls and I hear his paws thud onto the carpet. A few seconds later, the cat flap squeaks as he leaves.

The next morning Trevor wakes me up with a present of the tiniest mouse. I gently prise it from him and see that it's unharmed, just petrified. I cup its trembling body in my hands. Then I shut Trevor in the bedroom and take the mouse downstairs and release it into the field at the back. As I turn, I hear water gushing from the downspout next door and look up at Graham's bathroom window. I'm suddenly aware that I've come out without my wig on. I dash back inside, hoping to God that Graham didn't see me. That would be one humiliation too far.

Jenny phones me at ten and says she's on her way back from a doctor's appointment and asks if it's convenient to call by. Her call lifts me. I can't remember the last time someone phoned out of concern. You don't get that from BT or British Gas.

'I'm really sorry, but I still think it was the right thing to do,' Jenny says as she follows me into the kitchen. Now there are no client/therapist boundaries she feels free to wander around my house like it's her own. She'll run herself a bath one of these days. I think she can tell I've not been managing well. My expression must be as easy to read as an advertising board. I've hardly been out, and I've not done any gardening in case I bump into Graham, or Angela. Watching the weeds re-claim the garden is killing me, but I'm not brave enough to resume gardening yet.

I watch as she pours boiled water into the tea pot. 'I'll do this. Go and sit down,' she tells me firmly. I don't resist.

She comes through with the tea tray and asks, 'Do you have any family left anywhere?'

'No, no family now.'

'You should have told him who you are when you moved in,' she says, as she starts to pour.

'He already knew.'

She stops with the tea pot in mid-air, eyebrows arched.

'No? What?'

I stare at the suspended tea pot, unable to meet her eyes.

'And he didn't say anything?' she says, resuming the pouring of the tea and handing it to me.

'He said he wanted to respect my privacy,' I answer, taking it from her and trying not to spill the overfilled cup. 'Something like that. I can't remember exactly. I was just so...' I feel re-traumatised by the remembering, and I don't want to say *humiliated* out loud. She's thinking it, anyway.

'God, humiliating,' she says.

There you go.

'What a blow. Have you spoken to him since?'

'No. He's asked Angela to marry him,' I say flatly.

'No?'

'Yes.'

'Has she accepted?'

I shrug, 'I don't know. Does it matter?'

'Come on.' She takes the cup from my hand, though I've hardly had a sip. 'We need some fresh air.'

It's a beautiful day, and it's good to feel a bit of sun on my face. I feel a certain honour in being in Jenny's car, in her personal space. Does this mean that we're becoming friends?

'So, what will you do?' she asks, as we turn onto the main road.

I sigh. 'I don't know. I've thought of moving.'

It's a test statement, really. I want to hear what she'll say. I don't want to move; too disruptive for Trevor.

'Why should you move?' she asks, echoing my sentiment. 'Anyway, they might get somewhere together, so I'd wait and see.'

Wait and see. I nod absently and wonder whether I'm strong enough to withstand waiting and seeing them living happily ever after, right under my nose. After a short drive, we stop at Etherow Park. In the car park, Jenny points to a motorbike.

'That's just like Mike's,' she says. It's the first reference she's made to herself today.

'It's nice,' I say. 'Beautiful, even.'

'It's a killing machine,' she answers, and I remind myself that it's a hot subject and I need to tread carefully.

We stroll past the seating area where the ducks and geese emerge from the water and squawk and caw as they parry for scraps of bread. A small boy with flushed cheeks laughs and points as strawberry ice cream melts down his cone and dribbles through his plump fingers.

'How are your family?' I ask, hoping to steer the conversation away from killing machines.

'Good, thanks,' she answers, as a flock of ducks waddle across our pathway and splash into the water.

The trail around the lake is a mix of stone and grass, worn bare and dusty by the busy footfall and the dry weather. A decoration of low-hanging boughs and huge fern leaves trims the water's edge. To our left, a steep canopy of oaks and sycamore, hazel, and hawthorn trees. Their aged barks weathered like the hides of ancient beasts; lovers' initials branded into them. I breathe in deeply. The earthy smells of pine needles, damp moss, and animal scents fill my nostrils, and I allow myself to absorb the atmosphere and be in the moment. Sound resonates on a different wavelength under this cloak, like the acoustics in a cathedral. The calls of moorhens and distinct rap of a woodpecker merge together with the delighted shouts and frustrated cries of children until they are indistinguishable from each other.

Jenny is ahead of me. She turns and waits for me to catch up.

'You okay?' she asks. I realise it's the first time she's seen my limp in action. 'You know,' she continues, 'because I don't have any evidence that I've had therapy, my op has been postponed.'

'I'm sorry,' I say. It's a reflex response. I'm pathologically apologetic. 'I didn't think about the implications for you. Are you still mad?'

'No, I might be a mental case, but I'm not mad.'

'But you can still have the op if you get therapy?'

'Yep, from a real one though, obviously.' She stops and turns to face me. 'You know, for what it's worth, I think you helped.'

We're walking side by side now. 'Well, we don't have to stop.'

'I can't afford the cat biscuits,' she says, smiling. 'Why don't you do the training, become a certified therapist? You'd be good.'

I search her face to see if she's joking, but she clearly isn't. Tears spring to my eyes without warning and I blink them away.

'It's lovely here, isn't it? We're lucky to have it on our doorstep,' she says.

This is the most relaxed I've seen her. 'You seem happy,' I say.

'Mike came to another meeting with me. He started to listen, and he's supporting me.'

We step aside for a family with a pram, two young children and a dog. They smile and thank us.

'It's not so bad that I have to postpone,' Jenny continues. 'One of the reasons Mike was against it was because the operation was timed for right in the middle of the school holidays. We usually rent somewhere.'

'So, you can go now?'

'All booked,' she says, 'Cornwall.'

On the return journey, Jenny stops off for groceries and I take the opportunity to buy some boxes of cat food and various treats for Trevor. We stop outside my house and Jenny offers to help me carry my shopping inside, but I decline. Graham's car isn't on his drive, but Angela's is outside her house. They could be out together. I don't want to prolong the time I'm exposed. Before I get out, Jenny puts her hand on my arm. 'Will you be okay?' she asks.

'I'm fine, honestly,' I say brightly. Still wondering how she can be so kind after what I've done.

I spend the rest of the day inside, even though I can see through the window that my peonies need dead-heading, and my borders need weeding. I wonder about Graham's plants and his ironing. He'll just have to manage himself now until he can get Angela to do it for him. I don't see that sitting very well with her ladyship. I put the television on and lie back on the settee. I didn't sleep well last night. I was too restless, my thoughts tumbling around in my head like bingo balls in a blower chamber. *Why didn't Graham say anything? Has he been laughing at me all this time? Has he told Angela about me?* I realise that he may have confided to Angela months ago about our history. I cringe as I remember the meal. Believing I was fighting for a Graham's love. What was I thinking? Angela doesn't need to fight for Graham. She can sit ringside and watch me bounce off the ropes.

These chaotic ruminations blur together as one idea comes into sharp focus. I jump up and retrieve my address book from the kitchen drawer. Tucked between the pages is Steve's business card. Surely, he should know that his ex-wife is planning to remarry. After all, he only has her best interests at heart.

I call him.

Later that day, Trevor lifts his head, awake and alert. I think someone is trying the bell. I should have it removed. Then there's knocking. I check myself in the mirror and open the door.

'Hi,' Steve says.

His appearance jars me, but I suppose I should have foreseen this. Now the lid's off the can, I wonder if he's one of the worms.

'Hi,' I answer and pull the door to me so he can't see inside.

'I was wondering if you had a minute?' He looks over at Graham's and then back at Angela's and I get it. He doesn't want to be seen. I look back at my front room. It looks okay. Nothing like Angela's obviously, and not what he'll be used to.

'Sure, come in,' I say and step aside.

'Thanks, sorry, I won't keep you.' He sees Trevor. 'Hey, you must be the famous Trevor.' He scratches Trevor on the top of his head and Trevor doesn't protest, but his large eyes scrutinise, unblinking. To someone who doesn't spend a lot of time around cats, their stare can feel enigmatic and disconcerting.

Like being stared down by a cheetah. Steve turns back to me, and Trevor resumes his position. 'Gorgeous cat,' he says.

Fussing Sir Trevor doesn't put Steve straight into my good books, but he's at least a page marker.

'I love this room,' he says, leaning a hand on the back of the settee. 'It reminds me a bit of my mum's house. Very homely. Bet it's cosy in winter?'

I look around. 'Yes, it's very cosy with the fire lit.' I'm not totally stupid, though. I can hear false flattery. Steve's got the patter off like a parliamentary candidate after my vote. If I had a baby, Steve would be holding it by now.

'How can I help?' I ask, as though it's the start of a session.

He moves towards a chair, then remembers his manners. 'May I?' he asks.

'Course,' I answer too readily. I admit, I'm intrigued.

Steve sits with his hands in a steeple, resting his chin on the ends of his fingers. In a pensive '*Where do I begin*?' pose.

'It's delicate,' he says, staring at the floor. 'First, thanks for giving me the heads up about the upcoming nuptials.'

I have the decency to blush. 'I thought you should know.'

'This is where it gets delicate. Please believe me, I'm not being confrontational, but I was wondering. Why would you do that? I know I asked you. But...'

I asked myself that question too. 'I felt sorry for you,' I answer, but it's a lie. I felt sorry for myself.

'For me?' He points at himself, incredulous. 'No, never do that. The aroma you can smell isn't cologne. It's because, and pardon my French, despite whatever shit life lobs in my direction, somehow, I always end up smelling of sugar. Now, if I can hazard a guess, I'd say that you and I share a common interest in ensuring that him at eighteen and her at sixty-one don't get their happy ever after.'

He holds a hand up at my intake of breath.

'Apologies if I've misread it.'

Heart racing. 'You mean Graham and Angela. Can we just call them that? Graham and Angela. We're not trying to break the Enigma Code.'

'Fair enough.'

'Where did you get the idea that I have a... that I'm interested in Graham?' I ask.

'Angie. She said she had a run in with you when she first moved in. Said you were more into him than he was into you.'

'Did she tell you she nearly killed Trevor?'

'Said it was a misunderstanding. Says you've got cat brain. Calls you a meow head. She doesn't like cats; they make the house smell. Not that yours does,' he hurriedly adds.

'She what?' I look over at Sir Trevor, insulted for us both.

'Yeah, she's not so nice at times.'

'What do you propose?' I ask.

'So, it's true?'

'Even if it is, there's nothing either of us can do. Love will have love. It's like water, it always finds a way. The more you try to stop it, the more insistent it gets.'

'Wow, that's deep for a meow head.' Seeing my disapproval, he says, 'Sorry, I don't think that. I can see she's got you all wrong. You can use that: being underestimated is always an advantage.'

'Use it how?'

'Well, that's why I'm here. Angie's using Graham to get at me. It's not right. He should know. And if he did…' He looks down, examines his shoes… 'I can't tell him, obviously, but coming from you...'

'And are you more into Angela than she's into you?'

'Ooh, touché.'

'Well?'

'Let's say she's easily persuaded.'

His comment makes me cringe and I wonder about my own willingness to let him into my house.

'You know,' I say, 'I saw you coming out of her house late one night?'

He leans forward. 'Well, that's my point exactly.'

After he's left, a pick 'n' mix of decisions parades before me. Absentmindedly, I pull one of the cushions from the settee and sniff it.

Chapter Thirty

Bella

The following morning, I wake up and listen carefully to sounds from next door. It's been very quiet for the last couple of days. Maybe Graham is avoiding me, too?

I have a bath and set Audrey in rollers. I pull together a skirt and jumper, then go downstairs and move through my morning routine. Feed Trevor, that's the first thing. If it weren't for him, I probably wouldn't get out of bed. I try to move quietly through my chores. It's very wearing. In the days before, I would clatter around, sing along to the radio, put my music on, reminding Graham that I was here, like a kind of echogram, sending the 'vibes' through the wall. In those days, I heard more of Graham, too.

It would be a good gardening day, but my courage is too depleted. I couldn't make small talk with Graham if he came out. Small talk feels too big.

The morning paper arrives, and as I turn the page, Trevor jumps onto my knee. He likes the feel of newspaper. He kneads my jumper and reminds me why I always buy them from the charity shop. Despite his protracted claws, they don't pull the thread too badly. I think it's because they're very sharp; they make clean incisions into the wool rather than shredding it.

'What should I do about Zeta and Phil?' I ask him. He continues to purr and knead and bats me a slow blink. 'I could tell them I have an illness and I'm retiring? But they could tell the doctor and it might cause too many questions.'

Like many times before, I imagine Trevor speaking to me in a calm, patient tone, laden with wisdom and knowledge. '*Trust your gut instinct,'* is his counsel. Eventually, his purring quietens. He circles again and eventually settles. After a few minutes he's snoring, laid on top of my newspaper, with not a care in the world.

I spend the next half hour concentrating on stroking his fur and attempting to be mindful. Breathing in and out and staying in the moment. It's much harder than it sounds or looks. I think, if anyone has ever mastered it, it's because they have never pretended to be someone else.

Phil arrives for his appointment carrying a large leather holdall from which he produces a foil-covered plate. The smell of fruit charges the air. 'Mum made this for you. She's a feeder.' He pulls the foil aside to reveal a golden crusted pie with a crimped edge. 'Blueberry,' he adds proudly.

Purple juice oozes from a 'V' shaped incision which is flanked by two decorative, pastry leaves.

'It looks delicious,' I say. 'Would you like a piece with a cup of tea?'

Phil looks at me like it's a trick question. 'I, er…'

'It's not a test,' I add. 'Just a small slice.'

'Go on. I can tell Ma I had some then.'

I take the pie into the kitchen. 'Does your mum bake a lot?' I call. Thinking that this may be part of the problem, but warning myself not to jump to conclusions.

'All the time,' he calls back. His tone changes, 'Hello, you must be the famous Trevor.'

I put my head around the door. 'There you are.' I say to Trevor. He comes over with his little strut and meows. It's a hungry call, and I'm reassured by that. He's been very hard to please lately and looks like he's lost a bit of weight. I've changed things up and tried a very expensive vegetarian option, but he wasn't impressed. He picks at the contents of his bowl, then walks over to his basket and climbs in. He stares at me, and I lean down and stroke his forehead. He always seems to find that very relaxing.

After a couple of minutes, his eyes close. He seems fine, but something niggles.

During the session, it becomes clear that Phil's mum bakes for him as a thank you for his caring.

'She doesn't get out much, so I go for my dinner every evening and it's like she's still cooking for five of us.'

'Where are the others?' I ask. You can ask anything when you're a therapist and it's never considered rude or nosey.

'I've got an older brother, Nick, who emigrated. An older sister, Rita, who doesn't speak to us. And a younger brother, Martin, who lives miles away. Martin comes at Christmas and sometimes invites us to stay at his.'

'Do any of them help you with your mum?'

'God, no. I gave up on that a long time ago.'

He tells me that his mum has chronic obstructive airways disease. Home helps attend three times a week. She can manage the toilet and to keep clean but can't get in and out of the bath and gets very breathless.

Before we end the session, we explore ways that Phil could eat less of his mum's cooking without insulting her. It's a problem-solving approach, all the rage. I've not tried it before, but it seems to be working. Phil writes a list of possibilities and agrees to have a talk with his mum about his weight. Something he's never done before. I tell him he can ring me if he wants me to talk to her. He says an effusive 'thanks' to this and I wonder if it's wise to involve his mum at this point. I think I'm overcompensating out of guilt.

As I collect the plates, Phil stands to leave, but I ask him to stay seated for a moment. I stutter my way through this request and can feel the blood drain from my face.

'It's okay. It's nothing you've done. I need to tell you about something I've done. I've not been totally honest with you.'

Then I tell him.

When Phil has gone, I sit in the armchair and spend a

minute going over the conversation. I explained how it came about that he knows me as Angela but that I'm Bella and I'm not a therapist.

He considered me for a moment and then laughed and said, 'For real? That's one of the funniest things I've ever heard.'

'I didn't plan it,' I explained.

As the implication dawned on him, his smile disappeared. 'Does that mean I can't come anymore?'

I repeated the finer points, emphasising that I wasn't a qualified therapist in the way that Angela was. I showed him my certificate and a few of the books I use. After reading my certificate, he placed it down on the coffee table and said, 'That's good enough for me. What should I expect for free? Carl Jung? The way I see it is there's no harm done. And where else would I get to talk with someone for nowt? If it fits with you, I'm okay to carry on. I don't give a monkey's what your name is. Hey, I can pass some of Mum's bakes on to you.' He taps the side of his nose. 'See what I did there?'

The session has left me exhausted, but I feel better for being truthful. 'Two down, one to go,' I say to Trevor, who is asleep on the chair. My hip has started to spasm, so I knock some pain killers back and lie down and close my eyes. I wonder what the human equivalent of a cat's purr is.

Chapter Thirty-One

Angela

The Health Centre has been open for four years, designed to be an airy, welcoming space with clean lines and clear signage. As Angela walks through the foyer, she becomes acutely aware of how much she's missed it. She'd held a clinic on the first floor, right next to the secretary's room. A coffee and a chat with 'the girls' used to be a highlight of her day. Not a one of them was under forty, but they were always referred to as 'the girls.'

A year ago, she'd discovered that Steve was having an affair with a Carolyn someone-or-other, one of the physios on the ground floor. What followed were three of the biggest decisions of Angela's life. Divorce Steve. Buy a house. Set up a private practice. There was a fourth, which was to punch the physio in the car park. Apart from punching the physio, she's achieved them. 'If I'd have punched every person Steve had a fling with, I'd hold a title belt by now,' she thought. Later, she'd learned that the Carolyn person had left too.

The receptionist smiles at her and after a quick call to Nadia, says, 'You can go on up.'

As she mounts the stairs, she becomes aware of a distant ringing, and on checking her phone, sees that the caller is Steve. She puts the phone back in her bag and a minute later it pings. He's left a message, and a long one. She regrets that she hasn't changed her number, but this is the one her practice is registered to. Still, changing it probably wouldn't be as much of a ball-ache as all the calls from Steve, which have increased over the last week.

As she climbs, she notices the scuffed paintwork. The wear and tear have nowhere to hide from the startlingly bright spotlights set at intervals in the vast barn of a ceiling.

There are numerous groups held here. Mums and toddlers, drugs and alcohol, diabetes, heart disease, sexual health, counselling, and minor surgery. The vibrations of these human interactions and activities whorl around her. She feels part of something again, revitalised by it.

Nadia is tapping on her laptop when Angela enters. She looks up from her desk, smiles and says, 'Come in.'

'Hi, thanks for this. I know you're busy.'

'No problem, have a seat.'

Angela sits down, feeling like a patient in for a consultation.

'It's always nice to have visitors, breaks the day up. You want to talk about the group sessions?'

'Yeah, I'd be interested, if you think there is a need.'

'Absolutely. Like I said, we could use you, but unfortunately there's no money in the budget.'

'I would do it pro bono. As much for my own sanity. And I might get a few patients who want to book a one-to-one.'

'I mentioned it to the dietitians, and they will bite your hand off, if you'll pardon the pun. They have some training in CBT but not accredited or anything.'

'I don't want to step on anyone's toes, but I'm a bit stir crazy. Missing the chat, all of that. I think in retrospect that I made too many changes too quickly.'

'Do you want to grab a coffee? I have half an hour to spare.'

The coffee house is the same room they use for the bariatric meetings. Aromas of coffee and bread rise on the air conditioning. It's a busy morning, many of the tables are taken by men and women wearing the same blue and grey identity lanyards. The counters are laden with all the food groups. Meatballs, pasta, vegetarian quiches, salads, and fish. The dessert counter looks as colourful and tempting as any Angela has seen in the nicest restaurants, she's been in.

'No wonder the centre can't afford me anymore,' Angela says

as she moves her tray along in the queue.

'The NHS marches on full stomachs,' Nadia answers.

Angela offers to buy the drinks.

'Great, I'll have coffee. I take it strong and black, like my men,' Nadia jokes.

Angela laughs. 'I have mine weak and white.'

They find a vacant table by the window. Angela notices that the cream blinds take the brunt of the sun. Once a coffee colour, now the side turned outward has been bleached white by exposure to the UV rays.

'So, you're a bit stir crazy?'

'And some. I don't know if you know, but I left here in a bit of a hurry.'

'No?'

Angela fills Nadia in on what happened.

When she's finished, Nadia says, 'Sounds like the group will be a good way to get you back into that side of things. You might get some referrals, can't promise though.'

'I was meaning to ask. You know the person you said you'd referred to me?'

Nadia taps her nails on the side of her cup as she thinks, 'Jenny Moorfield. I didn't refer her. That was another lady. Jenny found you herself. It was actually Jenny who gave me your number.'

'Have you got the number she gave you? I just need to check it's the right one.'

'Sure, it's in my diary. Let's finish up here and I'll find it.'

Chapter Thirty-Two

Bella

The CBT manual says that to access the thoughts around painful memories, you need to get close up to them. Morrisons is as close up as it gets for Zeta. I spoke to her on the phone and ran my idea by her first. She asked if she could bring her granddaughter for 'mortal' support. Following the protocol – *listen to me, protocol!* – I advised that her granddaughter could wait in the car but that it should be just us who went into the store.

I have half an hour to get there. I should make it in plenty of time. I check to see if Angela's car is parked outside. It isn't, but Graham's still home. The longer route by the main road adds another ten minutes. So, I steel myself and step outside, wishing for once that it would throw it down and I could hide behind an umbrella.

When I arrive, I queue for tea and order one for Zeta. I pick up a packet of digestives for us to share, but then remember that Frank bought digestives when he was last here. I can't figure out if it would be good therapy or not to buy them, so I leave it. I remember though that she has oat milk. It's amazing what they can get milk out of nowadays. When she arrives, she looks fragile. I know she's been in here many times before, so it's not a first for her, but what we're about to do is. I've decided that I'm going to go through the session, then I'll tell her the truth about me and take it from there. Being deceitful is turning me into someone I don't like. I've not been myself since I've been Angela.

Zeta takes a seat opposite me and thanks me for the tea.

'I got you oat milk,' I say.

'Oh, thanks, that's very thoughtful of you,' she says, offering a weak smile.

'How are you doing?'

She rubs at her stomach and says, 'I feel like I've got something lodged right here. Something undigested. It's been there for weeks.'

'Have you any other symptoms?' I ask, suspecting it's anxiety, but I'm no expert. As we know.

'No.'

'Have you seen a doctor?'

'He says there's nothing physically wrong with me.'

I'm hoping that today will help to reduce her anxiety. I recall that day at the barbecue when I asked Angela how hard could therapy be? Well, now I know. I only hope I'm doing no harm.

When she's finished her tea, I say, 'Okay, Zeta, let's go for a walk through the store.'

She nods, 'Righto,' and we leave the café.

We stroll along the aisles of cereal and dry goods. She links her arm through mine, and I place my hand over hers. 'Now, tell me what's going through your mind. What thoughts are you having?'

'Well,' she says, looking up towards the end of the aisle, 'I think I'm going to bump into Frank, maybe at the end of here.' We stop and I see that we're in front of the tea bags. 'Look,' she says, pointing shakily. She reaches up and touches a box of Earl Grey tea, then another. She runs her hand along them.

'What are you feeling?'

'Sad. I want to see him again.' She looks down and moves away. I allow her to lead, keeping my hand over hers. 'He got the milk next,' she says, pointing to an aisle on our right. 'That was our routine.'

'How often did you shop together?'

'Oh, every Thursday. Never missed.'

'But you said that was a Tuesday, right?'

She stops, then points her gloved hand at me, remembering, 'Oh yes. I did, didn't I?'

She reaches in her pocket for a tissue, and I release her other hand so she can blow her nose.

'I know this is hard for you, Zeta, but you're doing so well.'

'It doesn't feel like it,' she says, pushing the tissue back in her pocket.

'Why weren't you here that day?'

'Can we go and sit down?' she asks, suddenly looking even paler.

'Of course.' I guide her back to the café, and we find a quiet corner. Zeta searches through the misted window, presumably for the car she arrived in. Then she sits back and sighs.

'I was here that day,' she says. 'I followed Frank.'

'Oh?'

She starts to speak, but the words come out as a croak, and she clears her throat.

'Do you need some water?' I ask, and she nods. I realise as I move away that I should have kept her in the moment. I buy the bottle of water quickly and forget the glasses and return to the counter, then limp back. I pour us a glass each and she takes a sip.

The café isn't busy, and one of the assistants begins to clean the tables. She squirts some purple liquid onto a table opposite and I watch as she spreads crumbs of food around with the cloth. When she moves away from the table, the brown particles drop from the cloth onto the floor. She approaches and enquires with all the enthusiasm of a deflated balloon if we want a 'wipe down'. We decline.

Zeta swills the water around in the glass and says, 'I feel such a ninny.'

'Do you want to tell me? I promise you I'm not judging you.'

I wait.

She leans forward, lowers her voice, and says, 'There's a lady in our Monday bridge club called Annie. She lost her husband about a year ago. She latched onto us. I didn't mind at first, I felt sorry for her, imagining the pain of that…' she pauses.

'Go on.'

'But then it was all times of day and night. One of my other friends said Annie had a glint in her eyes when she spoke about my Frank. She kept making these insinuations. Frank said he was just helping Annie, that I should be more gracious. He said he'd stop if I wanted, so I said yes, stop. Let her find someone else to importune. We had a bit of an argument about it, and he left the house without me on Tuesday. He said he needed to recompose himself. I followed him. I thought he might be meeting her, but he wasn't. He was just getting my biscuits and milk. When I saw him pick up a bunch of freesias, my favourite flower, I knew that was the real reason for his shopping trip. Typical of Frank. He was a real love. I felt awful, so I turned around and made my way out. I was half way up the road when I heard the sirens approaching, and I just knew.'

Her words are barely audible through the emotion. I try to hold my own in check. Tears spill down her face and she blows her nose. 'I hurried back, but they were already putting him in the ambulance.' Her voice rises at the end of the sentence. 'They let me get in with him and the girls gave me the shopping. But he never regained consciousness. I could never tell him how sorry I was.'

When she's finished, she blows her nose again and has some water. She doesn't look at me until I take her hand and say, 'Thank you for telling me. I can see that was hard for you.'

'Do you think I was punished for being mean to Annie?' she asks.

I think about this for a minute. I try it on as a CBT therapist. I should ask Zeta to challenge her thinking, ask her how these thoughts help. I think of all the things that have happened in my life, some a possible consequence of my actions, some apparently random. But how much do we really influence our lives and how much is chance? It seems to me that life walks a few paces ahead, clearing the way. We follow, trusting that everything will be okay. Then out of the blue, life turns on us, gives us some hard truths, puts us in our place.

Zeta is still waiting. God, it's such a responsibility being a therapist. I'm really stretching myself, finding answers I didn't know I had.

'What it sounds like to me is that you have had a great love in your life and a great shock. You're trying your best to deal with it, but guilty thoughts are twisting you up. Was it so bad to think that another woman might love your Frank as much as you do?' An image of Angela and Graham flashes up before me in a moment of recognition.

'You don't think I'm wicked.'

'No, I don't Zeta. I think you are both very fortunate to have had the loving relationship you did. That you each cared about the other so much. Many people can only dream of that.'

Zeta looks up at me. Her blue gaze is too wise. I need to get myself back on track, so I ask, 'What do you hope to get from coming here and re-tracing Frank's footsteps?'

'To be close to him. This was the last place he was alive, and he was without me.'

'What about in the ambulance? How long did Frank live for?'

Zeta looks out of the window again and says, 'He was unconscious when he got in the ambulance, but I talked to him.'

'Can you remember what you said?'

'I said that I was there for him, that I loved him.' She thinks for a minute and wipes her nose with a crumpled tissue. 'You know, he did squeeze my hand. I'd forgotten that.'

'It must have been very reassuring for him to have you there. He thought he was on his own, didn't he?'

'That's true,' Zeta says, as her composure crumbles. She covers her face with her hands and sobs. I move my chair next to hers and put my arms around her shoulders. It's like holding a child. Music plays cheerfully in the background while grief wracks Zeta's tiny frame.

After a few minutes, I offer her the water and she sips. The café is still quiet, and I'm grateful for that.

'You're right about that,' she says. 'I think he knew I was with him. He must have thought he was dreaming, but I was there with him.'

'You were.'

After a moment, she squeezes my hand and says, 'I wish I'd said sorry for accusing him.'

'Well, why don't you say sorry, anyway? It won't do any harm.'

She looks at me with a frown. 'What do you mean?'

'I bet you talk to him all the time.'

'I do.'

'Well, just tell him. We could do it in our next session if you want?'

My words reach her ears a nanosecond before they register with me, like an email pinged over from my conscience. I'm supposed to be telling Zeta the truth. I add quickly, 'Rather than leave it another week, we could continue tomorrow. That way, it's still fresh.' *And I only have to lie to you for another day.*

'I'm not adverse to it,' Zeta says, 'and thanks for today, Angela. Even though I feel I've been through a wrangler, I feel a bit better.'

Addressing me as Angela jars me again, reminding me that, when I reveal who I really am, every heartfelt word I've spoken since we met will be viewed as phony, every action deceitful.

My mum used to say I was good at self-deceit. She said I never let my left hand know what my right hand was doing. What she meant was that I never let *her* know what I was doing. She hadn't cultivated that kind of relationship with me. She thought I simply owed it to her to tell her everything and made my reluctance to share with her seem pathological. Even though there were times in my life that I desperately needed her to be a mother, my instinct was to keep my distance. I must admit that this situation is starting to feel too close to my mum's characterisation of me. I need to claim myself again. Separate myself fully from Angela, like a snake from its old skin.

As I walk home, daggers of pain in my hip and head thrumming, I recall my comment to Zeta about it being understandable that someone else would also be attracted to Frank. He sounds like a lovely person. I can see people being envious of what Frank and Zeta had. Envy has the capacity to destroy what it can't have. Though I haven't done it yet, Steve suggested I should sew a grain of doubt in Graham's head by telling him about the night I saw Steve coming out of Angela's. He said it would be for Graham's own good. Am I hoping to sabotage Graham's happiness because of my envy? I know the answer and it feels like a truth coming home.

As I approach my house, I see Angela's car parked up. Despite my pain, I quicken my step and, with a few nimble-ish moves, I'm through the gate. I have that primitive sense of something approaching from behind and an urgency to gain safe harbour. I step into my house and shut the door. My mouth dry and neck pulse beating against my collar, I pause with my back to the door and wonder why I've got myself into such a state? I have an image of Angela and Graham laughing at me as I pass them, their features distorted like something from *Theatre Macabre.*

'You're being ridiculous,' I say, as I pull my coat off. 'A complete ninny, as Zeta would say.' Has CBT taught me nothing? I need to stop, re-think. A thought is not a fact.

I find Sir Trevor and say, 'Hello, baby boy.' He opens his eyes and blinks at me, and I blink back. The surge of love is calming. 'Go back to sleep,' I say.

As I flick the kettle on, I notice that Trevor hasn't touched his food, so I throw it away and put fresh out. I bought some salmon sticks, which he loves. With a cup of tea in hand, I make my way over to the settee. I feel bent in half with exhaustion. I take some pain killers and close my eyes. With each session, I expect more from myself. I feel like the therapy *is me*. I don't have the skills to keep it at arm's length. It really is time to stop.

I wake from an analgesia doze when my phone rings. I've

been slumped to one side in an uncomfortable pose. It takes me a minute to straighten my arm. It's a number I don't recognise. Another client?

'Hello,' I answer.

'Hello, is that Angela Maynard?'

The voice sounds official, sharp. I think about putting the phone down. My heart is beating fast, and my mouth is dry. 'Who's calling?' I ask, barely.

'I'm Dr Halder. One of my clients gave me your number. Jenny Moorfield.'

'Ah, I see, yes. Sorry, but I'm not taking anyone new on now. I'm retiring.'

Silence

'Oh, that's very strange. Can I check I've got the correct details? Could you give me your address?'

'Well, as you won't be referring now… I don't think…' I put the phone down.

I draw the curtains and turn my phone off. An hour later, I hear knocking. I go down into the cellar and peek through the mesh. It's Graham. He knocks again. I hold my breath and stay very still. His footsteps retreat like a sound effect on the radio, and I hear his front door close.

I have a restless night. Zeta's possible reaction to my upcoming confession and the phone call from Dr Halder loop around in my head in quick succession. Eventually I nod off, but the worry stalks my dreams and sleep brings no rest.

The following day, Zeta arrives at the agreed time. I've prepared a tray of tea and pour for us both as Zeta makes herself comfortable. I feel unusually calm. Maybe my nerves have peaked, or I'm just exhausted.

I clear my throat. I've written some notes out to help me begin and I refer to them now.

'Zeta, I need to tell you something which might surprise you.'

She places her cup down. 'Oh?'

'You think that my name is Angela Maynard, but it isn't. My name is Annabelle Pearson.'

Different expressions cross her face. 'Pardon me? Your name isn't Angela?'

'No. I'm very, very sorry. Please hear me out.'

I spend the next half an hour explaining to her how a misunderstanding meant that I came to be Angela for a short time. I omit everything about Graham. I explain that Jenny came to the wrong address, and that I invited her in.

'When you phoned, Zeta, I didn't want to turn you away. I should have. I'm sorry.'

Zeta listens, every now and then checking that she's heard me correctly. When I've finished speaking, she sits with her hands in her lap.

'I don't know what to say,' she murmurs, shaking her head. 'You're a funny onion, aren't you? Where does that leave me now? Like a cake out in the rain?'

'If you'll let me, I'll carry on with the therapy. We can call it chatting instead. I'm learning all the time and, like I said, I'll never charge you anything.'

'I trusted you. With Frank.'

'And I'm honoured that you did. I can't apologise enough, and I hope I caused no harm.'

'I thought you were real.'

'I am, Zeta. I promise I took this more seriously than anything in my life. Look.' I've brought my books upstairs to show her. I hand her my certificate: 'The Therapeutic Principles of CBT,' my name printed across it in bold capitals.

'How do I know you're this Annabelle person?'

I'm back up again. I scrabble around in the kitchen drawer and find my PIP statement from HMRC. I spread the pages open for her. Not caring that my payment schedule is revealed.

'I can ask Jenny to come and talk to you, if it would reassure you?'

Zeta stands and goes to the window. 'Which is Angela's house?'

I join her, dreading where this might go. I lift the curtain and point and say, 'Over the road, the one with the green door.'

'Does she know?'

I knew this was coming. I'm totally exposed. The control I thought I had, an illusion, 'Not yet, no.'

'You think the real Angela won't find out?' she asks, turning as I drop the curtain back in place.

I think of the phone call last night as my breakfast threatens to make a comeback. 'Probably,' I answer.

Zeta walks to the settee and picks her handbag up. 'I need to go.'

I follow her to the door. 'Zeta, please forgive me. I'm very sorry. Have a think if you want to chat again.' I feign brightness. 'After all, I think we're getting somewhere.'

She stops at the door, lands those eyes on mine and says, 'I've been coming to talk about my problems to someone who needs more psychopathic help than I do.'

I watch as she opens the door and makes her way towards her granddaughter's car. She opens the car door and speaks for a moment, then closes it and proceeds to cross the road. I rush out and call after her. The granddaughter watches, frowning as she pulls an earpiece out. I signal for her to stay put. I mouth, '*It's fine,*' and somehow pull my face into a reassuring smile.

'Zeta,' I call.

Zeta reaches Angela's gate and turns around.

'Please, Zeta.' I lower my voice as I get closer. 'Don't say anything. I will tell Angela. I promise.'

She has her hand on the gate. She stops and says, 'I'm not going to tell her. I just want to make an appointment. Like I thought I was doing when I phoned you.'

'Oh.' My sails deflate. I suddenly feel exposed having this conversation outside. God knows what her granddaughter is making of this. I turn around and wave at her. She doesn't wave back. 'Of course, by all means, but Angela will charge you seventy-five pounds, minimum.'

'But at least I'll be sure who I'm talking to.'

'I completely understand. I'm so very sorry, I will tell her…' I pause as Zeta peers around me at the sound of an approaching car. I hardly dare look. When I do, I'm glued to the spot as Angela parks up and gets out of her car. 'Extremely soon,' I add.

It's like a Mexican stand-off. For a moment, no one speaks.

'Hi, Angela,' I say brightly.

'Hi,' she says hesitantly, looking from me to Zeta. I notice that Zeta has taken her hand away from the gate.

'This is my friend, Zeta. Oh, sorry, we're blocking your gate. How are you, Angela?' I babble. The excruciating awfulness of the situation like one of the un-funny comedy sketches my dad used to watch.

Zeta looks from me to Angela, then walks towards her granddaughter's car and says, 'I'll toddle along and leave it with you, *Annabelle*.'

'Perfect,' I say, confused by her change of heart, but grateful for it.

She climbs into the car, and they drive away. Angela hasn't taken her eyes off me.

I've only been home long enough to pick Trevor up for a cuddle and to wait for my heartbeat to return to a less threatening tempo when there's a knock at the door. I know instinctively who it is.

'*What do I do? What do I do?*' I repeat into the Trevor's fur.

'I think you and I need to talk,' Angela says, when I eventually respond. 'Can I come in?'

So, it's finally here. I feel a brief wash of relief, but my heart is in my mouth and I'm trembling. I lower Trevor onto the settee.

'Come in, sit down,' I say.

'I won't stay, thanks,' she says.

No, you won't.

Trevor jumps off the settee. He makes a noise somewhere

between a hiss and a growl and flies into the kitchen and out through the cat flap.

'He seems to have recovered well,' she says, and I feel my hackles rise. 'Anyway, you probably know why I'm here, and if you...'

'Look, Angela,' I interrupt – I can do that in my own house. 'It's a relief that you know. I was honestly going to tell you, but I was too scared. All I can say is I'm very, very sorry. It all got out of hand. I'm going to stop. I have stopped.'

She looks wrong-footed by my gushing confession. Her frown clears momentarily, then returns. She wants to milk it. 'The trouble you've caused me,' she says angrily.

'Please, sit down. Tea?' I ask. It's the last thing I want to do for her, but making tea will give me the break I need. My heart's pounding and my hip's in a spasm. I have never been able to handle confrontation. Surprising really, considering my exposure to it. But Mum died before I'd built up enough antibodies.

Angela perches on the arm of the settee, halfway between a sit and a stand. Her hands are clasped low, as if she'd going to offer me a 'leg up.' Her hair is pulled up in an untidy ponytail and she looks tired, less than perfect. I notice her jeans are ripped at the knee and her white t-shirt has a small stain on the front that looks like tomato sauce. 'Just half a cup then,' she concedes.

I hurry away. In the kitchen, I pour a glass of water and take a couple of *Ibuprofen* as I lean on the sink. I always wondered how my deception would be discovered. Now Angela is here, in my home. It has a very unreal quality to it. I'm not a sweary person. Swearing is crude and evidence of low breeding, but I have a few swear words lined up for just such an occasion. I only ever think them though, never say them out loud. I mouth two of them now in quick succession.

I carry the tea through with trembling hands. Hooking a slender finger through the handle, she takes the cup from me with a reluctant, 'Ta.'

I remain standing and repeat, 'I'm sorry, Angela. I'm trying to put things right. That lady this morning…Zeta.'

She cuts me off. 'I don't see how you can now. Stevie's already phoned me about ten times.'

Stevie?

'He's threatened to tell Gray himself.' She waves her free hand over to the adjoining wall. 'I mean, what did you hope to gain by stirring it all up?'

I'm confused.

'I didn't tell Gray about Stevie coming to mine,' she explains, with a roll of her eyes, 'because it would be playing into Stevie's hands.'

'Well, maybe you should have thought of that,' I say. 'I don't like to see Graham used and treated like a fool.'

'Really? You told Stevie about me and Graham getting married because you are protecting Graham? I don't think so. You wanted to stir things up. If you knew what I'd been through…'

It seems she wants to say more, but she stops mid-rant. My heartbeat slows to a healthier pace and my brain unscrambles, allowing me to comprehend. Angela isn't here about me stealing her identity and her clients. She's here because I phoned Steve and stirred things up. Thank God I haven't spilled the beans and revealed my real crime.

The reprieve allows me to compose myself and reply, 'Did Graham tell you we were engaged to be married? A long time ago, true. But I've never been under any illusion that we'd pick up where we left off.'

'You sure?' She swirls the tea around in the cup, the beginnings of a sly smile at the corner of her mouth. It's very annoying, I have a visceral reaction to it. I'm not a fighter, but God, I could poke her in the eye right now.

'No.' I say, with a calmness belying my thoughts of bodily harm. 'Me and Graham are *so* in the past and keep going. I admit I didn't like the change when you came on the scene and almost killed Trevor. But I never meant to cause any problems. I'm sorry for telling Steve about you and Graham, but I don't understand why you can't just be honest with him. You should have told him about Steve being at yours all night.' Here's me lecturing Angela about honesty.

'Look, whatever you thought you saw, you didn't. You can tell Gray if you like, but it will just show you up for who you really are.'

She has me off guard because there is truth in her reasoning.

She gives me a closed-lip smile, a millimetre away from a grimace. 'I appreciate the apology though,' she says, rising and looking for somewhere to put her cup.

I give one last jab. 'It seems obvious that Steve is still holding out for you, though, and he wouldn't be doing that without your encouragement.'

Her smile disappears. 'Stevie holds out only for himself. My advice to you would be to steer well clear.'

I take the cup from her, and she walks to the door. 'What did you want to tell me about Zeta?'

'Sorry?'

'The lady outside my house.'

Caught out, I scrape around for explanations. 'Oh, yes. I forget now. Must have been a lie.'

Chapter Thirty-Three

Bella

Trevor cries constantly. It breaks my heart. In the taxi, I strap the seat belt around the carrier and wrap my arm around it to give it more stability against the bumpy road, and the stop-start lurch of the cab. He pokes his paws through the bars, and I risk a clawing by sliding my fingers in and stroking his head.

'Soon be there,' I say, trying to maintain a calming tone. But he's a cat, and he doesn't like being in a cage, or a taxi, or going to the vet. The soothing words are for me, really.

I've placed some of his favourite snacks in the food compartment, but he doesn't give them a second sniff.

When we arrive, we're directed to the 'cat area' by the receptionist and I take a seat opposite another lady who has a cat box on the chair next to her. Trevor is still complaining, and I open the top of the box a smidge so I can scratch his head. He looks at me imploringly, and I feel that awful sense of helplessness, which comes with the inability to explain. All I have is his trust and each time I bring him to the vets I feel like I've betrayed it.

'What breed is he?' the lady opposite me asks, smiling sympathetically.

'He's a British Blue,' I answer.

'Ah, he's lovely.

'And yours?'

'Tabby.'

'She's very well behaved.'

'She's sixteen,' the lady explains. 'Deaf and nearly blind, so she don't get too bothered. Do you, my darlin'? I know I won't have her for much longer and I'm dreading the day.'

The vet emerges from her room and calls out, 'Tabatha Webber.'

'That's us, Tabs,' she says, shifting to the edge of the chair and then standing. Lifting her cat carrier, she says breathlessly, 'Well, bye love.'

'Bye,' I answer. 'Bye, Tabatha.'

Eventually, we are called into the clinic. The room is small and bright with a spotless white examination table. I carefully lift Trevor out and he reluctantly sits on the counter. The vet, Sharma, asks me to place him onto the scales and I let go of him momentarily while his weight registers. He meows and looks at me, then the floor. He would be out of here like a shot if he had the opportunity.

'Good boy,' I say repeatedly, stroking his head, scratching him under the chin.

'You are beautiful, Trevor. I could take you home,' Sharma says. 'He has lost a little.' She examines his teeth, his eyes and ears. Then feels around his legs and tummy and listens to his heart and lungs with a stethoscope.

'So, let's give him his booster and we'll take some bloods. Just to be sure.'

My heart has just bounced off my rib cage. 'Why? Is there something?'

'No,' she smiles, showing beautiful white teeth. 'It's just with him losing weight and being off his food. Bloods will tell us if there's anything underlying.'

'Does your foot hurt very much?' Jenny asks when she calls around the following day.

I stop what I'm doing and try to decipher the question. I've not told Jenny about Angela's visit. I realised that Steve used me, trying to get me to stir things up. But there's no smoke without fire, and no fire without fuel.

'You shot yourself in it.'

'Ha. Very funny.'

'If you hadn't phoned Steve, then they wouldn't have needed to get away and left you tidying up for them.'

She's referring to the fact that Graham and Angela have gone to Malta for two weeks. 'To get away from the stress,' as Graham put it.

'It's not for *them*, it's for Gray... ham. And I need the money.'

Trevor comes in from his morning jaunt and goes to his bowl. He sniffs the food, then scratches at the window. That usually means he doesn't like what's on offer. I tip it into the bin and search for a tin of sardines and put a small amount out. He sniffs again, then eats a little before walking away.

'I don't know what's wrong with him,' I say. 'He's off his food.'

'Has he done that before?' Jenny asks, leaning down and stroking him. He leans his neck into her hand and closes his eyes, his expression one of sheer pleasure.

'Oh, he's a cat. He has his fads. I'm just waiting for blood results.'

'He seems happy enough,' she says, as we watch him pounce on his small stuffed mouse toy and throw it in the air.

We both laugh at his antics until he gets tired and jumps up onto the settee for a nap.

'I came to tell you something,' Jenny says, standing in the kitchen doorway, looking like a trendy mum in a black baseball cap. Her hair is pulled through the back opening in a thick ponytail. She's wearing black jeans and a black loose t-shirt under a soft leather biker style jacket. I wonder if she's subconsciously yielding to Mike's motorbike enthusiasm.

We carry our mugs over to our respective chairs as though we're about to start a therapy session.

'I spoke to Mike about you pretending to be Angela,' she says.

I almost spill my tea. 'What!'

'I asked *hypothetically*,' she makes speech marks with her fingers, 'What would happen if someone pretended to be someone else?'

I'm on the edge of the chair.

She continues, 'It's not illegal as long as you haven't done or said anything that would be considered defamation of character, or libel, or slander.'

'What does that mean?'

'Well, as long as you didn't say any nasty things in her name, or do anything that would give Angela a bad rep.'

'By doing what?'

'Oh, I don't know, like killing clients and burying them in your back garden. Or making them dance to eighties disco music. As far as Mike's concerned, you've not actually broken any laws. Also, anyone can say they are a therapist apparently. There is no actual regulation of that in the UK. You can do some two-bit qualification in it and set yourself up. Like you did.'

'Blinking heck.'

'You *could* just have googled it, stopped you worrying.'

Jenny's kindness always heightens my guilt. Why would she go to this trouble? Zeta's reaction seemed more fitting. I could almost imagine her spitting at my feet.

'Why do you help me like this?' I ask. Why would you ever speak to me again?'

'I'm not saying I'm not angry at you,' she answers. 'It might not be illegal, but it's not ethical either, is it? I'm here to make sure you're true to your word and stop seeing the others.'

'I will, I promise.'

'I think talking helped, though. I looked forward to the sessions. Apart from the dancing. That was a bit of a stretch.'

'I really looked forward to you coming.' I pull a tissue from the box. 'Sorry,' I apologise for the sudden, sprouting tears. It takes only a minute before they're dropping heavily, like thawing snow. 'I can't stop them,' I say, as I pull another tissue.

'Bella,' Jenny says. The concern in her voice overwhelms me, and I hide my face in a bundle of wet tissues. She grabs my hand. 'It's done. You're going to stop it.'

'It's not just that. It's Trevor. I'm worried about him.'

'Well, he isn't worried, is he? He's out there sniffing on some other cat's butt.'

'Jenny!' I chide, though she has made me smile.

'What would you say if it was *me* worrying about Trevor?' she asks.

So, she has been paying attention.

I sniff back and focus on her face. 'I'd say you should wait for the results.'

She pushes herself upright and says, 'Good advice. Now take it.'

When I've eventually composed myself, I tell her about Zeta.

'I wonder why she didn't say anything to Angela?' Jenny asks.

'I don't know. I was convinced she would.'

'You know,' Jenny adds, 'Dr Halder phoned me and asked me for your address?'

'Yes, she called me. I'm afraid I put the phone down on her. You didn't tell her, did you?'

'No,' she answers, as she picks at a thread on the arm of the chair. 'I don't know why I covered for you. I had to say I'd lied about attending any therapy appointments. I said I had an initial appointment with Angela, the *real* Angela, but I didn't go.'

'Oh dear, I'm sorry. She asked for all my details, but I told her I was retiring.'

'What? So, you told her Angela Maynard was retiring? She knows Angela.'

'I was put on the spot.' I say defensively.

'Jesus, what a…' She sees my expression and pauses. 'Anyway, I'm not going to have the surgery this year, so it's not as important. Maybe next year, I'll figure something out. You, missus, just need to let a bit of water run under the bridge. I'm going to carry on like, eating regularly. Seems to be helping.' She turns and looks out of the window. 'Dr Halder gave the same details to Zeta, remember, so you're not out of the woods yet.'

Chapter Thirty-Four

Bella

Sue opens her front door with a flourish, as though she's about to make an announcement. 'Hi,' she says, smiling, tanned. 'I was just thinking of you and here you are. Come in, lovely.'

My day suddenly brightens.

The house smells musty, like the soil on new potatoes. I notice the parched reed diffuser in the hall, which must have dispersed its last vanilla bloom while Sue was away.

'I thought you must be back. I saw the food delivery,' I say.

'I'm just unpacking it now. Got fresh milk in here somewhere if you'd like a cuppa?'

Molly is curled up asleep in her basket.

'If it's not too much trouble?'

'None at all,' she answers as she prises the lid from the coffee jar. 'One of the great things about coming home,' her voice strains as she reaches for the cups, 'is that I get to catch up on the gossip all at once instead of on the drip. Now, hang on 'til we're sat down.'

I begin by asking her about her holiday. It sounds idyllic. Sue tells me that she and Julia bought the house together and planned to retire there one day. 'I've got two years to go, then I'm off.'

'You'll still go?'

'It's the only reason I'm still working, making sure I've enough to live on when I move. Now, do tell, what's been happening here?'

I keep my eye on the time while I fill her in on developments. Of phoning Steve; my confrontation with Angela. And I don't know why, but I confess to doing therapy under Angela's name.

For some reason, it makes me cry. When I stop speaking, I can't look at her.

'Jesus Christ, Bella, I go away for a couple of months…'

'I sound like a bad person, but I'm not. I'm not carrying on with it. I'm going to tell the truth.'

'To Angela?'

'I don't know.'

'Why have you told me?'

'I don't know. I think it's…'

Sue leans forward, waits.

'I think because you won't judge me,' I answer. 'You'll give me time to explain. Oh, I don't know.' I lean my elbows on the table and put my head in my hands. Tears drop onto the wood in front of me. 'It's Trevor…' I lift my head and the words come out sludgy. 'I think he's ill. I need to focus on him. All the deceit, it's too distracting.'

She leans back into her chair. 'Oh no.' She shakes her head, looks at me, sighs and says, 'Christ, what a brain mash.'

I don't put the tv on as I don't intend to be in Graham's for hours. Trevor seems a bit listless this afternoon and I don't want to leave him for too long.

I notice a little 'Swedish Ivy' with cascading stems and rounded leaves on the kitchen windowsill. I wonder if it was a gift from Angela. Everything in this house is now Angela-tinged.

As I'm dusting, my eyes are everywhere. Eking out details, playing spot the difference. I find a pair of diamond stud earrings in a little dish on the coffee table. I wanted proof of their relationship but now I find it. I feel a fresh jab of pain.

All the intimacy of cleaning for Graham has vanished. I used to have a sense of reassurance from my proximity to him, especially at night. His newfound passion has ripped a hole through that. I had been convinced that my feelings would eventually be reciprocated. All the while, Graham was writing his own story, and I only featured in the margins.

Everything feels different for me. For Graham, nothing has changed. My role is, and always has been, one of cleaner, plant reviver, creator of pressed pillowcases and crease-free shirts and the occasional home-made pie or pasta dish. That's what it's always been, 'End of,' as Jenny would say.

I pick an earring up and twirl it around. Angela doesn't strike me as someone to forget things, and I believe she has purposely left these out to remind me of my place, or rather hers. I'm not prepared for what subtle boundary-marking she might have left upstairs so, even though I'm tempted, I don't go there.

They took off for Malta three days ago. Graham asked me to look after the house again. He clearly didn't know about Steve staying. He said that he and Angela needed some time away.

I bet anything you like that Graham paid for the holiday, too. It's funny that they're waiting for the dust to settle while I'm here doing their dusting, kicking it all back up.

It suits me that Angela's off the scene for a while though and can't confront me with anything else. I need to take Jenny's advice and let that water flow under that bridge.

I use CBT to divert my thoughts from this subject matter. I wonder how it's going with Phil and whether he's spoken to his mum. I'll find out soon enough as he's coming back for another session in two days. I haven't heard anything from Zeta, and I'm truly regretful about that. I wonder whether she's still going into Morrisons?

The CBT diversionary tactic only lasts until the next unwanted thought comes barging in like a big bully, elbowing every other thought out of its way. As the steam rises from the collar of Graham's shirt, I think of all I lost. All I haven't told him.

As soon as I get back home, I check on Sir Trevor. He's curled up on the settee, his tummy rising and falling, his eyes closed. He appears to be in a deep sleep. I fill up with love for him. I remember watching a programme about an animal rescue centre. A little girl aged around five had been introduced to her new kitten and instructed by her mum to be very gentle when she picked him up. The little girl had replied, 'But Mummy, he's *so* cute. I want to squeeze him very hard three times!'

It had really made me laugh, but I completely understood that urge.

My phone rings. It's the vet.

I can't take it all in. Sharma said something about Trevor's blood results showing some abnormality and that he would need to come back for "'additional tests". I heard the words 'lymph nodes'. Sharma was still talking when I put the phone down. It rang again a few minutes ago, but I didn't answer it. Denial is a useful strategy and I'm very good at it.

The day draws in and the evening birdsong begins. I hear a car pull away on the road and rain starts a soft patter against the window. As Trevor snores gently on my knee, I rub his head and talk to him.

'It's okay, baby boy,' I tell him. 'I've got you.'

I'm still on the settee when I awake the following morning. I don't remember removing 'Audrey', but I clearly did because, when I put my glasses on, I see that she's on the floor under the coffee table, looking uncannily like an abandoned guinea pig. I grab her and shake her back into shape.

The click of the cat flap. Sir Trevor has either just gone out or has just returned. I take that as a very good sign and wonder if I dreamed the call from the vets. It's very possible because I've been having vivid dreams. Mostly about the accident. I awake to the sound of screeching metal, sometimes the sound of crying. The screeching always feels so close but stops when I open my eyes. And it's me who is crying.

Trevor appears at the doorway and meows softly. His bowl contains the untouched food from last night, so I bin that and bring him a tube of cat yoghurt. I sit on the kitchen chair, and he jumps up onto my knee. I tear off the top and hold the end to his little mouth. He sniffs it first, then laps at it, eyes almost closing with pleasure. Surely that's a very good sign? I try him with his feather bird toy, but he's not interested. Same with the tunnel game. His expression says, '*you* like it so much, *you* play with it'.

I feel brave enough to phone the vet.

After a short wait, Sharma comes on the line. 'Mrs Pearson, I'm so glad you phoned. I tried to phone you back.'

'Do you think you could have made a mistake? Trevor seems fine today.'

'Well, there're rarely any mistakes with the blood results, but we can't tell everything from them. Sir Trevor will need to come in for more tests.'

'He hates that.'

'I know. I'm sorry…' My heart quickens. Is she saying sorry because it's incurable, or sorry because he needs to have more tests? 'But he will need treatment and the sooner we do the tests, the sooner we can stage that treatment.'

'What did you say was wrong with him again?'

A pause. 'It looks like it might be Lymphoma. But we can't be sure as we–'

I cut in. 'That's not good.' If she could see me, she'd see I'm sort of marching on the spot, as if I'm desperate for the loo.

'It would be better if you came in. Then we can talk properly.'

'But what are you saying?'

Another pause. I hate the pauses. I fill them with images of operating rooms and drip stands and machines that bleep.

'I have time this afternoon at two,' she says.

Sue drives with extra care. 'Road bump coming up,' she says.

I cling on tightly to Trevor's carrier, covered with a blanket, corner lifted so he can see me. I blink slowly to reassure him. It doesn't work; he cries and thrusts his paw through the bars. I hold it. I don't care if he scratches me, but he doesn't. He would never deliberately hurt me. Not like I'm hurting him by doing this.

'Stopping,' Sue says, as the car comes to a slow halt at the lights. Then starts off again, no jolting or jumping. 'You both okay?' She regards me through the rear-view mirror.

I nod and smile. Stupid question, but she's only showing concern. She drops us at the door and goes in search of a parking space.

A couple of people waiting in the 'dog area' of reception. Faithful friends, some wagging wildly, some whimpering, one with powerful shoulder muscles, stressed, panting and straining at the lead. A lady in front of me holds a spaniel with an Elizabethan collar around his neck to stop him scratching at stitches. He looks very sorry for himself, and I smile sympathetically at him.

Sharma's ready for us. It's a different room this time, larger, with a desk and chairs in it. There's an examination area and some medical equipment to one side. Trevor is quieter now he's out of the car. I lift him out gently and sit him on my lap.

Sharma kneels in front of us, scratching Trevor under the chin and around his ears. 'How are you doing, boy?' she asks.

'He's had a little food this morning and been outside,' I answer, because Trevor's not going to, is he? If he could speak for himself, he'd brush our concerns off and tell us he's positively splendid. He's a stiff upper lip sort.

'I was thinking maybe you looked at the wrong results,' I add hopefully. 'Maybe they belong to another cat?'

Sharma returns to sit behind her desk. 'So, here's the thing.'

A light tapping on the door and Sue appears.

'This is my friend,' I say. It lifts me to have her here Whenever Graham has brought me, he's waited in the car park.

Sharma continues, 'The blood test showed cancerous cells.'

The 'cancer' word has been floating around, sidestepping left and right. Now I feel the full force of weight behind its punch. The room retreats as I focus on Trevor. He's unusually still in my arms.

Sharma's lips continue to move.

'Bella.' Sue touches my arm. 'Sharma is saying that there are lots of things that can be done.'

'We need to do some more tests, Bella. As you said, Sir Trevor seems okay in himself now, but because he's not eating…'

'Can he be cured?' My throat closes around the words.

'We need to do some scans and further examinations.'

Chapter Thirty-Five

Bella

'Do you want me to stay?'

'What?' I hear Sue, but I don't have the brain space to think. I've had to leave my little boy behind. Sharma said she'll conduct more blood tests and scans and such. Said it would be better to keep him overnight than make unnecessary journeys to and fro. Especially when he finds it so stressful in the car.

'No,' I answer. I sound abrupt and unappreciative, and I'm not. I force to my thoughts away from Trevor, like trying to switch a rusted rail track. 'Sue,' I turn to her and put my hand on her sleeve, 'I'm really grateful. I don't know what I'd have done…' It's no use. I flop down in the chair and cover my face. 'I'm sorry I must seem so stupid.'

'Are you kidding?' Sue says, perching on the arm of the chair. 'I know exactly how it is with cats. They're so trusting. They can break your heart.' She rubs my back lightly, then stands and says, 'Cup of tea, I think.'

Sue left about half an hour ago, telling me she's on the end of the phone if I need her. She's taking me to pick Trevor up tomorrow, and she's instructed me to try and rest in the meantime. Why do people say things like *'you need to eat something'* and '*try to get some rest?*' and *'try not to worry too much'*. What's too much? How much is enough?

Trevor's bowl still holds the food I put out for him this morning. I clean it away, feeling flat and empty. Then I traipse upstairs and think about having a bath, but when I think of the whole getting wet thing and having to dry myself, I can't the bothered. I put my nightdress on and get into bed, hoping that my exhaustion will mean I'll sleep until the vet phones.

As I lie here, I try to fight my fears, but who has ever been successful at that? May as well just let them in. So, I do. I wonder if I've missed Trevor's symptoms because I've been so preoccupied with Graham and with doing therapy. I probably haven't given the attention to him that he deserved. The tight grip of guilt in my stomach tells me it's true. Before all of this, there was just me and Trevor. Everything revolved around him. I never relied on anyone for anything. I took him to the vets in his carrier on the bus and he was never as afraid on the 330 as he is in a car. But he got heavier, and it became more painful for me. I started to order taxis, but then Graham noticed and offered to take us. I became reliant on him. Saw it as a sign that we were getting closer. Me and my signs.

Every night I watch the rise and fall of Trevor's breath and drop into a tranquil state before finally drifting off. But tonight he's locked in a cold cage, confused and afraid, believing I've abandoned him. I blame Angela. She gave Trevor a shock when he went under her car. And I'm convinced she has been his tormentor and was responsible for his tail pull injury. It would explain his uncharacteristic reaction to her when she came in the house. Is it possible that these shocks and her cruelty could have changed something at cell level, triggering his illness?

I curl myself into a ball and let the tears come.

The following morning, Sue picks me up, and while driving speaks with a forced brightness that I associate with early-morning radio presenters. When we arrive at the vets, Sharma invites us into her office, and we all sit. I expected Trevor to be here, but he isn't.

Sharma must see my expression because she says, 'I've left Sir Trevor upstairs. I just checked on him and he's sleeping. He had a stressful time yesterday, and it's taken it out of him.'

'Do you have any results?'

'We have the scan results, yes.' She clicks on her keyboard.

And begins the next sentence with the word '*Unfortunately*'. As she continues, her words move me closer to my most dreaded fear. With each sentence, my life changes.

'*Worse than we thought.*'

And again.

'*Very aggressive.*'

And again.

'*Tough decision.*'

I can't listen anymore.

'Can I see him?'

'Of course. He'll be very happy to see you too. I'll get him.'

The door swings closed behind her, and the room is still. Sue leans forward and whispers, 'She said there are treatments.' I turn my face to her and nod silently. I don't trust myself to speak, so thoughts chatter on inside my head. Sue continues, 'She said chemo.'

I nod again and feel a sob building, so I sigh loudly, and it stays at heel.

MasterChef used to be one of my essential evening viewings. Now I sit with Trevor on my knee, watching but barely registering it.

While we're here like this, it's easy to pretend that everything is fine, as if the last three days haven't happened, but I know I must face things. Sharma said surgery and chemotherapy were the most common treatment options. When Sue asked (because I couldn't) about the success of these treatments, Sharma answered that it was difficult to predict. The kick in the stomach was that without treatment, Trevor has about two months left. With it, he might have twelve months, maybe longer. But this would be spent with him on treatments and in and out of hospital. And chemotherapy would make him sick and weak.

Can I do that to my little boy?

I decide to leave it a few days before letting Sharma know. For the moment, I feel calm. Trevor seems to be more himself. He's tired, but that's to be expected. I shush him as I stroke and remember when he was a kitten. He loved to explore, finding holes that I hadn't been aware of, like the space in the kick board under the kitchen cupboards. I lost a good few tea towels to blocking holes with them until he grew too big to squeeze through. And as he grew, the place in my heart for him expanded likewise. He's eight now and in those eight years he's been my one true, constant friend and companion. The way people love can be fickle. They change, or you change. But, if you love an animal, you receive their trust and that doesn't change. Trusting you *is* love, to a cat.

Chapter Thirty-Six

Bella

They're back. I heard the taxi pull up early this morning and the dulled sounds of tread on the stairs. It's been quiet since then. I've watched the sun come up and a ribbon of light from the gap in the curtains move its way across the bedcover. Trevor slept on me all night until my bladder forced me to move. Then he stretched and shifted down the bed. It's gone ten o'clock now. Unusual for us both to still be asleep, but we're exhausted. I pull the covers back slowly, so I don't disturb him.

My reflection in the bathroom mirror tells a story. I look put together with flour paste. My eyes are bloodshot and swollen. I cried all last night. I did that inward crying with the sobbing contained in my neck and throat. Muffling the sound with the bed cover. Thoughts of Trevor going through all that treatment for the next twelve months foremost in my head. Sharma said chemo has a similar effect on cats as it does on humans. And that it's hard to know if a cat is in pain. She listed the symptoms Trevor might experience, both from the treatment and from the illness itself. She held nothing back. The night dragged slowly, but eventually I slept.

Back in the bedroom, I get dressed, then I kneel at the side of the bed and stroke Trevor's head. I don't want to cry again, but the next tear fall is just a blink away.

Knocking downstairs.

Graham? Jenny?

When I open the door, Phil's smile freezes.

'Are you alright?' he asks with concern.

'I'm fine.'

'What's wrong?'

I let him through. He's carrying a plate covered with foil. 'I'm so sorry, Phil. I'd forgotten. I mean, I remembered you were due today, then I forgot.'

'No, it's fine, you don't have to…' he looks down at the plate. 'Ham and leek,' he explains.

I root under my sleeve for a tissue.

'Are you poorly?' he asks.

'No, it's…' I flop down in the chair. Fear like iron weights in my legs. 'It's Trevor, he's ill.'

'Oh no.' He comes to sit down, then remembers the plate. 'Should I..?'

I ask him to put it in the kitchen and to thank his mum for me. Phil does this while passing on his mum's re-heating advice.

Returning to the lounge, he sits opposite me. 'Now, is there anything I can do?'

Phil leaves after I promise to keep him updated. It's only when I pass the mirror at the foot of the stairs that I comprehend the reason for his alarm. I've forgotten to put my wig on.

Chapter Thirty-Seven

Bella

The fiery orange leaves of a maple tree hang cheerlessly as autumn hovers in the air. The fine drops of morning mist cling to my cardigan, refreshing on my face as I walk along the uneven pavement.

As expected, Sue gets very upset when I tell her about the results. Her face crumples. I instinctively flinch as she opens her arms and hugs me and says, 'Oh, poor you, poor Trevor.'

I can't remember the last time anyone embraced me, or I them. This realisation shakes me. I tentatively lift my arms and put them around her. Sue's warm and smells of sponge cake. As an accompaniment to the tears, my nose starts to run. I pull away from her so that I don't dribble onto her nice cardigan. I find the damp ball of tissue up my sleeve and quickly wipe.

Sue gently rubs my arm. 'What can I do?' she asks.

'I don't know, Sue. I can't bear to think about it, but it's all I can think of.'

'Won't you come in?'

I explain that I don't want to leave Trevor.

'I'll come to you. I've fresh cheese scones. I'll bring them and we can have a chat.'

Previously, I would have made any excuse to avoid inviting someone into my house. But I inadvertently broke that fear barrier when I pretended to be Angela and Jenny crossed the threshold. Now it's a free for all. I can just hear my mum shouting at me for inviting a friend around, 'Why don't you invite the whole bloody street!'

Sue is at mine now, and Trevor is on her knee. I nervously passed him to her, like priceless China. She's stroking him and he looks so very content. It's a funny sensation, seeing him with other people. I'm looking at his little body in her lap while observing good manners and complimenting her on the scones. 'Lovely and light,' I say, but the words come out in a strange sob as though I'm in ecstasy at the taste. Sue knows, though.

I replace the scone on the plate. It's too much of an effort to eat.

'He's a strong boy. He knows he's loved and that will give him the strength to face whatever comes.'

'What about me, though?'

'Same,' she answers. 'We're all stronger than we know. You need to lean on others now. I'm here for you. Sounds like Jenny's here for you. Have you spoken to fella-me-lad?'

So much has happened since we talked about Graham. Sometimes change happens suddenly, and you need to adapt quickly. And some things change imperceptibly. You wake up one morning and realise that something you used to do a year ago has altered and you're not sure how.

'Not about this, no. They've just got back from holiday.'

'Ah,' she says, one eyebrow raised.

'I don't even know if Graham's my friend anymore.'

I could easily ask him if we're still friends because the following day Graham is at my front door.

'Hi,' I say. I don't mince my words.

'Hi.'

'Was Malta nice?'

'Great.'

It's evident. His eyes are shining reflectors, his crow's feet white against his tan. The grey at his temples bleached by the Maltese sunshine. We share the same sun, but she favours some over others.

'I bought you this,' he says, as he holds out a flimsy carrier bag.

I take it from him and peer inside. There's a small box. I wonder if it would be too rude to open it on the doorstep. Good manners prevail and I invite him in.

He steps inside. 'It's only a token.'

I hand the carrier bag back to him and pull the lid off the box. Inside is a tiny glass ornament of a cat astride a goldfish bowl.

'It's Mdina glass,' he explains.

It's beautiful, delicate, a perfect tiny cat with a cheeky face. I hold my nerve.

'It's lovely, thank you. Thank Angela.'

'Oh, she wasn't… I saw it and...'

'Thank you.'

'Is everything okay?'

I wonder what he's referring to. I need a hint nowadays. So many things are not okay.

'Why?'

'Just, it's nothing but…'

I'm still holding up the ornament. I start to put it back in the box, like my mum would have done. *Just what I've always wanted,'* she'd say. But I never saw anything I'd brought her used or on display.

'The back door was unlocked when we I got back,' he says, thumbs hooked into pockets.

My breath catches. 'Oh. Graham. I'm…'

'Everything's fine,' he says, holding his hands out, palms down, as if calming a frightened horse.

I recall the last time I was there I was worried about Trevor, distracted.

I sit down, holding the box close. 'Trevor's poorly.' I hate saying it. You tell someone, you become responsible for managing their reaction. Let's get this over with. 'Cancer,' I say.

'Cancer? You're joking.'

In the five years I've lived here, it's the first time Graham has sat down in one of my armchairs. He does so now. So, this is what it takes.

'When did you find out?'

'A few weeks ago.'

'Why didn't you say?'

'Why would I? It felt very difficult after everything Angela said.'

'What? When?'

'When she came around.'

'Here?'

'Yes, before you asked me to house sit. She came to see me. She told me off for telling Steve about you both. And she said you thought I was still holding out for you, and it was embarrassing.'

In the past, I'd have run a mile from being so outspoken. Too humiliating. But every emotion has paled into insignificance since Trevor became ill. My head doesn't have the storage space, so I'm having a clear-out instead of hoarding my thoughts and feelings.

Looking at the floor, shaking his head, Graham says, 'Look… Bella.'

Any sentence that begins that way is always going to be negative, so I interject. 'It doesn't matter, Graham. Steve came here. He asked me to stir things up for you both, to tell you about the night he stayed at Angela's.'

I can tell this is news to him. His healthy colour drains like a tv screen going from colour to black-and-white.

'I thought Angela might have mentioned it on holiday. Steve, he's a bit…' I'm not sure how to finish, but Graham's looking at me, waiting for the punchline. 'Well, a bit obsessed.'

He nods his head and looks at the back of his hands. 'He might be, at that,' he says.

'Graham, I'm sorry to land that on you, but I need to get on.'

'Sure,' he says, and stands up. He takes a deep inhalation. I notice he's put some weight on around his stomach.

'Where is the lad?' he asks, looking around.

'Asleep on my bed. The meds make him sleepy. I don't…'

'No problem. If there's anything you need. A lift to the vets, anything...' He places his hand on my shoulder and smiles sympathetically.

'I've got it covered, thanks,' I tell him. 'He won't be with us much longer, anyway.' My voice catches with the weight of the words.

'Come here,' he says and holds his arms out. I tense up but move into them hesitantly. 'I'm so sorry,' he says. His body feels solid and warm. I want to lean in, let him take the weight. He smells of washing powder and underarm sweat mixed with mint. It's not unpleasant.

'My boy,' I whisper into his chest.

'I know,' he says gently as he pats my back.

But he doesn't know. There is so much he doesn't know.

When he's gone, I take the figurine out of the box and place it on the mantelpiece next to the photo of Trevor.

As I climb the stairs, I think about the gift. Should I read something into it or is it just another crumb?

Trevor opens his eyes slowly and my heart breaks. He's losing weight so quickly.

'Hey, little boy, shush, go back to sleep,' I say as I rub his head.

I lie down and watch the rise and fall of his tummy and quietly weep. I've brought this on Trevor. This is my punishment for all the meddling and jealousy. The only time I believe that God has a hand in my existence is when something bad is happening. The continual drip, drip, drip of life's inhumanities being His vengeance.

Chapter Thirty-Eight

Angela

Angela phones Nadia Halder. She has her phone on loudspeaker as she removes her wash bag from her suitcase. 'So, you phoned the number Jenny Moorfield gave you?' she asks Nadia.

'Yes, I felt responsible. I mean, who have I been referring people to? Anyway, the woman who answered didn't say she *wasn't* you. She was evasive, wouldn't give her address. And said she was… *you* were retiring.'

'Cheeky cow,' Angela says as she skips swiftly downstairs, phone in the flat of her palm. 'Why not simply tell you you'd got the wrong number?'

'I have another client I referred to you. Zeta, I gave her the same number.'

'I've heard that name.'

'She's not from the group session. Lost her husband earlier this year. Tiny lady. It's delicate.'

'Oh, my God. I know her. She was outside my house! Said she was a friend of my neighbour. What the hell?'

'Well, got to go. Got a clinic list long as my arm. You've got her number now. It's up to you whether you phone it.'

Chapter Thirty-Nine

Bella

Crying has left my face ravaged and my scarring appears lividder than ever.

Sue's here now, making a brew while I sit with Trevor.

'You know, not looking after yourself isn't going to do Trevor any favours,' she says.

I look at Trevor, and he raises his head as though he's agreeing.

'I can't think of anything I want to eat. I never feel hungry.'

She carries the tea tray in and sets it down. 'Well, he's telling you the same thing, but you're not going to stop trying to feed him, are you?'

'Course not.'

'Well then.'

She's brought me a small stack of egg sandwiches and a salad. 'Come on,' she says. 'Eat.'

She's been coming round with little home-cooked meals for Trevor. He's tried bits here and there and received euphoric praise for every morsel that he hasn't spat out. I don't dare say it out loud, but I think he's put a little weight on. At least he's not lost anymore. I phoned Sharma with this news. I needed some professional reassurance, just a little hope to keep me going. It wasn't forthcoming, and I resented her for it. She said I could wait until Trevor showed clear signs that he was in pain. But that might be delaying the inevitable. She said he'd become exhausted and lose enjoyment in things, that he'd stop eating altogether, and that he'd be prone to more infections. That I should consider my options. I was sorry I'd phoned.

Chapter Forty

Angela

'It's such a shit show.' Angela says to Graham after the waiter has taken their order.

'Angie, do you have to?'

They are in the local Indian restaurant. Graham has been craving a curry since they returned from Malta. 'Get some proper British food,' he'd joked.

The restaurant is busy for Wednesday evening, but the service is always good. They are seated in a booth at the rear of the restaurant. Two tealights flicker behind purple glass holders, casting a pink light onto the tablecloth. The waiters are on hand in black Nehru jackets. The restaurant has an open kitchen and sounds of pots and pans and food sizzling on skillets add to the ambience. Traditional Indian music plays in the background. The sound of the sitar matched so perfectly with the smell of spices that fill the air.

'Yes,' Angela hisses. 'I'm livid and I can't believe you're defending her.'

'I'm not. But I think you need to be sure before you accuse her of anything. And with Trevor being so ill.'

'Not you too. He's a cat, for God's sake.' She sips her lager while the waiter finishes arranging chutneys on the white tablecloth. They both smile and thank him.

'Didn't you ever have a pet when you were a kid?' he asks, piling onions and mango onto a poppadom.

'No.'

'Explains a lot,' Graham smiles, trying to lighten the mood, determined not to let the disagreement spoil his appetite.

'Meaning?'

'Well, you'd know, that bond with an animal.' He bites into the crispy starter. It breaks in two, and some of the condiments fall back onto the plate. He scoops them up with a poppadom shard.

'Listen to Doctor Doolittle,' Angela answers, hiccupping. 'What did you have?'

'We had two dogs, a cat, and a rabbit called Pinky.'

'Give me a dog any day.'

Graham loads another poppadum and says, 'Bella said she thinks someone attacked Trevor, pulled his tail. He had a cut as well.'

'You're not accusing me?'

'No.'

'Good.'

'I didn't tell her what you said.'

'What did I say?'

'About putting poison down. If he came in your garden again.'

'Bloody hell, Gray. It was just words. I wouldn't…'

'Okay, okay… sorry, I mentioned it. Let's just...'

'Who would blame me, anyway? She encouraged him.'

'He's a cat.'

'Well, she's doing something. I told you what Nadia said. And that lady, Zeta, being at her house. It's too much of a coincidence. And some things you just know. Like it was her who answered the phone.'

'You don't know.'

She holds her mobile phone up to him. 'Check that against Bella's number in your mobile if you don't believe me.'

He nods toward the food on her plate. 'You need to eat.'

'You won't cos you know I'm right.'

The waiter arrives with silver dishes filled with their main course. They thank him again.

'Looks good,' Graham says.

Angela lifts her phone again. 'Go on,' she says.

'Can we eat?'

'Give me your phone and let me look.'

'Leave it, please.'

'Just give me your phone.'

Graham places his cutlery down and wipes his mouth, then signals for the waiter again.

The waiter approaches. 'Yes, sir?'

'Can we have the bill, please?'

'Is everything alright with your food?' the waiter asks, looking concerned. An older waiter hovers in the background.

'Could we take it with us, please? We need to leave, an emergency.'

The older waiter approaches and nods to the younger as he helps him to remove the dishes. 'It will be one moment, Sir.'

Angela looks on with an incredulous expression. 'What are you doing?'

'Take-out,' he answers.

Chapter Forty-One

Bella

Sometimes I get a rebound headache from the pain killers. But this feels different. I'm weak in my bones, cold to the marrow. I wonder if I'm coming out in sympathy with Trevor. I think I've left the radio on, so I go downstairs, squinting against the pain. The noise is coming from next door. I fill a glass with water, then sit at the kitchen table.

'She!' I hear Angela's voice, loud, distinct. And I know intuitively that the 'she' referred to, is me.

There's a muffled response and the sound of a chair scraping back. Then Graham's back door opens. I look up as light is cast over the adjoining fence and trellis. There's a sharp rapping at my back door. I jump so hard that I almost leave the chair. Some water slops down the front of my dressing gown.

'Angie!' I hear Graham shout. I've never heard that tone from him.

The rapping again. I pull my dressing gown together and reach up to my head. No Gloria. I look at the window and am struck with the image of Angela looking in and catching me in this state. I rush upstairs as the rapping continues. Trevor remains asleep on the bed. I pull Gloria on and tread carefully downstairs. I check the time. It's eight o'clock, but it feels much later. My mobile phone rings. I know immediately who it will be, so I turn it off and hide it under a cushion. The tapping on the back door again. I wonder if I should call the police, but think about Sir Trevor and decide against it. He needs peace.

With my head banging, I sit tight in the dark. After ten minutes,

I hear voices in Graham's back garden. The top window is slightly ajar, and a faint whiff of cigarette smoke reaches me. I go upstairs and risk a peek out of the back bedroom window. Angela is standing in the beam of light, a cigarette in her hand, her face pinched, eyes narrowed. Her voice lower now, less hysterical.

I can only see the top of Graham's head. He's facing her. I can't make out what he's saying. Angela suddenly ducks and screams, batting her arms about as a large moth flies close to her head. Her ridiculous dance makes me smile. Graham turns his head to watch as the moth lands on the globe security light. I back up, not sure if he's spotted me.

A few minutes later, his back door closes, and the security light dims.

Chapter Forty-Two

Bella

The faint peal of bells from St Thomas's Church tells me it's Sunday. My head feels slightly better, although when I lean down, I have an odd sensation, like my skull is filled with the aqueous fluid of a lava lamp. It might be a head cold. I've been leaving the windows open because I'm having to carry Trevor to his litter tray. He's too weak to go outside. I carry him to it now and can feel his ribs through his coat.

'There you go, little boy,' I say. He does a trickle of very loose stools and meows weakly as he tries to scrabble the litter back over it. I pick him up and wrap him in his blanket, then take him over to the settee and lay him down. We spend the day like this. I light the fire and put the tv on. I encourage him with a little food, then I use a syringe to pipe medication into his mouth. 'We can't let our standards slip now, can we?' I say as I gently wipe syrupy drips from his fur.

I haven't spoken to Graham since he bought the present over. The last time I saw Angela was during their argument outside. Was that Friday? Days blur together. It's been quiet next door, until around one o'clock in the afternoon, when it sounds like Graham might have family around. Shortly after, his front door bangs, causing both me and Trevor to jump. I curse him for his inconsiderateness.

Monday passes quietly. I'm encouraged when Trevor seems to regain some strength. Around-the-clock care seems to be helping him. However, I've lost track of time and I'm barely remembering to eat. Sue has called regularly, checking on

Trevor and me like a community midwife with a sickly child and mother. She brings lemon buns which I nibble and forget, then guiltily feed to the birds, who peck away the evidence.

In the evening, I turn the tv on and note that Trevor's ears prick up at the sound of birdsong on *Country File.* I immediately log on to my laptop and search for 'birdsong, white noise'. I berate myself for not thinking of it before now. He doesn't spend any time in the garden now, and I'm suddenly convinced that sounds of nature would aid his recovery.

As I'm searching, the regional news comes on, and it's my turn to prick my ears up. I focus on the screen. A woman reporter wearing a grey skirt suit is standing outside the Greater Manchester Police building, a photograph of Angela on the screen behind her:

'Angela's' mother raised the alarm on Sunday evening, when she hadn't heard from her daughter for two days. She said she spoke to Angela every day and became concerned when there was no answer from her mobile or house phone. Police are holding a local man in custody for questioning, but there have been no charges. They are appealing for anyone who has any information…'

I experience a time lapse of information from ears and eyes to brain. I'm rigid. If someone were to prod me, I would rock like a teetering doll. I stare at the remote control in my hand as if it's just materialised. A stream of odd thoughts tickertape through my head. Moths, blue paint, the tv reporter's suit, too small for her. *A local man in custody.* I pick the phone up and call Graham. There's no answer on his landline, so I try his mobile. Nothing…

Chapter Forty-Three

Bella

On Tuesday morning, I answer the door to a young man and woman. The man has dark wavy hairand is wearing a grey suit. He holds a badge up like they do on *CSI*.

'Hello, sorry to disturb you. I'm Detective Inspector Robert Kenny from Greater Manchester Police. This is my colleague, Detective Sergeant Alice Greenwood. I wonder if we could ask you a few questions? Can I check your name?'

'Annabelle Pearson,' I answer, quietly.

'We're canvassing the area, asking about your neighbour, Angela Maynard. Can we come in for a moment?'

I feel suddenly faint. They either know about me and Angela, or they are about to find out. I try to maintain a calm exterior. I step back and he enters. I catch his after shave and feel repulsed by it somehow, like he's trying to cover something bad. He stands just inside the room. The back of his head is reflected in the mirror. He has a small bald patch. DS Greenwood follows. She's taller than him and has a friendlier expression.

My hip hurts and I rub it.

'Do you want to sit down?' DS Greenwood asks kindly.

'Can you remember the last time you spoke to or saw your neighbour?' DI Kenny asks, opening his notebook. Confident in his role. Knowing I won't object as he takes a seat on the armchair. He doesn't look twice at Trevor, though he's curled up on the settee. The detective's opportunity to build trust and he didn't bother.

DS Greenwood remains standing. 'Been sat down all morning,' she explains.

I sit next to Trevor and try to breathe. Trevor lifts his head, then lowers it again.

'How old are you?' I ask DI Kenny. He looks surprised. I'm glad I've got him off balance, reminded him that I'm not just a middle-aged woman set to receive, that I can ask questions too.

'Twenty-eight,' he answers. 'We're getting younger every day, aren't we?' he adds. A smile flits between him and his partner.

'Would you like a drink?' I ask. I'll give him an old mug from the back of the cupboard. He declines.

'I will,' DS Greenwood says, and follows me into the kitchen.

'So, are you friendly with Mrs Maynard?' she asks.

'Erm, not *really*.' I turn my back on the detective as I pour the hot water and try to get control of my voice.

'We know Angela had a clinic at her house. Did she ever mention anyone to you who might be dangerous, or anything like that?'

'No, sorry. Like I said, we weren't close. She wouldn't have confided in me.'

'So, you didn't socialise?'

'No.'

I can see DI Kenny wandering around the front room. He disappears from sight as he moves towards the mantelpiece. Then he moves over by the cellar door. I desperately try to recall what I've left out in the cellar.

'I've lived around here for twenty years, never even knew this road existed,' he says.

I carry the tea tray through and realise my mistake in offering a hot drink. Now the DS can take her time sipping it, while her partner snoops.

'It's a conservation area, isn't it?' DS Greenwood asks.

'Yes, the entrance to the road is concealed with all the trees,' I say. 'It's got its own eco-system.'

DS Greenwood raises her eyebrows and says, 'Nice,' then looks around the room as if she's considering buying. 'No milk, thanks.'

Great, her tea will stay hot for a week.

'So, when did you say you last saw her?' DI Kenny asks from his position by the cellar door. Pencil poised.

I'm trying to gather my thoughts. 'Sorry,' I say. 'This feels so strange. To be honest, I feel a bit shaken. Poor Angela. What do you think has happened?'

'We don't know. She's probably fine. Just take your time,' DS Greenwood reassures.

'Yes, well. The last time I spoke to her would be just before she and Graham went on holiday.'

'Graham Dewsnap?' DI Kenny asks.

'Yes. They went to Malta.' I point at my miniature figurine. 'He brought me that back.' They both glance at the mantelpiece. 'The glass cat.'

'And why exactly did she come over?' DS Greenwood asks.

'To check, I would be looking after Graham's while they were away. I have a key. I clean, do his ironing. They went to get away from Steve, Angela's ex. He's been harassing her.'

'She told you that?' DI Kenny asks.

'Erm, I don't recall. It might have been Graham. Steve found out they were getting married. I got the impression he was a bit obsessive.'

'You met him?' DS Greenwood asks. I feel like piggy in the middle. The ball of questions flying back and forth between them.

'Briefly. The first time was a few months ago. He was leaving Angela's at around two in the morning.'

'You're sure it was him?'

'Positive. I can't be certain of the date. But then, a few weeks later, I met him outside her house. I think I stirred it up a bit because I told him that Angela had gone away with Graham.'

'How did he take that?'

'I thought he would already know because they were still obviously close. But he seemed put out.'

'Do you have keys to Angela's house as well?'

'No, we got off to a bad start because she nearly killed Trevor.'

They both stop and look at me.

'Trevor?' DS Greenwood asks.

'Yes, sorry. This is Sir Trevor McDonald, my cat.' Trevor rises on shaky legs and comes and sits in my lap. My poor boy.

'Sir Trevor McDonald after the newsreader?' DS Greenwood asks and reaches over to stroke him.

DI Kenny smiles for the first time. 'No way,' he says.

'Careful,' I say. DS Greenwood pulls her hand away. 'He won't scratch. He's just very poorly.'

'Oh, sorry.'

'It's fine,' I say, but tears come very quickly. 'Sorry, it's not you,' I explain as I reach for a tissue.

'So sorry, he's lovely,' DS Greenwood says, and finally sips her tea.

Just when I think I've distracted DI Kenny enough to get him away from the cellar, he turns on his heel. 'May I?' he asks, pointing to the door.

I'm tempted to say, 'Not unless you've got a warrant', but it will just only make me a person of interest and I can do without that.

'Hang on,' I say. I replace Trevor carefully on the cushion and rise too quickly. A sharp pain shoots up through my hip and I catch my breath. I take a step forward, the urgency overriding the pain. 'I'll put the light on.'

I reach up past him and flick the switch. The accusatory light reveals everything. I scan around as I follow him down, anxious about leaving Trevor upstairs. *Overcoming Depression* lies face up on my desk. I've already disposed of any notes and certificates in Angela's name. But maybe these detectives already know about me and are after confirmation. It's an extremely unnerving thought.

'What a great space. What do you use it for?' DI Kenny asks.

'It's a change of scenery sometimes. You know.'

He picks up the book. Considers it. 'Helpful? he asks.

I nod. 'Think so.'

He wanders over to the chest of drawers, which now contains some of the books and CBT paraphernalia I've accumulated. He stops and lifts the coverlet, then lets it drop again.

'So, Steve. Angela's ex. You think he might be jealous?'

'I got that feeling. He was calling around, phoning her. You could check her phone.'

'That's a very good idea, Mrs Pearson, thank you,' he answers.

His sarcastic tone is so irritating.

DS Greenwood appears at the top of the stairs. 'I think you'd better come up. Your cat…'

I rush back up and find Trevor retching on the settee, his small back arched with the effort. Both detectives look on, as I pull a wad of tissues from the box and place them under his chin.

'It's okay, boy,' I say as he heaves up a small amount of bile.

'We can come back later?' DS Greenwood suggests.

'Okay,' I answer distractedly, worried the retching will strain Trevor's heart too much. I hardly notice as they let themselves out.

After they have left, Trevor falls into an exhausted sleep. I pace up and down. I never really believed that people wrung their hands with worry, but mine are clasped together. The skin rasps and bones crack as I knead them together.

Chapter Forty-Four

Bella

I knock at Graham's door. As I wait for him to answer, I glance down the road and see the detectives at Sue's house. This time, DS Greenwood is the one in the lead doing the introductions. They must take it in turns. How DI Kenny must hate that.

When Graham answers the door, I'm shocked at how dishevelled he looks. He invites me into the front room and sits heavily in the armchair.

'How's Trevor?' he asks.

'Holding up, thanks. The police have just been to mine. Why didn't you tell me? You should have come round.'

'They took my phone and laptop when they took me in for questioning.'

'Oh no.' I lift my hands to my mouth. 'What, did they think...? But they've let you go?'

'They didn't charge me, but they have my passport.'

'You should have told me.'

'I didn't want to bother you,' he says, rubbing the three-day beard growth. His tan has faded and under his eyes was a pinkish brown from lack of sleep.

'What did you tell the police?'

'Me and Angie had a big row. We moved on from you and onto Steve. She had one of those moods on her. She went home, had to sort some stuff out. We didn't speak the next day. It was so stupid. I went into work. On Saturday night, I went round and couldn't get an answer. I left it for a bit, then her mum phoned. She'd not heard from her and thought her phone might be dead.

'Is it?'

'Yeah. Her phone was still there.'

'What do they think happened?'

'They are not saying. But she'd never go without her phone.'

'Or her car.'

'Exactly,' he answers as he leans forward. Resting his elbows on his knees, he kneads his eyes with the heels of his thumbs.

I feel pressure to find the right words. Something that will resonate and reassure, but Trevor's my priority and I need to get back. I stand and place my hand on his shoulder. 'I'm so sorry.'

He sighs, 'Sure.'

In the evening, I climb into bed and place Sir Trevor as close to me as I can. I feel badly shaken. The events of the last few weeks are catching up with me. I take Diazepam to help me relax. It's prescribed for pain, but the Diazepam doesn't know that does it? I repeat the old Apostles' Creed over and over in my head. '*I believe in God, the Father Almighty, Creator of heaven and earth… He will come again to judge the living and the dead…*

By Thursday, the news of Angela's disappearance has gained traction. There have been a couple of camera crews outside her house. I keep my curtains closed and text Graham to tell him to do the same. I tune into the lunchtime news. A reporter for *News Northwest* sits behind a wrap-around desk, a picture of Steve, Angela's ex, on the screen behind her. I grab the remote and turn the volume up slightly.

'*…was arrested yesterday by Greater Manchester Police in relation to the disappearance of Angela Maynard…*'

A photograph of Angela appears on the screen. It doesn't flatter and I have a twinge of satisfaction, then feel terrible that I'm capable of such a thought.

'*Angela was last seen on Friday,*' the reporter continues. '*Greater*

Manchester Police have issued a short statement.'

Angela's disappearance is now covered by all the local radio stations and loops on every channel. But I've stopped watching. My every minute is absorbed by caring for Trevor. I realised that playing birdsong might feel torturous to him, so we've been listening to classical music instead. I sit up with my boy and stroke his head until sleep asserts itself, and I waken in a betrayal of morning light. My chest is tight with the pain of what's to come. What must be done.

Chapter Forty-Five

Bella

Sharma is coming, and she's going to put my little boy to sleep. I can't look at him and I can't believe it's going to happen. I phone Sue and ask her to come and be with me. I'm shaking, and I can hardly get the words out. My heart is breaking. Can someone please stop me from doing this? Surely Sharma will see my distress and talk me out of it but, when she arrives, she's kind to me, too kind and I know she's not going to stop me.

'Am I doing the right thing?' I ask again, hoping this time she'll say a clear 'No.'

'All I can say is I've looked very carefully at the results. You can, of course, continue with chemo. But this is an aggressive cancer. It will only be a temporary reprieve. I think this is the right time. Before he's in too much pain.'

'I think you're doing the right thing,' Sue says. 'If Sir Trevor could speak, what do you think he'd say about it?'

'Oh, he'd say something like, "'don't worry old thing…'" I can't continue.

Sue knows I want him to be cremated and I want his ashes returned so I can keep him with me. Jenny has arrived too. She is here with us, and she's calm and composed.

I have Trevor on my knee on his favourite blanket. I can't see what Sharma is doing as she has her back to me, but I catch a glimpse of the needle as she draws liquid into it.

'It will be painless,' she says, 'like he's just nodding off.'

As she injects him, he looks at me one last time then, closes his eyes for ever. He looks like he's in a peaceful sleep. His beautiful face relaxed, his whiskers very still. Eventually, Sharma checks his heart with a stethoscope and nods at me.

'He's gone,' she says.

My beautiful boy is no more.

He's so still. His tiny tongue lolls from the corner of his mouth. I kiss his head and sob into his fur. I feel someone's hand on my shoulder and hear sniffling behind me. I sit like this for a time, until Sue tells me the cremation people have arrived. As the warmth of his body ebbs, I cover him snugly with the blanket.

Sue asks, 'Do you want to say a prayer or something?'

I nod. Not sure how the words will come out, I say, 'Thank you, Sir Trevor. Thank you for being my friend all of these years. I hope you had a happy life and I hope I did the right thing for you. Please forgive me.'

I kiss him one last time. Then I stand and carry him to the door where the cremation specialists are waiting. They smile kindly as they take him from me. My arms feel suddenly cold. Afterwards, I follow Sue inside and she asks me if I've eaten. Someone has taken the leek and ham pie Phil bought out of the fridge. It sits alongside some of Sue's cheese scones. I see Trevor's bowl with the food in from this morning. My legs feel heavy, and my head starts to spin. I feel no pain when I hit the floor.

Chapter Forty-Six

Bella

'Bella, can you lift your head for me, please?'

It's a voice I don't recognise. The sounds around me have an odd echo. There's a strong smell of something I can't place. My vision clears and I see the end of a bed that isn't mine. My body feels heavy again. I'm holding a small bundle. I look down at the face of my sleeping baby. I hold him as we fall through a hole in the mattress and then on and on, through one floor and the next, on and on we fall.

I've welcomed the embrace of the medication. It's draped a protective membrane over me like a fine pashmina. This place I'm in feels like a separate realm. One where I'm allowed to be vague, to be fragile. I respond to the care of the nurses. They wash me, dress me, re-arrange me. I could probably do more, but I'm consciously regressing, giving myself up.

The next time I open my eyes, I'm on my side and looking at a drip stand. I follow the tube to its destination in the crook of my arm. I can't figure out if I'm infusing the drip stand or it's the other way round. There's a person-shaped mound of hospital covers in the next bed. I can't make out much about them, but they are snoring very loudly. I lift my head and scan my covers. But Trevor isn't here. I've done something terrible. The emotion falls back inside me, displaced, like the sea falling into the abyss before the waves come crashing back. I close my eyes again.

Rattling wheels awaken me from my doze. It's Bozram, the lady who does the rounds with newspapers and sweets. 'Want anything, my lovely?' she asks. The cart holds a colourful array of confectionary: packets of Starburst, Murray Mints, Blackcurrant and Liquorice. Mars Bars, Mint Aero's, and peanuts, alongside the 'healthy option' yoghurt bars. Too much choice. I say, 'No thank you', but it comes out as a dry claggy sound. She moves on to the next bed and places a newspaper on the bedside table. A face on the front page catches my attention. It's a face I know, an image from another life.

Chapter Forty-Seven

Bella

'Hey, Missus,' Jenny says.

'Hey,' I answer, sitting up. I look for Bozram and the newspaper. But she's gone and I wonder if she was ever here.

'How are you doin'?'

'Good, thanks.' I answer, aware I have no wig on and no make up on my scar, but I don't seem to care.

'You look better than last time.'

'Last time?

'Yeah, I've been, and Sue's been. We haven't stayed long. Haven't you read your cards?' she asks as she approaches the bedside cabinet.

'Are those mine? I thought they were for the lady in the next bed.'

'Yeah, these are yours,' she says, looking nonplussed. She picks one up and reads, '"Get well soon, Bella. You have a cottage pie to work through", that's from Phil. There's one from me, one from Sue.' She holds up a small blue card with the picture of a vase of flowers on the front. 'You will never guess who this is from.'

'Who?' I don't like guessing games.

'Zeta.'

'Zeta?'

'She came to see you on the afternoon you… you collapsed. Pure coincidence. She was worried about you when I said we were waiting for an ambulance.'

'I don't remember.'

'You were out of it.'

Jenny hands me the card. Inside, in a shaky but elegant hand,

Zeta has written, 'Annabelle. Hope you are soon back in the pink. Zeta xxx'

'I didn't know you'd been.'

'I know, how rude. I've forgiven you, though. Pneumonia, the nurse said.'

I've been told pneumonia is normally a three- or four-day stay. Because of my other problems, I've been in now for seven days. I still don't feel one hundred per cent, but I think it's due to grief and guilt.

'I told them at the nursing station I was your sister. Hope that's okay?'

'I couldn't think of anything nicer,' I say. My eyes fill again. I sniff back.

'You'll be home soon.'

I nod. There doesn't seem to be much to say to that.

'Have you seen Graham?' I ask.

'I think he's a bit busy. You won't know, will you? They've charged Steve Cross, Angela's ex. They suspect him of being involved in her disappearance.'

It was real then, the front-page picture. Steve.

'Good God,' I answer. I feel like I've been asleep for years and the world has changed around me. 'They haven't found her, then?'

'No, sorry, I should've broken it to you more gently. My bedside manner needs some work.' She reaches up and swings the suspended tv contraption away. 'Don't suppose you've caught up on the news?'

I shake my head.

'Have a sip of this. You've gone white,' she says as she passes me my glass.

'Poor Angela. Poor Graham,' I say.

The nurse appears and says, 'You can go home this afternoon, Bella. I'll get your script written up and some follow-up sorted. Is your sister giving you a lift or will you need transport?'

In the car on the way home, Jenny brings Graham up again.

'I don't think he's coping,' she says. 'It must be hard. I shouldn't tell you this, but Mike said, before they arrested Steve, they questioned Graham for hours before releasing him. They still haven't a clue where Angela is, but they think Steve knows. He's got himself lawyered up.' She points to her handbag. 'Your house keys are in there. I kept hold of them so I could water plants and look after things. I didn't go upstairs or snoop around.' She throws me a bright smile. 'I didn't know how long you'd be in. Hope I did right.'

This surge of emotion, sometimes it's so strong it cancels itself out and leaves me blank.

'You're very kind,' I answer.

I think of all the things that meeting Angela has given me. I would never have Jenny as a friend had I not impersonated her. Maybe my friendship with Sue wouldn't have developed had I not seen her at Angela's barbecue. Yet it has taken so much from me. Like a deal with the Devil. I have what I wanted, but I lost what I loved. And the true reckoning has yet to be realised.

I watch the scenery. The shoppers on the high street, the new build of houses where the old school used to stand. Life insisting on itself.

Anyone who had pets and has lost them knows a home feels different without them. Emptier, yes, but something else indefinable. The house itself misses Trevor. The settee, the windowsill, the bed, all feel his absence.

'By the way, this came.' Jenny says, handing me a small grey bag, not unlike a draw string pump bag I used to have at school. It bears the letter 'T' on it in gold thread. Trevor's ashes.

'I asked them to deliver them to mine.'

'Thank you.'

Inside the bag is a small mahogany box. Inlaid on the front is an elegant carving of his name and dates of birth and death. I hold the box to myself and breathe in deeply. 'You're home now,' I say.

I bought a similar one from the charity shop years ago, just because it was so beautifully carved. It had been my intention to put Trevor's ashes in it and bury him in the garden, but I'm not ready to do that. I feel comforted by having him with me. I decide to use it to make a memorial for him in the garden instead.

I tell Jenny of my intention and she helps me. I've collected some photographs and some of his toys. I place them into the second-hand box with some lick-e-lix and his old collar and harness. I dig a hole under the fir tree where he liked to bask. When I go outside, I see Jenny has lined the hole with a black bin liner. I place the box into the ground and slowly stand. We back-fill the soil with our hands, and I mark the spot with a stone cat. I think Trevor would approve.

As Jenny puts the kettle on, I notice his food bowls stacked on the draining board. She sees me looking.

'Sorry, I didn't know what to do with them.'

'It's okay.' I take my bag and Trevor's ashes upstairs. It strikes me only now, that Jenny must have packed a bag for me. She must have seen Audrey on the dressing table. She obviously knows about my hair now anyway, but still embarrassing for someone to see my wig.

When I return downstairs, she's at the fridge sniffing a carton of milk. 'I think something's off in here. I could smell it while you were in hospital but can't find the cause. I should have left the door open. I brought you some fresh, anyway.'

'Could you help me do something with my hair?' I ask.

'Course,' she answers, as the fridge door swings shut.

I reach up and feel the fine strands, so insubstantial and fragile.

'Your hair's a lovely colour,' Jenny says.

'It fell out when I was twenty,' I explain. 'Stress, they said. I pulled a lot of it out and it never recovered properly.'

She passes me tea in the mug I gave to DS Greenwood.

'I did wonder.'

'Was it obvious?'

'No, it was good, suited you.' She considers my hair through the steam as she sips. 'It's not as bad as you imagine. I've seen a lot worse. I could definitely do something. When do you want it done?'

'I have a few matters to attend to, but later this afternoon?'

Jenny checks her watch. 'Okay, I need some shopping anyway. I can get back at two?'

Before Jenny returns, I call at Sue's. I'm always buoyed up by her welcome. She treats me like we've been close friends for years and I love her for it. When she answers her door this time, she throws her arms up in delight.

'You're home!' she exclaims. 'How wonderful, come in.'

She ushers me into the kitchen and pulls out a chair. I still haven't spoken a word.

'You had us all so worried,' she says. 'Are you fully recovered?'

'I think so. I feel better than I did.'

'We need to make sure you look after yourself now. Take better care. What have you there?' she asks, pointing to the casket which I'm clutching to me. 'Is that what I think?'

'Yes,' I answer, holding him even tighter. 'And I have a favour to ask.'

Chapter Forty-Eight

Bella

As promised, Jenny returns, and washes and styles my hair. She shows me how to use 'products,' to thicken and strengthen it. They are a revelation; my head feels light and clean. It isn't as lush as Audrey and doesn't offer the same thick screen to the side of my face, but the benefits outweigh the negatives.

When she's finished, she asks me if I want help to find out where the smell in the kitchen is coming from. She doesn't want me on my hands and knees scrubbing. She instructs me to rest; I promise her I will. Though she appears dubious about my assurances, she packs her equipment up, leaving behind some hair products for me to practice with, and departs.

When she has gone, I have a quick check around the house and make sure everything is in order. I don't know what's going to happen next, or how long I will be away.

Graham answers my knock, and I don't know who is the more shocked. He's lost so much weight; he'd hardly cast a shadow.

'Hi,' he says. 'You better?'

'I need to talk to you.'

'Okay, but excuse the mess. I've not…' His sentence peters out as he walks into the kitchen. I notice that he's sockless.

He isn't exaggerating about the mess. The sink is full. There are dirty cups on the table and a few empty wine bottles by the back door.

'Tea?' he asks.

'No, thank you.'

He nods and moves some papers from one of the kitchen chairs and clears some pots away. 'Sorry I didn't come and see you. I rang the ward. They wouldn't tell me anything, just that you were settled.'

'I know it's a bad time, but I need to talk to you. There's something I should have told you a long time ago. Something that might explain everything.'

'Bella, you don't have to.'

'I do. And it might seem self-indulgent, but I need you to listen.'

'Okay,' he says. I hear the scratch of bristles as he rubs his hand across his face.

'Years ago, you and I, we had something special. Didn't we?'

'Bella, I can't do this.'

'Please. It's very important. I know that it must be terrible for you with Angela and what have you. But please.'

He sits forward, hands clasped together on the table. 'Okay.'

'We were going to get a flat. Remember?'

'The grotty Market Street flat. Yeah, yeah sure. You went on holiday, though.'

'Yes, Wales. We'd agreed we would keep it a secret while you got everything sorted out. We would tell our parents when I got back. It would be a *fait accompli*. I knew there would be an almighty argument, but I'd be able to pack a bag and come to you.'

'I remember.'

'Well, you know what happens next.'

'The accident.'

'The accident. Would you at least agree that it changed everything?'

His forehead furrows as his eyes widen. 'Course it did. We were all set.'

I breathe out. Thank God, at least I've not been wrong about that. 'I was so excited,' I say.

'Hang on,' Graham says. He gets up, searches in the cupboard, and finds two glasses. He grabs a bottle of whisky from the top of the fridge and pours himself one and a small one for me without asking.

I take it from him and knock it back. It has a burnt unpleasant taste, but it warms the back of my throat. I breathe the spicey aroma out through my nose. 'I know it's a long time ago,' I continue. 'I've only now come to understand it myself. I've had flashbacks and nightmares. Stuff I'd long ago buried. The crash. Dad's death.'

'I remember your dad well. He was always fine with me. Quiet; I never knew what he was thinking. Your mum, though. She made sure you knew what she was thinking.'

'That's true. I always thought my dad didn't like me. I couldn't figure out what I'd done wrong, where the change had happened.'

'He probably just wanted an easy life.'

'You know, in those final minutes, Dad stuck up for me. I'd completely forgotten it. But I've been having weird dreams, and I remembered. Just before we crashed, my dad stuck up for me. He shouted, "For God's sake, leave her alone", and grabbed Mum's arm.'

We are both quiet for a moment. I look down at my glass and twirl it on the table, watching the dregs slide back and forth, wondering how to continue. 'I know it's hard for you with the situation at the moment.'

'Yep.'

'I need to explain, though. I lost everything because of the accident. My parents, my health. You only need to look at me to know how it affected me.'

'Yeah.' He looks away.

'Then I lost you.'

'Bella, I…'

'I don't expect you to remember this like I do. I know it didn't have the same impact on you, and that's okay. I don't know if you remember, but my aunty bought me a kitten at that time. Cleo. She helped me through.'

'I know you've always loved cats.'

'Well, then I got Trevor. He was special to me. More than a cat.'

Graham nods and smiles. 'What's that saying? In Egypt cats

were once worshipped as Gods and they've never forgotten it.'

'So true. I've had Trevor since he was three months old. He made me smile every day, sometimes laugh out loud. He kept me sane, stopped me from being lonely.'

'Where…'

'Just bear with me. When he got poorly, I felt it was retribution.'

'For what?'

'I've been pretending to be Angela.'

'You what?'

'A lady called Jenny came to my house by mistake. She had a therapy session booked with Angela. She thought I was Angela. I just went along with it.'

His chair scrapes across the floor as he pushes back from the table. 'Christ, she was right. She thought you were up to something.'

'It was wrong of me,' I say earnestly. 'But Angela did nearly kill Trevor and I'm positive she was the one who injured him. I think that cruelty might have triggered his illness.'

'Yes, but–'

'Don't stick up for her, Graham,' I jump in too quickly. Him defending her triggers something. The absence of affection, always having to argue my own corner, the lack of care. It stirs up deep stuff. 'Just… let me explain.'

He puts his hands on his head and leans back, looking at the ceiling. Finally, he looks at me. 'Go on.'

'It's been one of the worse times in my life. First Trevor's illness and then losing him. I…' I want to keep a grip, but that tsunami again. Whenever I think of my poor little boy's body. The tears drop onto my lap. I keep my head down. 'You wouldn't understand.'

'I had a soft spot for the little lad, too.'

'I had to put him first. I had to be there for him.'

'Course?'

I can see his confusion. I lean forward. 'You need to call the police,' I say.

'What?' He does a small hiccup of a laugh. 'Bella, you've been through a lot, and I hardly think they'll be interested.' He pinches the top of his nose between his fingers.

'Graham.'

'Yeah,' he says, dropping his hand to his glass.

'I need to tell them where Angela is.'

Chapter Forty-Nine

Bella

I can hear Graham as he calls the police from the front room. I walk to the back door. Graham rushes in, phone still in his hand. 'You have to wait here. Please, Bella.'

'I'm not going anywhere,' I tell him calmly.' I was just looking for Trevor.'

He ends the call. 'Trevor's dead, Bella,' he says gently.

'I know. I meant I can see his memorial from here. I put some of his things in a little casket, in the spot where he liked to lie. You'll look after the garden for me?'

He steps towards me, and for the second time in a month, he hugs me. 'You don't need to do this…'

'It's the right thing.'

'You're not doing it because you think I… did something?'

I bat him softly on the chest with the back of my hand. 'What? No, don't be daft.'

He sighs, turns away from me, and begins to clear the table. He lifts the pots with care, avoiding abrupt movements or clinking of plates. As though any sudden start might scare me off. I remove my jacket and help him stack the dishwasher and wipe things down as though we're expecting a visit from his parents. A world that might have been.

My preference would be to have an officer with the ability to empathise take my statement, so my stomach drops when DI Kenny arrives. He holds his notebook in one hand and slaps it against the other while he contemplates me. DS Greenwood squeezes past him and takes a seat opposite. Graham asks if they want a coffee. They decline.

I say, 'I'll have one now, please,' but I don't think Graham hears.

'Mrs Pearson. You have some information on the whereabouts of Angela Maynard?' DS Greenwood asks.

The dishwasher churns, and the kettle generates energy to boil. There's a faint trill from a blue tit outside.

'Yes,' I answer. 'I'm sorry, I should have told you sooner. I couldn't because Sir Trevor was dying. And I've been very poorly...'

DI Kenny has stopped slapping his notebook and Graham is leaning against the counter, arms folded. They wait for me to speak.

It takes me a moment to find the words. Saying them out loud will give them life. I breathe them out, 'Angela is in my cellar.'

Graham steps forward, 'What the–?'

'I'm so sorry. It was an accident,' I say, feeling the change in my world.

Graham's face is grey, his eyes, blue flames.

DI Kenny turns away and says something into his phone.

'In the fireplace,' I tell him.

He rushes to the door. A second later, he's back. 'Key?' he asks, breathless and pale.

'Unlocked,' I answer.

The kettle boils, but Graham doesn't move. My mouth is dry, stripped. *'Think of biting into a lemon.'* It's one of the experiments used to demonstrate how an image can trigger a physiological response. I should be thinking about poor Angela. Her poor mother. Graham. I've thought of nothing else over the last few days. But my mind is surprisingly blank now, except for the lemons.

Raised voices, banging, doors slamming.

Silence.

'If you don't mind, I'll have that coffee now,' DS Greenwood says, twisting around to address Graham, who hasn't moved. 'I think Bella will have one too.'

I nod.

I feel DS Greenwood's eyes on me. Eventually, she turns and looks out of the window.

Graham delivers the drinks to the table. 'Sorry, no milk,' he says flatly.

'No matter,' the detective says, drawing the hot mug to her.

I leave mine where it is.

There is a loud thwack from next door. The reverberation trampolines the moss of crumbs, cat hairs, and detritus from the gaps in the kitchen floorboards.

DS Greenwood turns towards the adjoining wall. Graham moves to the door, but she calls him back.

'You need to stay here, sir,' she says. 'Just for the time being.'

As I'm led towards the waiting police car, I see my belongings being carried from my house and loaded into a black van by white-suited people.

Sue has come out of her house and calls to me, 'Bella, Bella, what on earth?' She's asked to step back by a female officer. If looks could kill. 'How dare you,' I hear her say to the officer. 'What do you think I'm going to do, pass her a bump key?'

I wonder if I've misheard. Before the officer can respond, I'm in the car and we're moving towards the main road. I have a momentary panic when I wonder who's going to look after Trevor.

Chapter Fifty

Bella

Lilian Healy introduces herself and informs me breathlessly that she is the duty solicitor. She's about my age and reminds me of my old PE teacher, Miss Eccleston, who eloped with Mr Brown, the married science teacher.

Lilian has short blonde hair, a narrow face, and a sharp chin. She has interesting blue-grey eyes, and she's wearing little make up. I notice she has a small stain between two buttons on the front of her white blouse. If this were first thing in the morning, I would take it as a sign of slovenliness. But, as it's now mid-afternoon, I think it's a fresh drop of tea, hastily gulped before she grabbed her bag and rushed across to warn me to say nothing without her present.

'Say nothing without me present,' she instructs.

We are seated in a small grey room with four chairs and a desk. Just like the ones I've seen on television police dramas. I look around, but don't see any sign of a two-way mirror and think I'm probably not interesting enough for anyone to want to watch. The room has a slight smell of disinfectant and I try not to think about what might have been spilt in here.

I imagined I'd have more time following my confession, but proceedings have evolved so quickly. My head is spinning and there's no time to think. I'm simply following instructions voiced from impassive unreadable faces. All of this, I tell myself, justifies my reasons for not contacting the police immediately.

'Okay,' Lilian says, drawing the word out. She wets her thumb and uses it to flip the pages on a large notepad until she finds a clean sheet. 'Let me check you are Mrs Annabelle

Pearson, right?'

'I am.' My voice sounds very contained in the room. There's no echo or bounce back.

'Right, here's the thing. You've told the police that the victim,' she checks back, flipping over pages again, 'Mrs Angela Maynard, fell down your cellar stairs, is that correct?'

'Yes, it was an accident.'

'Have you told them anything else?'

'No, except that I didn't report it because of Sir Trevor, my cat.'

Lilian stops, pen poised, then makes a note. 'Okay, anything else?'

'No, just that, and where I buried her.'

'Shall we start from the beginning?'

'Do you have a cat?' I ask.

Chapter Fifty-One

Bella

Lilian is a self-assured woman with no pretensions. She goes through some questions about my income, to determine whether I will be eligible for financial help towards cost. She says she will bring the appropriate forms for me to complete, and not to worry about it for now.

I spend an hour filling her in about Angela's arrival at Elmwood Terrace and her insensitivity about almost killing Trevor. Telling my story helps. It's the first time I've put my voice to these thoughts. Lilian's hard features soften when she smiles. She's an alpha female, scary but charming, someone you'd want on your side. She encourages me, saying things like, 'I hear you', and the occasional nod or shake of her head. I feel safe telling her. She's like a sturdy guide rope that I grip as I take us down the steep decline of the past six months. I omit some things. Like the depth of my loathing for Angela or the breadth of feelings I had for Graham.

Talking about Sir Trevor makes me cry again, and Lilian waits patiently for me to gather myself. She puts her pen down, leans her elbows on the table and tells me about her cat.

'I called him Dirk, after 'Dirk Wears White Socks' by Adam and the Ants, you know?'

I don't.

'Anyway,' she continues, 'Dirk was a strong old thing; brought a magpie in once. It panic-crapped all over the curtains. Dad eventually caught it and set it free. The bird, not the cat.' She leans back. 'Cats aren't for wimps. Now, Bella, the detectives want to interview you. I'm here for you and we can always break if you need to.'

I nod. 'Let's get it over with.'

DS Greenwood and DI Kenny enter.

Chapter Fifty-Two

Bella

Four weeks earlier, Saturday night

I'm treading on eggshells.

After last night, it's clear that Angela wants a confrontation with me. It's been very quiet at Graham's since, and I'm hoping I'll have some peace so I can concentrate on tending to my little boy. By around eight in the evening, Trevor seems to be comfortable and is sleeping on my bed when there's a short, sharp rap at the door. Angela's signature knock.

'I know it was you,' she says, as she stands at my door, adrenaline making her voice shake.

So, here it is, finally. She's no Hettie Wainthrop, that's for sure.

I've had a bad headache since I woke up, and Trevor is too poorly to expose him to any stress. I can do without the confrontation, but I don't want the street hearing us. I certainly don't want Graham involved.

'If you promise to stay calm, you can come in and I'll explain everything.'

She steps inside. 'You got a phone call from Dr Halder, didn't you?'

I consider the question before I answer. From what Jenny has said, neither she nor Phil have told on me. There's only Zeta who might have done, but some part of me tells me she hasn't. 'I got a call from someone saying they were a doctor, yes,' I answer.

'You told her I was retiring,' Angela says.

My headache puts me at a disadvantage, like I'm fighting with one arm tied behind my back. Still, at least I'm on my home turf.

'Yes, I said something like that. I'm sorry, I don't feel well. I can't think straight.'

'You said you weren't taking on any more clients. Why would you say that?'

'I can't remember exactly what I said,' I begin. I breathe out and note that the pain in my head has moved to just above my left eye. 'But she phoned me. I have crank sales calls all the time. The last one wanted to sell me insurance for my boat.'

'Oh, come on, you've been pretending to be me, taking my clients.'

I close my eyes and wait for the right words to come. Deceit is exhausting. 'Yes.'

Her eyes widen. 'I knew it!'

'Please keep your voice down. Firstly, I've stopped it, and secondly, I didn't ever say anything to put you in disrepute.'

'My God.'

She almost allows herself to flop onto the settee, but remembers herself and stays upright.

'It just happened. I didn't plan it. A lady turned up here thinking I was you and I went along with it.'

'Jenny Moorfield.'

'Yes.'

She looks around the room, a full mine sweep. 'Unbelievable.'

'I've said I'm sorry, and I stopped.'

'Christ, you're not right in the head. You know that?' She stands leaning over me, her finger at her temple.

'Well, that's not nice.'

'Not nice? You stupid woman. And how could you *not* have put my name in disrepute? You don't know the first thing about Cognitive Therapy.'

'I do, though. I'm self-taught.'

'Self-taught, my arse. You know you have a major problem, don't you?'

I look towards Trevor's basket, remembering the trigger for his illness. The tail pull, his bloodied coat, his sickness from possible poisoning. The trigger for all of this: Angela. If Trevor wasn't so ill, I'd be tempted to bat her one over the head with the chopping board. Loathing rises from my gut into my throat and out of my mouth. 'That's what you tell yourself. But it's you who has the problem.'

'Hmm, don't think so.'

I feel space opening inside my head, relieving the pain. 'All that knowledge from doing therapy, all that rhetoric and waffle.' I do inverted commas and quote her: '"*I could tell you, but I'd have to kill you.*" Real people, they are, Real people with real problems. You use their misery for dinner party entertainment. You don't believe a word of what you preach to your clients. You're a shallow, empty woman who only values money.' I knew where I was going with my money analogy, but I lose the thread. 'You could never understand real love and friendship.'

'And you're the real thing, I suppose?' she shouts. 'What did you do, make your own certificate?'

Although this is intended as a joke, I can't hide my shame and she's on it. Her features distort, her mean mouth crimped at the edges. 'You did! You actually did!'

'Stay here,' I instruct.

I descend into the cellar and rummage around, tears starting. My certificates look so pathetic. I have one of those moments of insight when I can see myself as she will.

Angela's at the top of the stairs. 'Well, will you look at this?'

She steps forward. I brace myself for total humiliation.

'All this–' She stops, surprise on her face as her heel catches on the top step. She's thrown forward and lands, knees crunching on the concrete. I stand, reach out. Simple laws of gravity propel her forward. One hand thwacks the wall as arms flail around for purchase. It's over so quickly. She lands at the foot of the stairs, the sound like the snapping of a wish bone, then still. So still, I wonder if she might be playing possum.

Chapter Fifty-Three

Bella

Present

'*Please*, could I have some more water?'

I feel that the re-telling has de-humanised me in their eyes. How could it not?

'Of course,' Lilian pours some for me. 'Do you need a break?'

I shake my head. 'No, thanks.' I need to get this done. That was the easy bit. The next part feels like the wall on an assault course. I'd really like to go around it.

'What then?' DI Kenny asks.

'Her head was at a funny angle. She was dead.'

'Did you check her vital signs?'

'I felt her wrist. Then,' I put my hand up to my neck, 'I felt around here.'

'You have medical training?'

'No, but I've been very ill. I've been through the wars, as they say. I know how to find a pulse.'

'You're sure she was dead?'

I'm shocked. 'What? My God. She was, wasn't she?' My stomach lurches. I place my hands over it.

'It's okay,' DS Greenwood says, glancing at DI Kenny. She reaches over, hand palm down towards me. 'We don't have all the forensics back yet. We're just asking.'

'Good God, yes, she, Angela was dead, very dead. Very, very extremely dead.'

Detective Kenny sighs, 'Okay, she was dead. Continue.'

'Well, I went upstairs, fully intending to phone the police. Then I stopped and thought of Trevor. If I went to prison, what would happen to him?'

'But it was an accident at that point.' This from DS Greenwood.

'Yes, it's an accident at any point. But haven't you read any Perry Mason? You are a suspicious lot. I would have been taken into custody for questioning. Trevor would have died alone, while I was asked the same questions three ways until Christmas.'

'So, you decided to hide her body?'

'Well,' I clear my throat, about to shatter any illusion of decency that Lilian has of me. That I have of me. 'The fireplace has always needed bricking up. The bricks were there, the mortar was there. I'd never had the motivation before. *So*, I moved the chest of drawers away.'

'Then what?' DI Kenny asks.

'I, er, I brought all my plastic carrier bags down to the cellar and laid them on the floor. Then I taped them together with masking tape.' I have an image of the Morrisons and Lidl carrier bags taped haphazardly around Angela's body, and I remember thinking she deserved better.

'And?'

'I rolled Angela onto the bags.'

It feels unreal now. Angela was a vibrant, living, breathing person, and then she wasn't. When I rolled her onto those bags, it was the first time I'd ever touched her. I recall the cellar and the bag of lime and point towards it as if it's in the room with us. 'I took the bag of lime and covered her with it.'

'You had the lime?' DI Kenny asks.

I'm wearing a thick jumper which itches along the neckline, adding to my overall discomfort. I sip some water before replying. 'I needed to brick the fireplace up. Sir Trevor had been stuck up it. I asked for Graham's help, but he was too busy, so the lime and bricks had been there for some time.'

Lilian leans towards me and whispers, 'Keep it simple.'

'Can you provide receipts for them?' DI Kenny asks, leaning his elbows on the desk.

'I'm not a thief,' I reply indignantly.

'To show when you purchased them.'

'Oh… I doubt it.'

'Right, so you conveniently had the lime mortar and the bricks.'

'It's true, and yes, it *was* convenient, not planned, as you are insinuating. I pulled Angela over to the fireplace. It was a struggle, but I managed to bend her knees and sit her in sideways. Then I watched a video on bricklaying and bricked it up.' I can't believe it myself. I pretend I'm describing someone else because it's excruciating to be me right now.

They sit back, except Lilian, who is studying me side on. Her scrutiny prompts further explanation.

'Can I just say, I feel terrible about what I've done? I can't believe it myself. But Angela was dead, and Trevor needed me.'

'Why didn't you come forward as soon as the cat died? Give Angela, a *human being*, a decent burial?'

I make an effort not to rise to the insult to Trevor. 'I was in hospital, as you must know.'

'So, you were impersonating her, stalking her,' DI Kenny says without looking at me.

I hadn't realised how slumped I've become. I push with my feet and slide back in the chair until I'm more upright before I answer. 'I live over the road from her. It's hardly stalking, and I do have legitimate certificates.'

'But you only got the certificates later. And you had them made in Angela's name.'

'True. I got a bit carried away.'

'Angela must have been furious.'

Lilian places a hand on my arm. 'I think my client has explained the situation thoroughly. If you're going to charge her, please do so.' She checks her wrist and swivels her watch strap around, face pointing up.

I allow a slow breath out, thinking it's over for now.

But DI Kenny doesn't move. 'Where does your neighbour Graham fit into all of this?'

It must be a technique they use all the time. Find something to dislodge the interviewee. I frown. 'Graham doesn't fit in anywhere.'

'When Steven Cross was arrested, the first finger he pointed was in your direction. You and Graham Dewsnap.'

The detective's words flap around the room like an annoying bird. I want to bat at them.

'Don't be ridiculous,' I say, simultaneously insulted and flattered that they could imagine I possessed the guile to coerce Graham into committing a crime. 'Graham had nothing to do with it. It's exactly as I said, an accident.'

Later, I'm seated on a hard bed in a small holding cell. Lilian has gone home but said she would come back to see me this evening. I have no idea what the time is. There is a small rectangular window set high in the wall. Green glass with a cross-hatched pattern and it's firmly shut. Which is a pity, as the smell from the chemical toilet in the corner is so overpowering it's chewy. It's the smell of wet steel, of salty ammonia soaked into the cracked tile floor. I take shallow breaths, but it's no use: the stench prickles the glands on the side of my neck.

An officer brings me a drink and a sandwich. With a sympathetic smile, she asks if I need anything else. I ask her for a blanket because I can't think of anything else, and I don't want to appear hard-faced like one of those seasoned criminals on television. She says she'll see what she can do. I sip the drink, but I can't bring myself to eat anything. I cross my arms and legs and wrap my lower leg around the other, tight as a knotted rope. I keep my head still and gaze into the air space between me and the facing wall. I think about Trevor and how impoverished I am without him. How devoid my house is without his sparky energy, his high-tailed sashay and soft call.

Any other environment is preferable to my home and the acute reminders of my loss. But I can't escape the pull of grief in the hollow of my stomach, and I can't escape this guilt. I wonder why I feel only grief for him and not for Angela. I'm sorry she's dead, but the pain is nothing compared to the death of Trevor.

The jangle of keys alerts me. Lilian is here.

The aroma of freshly roasted chicken has hitched a ride in the fabric of her jacket and fills the room. Such a welcome contrast. I breathe in and remember: Trevor loved a little roast chicken. Unexpected tears run down my face. I wipe at them with cold fingers.

I ask what our plan is. Lilian explains that I will appear before the magistrate in the morning. She says that I can put in a not guilty plea if I want, but that I should wait until the pathology report is back and we know what we are dealing with. She says she will make an application for bail and tells me there's a good chance I'll get it because I have no previous history and won't be considered a flight risk. I wish I was a flight risk. But I'm the exact opposite of it. I'm more at risk of being grounded. Of being in long-term storage while the things around me take off.

Chapter Fifty-Four

Bella

The court room is hard. Hard benches, hard clothes, hard stares. A mixture of fear and a night in a cell has depleted me and I find it hard to concentrate.

It's just as Lilian said. The magistrate is satisfied that I won't be on the next plane to Brazil, and I get bail, with three provisions. The first that I will need to present myself at the police station every day. The second, I must have no contact with any of the people identified as prosecution witnesses. And last, I must submit my passport. I tell Lilian it ran out years ago, and I never renewed it. We turn to leave, and I'm surprised to see a few of the previously empty benches are now occupied. A young woman with a notepad watches us. Shame heats my face and I lower my head like a five-year-old hiding behind her hands. *If I can't see you, you can't see me.*

Lilian links my arm and says, 'Let's get you home.'

When we arrive, I invite her in. I step in through the door and stop. Every surface is scattered with papers, electricity bills, appointment letters, a bobble-catcher, a Sellotape dispenser: all displaced and foreign.

'I tidied up a bit, believe it or not. The cushions were all pulled off the settee.' Lilian explains. 'But I wasn't sure with these...' she ends, distractedly picking up a pet bill. It only occurs to me now that I haven't claimed the costs of the vet bills through my insurance. I can't imagine being able to tell a disembodied voice at the end of the phone about the details of Trevor's passing. Reducing his life to a few bills and cancelling the monthly standing order, cancelling him out of my life.

'It's fine,' I answer, moving through to the kitchen. The mess isn't as bad in here and I manage to brew up while looking through the window towards Trevor's memorial.

Lilian explains over tea that, depending on the Crown Prosecution Service's decision, my case might go to Crown Court. Before she leaves, she says, 'So, I think Graham will be giving evidence for the prosecution.'

'Oh,' I answer.

'Okay? You understand what that means?

'Yes, don't speak to him.' In a way, it's a relief. I didn't know how I was going to face him again.

'Thanks for all your help,' I call as she retreats down the path. Then I shrink back into the house. I catch myself in the mirror. I'm creased and irrelevant as the discarded letters.

I 'tut-tut' as I tidy the mess away. I repeat 'no respect' and shake my head countless times to an empty house. Trevor's photograph is on the mantelpiece. His beautiful amber eyes see me and remind me of the serenity I once knew. I clutch it to myself and cry. I need to sleep and be warm, so I go upstairs and run a bath. The bedroom drawers are open, items spill out. I can't muster up the energy to care, so I cram it all back in and push them shut.

I awake to a grey morning. Mother of pearl light infiltrates the gap in the curtains. The urge to turn over tests me. Eventually I slide out from the covers and re-assemble myself into the Bella I present to the world, which today will be the police station to sign in.

Before I leave, I go into the garden, moving slowly. I'm still not a hundred per cent recovered and my limbs feel as heavy as wet clay. The stone grave marker is a rain-washed grey. I stoop to clear some debris away and hear a noise to my right. I turn and there is a woman at the back gate.

'Hi there.' She holds out a small business card. 'I was at the court yesterday.'

I don't approach and don't take the card. She retracts her

hand and puts the card in her pocket.

'I was hoping you'd talk to me. I'm a social media journalist. I have a blog, law and order, but spelled Laura, as in my name, you know?'

'Sorry?' I realise my error. I've engaged in conversation, a big mistake, like making eye contact with a street seller.

'Laur *and* order, only the two words spell out... it's... anyway.'

I turn and scurry away.

Once inside, I peer cautiously through the window. The woman is texting. She looks up at the house and I duck down again. When I eventually emerge, she's gone.

I check first that the front of the house is clear before I make my way to Sue's. Anxiety like pounding waves in my stomach. The urge to throw up is strong. This sensation is a constant companion now, a permanent feature. Sometimes it crashes in, other times it ebbs in and out, to and fro, up and down, the motion nausea-inducing.

The blustery October wind ruffles the branches of a nearby fir tree, dusting off old cobwebs and dead leaves. It turns its attention to me and blasts my hair from my face, pulls my cardigan open and blows my skirt against my legs so I appear to be wearing culottes. I pull my cardigan around me again and push on, head down. Violet wisteria petals scatter along the pavement and gather in clusters along the road. Winter isn't far off. I'm dreading it.

I hold my breath and knock.

'Come in, come in,' Sue says as she holds the door open. I breathe out slowly and follow her into the cosy kitchen, which smells of grilled bacon.

'You've come for Trevor?' she asks.

'Yes, please.'

She's referring to Trevor's ashes. It's the favour I had asked of her before I handed myself in. I had a feeling that the police would tip the contents of the casket out during their search, looking for anything incriminating.

She opens a cupboard door, leans down, and lifts out the wooden box. She approaches carefully and places it in my hands.

'Thank you.' I hold him to me and feel the bond surge through me again. A nullifier for all the negativities.

'He's been very safe.'

'I owe you an explanation.'

'Sit,' she answers and pulls a chair out for herself. No offer of tea or coffee. 'You don't owe me anything, but I'm too nosey to decline.'

I place Trevor with reverence on the chair beside me.

Unsure where to start, I stutter over my words. It's one thing to explain to the police: they've heard it all before. It's another thing entirely to disclose to someone who I've known for less than six months. Someone who considered me harmless, who advised me to assert myself. I look around the room and settle on the array of spider plants on the window ledge. One slender, gently arching stem has grown so long it stretches down the splashback and the rosette hangs into the sink bowl. The drip from the tap *plips* onto the leaves, then runs off slowly before falling into the sink.

'It was an accident,' I begin. 'She fell. Trevor was dying.' I look at the small box and feel his loss. Tears come easily now. They run through my veins instead of blood. 'It was instinctive. Don't let Trevor die alone.'

Sue makes a 'phhh' sound. Her cheeks puff up as she exhales. She stands and grabs a strip of kitchen roll from the counter and hands it to me before sitting down again. 'Honestly, I don't know what to think. I can see what you're saying, but you had Angela dead in your cellar when we were there? When the vet came?'

I nod and blow my nose. It's hard to hear her name spoken out loud. I've been trying to distance myself. I push the image away. 'Sorry, it's awful,' I say, wiping my face with the scratchy tissue. 'At the time, I told myself nothing could have been done for…'

'Angela,' she says with emphasis.

I try not to flinch. "Yes. She… was dead. And here was my boy, with only hours to live. I planned to tell the police as soon as

Trevor passed away. I was barely getting through the minutes.'

'What do the police say?'

'I get the impression they don't think it was an accident. I'm on bail and I need to sign in every day.'

'And you have a lawyer?'

'Yes. She thinks I have a chance if I go before a jury. I don't have a date yet.'

Sue stands and finally puts the kettle on. I peek at Trevor's casket and place my hand on it.

'I don't know if you've seen any coverage, but it's been on the local news,' she says, as I watch her spoon tea leaves into the teapot. 'It was only a short report, mostly about Angela being found. There's a picture of you coming out of the court. It's not like a full head and shoulders, though. I don't imagine you'll be recognised in the supermarket.'

Dread bubbles up at the thought of being pursued by journalists. 'Someone was at my house earlier; they'd been at the court and wanted a comment.'

'It might be an idea to stay with a relative, if you can, until it blows over,' Sue says, as she places the cups on the table.

'Can I do anything?' I offer, half rising, straining my stomach and leg muscles.

'Get the milk?' She gestures to the fridge behind me.

I locate a bottle of semi-skimmed. 'I don't have any relatives,' I explain, as I pour milk into a small jug.

'You could stay in my house in Spain.' She looks at me briefly, then takes her attention back to pouring the boiling water into the teapot.

I turn away and replace the milk, so taken aback that I can't think of anything to say. It's the grandest gesture anyone has made on my behalf since my aunty came to look after me following the accident. I feel tears welling and close my eyes for a beat, until I've composed myself.

'That's very kind, Sue. But I can't leave the country.'

'Oh, sure. Well, maybe when it's all over.' She sits down, looks over at the sleeping Molly and shakes her head. 'I can't imagine.' She pours tea and I thank her. 'How terrible for everyone,' she says as she lifts her cup to her lips. 'Why don't the police believe it was an accident?'

I try to breathe in, but my nose is too blocked. Keeping my eyes fixed on the spider plant, I tell her about impersonating Angela, that the police think it points to motive. The telling and re-telling makes it no less strange. I'm loath to say how lonely I was. That's an excuse, a justification.

'It was a split-second decision to impersonate her. I regretted it immediately but didn't know how to reverse it.'

'Wow, crikey.' She's thoughtful, quiet for a moment. 'So, you did therapy? Actual therapy?'

I squeeze the words out. 'I read around it. I didn't take any money.'

'Good Lord, whatever possessed you?'

I don't say it was her suggestion that I find another interest, which put the idea in my head.

'So where are the people you saw? What happened to them?'

For the last ten minutes my heart has beat faster. In my own house, I've been cocooned and able to fool myself. In Sue's house, I feel cut loose. In the real world.

'To be honest, I'm not allowed to say, because of confidentiality.' This is true and momentarily gives me some collar room. But I've left myself open.

'So, there was more than one?'

I nod. I pick up my teacup and drink, hiding my reddening face behind the cup.

'Will they speak for you?'

'I'm hoping so.' The words come out in a low croak. I sip again before saying any more. 'Lilian, my solicitor, is speaking to them.'

'What about the *homme fatale*?'

'Graham?' It stings to say his name. He's like a phantom pain. The limb might be gone, but it still itches. 'He's for the other side.'

'Oh, course.'

'That's another reason I'm here, actually.' I pause. I need to ask her another favour, but I'm afraid. How can Sue think the same of me now? 'I was wondering. Lilian said I should ask. Would you give me a character reference if needed?' I close my eyes again. Waves slosh around. I think I might be sick.

'Oh? She's aware that I've only known you a short time since the barbecue, really?'

Resigned to her refusal, I open my eyes again and I'm dazzled by the brightness of the kitchen. 'Yes,' I answer, 'don't worry.'

'I can't see why not; I believe you when you say it was an accident.'

Even Lilian hasn't said this. As the impact of her words hits home, I feel overwhelmed and grateful. Crying again, I stand up and approach her. I hug her awkwardly. The corner of the table sticks into my thigh, and I inadvertently dip the corner of my cardigan in her tea. I apologise as I wring it out in the sink.

'It was going cold, anyway,' she says.

Now exhaustion hits me. My eyes feel swollen and sore, and I need to take some pain killers. I dread to think how I look.

'I need to go,' I tell Sue. 'I have to sign on at the police station this afternoon.'

Before I leave, I pick Trevor's casket up and tuck it under my arm. Time to take him home.

Chapter Fifty-Five

Bella

I try to nap before going to the police station today, but closing my eyes holds nothing at bay. I'm dreading signing on. I complained to Lilian, but she countered by saying it was a luxury compared to the alternatives, so I should put my 'big girl pants on'. I've only ever worn big girl pants. I wouldn't dream of buying those torturous-looking 'g-strings'. I'm baffled why any woman would wear them unless they're atoning for something.

It's started to rain. I'm grateful, as it means I can hide under my umbrella. I click it up and move down the pathway and close the gate. I assume Graham's either away on business or staying at his brother's, because I haven't seen him. He must loathe me; I'd be an idiot to think otherwise.

I look towards Angela's. The drawn curtains are like closed eyes. I think of her family. Her mother must be beside herself with grief, and it's my fault. Yet here I stand, living and breathing, in a brown bucket hat and beige raincoat. I pass by as quickly as I can, sensing the judgement from each front room of the neighbouring houses.

The police station always smells of wet wool and pine disinfectant. Today, a couple in their early thirties are seated on a bench to my left. The man's knee is pumping up and down in an agitated way as he examines a closely bitten thumb nail. A poster behind them warns me not to leave valuables on show in my car. I don't have a car, or any valuables to leave in it, so at least that's two less things to worry about. They look up as I enter. The man's leg pauses, and his thumb has a reprieve, as he looks me up and down. The woman leans forward and rests her elbows on her knees. She smiles at me and says, 'Hi.'

'Hi,' I answer. It comes out an octave higher than I intended.

In front of me is an oak door with a keypad entry mechanism. To my right a sign reads 'Reception,' though it's no more than a sliding window that fronts a modest office housing a couple of laptops and swivel chairs. It's occupied by a woman police officer I haven't seen before. She's side on to me and doesn't look up. I wait as usual, it's a short procedure. I show my I.D and sign a document to say I've attended. Above my head is a zero-tolerance sign. I switch from one foot to the other and cough into my hand. The officer doesn't flinch. I watch as she clicks the return button on the laptop. I have the feeling that I'm one in a long line of visitors who have had their tolerance tested at this window.

As I'm wondering if tapping on the glass will be construed as abusive, the door to my left opens and a man in a smart grey suit emerges. He's tall and has dark hair, threaded with greys.

'Mr Atkins?'

The couple stands.

'Detective Chief Inspector Mike Moorfield. Do you want to come through?'

My face heats up. This is Mike Moorfield, Jenny's husband.

Before he takes them through, he turns to me. 'Are you being seen to?' he asks.

I see the subtle change in his expression as he registers who I am.

For the remainder of the day, I sort through a few cupboards and check the dates on food in my fridge. I don't have any therapy sessions to prepare for and I wonder how I filled my time before Angela. It's true what they say about not knowing what you've got until it's gone.

Almost two months have passed and since the accident, and I still haven't ventured into the cellar. There are things that need sorting through. All the remnants of the stupidest, most destructive lie of my life. I shudder at the thought of Angela's body: the smell, the flies.

My mobile rings. Even before I look, I know it will be Jenny. I spend a few excruciating seconds staring at it. Only when it stops ringing do I pick it up. There is a voicemail message. *'Hi, just erm* [pause]. *Mike said he saw you yesterday. Hope you're okay*? [pause]. *Your solicitor contacted me* [pause]. *Just thought I'd let you know. Will ring back.'* Her voice is stretched thin. I imagine what's unsaid.

It rains during the night, pelting against the windows, building to an angry thrashing, so much so I fear a windowpane might break. At one in the morning, I go downstairs and make a drink. The front room feels different: still and patient, despite the mutinous weather. I turn the fire on to inject some warmth, and I sit on the settee. The absence of Trevor is an acute pain. Grief isn't confined to the physical: it surrounds me, imbued in the furniture, in the air, each room I enter, each time I go outside. As though all the places Trevor frequented are missing him, too. No wonder they call them 'old haunts'. It reminds me of Zeta and her trips to Morrisons after Frank died.

As I stare into the fire, I think about my visit to Sue's. If I found *that* hard, how am I going to cope in front of a judge and jury? As I'm considering this, I feel the draught from under the cellar door. I know the window has been left ajar down there, but I've still not garnered the courage to go down. Now the door takes on a prominence disproportionate to the room. No matter where I sit, even with my back to it, I can sense it looming, bidding me to come, investigate. A small part of me says, *go, do it now, get up, go into the cellar.* I know I should face it, confront it. It will help me to process the awful memories. I use CBT thought challenges. *What's the worst thing that could happen? What would you say to a friend?* Well, the worst thing that could happen has already happened. And to a friend I'd say,

'Do not go into the goddam cellar.'

Unable to settle, I return upstairs and lay Trevor's casket on the covers at the foot of the bed where he liked to sleep. It calms me and I drift off.

As I don't have a reason to get out of bed in the morning, I've taken to staying in it and listening as life goes on outside. With the window ajar, I can hear the faint thrum of traffic from the dual carriageway. Sometimes it sounds like waves crashing and retreating on a beach. I've never noticed it before.

I stare at the adjoining wall. I used to imbue that wall with an energy of its own, imagining it as a gossamer sheet between me and Graham. Now the space behind it is as unfamiliar to me as Graham is. It's weeks since I last spoke to him. It's unlikely I ever will again.

My bladder insists it's time to get up, so I do. I wash and dress slowly and go downstairs to a glowing fire and a stiflingly hot room. I must have forgotten to turn it off. At the back of my mind is the niggling thought that Angela is somehow behind it. I know this is absurd and melodramatic; she isn't haunting me. Nevertheless, for the first time since buying this house, I consider moving.

After breakfast, I go outside and tend to the weeds around Trevor's memorial. So many things run through my head. I have lots of appointments to attend. Time is passing so quickly, I feel I'm being left behind somehow. I have appointments with Lilian, with the psychologist, at the police station. My life has never been so busy, yet so empty. I have a nice wall calendar. I could record everything on it like I used to, but it's in the cellar. I take courage from Trevor and his indomitable spirit and, without over-thinking, I walk back into my house and open the cellar door. The musty smell of bricks and concrete hits the back of my nose. No matter how many layers of paint and air fresheners I've used, the smell always re-establishes itself, like a personality trait. Careful of the top steps, I tread cautiously, hand tight on the wooden rail. Overflow from the gutters drips onto the unlatched window and sounds like someone is popping bubble wrap. My eyes are fixed on the foot of the stairs. There's no evidence of Angela's fall, but the surroundings trigger my memory, unify my senses, connect dots in my head. A shudder ripples through me as I hear her cry out, see her fall, remember her still body, beautiful and bent on the cellar floor. My courage almost fails me, but I push on. If I let wild imaginings consume me, I would never be able to be alone again. Everyone must grow up, learn to sleep with the lights off, particularly with the cost of electricity these days.

I reach the foot of the stairs, step over an imaginary line and move towards the fireplace. There's a plastic sheet over it, maybe used to preserve the evidence. I lean down to pull it back but stop. The moment feels unreal; not my home; not my life.

I turn away and look at my desk. Oddments of paper, my books and a few pens lie on top of it, all covered in a layer of white dust. I touch it and rub my fingers together; it feels almost greasy. The drawer is open and contains only a stapler and a tub of paper clips. My wall calendar is gone. The police must have taken it along with my computer. I recall the joy I had making those entries. *Jenny at 12; Zeta at 2pm* and all the little things in between, things I would never have forgotten, but were nice to see written down. I sigh, a deep heavy sigh, that brings tears. Last year, me, Trevor, and Graham; all of us in rhythm. I was so content. My life still held wonderful possibilities. I'm certain Angela thought hers did, too. What plans she must have had. I weep, for Angela, for Trevor, for myself.

I return upstairs when there's a knock on my door. I've been ignoring callers in case it's journalists, but there's something about this knock. I know before I open it.

Jenny.

I have told myself that the deception all began when Jenny first came to my door. The idea to steal Angela's identity would never have entered my head had Jenny not appeared looking for help. I'm not blaming her, but sometimes I wonder whether she'd colluded somehow. I know it's irrational. The seed had been planted already; Jenny was simply the water. Now here she is again. And my whole world has changed.

'Hi,' she says.

'Hi, come in,' I say, then, 'I mean, if you want.'

I take her coat; it releases her perfume into the air. It's fresh, full of citrus.

'You smell nice.'

'Thanks, duty free. Issey Miyake.'

'Is he what?'

'No, Issey Miyake, the perfume.'

'Oh, course.'

She's lost a little weight. As I'm no longer her therapist, I don't mention it. She looks well though. I don't say that either.

'It's good to see you,' I say. 'I wasn't sure if… after…'

She helps me out. 'Mike said he saw you. He said I should come.'

It's amazing to me that I've found an ally in her husband. Maybe because of the motorbike thing.

'That's good of him.'

'Did you get my message?'

'Yes,' I say, as I indicate for her to sit. Normally, she would have done so without permission. She'd have the kettle on by now. 'Would you like some tea?'

'If it's no trouble?'

So formal.

'If making a cup of tea was trouble, I'd be scuppered.' I'm trying to find old ground, get some purchase.

I retreat into the kitchen and wonder if I should return and make small talk while it boils. Instead, I busy myself with the cups and milk, which takes all of two seconds.

When it's done, I carry it through and see Jenny is checking her phone. She's filling time too.

'Listen,' I begin, when we've settled into our positions, teacups in hand. 'I need to say sorry. It must have been terrible to realise that Angela was here all the time you were helping me with Trevor. I think I went a little mad. So… I should have said something. I just couldn't.'

She doesn't give me any indication as to how my words are landing. I only hope she can see how sincere I am because I have nothing else.

'Yeah,' she says. 'It was all a… a terrible shock. You must feel for Angela and her family.'

'Oh, my God, I do. Honestly, Jenny,' I say, emotion rising, tears escaping. 'It all feels like an unknown half of me was doing those things. But what should I have done? I couldn't let Trevor die alone, or with strangers.' I grab a tissue and blow my nose. I look to the mantelpiece, where his photograph and casket are.

She follows my glance.

'You could have gone to the police and asked me or Sue to care for him.'

'If it was your son, what would you have done?'

'I know, but, sorry Bella, Trevor wasn't a child, was he?'

'But what would you have done? If your child was dying? Had only hours left?' The tears come again. I let them. There will be more anyway.

'Honestly? I don't know. I'd like to think the police would be understanding.'

'You really think so? With a dead person in your cellar?'

We are both quiet again. I blow my nose and take a breath.

'Anyway, look. I came to tell you. Your solicitor, Lilian Healy, contacted me, and I'm being called to give evidence on your behalf.'

'Thank you,' I answer, humbled.

'Pillock,' she says.

Chapter Fifty-Six

Bella

I have a plea and case management hearing today, so I'm meeting Lilian at her rooms to run through everything. I've never been to her offices before and I'm nervous. Going to her place of business brings home the seriousness of the situation. My barrister will be there too. Lilian thought that having a barrister on side would reassure me, but it hit me on the head like a fairground mallet. You don't need a barrister if you've been playing dress-up. I'm slowly realising that my innocence is in my own head. And every new piece of information about my case and the trial is designed to make me feel more criminal.

Before I exit the house, I check out the road to make sure it's clear, then I kiss my hand, pat the lid of Trevor's casket and say, 'Bye, won't be long.'

As I leave, I notice the weeds growing though the paving and flower borders, and the sodden leaves sticking to my small lawn. Although the rain has stopped, the storm has left a mood hanging in the air like an unfinished argument. It's not quite done with us yet. Collar up and hat pulled down, I make my way to the bus stop.

The Christmas decorations are up. Lights twinkle in shop fronts and garlands are hung around doorways. I've not bothered with my Christmas tree or decorations this year: no energy or inclination. But it does cheer me a little to see Manchester dressed up like this. The Gothic architecture lends itself so well to Christmas. It's easy to imagine it in Victorian times with snow falling on horse-drawn carriages.

Lilian's office is just off Deansgate amid a row of Georgian houses. The imposing front door opens into a large tiled hallway. Regency mouldings and decorative cornices adorn the high ceilings. I think this must have been a grand and elegant house at one time. I would say it's like entering another era, but for the anachronistic fire exit signs and the extinguisher. A bowl-shaped vase of flowers sits on a walnut console table. I can smell the blooms, until I see that they are silk, and the scent is coming from a wall dispenser, which makes a shhh sound as it releases a blast of chemical magnolia.

To my left is a wall directory. Among the list of names, I find Lilian's carved black into the brushed metal. I've been busy with the journey and haven't acknowledged my nerves. Seeing her name with letters next to it, among all the other professionals, makes my mouth dry, my heart rate noticeable. I climb the carpeted stairs, grasping the wide balustrade.

As I reach the landing, a door opens and a young woman emerges carrying what looks like a carton of steaming noodles.

'Oh,' she says. 'Sorry, be with you in a minute.'

She disappears into an office, the smell of spicy chicken in her wake. The door is ajar and I can see the corner of a desk laden with papers. I hear Lilian's voice before she emerges, pulling the door wide and exposing more of the room. Blue carpet, marble fireplace.

'Hello Bella,' she says, as she pulls the door closed. She looks very smart in crisp white blouse and black trousers. 'I was going to suggest we use a room downstairs to save your legs, but we may as well stay up here now if you're okay with that?'

'Course,' I answer, too breathless to suggest she might have told me that before I arrived.

'There's an intercom on the front door. If you press that next time, I'll come down and meet you.'

I nod and silently refer her to my previous thought.

We're seated in a room at the back of the house, presumably

part of the old servants' quarters. The black iron fireplace is still in situ and I'm glad. It shows respect for old things. You don't just rip them out and replace them with the new. The thick blue carpet continues in here and the chair legs have left an impression. I try and line them up in the indents before I sit. No one will know I was here.

The young woman of the hot noodles introduces herself, takes my coat and asks if I'd like a drink. I say yes, please. Suffering with a serious case of dry mouth, I'm prepared to overlook the prospect of a cracked office mug if it contains tea. However, (I've forgotten her name already, so will refer to her as Noodles) Noodles returns with a tray, complete with China teapot, matching cup, saucer, and milk jug. Lilian has black coffee. She waits as I pour, the tremble in my hand evident.

'Alright then,' she begins, as I raise the cup to my lips. 'It's good to see you. How has it been?'

'Not brilliant.'

'No, sure. It's a difficult time.' She checks her watch. We have a defence lawyer called Constance Loveday. We've worked on a few cases together and I think she's a good fit. She is what we call a non-silk barrister, therefore less expensive, but still very able. She'll be here any minute now. You can meet her and decide for yourself.'

As if on cue, the desk phone buzzes and Lilian answers, 'Sure, ask her to come through.'

A moment later, the door opens and a tall black woman with hair pulled into a top bun appears. She's wearing a camel coat and carrying a smart burgundy briefcase, which looks like it cost more than my house.

I rise from my seat, unsure of myself. While I'm dallying, she takes my hand and shakes it, never taking her amber eyes from mine.

'Hello Bella. I'm Constance Loveday, your barrister. Today is all about putting our plea in. The judge will decide how much time to allocate to the case and whether to involve a jury.'

I know I should be concentrating on what Constance is saying, but I'm still processing her. The energy in the room has changed since she arrived. Her coat is draped over the chair behind her and she's wearing a black woollen dress and brown suede boots. A single gold wedding band is the only jewellery I can see. She's attractive, but there's nothing of a window display about her, like there was with Angela. Constance conveys confidence with her composure. Her clear voice sounds educated and knowledgeable. She gestures in an artful way, soft flowing movements like hand ballet.

'We'll hear the charges from the prosecution, and put in our plea, most likely manslaughter.'

'Oh.' My cup tilts and tea spills into the saucer. I breathe in and out, calming breaths.

'I think we have a strong case, Bella, and I don't say that to all my clients. The prosecution might come up with another charge. Maybe failure to provide a decent burial. We'll know for sure by the end of play.'

I've never heard of this charge before. It sounds horrible, but it's true: I failed to give Angela the dignity I sought for Trevor.

'I did fail in making sure she got a decent burial.'

'She'll have had a decent burial by then.'

'But I did fail to do it. I'll take the punishment. Should I say that when I'm being questioned?'

'Let's see what we have first. After today we'll have a clearer picture.'

'Is proving something untrue easier than proving its true?'

'Well, that's the whole crux of it. You don't have to prove you're innocent. The prosecution must prove you are guilty. This is called the burden and standard of proof. They have the burden of proving guilt and they need to prove it to a high standard.'

'How hard do you think it will be to prove my innocence?' It's the only question there is, isn't it?

She glances at Lilian and turns to me. 'The forensics appear to be inconclusive, so we can exploit the lack of evidence.

However, impersonating Angela speaks to motive, and the prosecution will certainly use that, and the fact you didn't call the police immediately. If they're not successful with the manslaughter charge, they'll go for the lesser charge.'

'Do you believe it was an accident?' I hold her gaze in a way I believe a guilty person couldn't.

'I always tell my clients it doesn't matter what I think.'

Lilian leans back in her chair, pulls her jacket straight and clears her throat. 'Having spent more time with you than Conny, I don't believe for one minute that you pushed Angela down the stairs.'

My heart thrums in my chest, and I have a strange sensation in my throat. I look at my teacup and regret not asking for decaf. I didn't want the noodle girl to think I was a demanding person as well as a murderer. 'I couldn't kill anyone,' I say. The words feel compacted inside my head as the room spins.

Constance is at my side. 'Are you alright?' She takes the cup from my hand, and tells me to lean my head between my knees. I do as she says. A moment later, I hear the door open and I feel the brush of air around my feet and someone's hand on my back. When I raise my head, the room is still, the sounds normal, the panic has passed.

'I'm getting the first-aider.' Lilian's voice.

'No, I'm fine.'

She crouches at my side. 'What have you eaten today?'

I try to remember, then feel foolish when I admit that I haven't.

'Right.' She leaves the room. Soon she's back with a plate of biscuits. 'This is the only thing I could find. You wouldn't believe what crap my colleagues eat.'

'Ha,' Constance says. 'I've seen, I believe.'

Lilian pushes the plate across the table towards me as she sits down. I take an unoffensive-looking shortbread. After organising the delivery of sandwiches for the three of us, she says, 'You need to look after yourself. You need to be strong. Think of this as training for a triathlon. For facing the prosecution, the court process, the aftermath.'

'You mean journalists?'

'I'd like to sugar-coat this, but I've learned that clients want honesty. Once the court case starts, you could be doorstepped, pursued. You might read things about yourself that are untrue. People come out of the woodwork.'

'I've already been approached.' I tell them about Laura.

Lilian leans back in her chair. Fine ruffled lines appear around her mouth as she purses her lips: 'Hmm.'

'There will be more,' Constance adds. 'Say nothing. If you feel the need, simply say *no comment*. I'll make a statement after the verdict, and we stick to it.'

Leaning forward again, Lilian eyes the one remaining shortbread, then considers me. 'How are you feeling now?'

'Much better, thank you.'

'Ready?'

I nod.

Constance says, 'Has Lilian mentioned we will need a mental health assessment?'

'But…'

'The prosecution will ask for one, anyway.'

Lilian picks up a piece of paper, leans her elbows on the desk as she reads. 'Next, you need to know… it's Angela's funeral tomorrow.'

A silence, broken by the sound of a door opening down the hall and a distant ringing phone. Their eyes are on me, watching for my reaction, like waiting for a photograph to develop. Angela's funeral. Her funeral makes it so real, so unshakeable. My shame and dread are so acute I want to pull my head inside my body.

Constance leans towards me. 'You may hear on the local news.'

'Should I send my condolences?' I ask, then admonish myself for the silly question.

'No. No contact with the family. You'll get the opportunity to say sorry in court. Now…'She checks her watch. This puts me in my place, reminds me this is business as usual for her. 'Before we leave for the hearing, I need to take some more in-depth information. How you first met Graham. How you met Angela. What series of events led you to impersonate her. Let's begin with Trevor. Tell me all about him. What makes him so special?'

I tell her.

From my seat near the back, I watch people board and alight the bus from Manchester to Stockport. A boy of about eight in his school uniform wanders up the aisle and lies across a vacant seat. His mother repeatedly asks him to sit down next to her. He does for about a minute, then he's up again. In my opinion, his trousers are much too tight for him, pulled up high into his groin. No wonder he doesn't want to sit down. When he disobeys, and he does, repeatedly, she asks again in a sweet calm voice and calls him 'Darling.' I suspect the boy knows she won't shout at him in public, but I bet he'll pay for this when he gets home.

Needles of sleet hit the window as a matching pair of middle-aged women get on at the next stop. They are the same small, stocky build and fit snugly onto the seat across the aisle from me. Though I've never spoken to them, I know them as the Barber twins. They are a familiar sight in the village. Both hold shopping bags on their knees, both wear light-coloured raincoats dappled with globs of rain. They clearly disapprove of the boy's behaviour. When he lies across the seat in front of them, they stare straight ahead. When he moves back next to his mother, they exchange a quick knowing glance. I wonder what it would be like to be in sync with someone like that? I park the thought as the bus approaches my stop. I get off and put my umbrella up. As the bus moves away, the women watch me from their seats. The forward motion forces them to turn. They track me in unison, as if their heads share the same shoulders. I imagine them at some point soon, as they watch the evening news: *'Isn't that...? We were sitting next to her just a few weeks ago.'*

Recalling what Lilian said about looking after myself, I open a tin of leek and potato soup and eat as I watch the tv. The chill dominates the weather, a cold front moving up from the Atlantic. I wash the pots and check around the kitchen before I turn out the light. It's been a long day. The pre-trial hearing went as Constance predicted; the judge set a period of three days for the trial, which is on the twenty-eighth of June. I put in a plea of not guilty to manslaughter and guilty to failure to provide a decent burial. Constance advised me to plead not guilty to both, but my conscience wouldn't allow it.

I know I didn't plan for Angela to die, and I know I didn't push her. But when I remember the truth of what happened, my heart closes around it, like rose petals at sunset.

Chapter Fifty-Seven

Bella

My first impression of Dr Ruth Bjarni is that I won't be able to warm to her because she's too beautiful. Thick black hair and deep brown eyes, set in skin so clear it appears photoshopped. She smiles as she offers me a seat, seemingly oblivious of the impact she must have on people at first meeting. I estimate her age to be around thirty-five and, rather than the qualifications which adorn her wall, I wonder what valuable lessons life has taught her. I do know her services are in demand because I've waited for weeks for this appointment.

Ruthi begins by telling me about her background as clinical psychologist and explains that this isn't a therapy session. She is an expert witness and has been asked to provide a psychological report. The information therein will be used to assess my state of mind at the time of the offence and will be made available to the court.

She provides me with some questionnaires and asks me to complete them as she leaves to make us drinks. When she returns with our coffees, I notice for the first time that her left arm tapers into a stump. I immediately re-evaluate her and her life experience and feel an affinity with her. For some strange reason, the arm emphasises her beauty. I'm wondering about this when she slices into my thoughts.

'Can you tell me a little about yourself?' she begins.

I find it odd talking about myself. In my forty-two years, there have been very few people in whom I've confided. I only opened up to Constance because she pushed me to talk about the accident. Afterwards, she told me it was crucial to share my revelation with the psychologist.

I'm humbled when I realise the level of trust that Jenny, Zeta and Phil put in me, a stranger. I need to take a leaf from their books and do the same with Ruthi, a bone fide, time-served clinical psychologist. But I'm unprepared for the earth-shifting experience of having a skilled practitioner scrutinise my life. Ruthi is like a prospector sifting through mud and silt for gold nuggets; the moments in my life that define me, that I've hidden from myself and others.

'Tell me about when you first met Angela Maynard.'

I start off easily. The memory so vivid.

'She nearly ran my cat Trevor over. Trevor means the world to me. He was with me through thick and thin. Always by my side. He had my…' It sounds ridiculous to say he had my back, which is what I was going to say.

'He had your..?'

'He had my love, *has* my love.'

'Of course. We love our pets, don't we? More than we love our human family sometimes.'

'Trevor was my only family.'

'Where are your parents? Siblings?'

'I'm an only child. We were all in a car crash. Dad died at the scene. Mum died a year later. My aunty moved in and looked after me. My injuries, you know,' I say, pointing to my face, as if it isn't obvious. 'She died a few years ago.'

'And Angela threatened your only other family member, Trevor, by nearly knocking him down with her car. It must have triggered a lot of unhappy memories for you.'

I'm stunned by this comment. I have never made the connection. Ruthi is offering me something. Insight? Her compassion floors me. I start crying again. I fear that tears will soon rise up through my pores like excess surface water.

'I've never thought of it like that before,' I sniffle.

She passes me the box of tissues. Where would therapists

be without their tissues? I often found that passing them to a distressed client covered up for the fact that I had nothing else to offer but three-ply ultra-soft.

'Do you have memories of the accident now?'

'I've started to have weird dreams. I hear it again.'

'Have you heard of post-traumatic symptoms?'

I ask for a break and go to the bathroom. I run the tap and splash my face with cold water, a lovely momentary relief. I pull a wad of tissues from the dispenser and blow my nose again. I catch myself in the mirror. Red eyes, swollen. This is becoming a 'look' for me.

'Are you okay to continue?' she asks when I return.

I nod.

'You're doing really well, and I really appreciate your honesty, Bella,' she says kindly. 'Okay, can you tell me about how you came to be providing therapy for people as Angela?'

I explain about Jenny knocking on my door and how the therapy sessions unintentionally snowballed.

Ruthi takes notes, nodding encouragingly. 'And Angela eventually found out?'

'Yes, she came to my house. She was shouting, threatening, laughing at me.'

'Did you push her?'

'No.'

'How do you feel about what happened?'

'How do I feel?' I haven't been asked this before. Isn't that shocking? 'I think I've grieved so much for Trevor. My grief for Angela took a back seat. But I'm sorry she died, and I'm sorry I didn't call the police sooner. As you must know, I intended to. But I couldn't leave Trevor. Then I ended up in hospital.'

'Would you do the same again?'

'I've asked myself that over and over. I should have put a human being first…' I run out of words because I have only emotions. 'On a rational level, I know it was wrong, but my grief for Trevor overrode everything. I'm very sorry, I didn't plan to be ill.'

'What did you think of Angela and Graham's relationship?'

'I was happy for them, for Graham, anyway. He'd been alone, you know. Lonely. I tried to help him out, do ironing, be there for him.'

'I've read Jenny Moorfield's account. She said she knew you both at school. You were an item?'

'Oh.'

'Can you tell me about that?'

Outed, I take a breath and tell her.

As I make the journey home, a dusting of memories billows around me. My body occupies the bus seat, my mind occupies 1994.

Inserting the key into my front door brings me home and back to the present.

After dozing on the settee, I lumber upstairs, feeling the strain on my muscles as though I've toiled in a field. I undress and have a bath, then crawl into bed. Trevor's casket is at my feet. I say goodnight to him, then close my eyes and hope for sleep. I was with Ruthi for three hours today and I told her everything. Things only four people in my life know; and two of those are dead.

Chapter Fifty-Eight
Bella

Six months later

June 28th is the first day of the hearing. Lilian and I are walking from her office to Manchester Crown Court in Spinningfields, a trendy grey-paved area where tall glass structures draw the eye up to a cloudless blue sky. Two planes leave white trails that resemble shuttlecocks in flight.

We pass a shop with a beautiful display of ladies' silk undergarments. I'm drawn to a long gown in earthy tones with very fine straps, implausibly flimsy and unwearable; but a thing of beauty, woven full of daring and escapism.

Lilian walks with purpose, her light cream mac fluttering behind as though it's hanging on for dear life. We dodge around people who wear the same ungainly white trainers, carry coffees and gaze at their phones, noticing nothing. She's talking away and does a double take before realising I've fallen behind.

'Sorry,' she says. 'I've had three strong coffees and my feet move at the same speed as my mouth. I was asking if you had any plans for Summer?'

I tell her I don't – other than being in my own home, spending time with friends, sharing lemon bun recipes, not toilet paper with a cell mate.

We mount the steps up to the court building. 'You'll be home,' Lilian says as she ushers me in. 'Have confidence.'

Is she serious? I am here. This is happening. I doubt I'll ever feel confident again.

We take the lift to the second floor. I can't get my breath; it feels like my lungs are shrinking in my chest. Then the lift doors open; air again. The hallway is high and broad, seats are dotted along its expanse and large windows give the feeling of an airport lounge. We are in Court Two. Behind that oak door is a world I only know from television. My head feels strange, my face tight. This is it.

Lilian takes me into a small side room and asks me if I'm okay. I tell her I'm fine.

'You can leave your things in here,' she says. as she searches her pockets. She produces two wrapped yellow sweets and hands me one. My mouth feels stuck with flour glue, so I take it. I peel the paper away and pop the sweet into my mouth, then squinch my face up at the hit of citric acid.

'Remember, if you see Angela's family, just keep looking forward.' She puts the sweet into her mouth and manoeuvres it around. I hear it clack against her teeth. Searching again, head down, peering into her briefcase, she brings out her mobile, reads a message and then replaces it. I notice a gathering of fluff in the corner of the room and wonder how often it's cleaned. 'Phone off,' she says.

I shrug my jacket off, then pull my mobile out of my bag. The police have my old one, so I bought a replacement. Sue started a WhatsApp group for me, and I invited Phil and Jenny. Zeta declined.

There are a couple of messages. I sit down and read.

'You will be fine,' from Jenny.

A thumbs-up emoticon, from Sue, who provided a written character reference for me.

Grateful tears warm my eyes. I'm thankful for these small things. This group has kept me going over the last few months. We've met up several times, at Sue's – never mine. My own weight loss is evidence enough that having had a body in your basement doesn't facilitate a hearty appetite. 'The deep doo-doo diet' Jenny called it, only she didn't say doo-doo. The friends asked lots of questions, listened to my answers. I believe humankind has a primitive, inherent sensibility for recognising the truth. They said they believed me when I told them Angela fell. The sticking point has always been why I didn't call the police immediately if I hadn't committed a crime. I can only tell them what I tell them. I say, *'You had to be there,'* but they are clearly glad they weren't. Despite what happened, I've always strived to be a good person, but maybe I'm deluded? There must be lots of people in prison who once baked cakes for the church fete.

'Time to go,' Lilian says.

I feel a drench of fear and take a deep breath.

Out in the imposing corridor again, I look around. A young man in a grey suit, his 'first day at school' expression a big giveaway: not so tough now. A woman in ankle boots, a shapeless leg tattoo peeping over the top. I have nothing much in common with these people, yet we are all connected. Here, where people lip chew and imagine their futures through stereoscopic vision. Right eye and left eye depicting different outcomes. All dependent on a judge and jury.

We move towards the doors. To my left, I see Graham talking to a smartly dressed man. If he's seen me, he doesn't let on. I grab at Lilian's arm.

She turns and glances over her shoulder. 'Don't worry about him. You'll be fine.'

Easy for her to say. It's strange to think it, but almost a year has passed since I spoke to him, since I confessed in his kitchen. So much water has flowed under the bridge since then and taken us towards different horizons.

It's all light oak inside the courtroom. It has that atmosphere which churches and libraries share. It's a whispering gallery; people speak with lowered heads and voices. Some glance up at me; some eyes stay a little longer. I look away but still feel their stares crawl across my skin like sci-fi scanners. All the while, I move forward, surprised that my brain has the capacity to operate my body. There is a viewing gallery in the gods at the rear of the court. I can see people shuffling, crablike, to take their places.

Lilian leaves me to take her seat next to Constance and I'm passed like a baton to the usher, who escorts me to a booth with glass on three sides. It reminds me of a fish tank. I sit heavily on the wooden pew, and pain shoots through my hip and into my neck. I place my palms one it either side of me, steadying myself. The seat feels tacky to the touch, so I quickly remove them. There's room for about ten people in here and the space emphasises my segregation and heightens my senses. Hearing my own short breaths in close-up makes me fearful. It's similar to seeing my own blood. I look around the court. I see the witness box to my left and a couple of desks to the side of that, where the usher sits. Across from her is another woman, maybe the court stenographer whose job it is to record every sorry word. They both wear black gowns.

Four rows of benches stretch across the width of the room. Everyone seated at them has a computer screen and a large television is fixed to the wall. Facing me, at the front of the room, is the raised judge's bench, unyielding and inaccessible; above it, a coat of arms which reads: '*Dieu et mon droit.*' Slowly, I begin to meld with the room; it doesn't feel so set apart and it offers some protection. I decide to deliver myself up to whatever comes.

Constance is seated to the left in front of me. She's wearing barristers' robes and a white wig; she told me the wig's official name is a 'peruke,' as if wig wasn't a silly enough name already. On the opposite side, the prosecution barrister, Paul Jackson Proctor (to Constance and Lilian he is PJP), a tall man with broad shoulders. He's incredibly handsome in his black gown. His eyes are dark, his nose straight, his light brown hair peeps out from under his peruke. He isn't what I expected. Neither Constance nor Lilian commented on his good looks, but maybe that's progress. He smiles at Constance and glances up at me.

He gives me a full two seconds, then gathers his robe in and sits down. He lowers his head and leans in to speak to a young woman in a grey suit. She mirrors his posture as she listens, then her eyes dart straight up and meet mine. She looks away again quickly. A second later, she nods and says something, and he smiles. He's very comfortable here, this man who will try to ruffle me, who will encourage everyone to believe I am a despicable person.

Constance turns, gauging me. I meet her gaze; she smiles and nods her head, which makes me want to cry: no kindness please, not now.

'All stand,' the court usher instructs.

The door at the side opens, and everyone gets up. My legs tremble when I stand. I sway backwards, but the hard bench against the back of my knees keeps me upright. A tall woman in a black robe and white peruke enters. Her Honour, Judge Abilene Blanchflower. According to Constance, she's a fair-handed, no-frills judge who has an excellent reputation.

When everyone is seated, Constance and PJP approach the judge's bench and speak in whispers. For the first time, I notice a curtain is drawn across the window to my left. This must be so the people in the family seats and viewing gallery can't see me, nor I them. I breathe out and try to ease the tremble that ripples through me like a Mexican wave every few minutes.

'Are we ready for the jury?' the judge asks, as Constance and PJP return to their seats. They nod and the usher opens a door. The jury file in. My first impression is an equal number of men to women, some young, some middle-aged. Not one of them looks my way. They are sworn in and then the judge addresses them directly.

'Good morning. May I remind you all that your role here is to assess whether the evidence you hear proves the defendant's guilt. It is your job to consider the evidence, not the law. I will guide you on points of law. Prosecuting counsel will now open the case for you.'

PJP stands. He pulls his gown together with a flourish and keeps one hand clutching the fabric at his chest. It gives him an arrogant, swashbuckling air. 'Your Honour, members of the jury, I appear for the prosecution. My learned friend Mrs Constance Loveday, appears for the defence. It is the prosecution's responsibility to prove to you beyond any reasonable doubt the facts of the offence.' His educated accent sends the message that we are in the presence of our betters, and we should listen and learn. 'The defendant, Miss Annabelle Pearson, is charged with the manslaughter of Miss Angela Maynard, and for failing to provide a burial. The crown's argument is that Miss Pearson killed Angela Maynard, a qualified psychotherapist and her neighbour, by pushing her down cellar stairs. She then hid her body in her cellar. There is no dispute over whether Angela Maynard died at Miss Pearson's house. Let me give you a brief outline of the facts. On the afternoon of the twelfth of August 2022, Annabelle Pearson told her next-door neighbour, Mr Graham Dewsnap, that the body of Angela, who had been missing for two weeks, was buried in her cellar. The authorities were informed, and they subsequently recovered the victim's body. She had lain there for two weeks. The crown's argument is that Angela Maynard confronted Annabelle Pearson after discovering the defendant had been impersonating her. Yes, Miss Pearson admits she took Angela's name and acted as a psychotherapist, taking on real people, real clients.' He pauses before the jury and places a finger of his left hand on his chin as if in deep thought. I wonder how many people in the jury notice his wedding ring. He resumes his performance.

'Now, it is the prosecution's case that during the confrontation, fearing Angela would expose her to the authorities, Pearson lured her to her cellar and pushed her down the stairs, then hid the body. Now, my learned friend,' he extends his arm towards Constance like the host of a talk show welcoming his next guest, 'will ask you to have compassion for the defendant. She will tell you it was an accident. But then what were the defendant's actions following this alleged accident? You will hear that she dragged

Angela's body to the open fireplace in her cellar and, brick by brick, covered her crime. And why? If she was innocent? If it was an accident? Why? The defence will tell you it was because her cat was poorly. Now, I am an animal-lover. In my house, we have two dogs, a rabbit and two guinea pigs. I understand the need for compassion at the loss of a family pet. But to put the needs of her cat over the immediate needs of a human being? Yes, compassion has a place in this courtroom, but it belongs with Angela Maynard and her family.' He pauses, waiting for his words to land, then says, 'Thank you.' And sits down.

Constance stands. 'Good morning,' she begins. 'My learned friend has outlined the reasons my client, Annabelle Pearson, Bella, to her friends, is here, defending her good name and character, against the very serious charge of manslaughter. He is correct. We *will* argue Angela Maynard's death was an accident. When she fell down the stairs at the defendant's home, Bella felt herself to be in an impossible situation. She knew the demise of her cat, Trevor, was imminent. He had a terminal illness, and she had made the heart wrenching decision to have him put to sleep. Should she let her beloved cat die alone? Or could she wait, just a day or so before reporting the death? In the depth of her grief, she decided she would wait to inform the police until it was done. Not the best decision she ever made, because directly after her cat had been euthanised, Bella collapsed and was admitted to hospital with serious complications of pneumonia. This had terrible consequences for the defendant, for the deceased, and for her family. However, the day Bella was discharged, was the day she informed the authorities of the deceased's whereabouts. Which demonstrates it was her intention all along.

To understand this case, you first need to understand, to Bella, her cat Trevor, was her child, her boy, as she described him to me. She told me without him she wouldn't have got out of bed some mornings. You will hear from a psychologist; how central Trevor was in Bella's life. Now, the prosecution has the burden of proof to show Bella deliberately pushed the deceased down her cellar steps and then hid the body, hoping it wouldn't be discovered. They will tell you she had been impersonating Angela, that she was obsessed with her. Maybe she was. This doesn't prove she was capable of manslaughter. You, the jury, will meet Bella Pearson and hear in her own words, what led to those tragic events of September last year. And my learned friend is incorrect. I will not ask you to show her compassion. This case doesn't rest on your disposition to the defendant, only on your sense of justice.'

When she has finished, she nods to the judge, and the judge asks PJP if he is ready for his first witness. He tells her he is. The court usher says.

'Call Graham Dewsnap.'

Chapter Fifty-Nine

Bella

To hear Graham's name stirs odd feelings: something of the past that lingers in my memory but has no substance now. My future feels inaccessible and unknown. I should fear it because of that, but I hasten it on.

The doors open and footsteps sound. Heads turn, shadows move as if around a sundial. I track his position by them. He comes into view. Now he takes the oath, I'm able to look at him fully. He's wearing a light blue suit. It looks new, but he looks worn. He's grown a full beard and moustache. He's different, everything's different.

'Can you tell us how you know the defendant?' PJP asks.

'Sure, we met at school, dated for a while.' He leans into the microphone and is told it's unnecessary, the mic will pick him up.

'How long did you date for?'

He clears his throat and the sound echoes around the room. 'About three years.'

'And how did your relationship end?'

Constance stands. 'Objection, Your Honour, relevance, leading.'

'It goes to the relationship now, Your Honour,' PJP responds.

'Overruled,' the judge answers. 'Continue.'

'Oh, you know,' Graham says to the jury. 'It just fizzled out.'

'And afterwards?'

'Nothing, until Bella moved in next door about five years ago.'

He stands stocky and square, like a tin of condensed soup.

'Were you shocked when you discovered she had moved in next door?'

Constance again. 'Objection, Your Honour, leading.'

'Sustained,' Judge Blanchflower says.

PJP coughs and then tries again. 'How did you discover your new neighbour was Bella?'

'I knew it was her from the get-go.'

'Did you have any problem with that?'

'I thought it was a coincidence, but no problem, no.'

Graham's getting into his stride now.

'Did you talk about the past with her?'

'Not until these last few months.'

'And did you get on as neighbours?'

'Yes, good. Bella kept an eye on my house when I was away on business. Helped me out.'

'You knew her cat? Sir Trevor?'

'Yeah, he travelled between us if you like, that's how they are. But he was Bella's. She doted on him.'

'Did you ever discuss re-igniting a relationship with the defendant?'

'No, she didn't let on she knew me.'

'And did that change?'

'Yes, about a year ago. I said I knew who was she was.'

'In your written testimony, you say that you felt Bella wanted more?'

'Well, she wanted to talk about the past, about us.'

'Why do you think that was?'

'I've no idea.'

'And you weren't interested in finding out?'

'Didn't see the point; it was a long time ago.'

'It sounds like you had, as they say, moved on.'

'Completely.'

'Do you know what prompted her to come to see you on that day?'

'No.'

'And did anything change from there?'

'Not for me.'

'Thankyou. I'd like us to move forward to the recent past. Is it correct that you were engaged to the deceased Angela Maynard?'

Life is so much more than the words we use to describe it. PJP has deliberately glossed over how we lived, how we interacted.

'Yes.'

'Now, I know this is difficult for you, Mr Dewsnap, and I'll try to make it as painless as possible. What we know is that Angela disappeared on the sixth of September last year. Is that correct?'

'Yes.'

'And on the sixteenth of September, ten days later, Bella Pearson visited you at home and told you something.'

'Yes.'

Graham blinks rapidly. His gaze skitters across the room and finds me, then moves on.

'Can you tell the court what she said?'

'Bella told me she'd been impersonating Angela. Said she'd been seeing clients, doing therapy.'

'How did you respond?'

'Shocked because Angie had had her suspicions.'

'Objection, Your Honour, hearsay,' Constance says.

'I'll allow it this time for the deceased. Please continue.'

'What were her suspicions?'

'Angie said she thought Bella was doing something underhand, using her name somehow. She asked Dr Halder–'

'Objection.'

'Sustained. Please only tell us what you heard directly,' the judge directs Graham.

PJP takes up his questions. 'What else did Bella tell you?'

'She said Angela's body was in her cellar.'

The truth is brutal in the re-telling. My mother will be cosy in her grave with the satisfaction of knowing she was right about me.

'Thank you, that's all, Your Honour.' PJP sits.

'Re-examine?' the judge asks.

Constance stands. 'Yes, Your Honour.' She waits as Graham

drinks from his bottle of water.

'Good morning, Mr Dewsnap.'

'Morning.'

'First, can I offer my condolences to you over the loss of your fiancée?'

'Thank you.'

'I'd like to clarify a few things. Can you tell the court how long you knew Angela Maynard for?'

'We knew each other for a few months before we dated.'

'And how long did you date for?'

'I'd say six, seven months.'

'Quite a short time, would you agree?'

'You don't hang about when you're my age.'

This earns him a few smiles from the jury.

'You and Bella both saved and planned to live together when you were seventeen?'

'True.'

'So, your first real love?'

'Yes.'

'They say you never forget your first love.'

PJP stands. 'Is there a question, Your Honour?'

'Trying to establish the relationship history.'

'Well, move on, please,' the judge says.

'Can you tell the court how long Bella had lived next door to you before she told you who she was?'

'About five years.'

'But you knew who she was all along?'

'Yes.'

'So, in that five years you didn't acknowledge that you knew her, this woman whom you'd shared an important part of your teenage life with?'

'Like I said, I thought she didn't want to talk about it, and she looked, well, different. We both did.'

'You said you felt Bella possibly still had feelings for you?'

'I didn't say that. I said she wanted to talk.'

'Can I refer you to your statement, white folder, page twenty-three, line ten?'

She waits for everyone to catch up. 'Could you read that line out for the court please, from "Bella seemed"?'

'Yes, hm…' He uses his finger to guide him while he reads. 'Bella seemed keen to pick up where we left off. I had to let her down gently.'

'That is your sworn testimony?'

'Yes, but–'

'So, you let her down gently by allowing her to clean and cook for you? Is that correct, Mr Dewsnap?'

'Not at all. It was just a bit of cleaning and ironing when I was away.'

'Mr Dewsnap, it looks to me that you took full advantage of the fact that Bella Pearson still had some feelings for you, did you not?'

'That isn't…'

'In your written statement you say Angela sometimes made underhand, unkind comments about Bella?'

'It was just her sense of humour.'

'Can you give us an example of Angela's humour?'

'It won't sound funny now.'

'I understand. A case of you had to be there.'

'That's right.'

'Shall I read out the funny example you gave? The one which made you both laugh?'

'Erm…'

'Very well. In your statement you said Angela once commented, while Bella was in hearing distance, that her cat, Sir Trevor, probably hoped he didn't smell like his owner.'

I can't hear the jury, but I notice some subtle reactions. A shifting here, a lowered head there. I imagine this comment occurred at the barbecue. There had been some speech behind hands and some sniggering.

'It was a play on words, y'know...'

'I think we get it. Thank you, Mr Dewsnap. No further questions, Your Honour.' Constance sits.

'Prosecution, any clarifications?'

PJP stands. 'Just briefly, Your Honour.' He addresses Graham again, 'Did the defendant do your ironing and cleaning for nothing?'

'No, I paid her.'

'Can you tell the court how much?'

'Depends. Probably fifteen pounds for the ironing and the same for the cleaning.'

'And did *you* help *her* out as well?'

'Yes, she doesn't drive, so I'd take her to the shops, to the vets. Help her with stuff in her house.'

'Thank you. No further questions, Your Honour.'

The judge turns to Graham. 'You can step down now, thank you. You can leave or stay in the court.'

I anticipate he'll glance at me, so I look at my hands as he's escorted away. I'm still processing everything. Love makes either fools or heroes of us. I'm left with no doubt about which one I've been. Strike two for Mum. I listen for the doors, but there's just a bit of coughing and shuffling. He must be staying for the encore.

'Your Honour, the prosecution would like to call their next witness, Dr Nadia Halder.'

Dr Halder gives her account to the prosecution about how she and Angela discovered my deception. She says it began when Angela realised that Jenny Moorfield reported having sessions with Angela, yet Angela had never met her.

PJP takes her through the day Dr Halder phoned me. She says that Angela had asked her to pose as a client.

It's interesting to hear, but as Constance explained, I never claimed I didn't impersonate Angela. It's all there in my statement.

She does cross-question Dr Halder though as to the state of

Angela's' mind at the time of her death.

'Dr Halder,' Constance says. 'You have explained to the jury how frustrated Angela was at the idea that Bella might be taking clients off her?'

'Yes, she wasn't happy.'

'Can I refer you to your written statement, please? In the white binder in front of you. Page thirty, line five.'

There is flipping through white winged folders.

'You state, halfway down, that Angela was furious and gunning for Bella?'

Dr Halder looks directly at the jury and answers, 'Yes, well you would be.'

'No further questions, Your Honour.'

Dr Halder leaves and this time I hear the doors brush the floor as they open and shut.

'The prosecution calls their next witness,' PJP says. 'Detective Inspector Robert Kenny.'

With a sway to his shoulders, DI Kenny enters the court. He's holding a slim leather document case close to his chest. He's sworn in and PJP runs through his professional history with him. Impressive. I still don't like him.

'Thank you, Detective Inspector Kenny. Now can you describe to the court how you first met Annabelle Pearson?'

'May I?' he holds up a black notebook.

The judge nods, 'Of course.'

He flicks through the pages and looks as though he's been asked to read his homework out loud to the class.

Constance advised me not to react, to zone his words out.

He locates the page and clears his throat.

From here on, I focus on my own breaths and channel their words through a distant funnel.

'I met with Miss Annabelle Pearson for the first time on Tuesday, the eighth of September, at her home address: sixteen Elmwood Terrace, Stockport. She said the last time she had spoken to Angela had been just before Angela and Graham went on holiday. I checked the dates, and they were away from the twenty-fifth of August to the first of September.'

'So, the defendant claimed she had last seen the deceased, Angela, over,' he checks the calendar on his phone, although he clearly knows already. '-Fifteen days before your visit?'

'Yes.'

And you didn't search the property?'

'No.'

'Can you tell the court why not?'

'We didn't have a warrant, and we didn't think there was any reason to. Miss Pearson was very distressed over the cat. We called back the following day and there was no one home. We learned later that the defendant had been taken to hospital.'

He goes on, and on.

Finally, Constance objects. 'None of this is in dispute. It's all in Bella Pearson's statement.'

'Approach, please,' the judge instructs. Constance and PJP walk to the bench, where they speak in hushed tones. I've no clue what they're saying, but Constance turns away first and returns to her seat. She looks up at me briefly, giving nothing away.

'So, returning to your written statement,' PJP addresses Kenny. 'Angela Maynard went missing on Sunday the sixth of September and, as Miss Pearson has reported, that was the same date the victim allegedly died. Which means that on the eighth, when you were doing house-to-house enquiries, while you were standing in the accused's living room, Angela Maynard's body was in fact in the cellar, under your feet?'

This statement hits me like I've walked into a door. PJP goes red in the face for emphasis. I think he's been building up to this like a child with one line in the nativity. I wonder if the jury caught this or just me. PJP continues and I hear one long drone, though small snippets jump out: 'The accused cunningly misled you to take the attention away from herself.'

Even though Constance jumps on everything and has some of it scratched from the record, it still hurts me in the jury's eyes. So much is lost in translation. It's a very clinical process. I understand now why people stand up and shout impassionedly in court. I want to knock on the glass and call out, 'I am here, you know. I can hear you!'

'Can I ask the court to open their blue folder at page two please?' PJP says.

I watch as the jury members duly open their folders, expressions passive. I don't know which order the evidence will be presented in, but I've realised that the photographic evidence has a bigger impact on me than spoken evidence. Constance has talked me through this, but she underplayed it. It's excruciating. I watch the room's opinion of me slowly evolve. Shouldn't the defence go first if I'm supposed to be innocent until proven guilty? It seems contrary to that principle when all the negative information is the first the jury will hear or see. As each new piece of evidence is presented, neurons will spark, and new pathways will be forged as their first impression of me is created. How hard will it be then for Constance to challenge that new learning, those beliefs? I'm no neuroscientist, but I'm hoping those belief pathways are still wet like feather icing and can be flattened and re modelled with my evidence. Otherwise, I'm in trouble.

The photograph PJP refers to contains my certificates. 'Can you tell us about the photographs marked one, two, and three?'

'Yes,' DI Kenny answers, lifting the page by the corner. 'During the search of number sixteen Elmwood Terrace, we found framed certificates in a chest of drawers in the cellar. We seized the defendant's computer and were able to ascertain they were downloaded from it two months previously.'

'Could you read the details for the court?'

DI Kenny clears his throat and reads: 'Certificate in the basic principles of Cognitive Therapy.'

'And who is the recipient?'

'Angela Maynard.'

'Could the court turn to page four in the same folder?'

Flipping over pages. Flipping over heart.

'Tell us about the photograph in front of you marked four.'

'We found this alongside the previous certificate.'

'Can you read out what the certificate says?'

'Your Honour,' Constance cuts in. 'We have an intelligent jury who can all presumably read and we're using valuable time.'

'Sustained. Please be brief, counsel.'

'Yes, Your Honour.' He nods to a person out of my eyeline and the television screen and desk screens flash into life. 'I'd like the court to consider the significance of these certificates. They are all in your folder. The one on the right is the certificate the accused downloaded and falsified in Angela Maynard's name. The one shown on the left is the certificate that Angela Maynard was awarded by the BABCP, the regulating body responsible for ensuring that all therapists maintain professional, accredited training and supervision and work within strict ethical boundaries.... Batchelor of Science in Psychology; State Registered Nurse, from the Nursing and Midwifery Council. Now, you will recall Dr Nadia Halder gave evidence that Angela was, and I refer to her earlier statement, furious and gunning for the accused. I would suggest that anyone who had gone through such rigorous training and strived to maintain a high standard of therapy for her clients, would be furious and gunning for anyone who brought her name and her reputation into disrepute.'

'Is there a question for the witness, Your Honour?' Constance asks.

'Counsel?' the judge asks.

'Yes, Your Honour, there is.'

DI Kenny switches from right leg to leaning on his left. I switch from left to right buttock; it relieves my hip pain for one glorious second.

'DI Kenny, I'd like to move on to the day you discovered

Angela's body. Can you talk us through what happened when you arrived at Mr Dewsnap's address on the sixteenth of September?'

'Yes. The door to number sixteen had been left open for us and we immediately entered the cellar…'

I can't listen to him anymore; I zone out and retreat into my head for a short while.

'…found the body later identified as Angela Maynard.'

'Thank you, no further questions, Your Honour.'

PJP slides back onto the wooden seat, looking smug.

'Cross-examination?' the judge asks.

Constance is already on her feet, document folder opened in front of her. 'Good afternoon, Detective Inspector Kenny. I'd like to clarify a couple of things. You didn't search the cellar on your initial visit to number sixteen, because you didn't have a warrant?'

'Correct.'

'But you went into the cellar, did you not?'

DI Kenny blushes a deep red. The kind of red that makes other people uncomfortable.

'Well, yes. But I didn't search it, no.'

'In these circumstances, you don't need a warrant. You can simply ask permission of the homeowner, am I right? So, did you, at any time, ask permission of Miss Pearson to search her cellar?'

'No, she was very distracted because of the cat.'

'So, you didn't conduct a thorough search?

'No, she was in a state herself.'

'Can you tell the court what your observations of Miss Pearson's state of mind were at that time?'

'She was tearful, distracted. So, we went back the next day.'

'But on that first day you had full opportunity to conduct a thorough search. Miss Pearson was distressed and not thinking clearly, but not obstructive. Just a matter of the right approach by you, at that time and Angela Maynard might have been discovered, and her family and friends would have been able to begin grieving then, rather than ten days later.'

'She was...'

'We will never know, will we, detective? What we do know is, had Miss Pearson not come forward as soon as she came out of hospital, Angela Maynard would still be considered a missing person.' She closes her folder to show she's done. 'No further questions, Your Honour.'

The judge tells us to take an hour for lunch and we stand as she, then the jury, leaves the room. I watch them. They must be feeling the strangeness of it all. The steady deliberations and traditions. It's all so 'proper' here where the wheels of justice squeak and grind. Where good and bad collide, where there's little laughter and only quiet tears. Such a sharp contrast to the sensationalised portrayals I've seen on the television.

My knees feel like they've been set in cement and my hip reminds me it's time for pain killers. Fortunately, the public gallery has emptied first, and I don't have the awkwardness of having to face the family, or Graham.

Back in the dusty side room, Lilian asks if I'd like something from the shop. I decline because of the stew of stress in my stomach. My stomach gurgles and I hold my hand over it as if reassuring a disgruntled child. Lilian returns with a take-out salad and some plastic cutlery, which she digs into the lettuce like a pitchfork. Constance has a thermos flask, which she shakes intermittently. She tips her head right back to get to whatever's in it. Her peruke lies forlornly on the table. The ball of dust has accumulated more flotsam and rolls like prairie grass into the opposite corner of the room.

'How are you holding up?' Constance asks as she tips the silver flask from side to side.

'It all feels so fast-moving, a bit of a blur.'

'I think it's going well,' Lilian says, as she puts her half-eaten carton of food in the bin and tucks the plastic fork into her bag.

I'm distracted by these details. Their tepid half lunches, where food seems an inconvenience and isn't enjoyed, or even acknowledged.

'We've sewn a seed of doubt about the investigation already. We can build on that,' Constance says, as she stands and places her wig back on her head. 'Got to prepare a cross for the forensic expert.'

'That sounds a bit harsh,' Lilian says.

Constance smiles and says, 'Ha ha, the old ones are the best.'

She's out of the door before I've caught up with the joke.

Chapter Sixty

Bella

Miss Elspeth Graham, the forensics expert, looks about twelve and I find myself equal parts envious of her youth and education, and appreciative of her skills. Then a computer image of my cellar appears on the screen, and I'm reminded that this only half-lived woman is a threat.

PJP is asking if Angela's injuries were consistent with a fall. 'And can you say for certain that the deceased died in the cellar?'

'Yes, the evidence at the death scene was consistent with the victim dying in that room.'

'Can you talk the court through the pictures we have up here of the accused's cellar stairs?'

Miss Graham puts some trendy heavy-framed glasses on and replies, 'So, a fatal fall can be presumed from external and internal damage to the body, and other circumstantial evidence. I was officially asked to conduct experiments to elucidate possible falling patterns. I used what is known as 3D optical surface scanning... The accused said the victim had been forward-facing…'

She points a small gadget at the screen and rotates the model this way and that. One minute I have a bird's eye view of my cellar, the next it's as if I'm stood at the very top of the stairs. I feel disorientated, like I'm on the big dipper. A grey virtual figure appears on the screen and tumbles slowly forwards. I instinctively lean back. The figure slows down and catches its shoulder against the wall then rolls forward tearing off fingernails, trapping an arm under itself and hitting its head sideways on one of the concrete steps.

'…and fell from the top of the stairs to the cellar floor. So, I used that information in conjunction with the post-mortem findings, which revealed a fracture to the right forearm and abrasions to the arms and legs.'

I close my eyes. When I open them again, the figure is at the foot of the stairs.

'And would these injuries be consistent with a forward fall?'

'They would.'

Holding onto his lapels like a headmaster, PJP asks, 'Can the jury refer to the blue folder in front of them? Pages seven, eight and nine. I must warn you the crime scene photographs may be distressing.'

'Objection!' Constance calls out.

Her voice disrupts the controlled breathing I'm trying to tune into.

'A crime has not been established, Your Honour. That is for the jury to decide.'

'Sustained,' the judge answers, peering at PJP over her glasses. 'Can the jury disregard that last comment? Rephrase, counsel.'

'Noted, Your Honour. Can the jury refer to the death scene photographs.'

I close my eyes and try to separate myself again, concentrate on my breathing. The jury don't know me, breathe in. I didn't push her, breathe out. They will understand when it's our turn, breathe in.

The photographs they refer to are displayed in the open file in front of Constance. Lilian has one too, but she doesn't open hers. Maybe she's aware that I'm directly behind her.

Miss Graham is talking. 'The body of the deceased was wrapped in plastic carrier bags and a black bin liner. … remnants of lime cement… The body was decomposing but was well preserved because of the lime cement. I estimate the deceased had been there for approximately ten days. …cause of death was a cervical fracture.'

'And could you say that death would have been immediate?'

'The fracture was high up on the cervical spine making the injury fatal, so yes.'

'Now, can you tell the court the effects that lime cement may have on a body?'

'Yes, research has shown that general decomposition is slowed down by quicklime and hydrated lime. It may protect the body rather than destroying it. It may also help with hiding the odour of decomposition for a time.'

'So, it can be used to cover the smell?'

'Yes.'

'Miss Graham, is it possible for you to say definitively that the deceased wasn't pushed?'

She sets her shoulders straight and says a firm; 'No.'

PJP gives a slight nod like he's pleased with her, but because it's him I think it's more likely he's pleased with himself. I'm surprised he doesn't check himself in a mirror. I observe the jury: their features appear softened. I must admit, PJP chose the forensics expert well. Her prettiness and youth seem to be a vessel for truth.

He continues, 'And are there circumstances that make it harder to give a definitive answer?'

Constance is up. 'Objection! Leading!'

'Overruled. The witness may answer.'

Miss Graham looks from PJP to the judge then lifts a bottle of water to her lips and takes a sip before answering. 'Yes, when there is only one witness to the events.' At this, she fires a quick look in my direction. The implication hits me like buckshot.

'Thank you. No further questions, Your Honour.' PJP sweeps his gown up behind him and sits down. He doesn't even glance at Constance.

Constance stands and I'm reminded of her joke about the cross being prepared for this woman. I'm waiting in anticipation to see if she nails her to it.

'Thank you, Miss Graham,' she says with a smile. 'I just need to clarify a few things. Could you tell the court what injuries we would expect to see if the victim had been pushed?'

'So, the projection of the body when someone is pushed is different from that of a natural fall and it will often land further away.'

'And were you able to determine where the deceased in this case landed?'

'We found blood at the foot of the stairs which we determined was that of the victim and most likely indicated where she landed.'

'And did it correspond with the victim being pushed?'

'It's difficult. The body had been moved, and the ground had been disturbed.'

'Thank you. Would there be any other evidence that a victim *might* have been pushed?'

'Well, there would likely be transfer of skin cells, fibres etcetera on the back of the victim's clothing.'

'And, when you examined the victim's clothing, what did you find?'

'We found strands of synthetic hair, which we were able to match to a wig that Bella Pearson was wearing on the day of the incident. We also found fibres which matched the cardigan belonging to the accused. There were also several cat hairs belonging to the accused's pet cat.'

'Did you find any bruising on the victim's back?'

'Yes.'

'Could this have been sustained in the fall?'

'It's possible.'

'Did you find any skin cells belonging to the accused on the victim's back?'

'Yes.'

'Would it be possible, in your expert opinion, to conclude that those skin cells could have been transferred when the accused moved the body?'

Miss Graham pauses and glances at PJP. 'Possible, but–'

'Thank you. A couple more questions. Can you say definitively that the victim was pushed?'

'No.'

'And finally, do you recall my learned colleague asked you whether there were circumstances which made it harder to determine whether a victim was pushed or fell?'

'Yes.'

'And your answer was when there is only one witness to the event.'

'Correct.'

'Now Miss Graham, I'm assuming you have read the statement the accused made?'

'Yes.'

'And in that statement, has the accused given any evidence that has not been supported by the forensic findings?'

PJP is suddenly up, startled out of his superior complacency. 'Objection, Your Honour! Beyond the scope.'

Constance turns to the judge. 'I don't see how, Your Honour. It's a straightforward question relating to the forensic findings.'

'I'll allow it,' the judge answers.

PJP sits, forgetting to swirl his cloak about.

'Would you like me to repeat the question, Miss Graham?' Constance asks.

'No, it's okay,' Miss Graham answers. She glances at PJP and for the first time I see some nerves. She reaches a hand up to her forehead and touches it lightly, as though brushing hair away before answering. 'It's a long statement. I'd need time to read it again.'

'Well, wouldn't that be nice, Miss Edwards.' Constance smiles. 'No further questions, Your Honour.'

Chapter Sixty-One

Bella

Zeta looks lost in the witness box. Recently removed rollers have left white hollow swirls of hair. She's wearing a navy-blue jacket with a green silk scarf tucked into the neck which she loosens with pale fingers.

Her pink-ringed eyes make me think she's upset about being here. Why wouldn't she be? She's the only witness who looks at me for any sustained period. That slight shake of her head still there. It conveys a vulnerability but, from what I know of Zeta, she's a strong, forthright woman who I like and admire. To have upset her brings tears to my eyes and I search for my own tissue.

She's recounting how she came to contact me. I know all this, of course, but PJP wants to draw it out, play on Zeta's age, emphasise her susceptibility. But I can't throw stones, can I? I'm here, literally in a glass house.

'…and can you tell the court how you felt when you learned that the accused was not the Angela Maynard you thought she was, but instead was just a neighbour of hers called Annabelle Pearson?'

Since I've known her, Zeta has had handkerchiefs at the ready. She pulls one out of her pocket now and wipes her nose, a dab backwards and forwards. Then she pulls her shoulders back and answers.

'Horrified. I was horrified. I mean, how would *you* like it?' She looks directly at the jury, then at the judge, who sits back in her chair, her body language saying she wouldn't like it at all. 'I'd talked about my late husband Frank. He would have turned in his grave if he was alive today. Me telling a stranger on the street all about us. I was very angry at her.'

'What did you do immediately after you found out?'

'I told my granddaughter and my daughter. They said I should go to the police.'

'And did you?'

'I thought about it.' She folds one hand into the other and turns them over in a brief washing action. 'But no, I didn't.'

'Mrs Cronshaw, in your written statement you say that it took time for you to recover from this deceit. How did it affect you?'

'I felt foolish and embarrassed. I'd been taken in by a charlatan. I feared she would have spread what I told her all around the village. It made me scared to go to another mentalist. I knew I was a fruitcake over Frank's death, and I needed some help, but I couldn't bring myself to speak to anyone else.'

'We appreciate how difficult it must be for you,' PJP says. 'Can I ask, have you managed to find some help?'

'Yes, I have a very good friend called Malvine who I met at whist. Talking to her has helped a lot.'

'Thank you.' PJP turns to the judge. 'No further questions, Your Honour.'

Constance stands. 'Good afternoon, Mrs Cronshaw, thank you for coming. I won't keep you long.'

Zeta responds by producing her hanky and wiping her nose.

'Bella has spoken about you in her statement in very warm terms and I'd like to reassure you that, throughout hours of interviews I've conducted with her...' Zeta stops wiping her nose and waits. She seems to be holding her breath, alert as a meerkat, 'she has never divulged anything you discussed in your sessions.'

Zeta looks up at where I'm sitting. She doesn't say anything. There is an ever so slight shake of her head. The hanky goes back in her pocket as she turns to listen to Constance.

'I'm not going to ask anything about your discussions. I understand from what you have said here you have suffered the loss of your husband and I offer my condolences.'

Zeta responds with a sniff and says, 'Thank you.'

Constance says, 'We have heard how badly you were affected by Bella's actions. Can you tell the court how you found out she wasn't Angela?'

'She confessed. She said it was a situation she'd got herself into and couldn't get out of. She was very apologetic, but it was a shock to my system.'

'Of course. I'm sure the court can understand about the shock, but was there anything in those sessions, before you discovered who Bella was, that might have helped with the problem you'd gone to seek advice for?'

'Well, when Mr Proctor asked me to take the side of the police, I was happy to do it because I was so angry. But I thought back. It was good to talk to Angela, I mean Bella. She was very understanding. It made it harder in a way. I thought we would be friends.' Zeta turns to me. Some of the jury follow her gaze, see me through her eyes. 'I hope she gets some help,' she says.

'One final question,' Constance says. 'Did Bella ever take any money from you?'

'No, not a single penny. She asked me to give a donation to The Cats Protection League.'

'Didn't you think that was odd?'

'Well, odd is as odd does. Once I got to know her, it made sense. She loved her cat, Sir Trevor. Anyone who loves a cat like that can't be all bad.'

'Thank you, no further questions, Your Honour.'

'Okay, grab my arm and stay under the brolly,' Lilian says to me as we leave the court after the first day. It's only a fine summer drizzle and my hat is usually protection enough, but then I see her reasoning. Reporters.

With one simple flick of her hand the umbrella blooms out above us. It's a doorman's umbrella and provides an igloo of protection through which questions are filtered.

I hear the man ask, 'How did it go today? Will you be taking the stand? How did it feel seeing Angela's family?'

Lilian steers me swiftly on, using the umbrella like a medieval shield. All I see is the wet grey paving and the tips of my shoes as they kick up spittle's of water. Eventually the questions fade away and Lilian's umbrella arm relaxes.

'You need the hide of a rhino,' she says.

'How do you manage it? I'd hate to be on camera on television.'

'It's not about me, is it? I'm not the one on trial. Anyway, it's usually Constance who does the interviews. She's used to it.'

We meet up with Constance at Lilian's office and order from an Italian take-out menu. Lilian suggested we return here to go over the day's developments, and I didn't object because the thought of getting the bus back home kicks up a dark unease. It's become clearer to me that it's going to be impossible to remain in my house; the associations and memories are too disquieting. I can take Trevor with me anywhere I go. So, I make a pledge for myself, and the universe, whoever is listening, that I will move. I'll start again. I'll live a good life and repent for all the pain I've caused.

'Ham and pineapple?' Lilian asks, holding the lid of a pizza box open.

Chapter Sixty-Two

Bella

The following day I awake to dripping grey clouds and wonder if my pledge to the universe has influenced the weather in my favour. Rain means we can use the umbrella to avoid the press again. I ignore the fact that I live in Manchester. It rains here as often as the sun shines in Arizona. I double down on my pledge to put my house on the market and be a better person.

More luck: the courts are quiet on our approach, and Lilian and I slip in without notice.

The first witness today is Steve Cross, Angela's ex-husband.

Steve is a horse of a different colour. He stands confidently, addressing the jury as if it's a performance.

'Mr Cross,' PJP says. 'We have heard in detail from Detective Inspector Kenny about his interview with Annabelle Pearson, and how, as a result of that information, you came to be arrested in connection to the disappearance of the deceased.'

With the air of an affronted Jane Austin heroine, Steve replies, 'Yes, it was traumatic to say the least.'

'How was your relationship with the deceased?

'Me and Angie had a love-hate relationship, you know, passionate and complicated. I think she still loved me.'

He boasts that he and Angela still slept together occasionally after they split up. I cringe for her family, seated in the visitors' section. It's cruel of me, but I wish I could see Graham's face, witness his discomfort.

'In your statement you said that on the twelfth of July last year, Bella Pearson approached you outside Angela's house.'

'Yeah, like your friendly neighbourhood watch, wanted to know what I was doing.'

'What did you tell her?'

'I was calling on Angie.'

'Did she say anything else?'

'Yeah, she told me that Ange and Graham had gone away together. Said they'd been together for a while. Like she was trying to wind me up.'

'Objection, speculation,' Constance says.

'Stick to the facts, please, Mr Cross.'

'It is a fact. That's what it felt like,' Steve answers.

'Remove that last comment from the record,' the judge instructs. 'Just answer the questions, please, Mr Cross.'

'Sorry, Your Honour,' Steve says.

PJP continues. 'Now, Mr Cross, what did you believe her motivation was for that?'

'Objection, Your Honour!' Constance has hardly sat down since the last one. 'We've just covered that.'

'Sustained. The facts please. Counsel.'

'Apologies, Your Honour. How did it make you feel, hearing they had gone away?'

'Like she was trying to drive a wedge. To get Angie out of the way so she could have Graham to herself.'

It goes on in this vein. It's a role Steve looks comfortable in. He's frequently pulled up by the judge for adding his little insights. 'She's a nutcase… a meow head,' he says, referring to me and I see a couple of the jury frown. Constance and Lilian exchange a glance and I realise that Steve is doing the prosecution no favours.

When it comes to cross-examination, Constance asks him only one question. 'Mr Cross, have you ever had a restraining order issued against you?'

Steve falters, rocks back on his heels and then leans forward, very close to the microphone and answers, 'That's not–'

'I have it in front of me, Mr Cross. Would you like me to read it to the court?

'Objection, Your Honour,' PJP says, jumping up with his hand in the air. 'This witness is not on trial.'

'Overruled.'

It transpires that his previous partner had taken a restraining order out on him in the first few years of marriage. Steve describes it as a one-off, says she took him back.

Constance closes her files and clasps her hands on top of them like a paper weight. Thank you,' she says. 'No further questions.'

The days follow the same pattern. I zone in and out at court and try to hold on to the remnants of myself. Sue has had to go to Spain because of some maintenance issue with her house, but I think it's more to do with the fact that she has met someone there. She says they are only friends, but she's been a little more wistful, full of sighs and unsaid things. I think she will be living there permanently soon. It's over a week since we had our usual cuppa and catch-up, something I realise has been putting me back together after a day of being disassembled in court.

I sleep badly; the pain in my hip makes it impossible to settle. I become aware of my own limbs and feel the strangeness of being human, arranged the way we are with a head and arms and legs. I think how ugly we are. I realise these are strange thoughts and worry I'm going slightly mad. Last night I dreamed about a Victorian doll I once owned, given to me by my late grandmother. I named her Sophie; she was old even then, with long flaxen ringlets and a blue ribboned bonnet. I didn't much like the way one lashed eye stuck open while the other slowly closed in a lewd menacing wink. Her jacket, though, was made of deep red velvet, fashioned in the style of an Imperial Hussar, with swirling knots of braiding and gold buttons. I wanted to wear it myself it was so beautiful. In my dream I'm around six and I'm playing at dressing her. When I try to put her jacket on her, it gets stuck at an elbow joint. I attempt to yank it over, but the felt has perished, and tiny threads come away in my hands and float to the floor, like weightless strands of blood. Panicking, I struggle to hold the jacket in one piece with just the pressure of my hand. The more I try, the more the jacket disintegrates, and the yellowed, cracked doll chest is exposed. Just before I awake, I feel her chest expanding against my fingers. She turns her head towards me, and batting one vitreous eye, she exhales.

The dream lingers as I ready myself for the day ahead. I haven't thought about Sophie for many years, and I wonder what it means to dream of her now. I've grown accustomed to my memories. It's rare to discover a new one. I've no siblings to spark off, so I'm stuck with one story of my life. I hope my dream is not a bad omen.

Chapter Sixty-Three

Bella

Today it is our turn, and our first witness is Jenny. I hold my fingers tightly crossed as she takes the stand.

Beautiful Jenny, she has a calm confidence and a good energy, a stark difference to Steve Cross. She gives a little of her background. She mentions school. She tells the truth of our meeting. She came to my house by mistake. No, she didn't know I wasn't Angela and yes, she continued to come without being charged. Did I do any harm? Was she angry with me? No and yes. Constance keeps the questions short and simple, and I feel as though I'm being nourished by fresh water following a hard drought.

Then it's PJP's turn, and the questions turn to death.

'You were in the defendant's house when her cat passed away?' PJP asks.

'Yes.'

'It must have been horrific for you to find out later that the body of Angela Maynard–'

Constance stands. 'Objection, leading. 'I hear strain in her voice this time.

'Sustained.'

'What was your reaction when you discovered that the body of Angela Maynard had been in the cellar at that time?'

'Sick to the stomach.'

'And you still claim to be a friend of the defendant?'

I hold my breath as Jenny looks at the jury, and not PJP. I think she's going to give a long explanation, but she simply answers, 'Yes.'

As Jenny is ushered away, I see the red flourish of heat on her neck. I know how difficult she would have found it, having eyes roaming free over her curves, believing that strangers are judging her shape as harshly as she does.

As I'm observing this, I hear Constance say, 'Call my next witness, Annabelle Pearson.'

The usher opens the door for me, and I will my legs to work. My spine is stiff, so I lean forward to aid momentum. Like a nervous animal, I leave the safety of the dock. I'm at the witness stand and my heart is pounding, as if from a hollow cavity, as I deliver myself up to what will be.

Constance begins by asking how I first met Angela. I tell my story. I tell the truth, but it's not the truth apparently until a jury says it is. I recount the incident over Trevor. Then the barbecue. I explain how I learned that Angela was a psychotherapist.

Constance speaks gently, trying to break me in slowly with nursery-level questions, before PJP takes me to graduation level. I've been advised by Constance to address the jury, give them some appropriate eye contact but not to linger on anyone. Looking at them brings them closer in. I'm itchy under their scrutiny. I think they'll find me dull very quickly. Maybe they will find me innocent due to boredom.

The questions are unrelenting:

'Tell the court about the last day Angela came to your house?'

'And when she fell, what did you do?'

'Why didn't you call the police?'

I recount it all as it happened, leaving nothing out. I add I'm ashamed and I'm sorry and I hope the family believe me.

'I was deranged with worry over Trevor. I just couldn't leave him. I knew Angela was dead. I'm very sorry, I couldn't help her. I had already arranged for the vet to come and put my boy to sleep.' Tears fall down my face and I search for a tissue before I see it on the floor just beyond the stand. An image of Zeta comes, and I wonder if she is in the gallery, congratulating herself on her pockets full of handkerchief's. 'In my mind, I was going to phone the police as soon as Trevor was…'

'Can you explain why you concealed her body?'

'I don't know. I think I… I couldn't leave her there, and I didn't intend her to be in the cellar long. It was a very bad decision.'

Eventually the usher brings a small box of tissues and places it on the stand. I have another sip of water and rub my eyes. Now one tear has fallen, more will follow, like lemmings.

Constance moves on to ask me about my history with Graham. She has explained that we need to give the jury a strong context. I'm more nervous about telling this than anything. My mouth is dry and, although I've been allowed to sit, I want to stand for a bit to alleviate the pain, but I won't ask.

'We heard that you moved in next door to Graham and lived there for five years before Angela moved into the house over the road.'

'Yes.'

'We've heard from Mr Dewsnap that you initially met at school. Can you briefly describe to the court what happened to bring that relationship to an end?'

'Yes. We were about to move into a flat in the village together. Graham had saved a deposit. My mum suggested we – me, Mum and Dad, that is – went to Wales for a week.'

I can see the visitors' gallery from the corner of my eye, but I would have to turn my head to search Graham out. I know, somehow, he's still here and this will be the first time he's heard this. I've tried to tell him before. I hoped it would give me some sort of closure because it's a thing I've carried with me for so long. Grief is a tether to the past.

I take a moment to have a drink of water. It tastes sweet and cool. I replace the glass on the table in front of me and notice wrinkles on the surface water, induced by the quiver in my hand. As I continue speaking, Constance nods and smiles reassuringly. The courtroom is deathly quiet. If I closed my eyes, I wouldn't know anyone else was here.

'On the last day of the holiday, we piled everything into the car.'

'Clothes shoved hastily into my case. Stuff piled into the back.' *Dad couldn't see through the rear-view mirror, so he made us re-arrange it all so most of it ended up on the back seat with me.*

'We'd just got onto the M62.'

A song came on the radio. 'Eternal Flame' by The Bangles. I asked Dad to turn it up. Mum stopped him. She said it was their car so their choice of music.

'We had a bad accident.'

I explain it to the jury using conventional descriptions but, in my mind, I see it all as if it was yesterday…

'Don't you be giving your orders in this car,' Mum says, from the front passenger seat, head and shoulders stiff with irritation, sideways glance at my dad.

'I wasn't, I was just…' I catch Dad's eyes through the rear-view mirror. I know there would be no help coming from that quarter. He probably hasn't even heard me. It's like he disappears into himself when he's around Mum.

'When she pays the bills, she can have what music she wants,' Mum adds. She glances back at me with a look of satisfaction that she's stopped some enjoyment for me.

'Well, you won't have to worry about that anymore. I'm moving in with Graham as soon as we get home.'

'You what?' Mum says. 'You think so? You're a deluded little slut.'

'Hey, hey, language,' Dad says. He looks at me through the rear-view mirror. 'Is it true?'

'It's true, Dad, we've already paid the deposit. Graham's waiting for me now. With his parents' blessing.'

'Bloody slut,' Mum repeats.

'Oy, no need for the language,' Dad says. But Dad doesn't know what Mum knows.

'Oh, yes there is. Your daughter's got herself knocked up. Seventeen

and pregnant. How proud she's made us.'

'What?' He's looking at Mum, then the road, then his mirror and briefly meeting my eyes.

'I found her pregnancy test.'

Dad's eyes flit around. He indicates to move from the fast lane, but a car bips its horn and he swerves back.

'Bob, watch it, you idiot.'

Dad turns in his seat to try and get a look at me. Then glares through the rear-view instead. 'Is this true?'

'Course it's true,' Mum says.

'Yes, I'm having Graham's baby.' Saying the words brings a flush to my cheeks, but not of shame: of delight. 'I would have told you, Dad. I'm moving in with Graham when we get home. We're getting married.'

'I gave her chance to tell us while we were away, but no, she chose to hold her dirty secret to herself, glassy-eyed idiot. As if Graham's going to marry you, you fool. Well, I won't be bringing the little bastard up, I can tell you that for nothing.'

I watch the cars as we speed past them in the fast lane, willing Dad to put his foot down, imagining the flat, and me and Graham with our little family. I always imagined a boy first then a girl.

Mum turns around in her seat and I smile at her. We both feel it at the same time. My triumph over her, her loss of power over me. Her face puckers with anger and loathing. She leans over and slaps me on the legs, then she kneels up in her seat, bends over me and pummels. Dad is shouting.

The car hits the barrier.

'When I came to, the nurse told me that, as well as all my other injuries,' I point to my face. 'I'd suffered a uterine rupture. I was four months pregnant. Apparently, all the luggage on the back seat cocooned me, protecting me from more serious injury, but I lost the baby. I also developed an infection that meant I'd have difficulty conceiving again.'

Now I turn fully to seek out Graham. I find him. He leans forward and rests his forehead on his hands. Then he looks at me, eyes red-rimmed. Mine sting in response.

'And you never told Mr Dewsnap?'

'I didn't want him to stay with me out of pity.'

'Why didn't you tell him before you went on holiday?'

'I didn't put two and two together. I had irregular periods anyway, and it took me a while to get the courage to buy a pregnancy test, and then the courage to use it.'

'Who did you tell about your loss?'

'I told no one about the baby. My mum told my Aunty Betty who came to look after us. And I was offered some group support sessions, but I was too ill to go.'

'I know these are very sensitive questions, Bella, and I appreciate how difficult it must be for you. Are you alright to continue, or would you like a break?'

'No, I'm fine,' I answer. Though a break would be welcome, I'm afraid I might make a run for it: a slow walk for it, anyway.

'How did you feel about the loss of your baby?'

How did I feel? I felt and still feel like I lost part of myself and a part of something precious that I'll never know. I won't say this though. These feelings are mine alone. I'm already selling my soul here, bartering for my freedom. 'I felt devastated.' Saying the word brings the devastation back. It was total, absolute, like the bombing of a city. I grab the box of tissues and pull some out, which seems to trigger a conditioned response as tears fill my eyes.

'I can't talk about it.'

'Take a moment,' Constance says.

I blow my nose and sip water, then clear my throat and Constance continues.

'Did anything help you at that time?'

'Objection, leading.'

'Sustained.'

'I'll rephrase. Were there things that made it easier or harder for you at the time?'

'Yes, the emotional pain seemed to make the physical pain worse. I don't know if that makes sense. Also, I hid away from Graham. I didn't want him to see me looking like…' I falter and take another sip of water before continuing. 'I wanted to tell him about the baby but, as I said, I didn't want him to feel he had to stay with me because of it. I wanted to get better,' I look down and say quietly, 'to start again.'

'Anything else?'

'Yes, my cat Cleo, well my aunt's cat, really. She was old, the cat not my aunty, but she was old too… sorry, I've lost my thread…'

'And how did she help? Cleo the cat, not your old aunty.'

There are a few soft laughs from the jury, and it brings a lightness to the afternoon that I think everyone needed. I use the reprieve to take a breath and remind myself we are nearly through.

'She was a massive help,' I answer. 'She slept on my bed at night. The rise and fall of her tummy helped me to sleep.' I'm tempted to add, 'the cat, not my aunty'. I don't, because it's okay for Constance to bring a little light to the dark, but not for me.

Constance moves on to Trevor. 'When did you get him?'

'I got Sir Trevor seven years ago from being a kitten,' I explain to the jury. 'I called him Sir Trevor after the newsreader Sir Trevor McDonald. He had orange eyes and blue fur that was light grey around his nose and face. He was very beautiful. Trevor was my baby.' My voice breaks and I bury my face in a tissue again. This is excruciating. How is it possible to make myself cry, I wonder, when the words are my own, generated by my brain?

'Thank you, Bella. No further questions, Your Honour.'

I'm cross-questioned by PJP, and I answer honestly, without guile. This is a story I won't budge on, and I won't cover up, so it's easy in the telling. Even PJP's snide insinuations are acceptable to me. I don't expect sympathy for concealing Angela's body.

'Miss Pearson, were you angry with Miss Maynard?'

'No. I was nervous around her because I had been pretending I was her. I hoped to stop before she found out.'

'You were so worried and nervous about this that you had some certificates made in her name. You bought books and set up a small home office in your cellar, did you not?'

'It all got out of hand.'

'They say that imitation is the highest form of flattery, would you agree?'

'I don't know, probably.'

'Miss Pearson, I put it to you that you were in fact intensely jealous of Angela Maynard. She had all the skills you lacked, she was sociable and beautiful, and she had captured the heart of the man whom you had loved since you were a teenager. Who for five years had you cleaning and cooking for him, knowing all along who you were, while never acknowledging or returning your love.'

I'm shocked by this sudden attack. Heat rises in me, and I feel the sweat build under my glasses.

Constance stands and diverts the attention. 'Objection, is there a question, Your Honour?'

'Sustained.'

Constance sits down and PJP resumes. Eyes like a cat on the hunt. 'Were you jealous of Angela Maynard, Miss Pearson? Yes, or no?'

He's got me on the ropes. I have to say something. The truth resonates more when it's reduced to one-word answers.

'Yes,' I answer.

'Was Angela Maynard flattered, do you think, when she found out what you were doing?'

'Objection, speculation.'

'Sustained.'

'In your statement you said that Angela had followed you to the cellar. You were at the bottom of the stairs when she fell?'

'Yes.'

'Please could you describe to the court exactly how you

happened to already be in the cellar while Angela Maynard was stood at the top of the cellar steps?'

'She made a remark. I can't remember exactly, insulting, about me making my own certificates. I went to get them from the cellar. She followed me.'

'I see. So, during your argument you left Angela, the woman you were jealous of but not angry with, while you went to fetch the certificates.' He speaks slowly for emphasis. 'The ones you had made in her name?'

'Yes.'

It's not humanly possible to withstand the barrage of stagy overblown questioning for too long, so I cope by paying attention to my breathing. I've not recovered from talking about the accident and the loss of my baby. Despite being caught up between PJP's underhand slights, his courtroom wordy limbo, and the continual objections called out by Constance, I'm preoccupied by my own testimony, and the fact that Graham knows everything now. How odd it is that it has come out now, in here.

'No further questions, Your Honour.' PJP sits.

We have a break and, accompanied by Lilian, I hobble to the ladies' and swallow two pain killers. When I emerge from the toilet cubicle, I see Lilian at the washbasin. She's looking at me through the mirror, and shakes her head slowly, a warning. As I wash my hands, I hear a toilet flush, then the door opens, and Angela's mum comes out. She smiles at first, then recognises me and her expression changes so dramatically she looks like a different person, like her older, evil twin. Sounds crack like ice inside my head as I search to articulate some apology. Lilian grabs my arm and propels me towards the door.

'Come on,' she says, 'we need coffee.' She guides me back to the small side room and leaves to get refreshments. When she returns, she hands me a paper cup of milky sweet tea. I wonder when the word 'coffee' stopped meaning coffee and started being used as an invite for any hot drink.

'You did well in there with those questions,' Lilian says. 'How are you feeling?'

'Numb.'

'We bury stuff like this, and we hope it stays dead, don't we?' She flicks at the lid of her coffee cup, and I know she's remembering something. 'They lie dormant, zombies, no heartbeat, but Holy Moly can they jump out and scare the sh–'

She's interrupted by a sharp rap at the door and the usher tells us it's time to return.

'What I'm saying is, it's not too late to talk about this stuff, to a professional. But you already know the value in that,' she says, as she stands up.

Her words register and I check her face for sarcasm: there's none. She smiles and winks. She can carry a wink.

As we return to the court, I see a face I recognise. Sue has joined the short queue inside the viewing area. I focus my eyes on her, pixelating out the other faces in the gallery, afraid of what I will see. Sue sees me and nods as the usher directs her to a seat. I feel reassured by her presence, a counterbalance to the hatred from Angela's mum.

Chapter Sixty-Four

Bella

The next witness to be called is Doctor Ruthi Bhjani. She looks very official in a dark suit and white shirt.

Constance begins by asking about her qualifications. It's an impressive list: 'Chartered Psychologist with the British Psychological Society.... Published articles in scholarly papers... etc, etc.' In short, the real deal.

The court is now going to hear about my emotional stability. It's the oddest of sensations, waiting to hear this analysis, judgement upon judgement.

'Doctor Bhjani,' Constance begins. 'It is my understanding that you met with the defendant earlier this year to conduct a mental health assessment and to provide a report for the court?'

There's some toing and froing about who the report was provided to, and which measures were used. I was supposed to receive a copy but never did and I didn't chase it up. The sound system in the dock isn't great and Ruthi's voice is soft.

'The reason for my assessment was to gauge her feelings about her part in Angela Maynard's death and her current mental health.'

'And how did you do this?

'Through a combination of quantitative and qualitative research methodologies.'

'Please could you explain to the court what that means?'

'Yes, the qualitative research pertains to interviews, discussions, and observations, and the quantitative to the various clinical measures such as questionnaires which we use to interpret the severity of symptoms. Both used together enable us to develop a more rounded picture of the person.'

'Can you tell us about the different measures?

She reels off a list of assessments. I remember the day well. I was exhausted with the questions.

'Did you discuss the day of Angela's death in the defendant's cellar?'

'Yes. It wasn't my role to establish the facts of the day but to assess her state of mind. She was able to express sorrow and remorse for what happened. She maintained throughout that it was an accident. She reported that she'd hidden the victim's body because she worried her cat would be left to die on his own. She described feeling panic and horror. But there was no evidence of a loss of reality.'

'Thank you. I have read your report, which is twenty-five pages long and impossible to cover in its entirety here, but can you give the court an overview of your findings following your assessment of the defendant's mental health?'

'Bella was found to score significantly across the sub-scale of avoidance… evidence of untreated post-traumatic stress relating to the past and the present… moderate depression. She had been taking an antidepressant called Sertraline, and this hadn't been reviewed as it should have been.'

'You report that the defendant still displayed some residual symptoms of untreated post-traumatic stress. In your opinion, what would that be caused by?'

'We were able to ascertain that the car crash and the loss of both parents in 1994 were the triggering events for the symptoms of PTSD. The client still experiences flashbacks and nightmares, which are usually activated by stress. On top of that, the loss of a baby would be considered a very difficult life experience, and I found evidence that the client experienced a complicated grief reaction.'

'Can you tell us a little about complicated grief and how it might present?'

'Yes, it's recognised that people dealing with normal acute grief feel shock, disbelief, sadness, anger, hostility, insomnia, and the loss of ability to function as usual. These symptoms may dominate for around six months, then gradually ease until some form of normality is restored. In contrast, complicated grief is a state of being in which the griever remains preoccupied with reminders of their loss that are severe and pervasive and persist beyond six months and sometimes for decades after the death has occurred.'

'So, even twenty years after the terrible accident in 1994, the defendant was still experiencing symptoms?'

'Yes.'

'Doctor Bhjani, you said that stress could trigger these symptoms of nightmares and flashbacks?'

'Yes.'

'And was the defendant experiencing these?'

'Yes.'

'As you know, the defendant was conducting therapy sessions in the name of Angela Maynard. Did you explore this in your sessions?'

'Yes. Miss Pearson said it was a spur of the moment decision which she couldn't find a way out of.'

'Were you able to ascertain any reason the defendant might have got herself into this position?'

'She described feeling lonely and isolated. She had hoped more of a relationship would develop with her neighbour, but this was unlikely to occur.'

'And was there anything in your assessments which would shed light on this behaviour?'

'The long-term effects of untreated post-traumatic stress can be social isolation and withdrawal. This had been the case for Miss Pearson, the only light for her being her neighbour, Mr Dewsnap. It had been hard for her to come to terms with him falling in love with someone else. In my opinion, in simple terms, when a client of Miss Maynard's appeared on her doorstep, she naively saw it as an opportunity to make a new friend, to fill that emptiness.'

Her explanations for my behaviour resonate with me. I think we are obscured from ourselves in the moment of a bad decision. It's much easier to see ourselves retrospectively, especially when someone is describing us with such compassion. It makes me miss a mother, not *my* mother, but a mother.

'Would her stress levels have been affected?'

'Objection, leading,' PJP calls.

'I'll allow it,' the judge responds.

I feel like a dissected lab rat. Cut me open, this is what you find. I wonder if she will stitch me back up again.

'Yes, she scored significantly on the anxiety measures used.'

'And did the defendant talk about her cat?'

'Yes, she talked about her cat Trevor. Miss Pearson said she wouldn't have got out of bed in the morning on some days if it hadn't been for him. Trevor was a significant part of her life.'

'I read in your report that cats had been a significant part of the defendant's life for many years. Is that correct?'

'Yes, beginning with the accident. It was an important time to have developed a closeness with her first cat Cleo.'

'Objection, Your Honour, beyond the scope. Doctor Bhjani isn't an animal expert,' PJP says.

'We are discussing the defendant's connection to cats, Your Honour, not animal behaviour,' Constance says.

'Overruled. Please continue, Doctor Bhjani.'

'Doctor Bhjani, is it possible to say that the defendant's cat was a replacement in some way for her lost baby?'

PJP is up, 'Objection, Your Honour, speculation.'

'Sustained.'

'Doctor Bhjani, in your opinion, did the defendant treat her cat like her baby?'

'I wouldn't say she treated him like a baby, she allowed him to be a cat. He went outside and hunted, but in my opinion, she saw him as the closest thing to a child that she would ever have.'

'And, in your opinion, could this explain her justification for wanting to stay with him while he died, rather than risk being taken into custody and having him die alone?'

'Yes.'

'No further questions, Your Honour,' Constance says. She turns away and smiles widely at PJP.

PJP is up immediately.

'Dr Bhjani, can you refresh the court's memory, you are a psychologist, correct?

'Asked and answered, Your Honour,' Constance is up and at it from the get-go.

'Sustained.'

'Very well,' PJP continues. 'Many people, including myself, get confused with what a psychologist and a psychiatrist does. For the court's clarification, can you tell us the difference?'

'Yes. Psychologists can assess the psychological needs of their clients, as I have outlined here. Then they focus on providing therapy to help patients. Psychiatrists are medical doctors. They diagnose illness, manage treatment, and provide a range of therapies for serious and complex mental illness.'

'So, a psychologist doesn't diagnose?'

'No.'

'But haven't you just offered a diagnosis of the defendant in this court?'

'No, I offered my expert opinion based on time spent with the defendant and reliable assessments.'

'Ah, I see. So, a psychiatrist doesn't rely on opinion?'

'Objection, Your Honour, argumentative, asked and answered.'

'Sustained.'

'How long did you spend with the defendant conducting these assessments?'

'About four hours in total.'

'In your opinion, Doctor Bhjani, would you say you would get the same results on one day as you would on the following day?'

'Answers can vary depending on the kind of day someone has had, but–'

'Thank you, Doctor. Now, you testified earlier that the defendant had shown remorse for hiding the body of Angela Maynard in her cellar.'

'Yes.'

'Wouldn't it be quite easy for someone to fake remorse on a questionnaire?'

'These are designed to–'

'Answer the question please, Doctor Bhjani.'

'I'm saying that the questions–'

'Just a yes or no, please.'

'There isn't a yes or no answer, the–'

'Someone with a knowledge of psychotherapy would be able to fake their answers, yes or no?'

'Possibly, but the questionnaires–'

'Thank you. No further questions, Your Honour.'

Constance stands.

'Only a couple of clarifications, Your Honour. Doctor Bhjani, can you tell the court how many years training you have had in your specialism?'

'Yes, ten years.'

'Thank you. My learned colleague asked you if you might get different answers on your assessments on different days. How do you ensure your findings are reliable and not dependent on, say, a client's mood on the day?'

'The majority of reports ask how you felt at that time. And the assessments I used are found to be robust and reliable, meaning that, if I conducted the same assessment today, I would get very similar outcomes. The only differences might be on scores that ask about ratings for today.'

'Thank you, and how would you know if someone was faking

remorse?'

'I don't only ask questions – and I ask a lot of questions, using various assessment tools. I also look at other factors such as body language, congruity and consistency. Once I've established a base line for truthful answers, I use this to gauge honesty for evasive or untruthful statements.'

'And how did you find the defendant's responses?'

'In my opinion, Miss Pearson answered truthfully. She was open and candid.'

'Thank you. No further questions, Your Honour. And no further witnesses.'

Judge Blanchflower addresses the court. 'Very well, we can take a half-hour break and re-convene for summing up. Which will be led by the prosecution.'

Chapter Sixty-Five

Bella

There's no time to open and close a big discussion about my fate in the half-hour break. So, Lilian asks me if I have made any holiday plans. She's optimistic, I'll give her that.

Then we're called back into the court

PJP begins his summing up This is his moment, his stage, his court.

'The court has heard from the police investigation how Miss Pearson concealed the body of Angela Maynard in her cellar. She says she didn't push her; she says Angela fell. Yet she didn't contact the police.' He pauses to let that sink in and to allow the jury to stare at him at little longer just for the pleasure of it. Then he places a manicured hand on his chin as if puzzling about something. I find myself hoping he finds a solution to his problem. He continues, 'The defendant admits she disliked Angela because she had nearly run her cat over. She admits that she was impersonating Angela. You have seen the certificates she made in Angela's name. The defendant admits she was jealous of Angela because she stole the love of her neighbour, Graham, from right under her nose.' He leans with his hands on the wooden plinth in front of the jury, up close and personal: 'After five years of waiting, cooking, cleaning for him. Can you imagine that?'

Yes, I think. I can. And I'm listening to a man who can't.

He pushes himself away from the partition and continues. 'The defendant admits all of this, members of the jury, but she denies being angry. Why? Why does she stop there? It definitely fits the narrative, if not the defendant's version of the narrative.

Because surely all of these circumstances would culminate in feelings of anger. The defendant says there was a confrontation because Angela found out. Yet, she proposes that Angela fell down the stairs of her cellar and wasn't pushed during that confrontation. Forensics gave evidence that they couldn't be sure that Angela wasn't pushed. There were traces of the defendant's DNA on her back. And we are not talking a huge push, members of the jury. We are not talking the strength you would need to push someone over a cliff. You have seen those stairs. Just a gentle…' he lifts his arms, palm facing front and mimics a push, 'pushhh.' He elongates the word; it holds the attention. 'We heard from the forensics expert how it is highly suspicious when you have someone who has malice toward the deceased, or stands to benefit from the death in some way, being the only witness to…' he signs air quotes, 'the fall.'

The defence have brought a psychologist who says the defendant was suffering with untreated symptoms of PTSD and complicated grief. This may be the case, but it doesn't offer a robust defence. In fact, it might just give weight to the anger and frustration that the defendant felt at the time of the confrontation. The defendant says she was planning to confess to the police as soon as her cat died. But she waited over a week. They have telephones in hospital. Was it to give herself time to think of a story in case Angela's body had been discovered in her absence?'

He paces in front of the jury, meeting their eyes. 'I propose that she planned to conceal the body until she had the opportunity to remove it to another spot. She had gone to great lengths to conceal it. She had lime mortar, used as we heard, for the benefit of preserving a body and covering the smell. She hadn't planned on the hospital stay, and the body was starting to smell, the game was up. While I don't deny she may have had some depression and was grieving, she only grieved for herself. She lied to the police, deliberately misled the investigation. Indeed, if she had contacted the police immediately, she would most probably have been believed. I am no psychologist, or even a more qualified psychiatrist, but I would suggest that Miss Pearson has a deceptive personality. And her actions were born from rage and spite. In this case, you have no choice but to find her guilty of manslaughter.' He pauses again then bows slightly as he says, 'Thank you.' Then he turns to the judge. 'The prosecution rests, Your Honour.'

The main thing that saves me from being too stricken by PJP's summing up, is that I had a mother who used to enjoy a long negative rant about me to other people. It makes me wonder how much he gets paid for this stint, because I can tell you, my mum would probably have done it pro bono. He takes his seat while the jury's eyes are still on him, and I hope to God that Constance has the charisma to make them forget him.

Constance stands, looking professional and confident. The peruke and white collar of the court robes look striking against her skin. She walks across the breadth of the jury, cleansing their palette of PJP. She is equally as tall and imposing, but she has a less arrogant, more friendly air. She begins, and I hear:

'Bella didn't take any money …clients testified that she helped them.'

After five minutes, she stops, sips from a glass of water and says, 'Sorry, I'm a little hoarse today through shouting at my teenage son to get out of bed this morning.'

The jury smile, a couple of them laugh, grateful for the emotional break. PJP looks at his feet and his shoulders rise in a half laugh of understanding. Constance resumes, 'You heard from the psychologist about the terrible car accident in 1994 and its profound effects, both emotionally, and physically on the defendant. When Graham Dewsnap lost interest because of her injuries, she channelled that love into her cats, first Cleo and then Trevor. If any of you have ever had a pet, as I have, you know how attached we become. Then to make the decision to have your lovely pet put to sleep: it breaks your heart. Bella was also poorly at the time Angela fell, but she has never once used that argument to try to dodge out of her responsibility. She admits she should have contacted the police immediately. She admits she made a bad judgement of the situation, but she did not push Angela Maynard down her cellar steps. The evidence for this accusation simply isn't there. There is evidence of animosity from Angela towards Bella, and we've heard about the hurtful jokes that Angela and Graham shared at Bella's expense and Bella's fear that Angela was torturing Trevor. It's easy to see how they might have argued, and how Angela might have been the aggressor, and in her anger, mis-stepped, as Bella described in her heartfelt testimony.

Please remember during your deliberations that the police, who I admire and normally have a lot of respect for, had the opportunity to search the cellar. They had the opportunity, but they didn't bother. It's only because Bella went to them, as she had always intended to, as soon as she came out of hospital, that Angela's body was recovered, and the family were allowed to give her a burial.

Now, the prosecution has the burden of proof to show that Bella Pearson deliberately pushed Angela Maynard down her cellar steps. And the prosecution has brought no evidence to that effect. Their expert forensics witness said she could not say that the deceased had been pushed. No evidence, members of the jury. No evidence. So please, find Bella Pearson guilty of being an animal lover, of loneliness, of misguided judgement, but not guilty of manslaughter. Thank you. The defence rests, Your Honour.'

Judge Blanchflower takes her glasses off, turning to the jury, and says, 'You have heard the defence and the prosecution case. Now it is your task to decide: has the prosecution proved to your satisfaction that the defendant is guilty of the charge of manslaughter? And is the second charge of failure to provide a decent burial proven? Jury members, you must find you are satisfied and sure of the defendant's guilt. You must be one hundred per cent satisfied and sure. If you think the defendant might have pushed the victim, Angela Maynard, she is not guilty. If you think she probably pushed Angela Maynard, she is not guilty. If you are almost sure she did, she is still not guilty. Only one hundred per cent certainty will suffice, members of the jury.'

Now it's a matter of waiting and waiting.

After three hours, there is a short rap on the door and the court usher tells us the jury is ready. I feel nauseous already, but this is a new level. I do a low belch and taste bitterness in my throat.

Just before I am guided to the dock, Lilian grabs my hand and gives it a quick squeeze.

The clerk of the court addresses the jury. 'As to the charge of manslaughter, have you reached a decision upon which you are all agreed? Please answer yes, or no.'

'Yes.'

'And what is your verdict?'

My stomach seems to be scrabbling up my oesophagus in a bid to escape. I completely sympathise with it.

'Not guilty.'

It takes a minute to register. Constance and Lilian turn to me and smile, but we haven't finished. Still, the swell in my chest feels like tears on an incoming tide.

'As to the charge of failure to provide a decent burial, have you reached a verdict upon which you are all agreed?'

'Yes.'

'And what is your verdict?'

'Guilty.'

As the judge addresses the court, the verdict slowly registers. Those words resonate. I feel the power of justice delivered, a rebalancing of my character.

I refocus with some spare breath in my lungs as Judge Blanchflower delivers my sentence.

'I must take into account aggravating factors, of which there are two. The first is that you failed to contact the police and report Angela Maynard's death. Second, you hid her body in your fireplace, covering it with plastic bags and lime mortar. There are also mitigating factors. There is your previous good character and the circumstances of your mental and physical health.' She pauses and considers her notes, then continues, 'Therefore, it is my decision that you should receive a custodial sentence of fourteen days, suspended for six months, with the requirement that you undertake a treatment programme for symptoms of post-traumatic stress.'

She thanks the jury for their service and reminds them that talking about what was said in the jury room is illegal.

The court empties around me as Lilian approaches. 'How are you feeling? You okay?'

I'm not sure how I feel. It's like one of those times when I've walked somewhere but have no recollection of the journey. As I leave the box, weak-kneed, I cast my eyes up to the visitors' gallery. Angela's mother remains seated, looking bewildered, as those in the adjoining seats rise and wait patiently for her to move. I drop my gaze with shame. I'm stricken for her, but I think any apology will be like a slap in the face. I need to creep away quietly. Cool air wafts around me, beckoning me towards the open door.

As we leave the court, the press rush ahead to get to the cameras outside. A young woman I recognise holds back. She was at the magistrates' court when I was released on bail. Then outside my house. She offers a small wave and smiles. Outside, Constance heads the press off and Lilian steers me sideways, away from the cameras.

We return to her rooms on St John Street and wait for Constance. Lilian explains over a coffee that a suspended sentence means, if I break the law, even purloin a copy of 'Hello' from the Co-op, I will serve fourteen days in prison.

'It's suspended for six months which means after that time

you can start gun-running or dealing spice and you would still have to have a fair trial. Before that, they haul you off to Styal prison, no messing.'

I return home that evening and drag myself upstairs to undress. The euphoria of not being in custody has passed quickly because the image of Angela's mother keeps surfacing. I tell myself we could relate to one another's grief, but I know she'd be repelled by this comparison.

The only sounds I hear are the ones I create as I move through the rooms and contemplate my life now the case is over. My phone beeps and I see it's a message from Sue:

'Thank God it's all over. Call in for cuppa when able.'

Chapter Sixty-Six

Bella

The tropical fish tank makes an interesting focal point in the waiting room. The pretty fish waft around languidly with open mouths. One large shimmering goldfish comes up close to the glass, then suddenly darts off in another direction as though spooked by the sight of me.

As ordered by the court, I arranged ten treatment appointments with Ruthi. So, here I am. Little has changed about the consulting room, the muted colour palette and cream leatherette chairs. A white petal of soft tissue sprouts from a pastel-coloured box in readiness. If household goods were bestowed with a personality, tissues would most definitely convey characteristics of kindness and devotion to service.

I'm feeling more nervous today than I was in the assessment appointment. I suppose because 'treatment' sounds more ominous. This place feels like an operating theatre where I'll be cut open without the need for a scalpel.

Ruthi tells me about Eye Movement Desensitisation Reprocessing, which is a treatment for PTSD. 'It has very good outcomes,' she explains. I bristle at the word 'outcome': it feels too corporate, like guaranteeing value for money over value for health. But I suppose they amount to the same thing. She continues, 'You simply follow my hand movement with your eyes as we talk. It will help to process the memories. They have become stuck in a part of the brain called the limbic system and therefore are remembered as if they happened yesterday.'

'What if I don't want to forget?' I pull the box of tissues

towards me.

'EMDR isn't brainwashing. You will still have your memories, Bella, but the nightmares and flashbacks will end.'

We talk some more about the accident. 'We need to find a trigger for your symptoms,' she says. 'When you think about the car accident, what's the overriding memory? One that evokes the biggest physical reaction?'

The memory springs from my brain and boomerangs through me. 'It's a sound, the screeching of the car against the metal barrier.'

'Let's go with that,' she says.

I awake in the morning feeling hungry. The treatment appointment yesterday was challenging. I cried a lot, but I felt calm when I came out. Maybe it was just the relief it was over. Ruthi said I might have some odd dreams and to make a note of them, but I slept right through. I have been ruminating on something though; Ruthi asked why I hadn't acted on my feelings in the five years I lived next to Graham. I said I was embarrassed about the way I looked.

'So why move next door to him in the first place?' she said. 'Why expose yourself like that?'

I didn't have an answer, and she suggested I have a think about it. Which is infuriating. If she already knows, why not just tell me?

Bacon sputters under the grill as I hum along to the radio. I rinse a cup and watch as rain hits the window then slides down like melting sugar to gather on the ledge. Two morning presenters chat in the background.

'That was The Isley Brothers' with 'Summer Breeze.' Now, Julie, we know Summer is a lovely time for walking our dogs, as long as it's not too hot. You have a little dog, don't you?'

'Yeah, I have Dolly, she's spoilt rotten. At Christmas, she has her own presents, all wrapped, with bows and everything. She's family.'

'Does she have a place at the table?'

'No, but she'd like one. With silver service.'

They laugh, and I laugh with them, remembering Trevor and his lick-e-lix favourites which I used to wrap and put under the tree.

'How far would you go for Dolly, though? If you've heard the news reports, or been on social media this morning, you will know that a Stockport woman, Annabelle Pearson, was found not guilty of manslaughter yesterday, after failing to report a fatal accident in her house because she was worried about her cat dying alone.'

'Yeah, I read this, Paul, so sad...'

'What would you do for the love of your pet? Call us.'

I rush and switch it off. Hearing my name spoken on the radio is frightening. I'm breathless, stupefied. I sit down in the armchair and wish for the warmth of Trevor, for the presence of Graham, for things as they were.

I stand up and put a record on. As I watch the black spinning disc, the stylus lowers, the needle makes contact and Frank Sinatra's light baritone fills the room. I focus on the lyrics, puzzling over which regrets he's singing about. Still my brain throws out unbidden thoughts as I wonder who is listening to that station, hearing the idle chatter about my life. What a distasteful subject for a phone-in. Inane entertainment hiding the corrosion of human misery.

I look towards Angela's house at the 'For Sale' sign. It's been on the market for a few days now. Maybe the family were waiting for the court case to end before selling. What I'm not prepared for is the 'To Let' sign in Graham's Garden. It wasn't there yesterday. Of course, why didn't I see that one coming. His house has been unoccupied for months. I've heard sounds from inside and seen his car outside on a few occasions, but we've never spoken, and I've not laid eyes on him until I saw him in court. The smoke alarm beeps suddenly, and I remember the bacon. I open the back door and waft the smoke out with a tea towel. As the acrid air dissipates, I search in my bag and find the business card I picked up from a local estate agent. When I call them, the man who answers uses my first name too easily. I say I want to sell my property. His tone changes when he registers the address.

'Er, erm, yes, we can certainly do a valuation. Would tomorrow be convenient?'

I say it would. When I've finished the call, I fret about showing him around, especially the cellar. So, I pull my hat, coat, and boots on. I see the scarf that Graham bought me still hanging on the coat stand but I leave it there, deciding it will go to the charity shop when I'm packing for the move. Then I walk around to Sue's for the promised cuppa, stepping carefully on frozen paving, holding tentatively to the branches of the hedgerow as I move against the nipping crystals of rain.

Sue opens the door. 'There you are,' she says in surprise, as though she'd misplaced me.

When we're settled with coffee and cake, Sue asks me about my plans. I tell her I'm putting my house on the market and ask her if she could be there when the estate agent comes around.

'You can let the estate agent show people around. You don't have to be there.'

'I hadn't thought.'

'The estate agent can sort group viewings, too. Come here while they're shown round. Leave the experts to it.'

'Do you think people will be put off by … you know…'

'Some might come out of morbid curiosity, but these days you must have your own house on the market before you can view. I wouldn't worry. If it's priced right, it'll get snapped up.'

'I heard them talking about me on the radio.'

'Keep your head down and it will go away. I saw your barrister interviewed outside court by the way, and it's been on the local news, but it will die down. Ride it out. Have you had any thoughts on where you'll move to?'

'No, except I thought a fresh start. Somewhere where no one knows me.'

I spot her as soon as I pull Sue's gate closed. The young woman from court is waiting, leaning against a small blue car. She rubs her mittened hands together and blows on them. I cross over the road, head down. The sleet has almost melted and I'm surer-footed. I can nip around the back of the houses before she realises it's me. She's on my left, obscured by her car as I pass. When I get to the end of the road, I cross back. In my periphery I see her push away from the car and follow. *'Damn.'*

'Hey, hi, wait please,' she calls. 'I'm not with a newspaper.'

My hip hurts from the strain but I bear down and press on towards the opening of the cut through. In a few minutes I'll be 'barleys', a word we used to shout when playing tag. It told other players you were on safe ground and untouchable.

'I just want to chat,' she says, as she catches up, 'tell your side of the story.'

I move aside as a cyclist hurtles towards us in the narrow passageway.

'Hey,' she calls as the bike draws aside. 'People here on legs.'

The cyclist slows but we're still forced into the hedgerow.

'Unbelievable,' she calls after him.

I get a closer look at her. She can be no more than twenty-three or -four. I start up again. Aided by the springy branches, I almost bounce away and I'm at my gate in a couple of steps. It's a wooden, waist-high gate, not a rampart or drawbridge, but I feel immediately safer.

'I have a cat too,' she calls.

Enthusiasm curtailed, she turns away, following in the cyclist's wake. As I watch her retreat, I feel something soften. The guilt I'm carrying unwieldy, like I'm trying to balance a tray of water on one hand. It tips this way and that. It's an almighty effort not to spill any.

'Laura,' I call as I open the gate.

She stops, turns back, hopeful. 'Yeah?'

'Come on, I'll put the kettle on.'

Chapter Sixty-Seven

Bella

An ex-criminal lawyer, Laura tells me about her *Laurandorder* blog where she discusses high-profile cases. She holds the mug of tea in her mittened hands as she explains.

'I started the blog to keep me occupied, a reason to get out of bed in the afternoon. 'Open new pathways' was how my consultant had described it. It's morphed into a kind of rabbit warren I've burrowed with words; and been lost in for the last two months.'

Although I'm a little taken aback by her candour, I like the fact that she's not shy about talking about her mental health. It's my field, after all.

'I'm not really sure what a blog is,' I tell her. 'I'm not that way inclined.'

'Well, it's just like Facebook?' She says it as a question.

'Nope.'

'Well, it's like a newspaper column I write about stuff happening in Manchester, but people read it on laptops and computers or phones?' Still a question.

'I've heard of phones,' I say.

'Great, well, if you have an iPhone?' She scrawls through some items on her phone and shows me said blog.

I lean in and read a stream of messages about a speech that Megan made when she and Prince Harry visited Manchester.

'Interesting,' I say.

'You can see here,' she points a blue varnished fingernail to the number of followers she has, and I'm reminded of religious preachers gathering a flock. 'Almost a thousand in two months.

I need to keep the momentum going, so I've been at the courts, seeing if anything worthwhile pops up. Something engrossing, a story with real people, rather than wealthy celeb types. That's when I first saw you. I've been writing about you.'

'Oh. I'm not sure I like the idea of that.'

'Read it if you like. It's all balanced. Most people have an interest in the law, or cats. I have strict guidelines about what people can write and I audit everything before it goes out.'

'What do they say?'

She holds her phone up to me, but I pull away. 'You tell me.'

'Here look, a lady called Marianne writes, *This case should never have come to trial. There's not enough evidence for the prosecution. Just a waste of taxpayers…* I'll find a better one. Here, Jo writes, *I have a cat. I would like to say with certainty that I would put a dead person first, but if my cat was being put to sleep the next day I might hold on. I definitely sympathise.'* See, people are interested, and you do have support and understanding out there. Course it's not all roses but, if I interview you, we can offer your perspective.'

'Will Angela's family see it?'

'I can't promise they won't, but at least it starts a conversation.'

I'm still not sure what she means by 'starting a conversation' on a blog. 'And I won't be filmed?'

'Well, I'd prefer that you were. It adds authenticity.'

I lean away from the table and rub my hip. Although I like this girl for her enterprise, I get the feeling her ambition might persuade me to do something I'll regret.

Lilian told me that PJP said Angela's family have declined all press interest, and she advised me to keep a low profile out of respect. I wonder what she would advise about a blog. I decide to call her before I proceed. Laura seems disappointed by this suggestion but still, she asks if she can see the cellar. She has her phone in her hand and I suspect she wants photographs, or to film it. It makes me shudder and I tell her, 'No, the cellar is out of bounds.'

She doesn't give up easily, says she will leave her phone with me. By my third refusal I've seen through her and realised the mistake I made inviting her in. I open the back door for her as she gathers her things.

I stand and watch her retreat down the path. As she comes alongside Trevor's memorial, she points to it, turns to me and mouths an 'Aw' with her hand over her heart. Then she pulls out her phone and points to it, then at the memorial in a kind of mimed request to take a photo. I shake my head, another firm 'No', astonished by her guile and nerve.

When she's gone, I phone Lilian and tell her about my visit from Laura.

'Did she ask to go into the cellar?' she asks, straight off.

How did I miss that this girl was as much an opportunist as all the rest of them, yet Lilian grasps her motives immediately?

'I ask because you need to be careful. There's a fine line between interest and exploitation. My advice, as I've said before, is keep a low profile or no profile.'

'I thought it might be a way to say sorry to Angela's family again.'

'You could write a letter to her. I could pass it to PJP. Her family might read it, they might not. You'll probably never know.'

I make several attempts to do this, I really do. In the end I screw the letter up into a tight ball and throw it into the bin. To lose a daughter and gain an apology, what an insult.

Chapter Sixty-Eight

Bella

For the past week, I've gone over and over a question Ruthi put to me. Why did I move in next door to Graham if I was too embarrassed by the way I looked to tell him who I was? The answer came to me one evening. I sat up suddenly from a dream in which I had been transported to the nineties. The recall pierced my gut and head. I had been there, really there. I had just left a great day with Graham and our friends. The sights, sounds and smells were so strong, so evocative. I felt a sense of wonder. When the imprint faded, I wanted it back. When I couldn't evoke it, I cried. The tears overwhelmed me, wracked me like some great orgasm of self-pity. It was only afterwards that I realised the reason I moved in next to Graham despite the way I looked, was because I was hoping Graham would see me as the girl I was. I had bestowed on him the power to give me that time back. It wouldn't matter to him that I had changed. The memory of how things used to be would be enough. All that time. What a waste.

At our next session, I tell Ruthi.

She smiles and nods her head like therapists do, then she asks me if I'm sure I really loved Graham.

I'm annoyed because it is another cliff hanger question, asked right at the end of the session.

Chapter Sixty-Nine

Bella

The following week, I call into the police station and sign on, then walk to the village and call in at the Cats' Protection League charity shop where I volunteer one day a week. There are a couple of women looking through the clothes rails. Asha, the manager, is in the back office at her desk.

'Hi,' I say.

'Bella,' Asha answers as she rises. 'You look nice.'

'Oh, er, thanks. I just...' I've had contact lenses fitted, and bought some new clothes with Jenny's help, but I cannot get used to the compliments. My first thought is people don't mean them. Compliments have become a form of greeting, a space filler, like foam popcorn, used to fill gaps in conversation. I'm working on this cynicism.

'I'm doing the rota for next week,' she says, as she goes to the filing cabinet. The cabinet drawer sticks so she has to lift it and pull. I hear the exertion in her voice. 'Damn drawer. So, I've put you in on Tuesday if that's okay? Usual hours.'

'Perfect,' I answer. I've only worked here for the past month and, although I found it initially challenging, I'm enjoying it and I feel like I'm still doing something for Trevor. I did get a few stares and nudges to begin with, but most customers are regulars, and the novelty seems to have worn off.

On the way out I almost collide with someone. I make a swift apology and am about to move on when I recognise the man's voice and glance up to see that it's Graham. I'm as embarrassed for him as I am shocked and disjointed myself. He put his arm on mine when we collided, and he releases it quickly now.

'Bella,' he says.

'Oh,' is all I've got. I'm so shocked I don't move. Neither does he. He's lost weight so I might have passed him by had I not bumped into him.

'You okay?' he asks.

'Yes, you?'

'Not bad. I'm just…' He points behind me to the door of the charity shop as a small, slim, fair-haired woman comes out. She smiles at him and then looks at me as though awaiting an introduction. She doesn't get one.

I step aside as she links his arm.

'Well, see you,' he says.

And they walk away.

I hurry home, holding onto my breath as if I've got a long swim to the surface. My breathing returns to normal when I'm on the dry land, in my own front room. I think about seeing Graham and his girlfriend, or wife. As I'm wondering this, I realise something is different. I search my heart, my head, my groin. Could it be...? Because that incitation of longing, heightened after any encounter I have with Graham. The physical craving for more, the ensuing self-harming beliefs that I'm unworthy. Those spontaneous, love- and lust-affirming responses, they are not there anymore.

Chapter Seventy

Bella

Nine months later

The pretty town of Porto Cristo lies to the east on the island of Mallorca. I've been staying here for just over a month now and I'm getting used to the beat of the village and the way my body feels under the thermal comfort of a Mediterranean sun.

As predicted, my house in England sold quickly but I was held in a chain for five months, which meant I needed to rent a property for six months until my suspended sentence expired. Angela's house is now occupied by a family with two small children, and Graham's is being rented by a young couple who I hardly saw or heard. Maybe they kept out of my way, but that suited me fine. Elmwood Terrace is a different place now. It's been regenerated, it has a different vibe, as Jenny would say. Sometimes I miss it. I was very happy there with Trevor. Those few years before Angela were idyllic.

Sue's house is situated on the Carra de Cala Murta. A far grander house than I'd expected from her low-key description. It has three bedrooms and stands in a large plot of land where vegetation hums and crackles with wildlife. Fronds from overhanging palm trees provide shade on the south-facing balcony of my bedroom, and dusk is accompanied by chirping crickets and a sweet chorus of evensong.

Molly the cat has a large, shaded pen in the garden where she roams free during the day. She watches the birds with the stillness of a hunter. Occasionally they land inside the pen, but their visits are a flutter of hello and a swift ascent of goodbye. I think Molly is going to be happy with the plans we have.

It's the height of the season and I watch from my seat at the local café as tourists pass by on their way to explore The Caves of Drac. Sun glints off sunglasses and heats the buckles on backpacks as they hitch them up and refer to neatly folded maps.

I return to my writing, choosing my words to Jenny carefully. I write that I'm settling in, and I'm sending a postcard because I've never sent one before. I suppose postcards were the first form of text messages. A few clichéd phrases written under a rented sun. I know they're probably considered old-fashioned, but I feel bohemian, European, sitting here sipping coffee, which I ordered in Spanish: '*un café por favour*?'

I think of Jenny as a friend who stood by me through one of the craziest periods of my life. Though I still don't understand why she did, I accept it's something in her nature. Some people are simply good and kind. She never did have the planned surgery. Apparently, her daughter convinced her to wait for a year.

Of all the people I met through therapy, I identify with Zeta the most. I would have been enraged if anyone did to me what I did to her. She has accepted my apology though, and I'm still treading carefully. I think a postcard would be appreciated: she's of a generation.

When I've posted the cards, I walk to the harbour. There's a mix of serious sunbathers. Sun *burners*, if it's English skin on the beach. Children run into the waves; families gather under large umbrellas. Today the sea is blue taffeta shimmering with light. The sea puts us in our place. We dip a toe into its sunlit shallows, while being awed by its abundant depths.

As I stroll, I notice again that the pain in my hip feels less sharp. It's amazing what a bit of warmth can do. Or maybe it's that I'm less stressed. 'The warmth chills me out,' as Sue says. I spot her and her friend Paola outside the Flamenco restaurant. They are seated at a small table under a turquoise canopy, sharing a small carafe of red wine. Their heads are dipped towards one another as they talk, both holding the stems of their wine glasses. Then they laugh at something, heads tilted back, mirrors in the sun, perfect reflections of each other.

'We were just talking about you,' Sue says as I approach. 'Were your ears burning?'

'Everything's burning,' I answer, and they both laugh. Paola pulls out a chair for me and then disappears into the restaurant.

'Why were you talking about me? You can't be that bored.'

'You look happy. It's good to see.'

Paola returns with a third glass and places it in front of me. She knows the whole saga of what happened in England and has promised to keep it to herself. '*Cruza mi Corazón,*' she said. Cross my heart.

The wine tastes of blackberries and cherries, and leaves my mouth dry, full of summer fruits.

After sharing a platter of boquerones en vinagre we leave in Paola's old Fiesta. Our destination, a short drive to the Carrer de Llaut.

Despite what happened at my old house in England, I did well from the sale and have a good pot of money, but I need to *do* something. I had an idea and, after some research, discovered several centres in the west of Mallorca, but nothing on this side of the island. I approached Sue with my idea and suggested a fifty-fifty split of the business. It didn't take her long to come back with an excited 'Yes!'

When we exit the car, the heat draws the attention. I can see its work up close in the wearying tree boughs and frayed weatherboards. The property we have come to is a rundown finca with five acres of land which includes an olive grove and a well. It has mains connection and running water but needs some TLC.

We kick up dust and gravel as we wonder around my newly acquired home and our soon-to-be cat sanctuary, El Gato Azul.

The front door opens into a cool dark living room. A stone fireplace dominates the centre of the back wall, and a black wrought-iron chandelier hangs from the ceiling, draped with elegant webs.

'Settee will go here,' I say, marking out a rectangle with outstretched arms, like a runway marshal. 'The kitchen needs some work,' I add as Sue and Paola follow me.

'It's amazing,' Paola says. This is the first time she's seen it.

'Show Paola around,' I say to Sue. 'I need to do something.'

Sue nods her acknowledgement and pushes open some large double doors. 'Bella's dining room,' I hear her say as I go outside. I smile as I hear Paola respond with, 'Ooh, buena.'

I walk towards the rise of the olive grove. The sound of crickets and buzzing grows louder as Sue and Paola's voices fade away. I find the right spot, a rise in the hill overlooking the trees with a view of The Serra de Tramuntana mountain range, edges smudged by purple cloud. There's more of a breeze here. I lift my face to it and have one of those moments where I feel another force or agency urging me to remember this. I feel the ground under my feet, the warmth of the sun, the taste of wine in my mouth. Sue and Paola have wandered onto the back porch. I see them; feel connections firing, registering a feeling of wellbeing. I can't wait to bring all those abandoned and poorly cats to a good and loving home. I want to hold this new reality to me.

I lift the straw bag I've been carrying and gently remove the small casket. My boy Trevor. My companion. My entertainer. My friend. I've never told anyone what really happened on the day Angela died. Never mentioned, despite his illness, Trevor moved as lithely as I'd ever seen him. Just as Angela moved forwards on the cellar steps, he darted between her feet. She lost her balance and fell. It wasn't worth mentioning to the police, but I wondered. Maybe it was payback for her cruelty towards him. Perhaps, he was making sure I was safe. By the time I'd returned upstairs, he was collapsed on the floor, too weak to jump back up onto the settee. He only lasted one more day.

I place my hand into the ash of his remains and stay for a moment with the atoms of him against my fingers. I have no tears, only a calm mix of love and regret, settled somewhere in my body.

I lift my hand and let the ash blow from my fingers. 'You can rest here,' I say. 'We can both rest here.'

The End.

Acknowledgements

I have had the story for 'A Cat Lover's Guide to Murder' in my head for several years, but I knew it was more in the 'cosy crime' genre, and not 'psychological suspense,' which was the genre my debut novel 'Her Sister's Shadow,' belonged in. When my brother, Pete, became ill in 2022, I felt I needed a gentler paced novel to throw myself into, and I lay to one side the story I was working on (a dark psychological suspense novel) and concentrated on developing 'A Cat Lover's Guide' more fully. So- thank you to Northodox Press for allowing me to use this story as a kind of grief therapy. The dark psychological thriller is still planned for 2025.

At Northodox Press I would like to thank James for his support and input, and for hauling boxes of books around to various library events. I would also like to thank Michelle 'Shelly' Shine, and Sara Brylin, at Stockport Libraries for inviting me to those events and allowing me to talk with my talented fellow author, Caroline England, about our writing experiences.

I would also like to thank Criminal Lawyer, Lucy Kate O'Gara and solicitor, Dom Patching. You can only find out so much from a web search. They answered a plethora of questions and their help added authenticity and realism to the storytelling.

South Manchester Writers Group has been a continued source of sustenance for the challenges of writing, and especially the little group of supportive friends I have met through the group. We meet up for coffee and share the ups and downs of just about everything.

To my son, Adam, who understands the trials and tribulations of the creative process and can always chivvy me along. And to Ian, for always being there for me, and for all the great home cooked meals.

NORTHODOX PRESS

SUBMISSIONS

CONTEMPORARY
CRIME & THRILLER
FANTASY
LGBTQ+
ROMANCE
YOUNG ADULT
SCI-FI & HORROR
HISTORICAL
LITERARY

SUBMISSIONS@NORTHODOX.CO.UK

NORTHODOX PRESS

SUBMISSIONS

Northodox.co.uk

CALLING ALL NORTHERN AUTHORS!

DO YOU LIVE IN OR COME FROM NORTHERN ENGLAND?

DO YOU HAVE AN INTERESTING STORY TO TELL?

Email submissions@northodox.co.uk

- [ ] The first 3 chapters OR 5,000 words
- [ ] *1 page synopsis*
- [ ] *Author bio (tell us where you're based)*

** No non-fiction, poetry, or memoirs*

SUBMISSIONS@NORTHODOX.CO.UK

NORTHODOX PRESS

FIND US ON SOCIAL MEDIA

Printed in Great Britain
by Amazon

42136034R00209